I0838292

A JUNIOR RANGERS
INVESTIGATIVE CLUB NOVEL

TREASURE OFF THE COAST

NATHAN W. LANDRUM

Treasure off the Coast
a Junior Rangers Investigative Club Novel

This is a work of fiction. Names, characters, places, and incidents either are the product of the author's imagination or are portrayed entirely fictitiously. Any resemblance to actual persons, living or dead, events, or locales is entirely coincidental.

Copyright © 2022 by Nathan W. Landrum

All rights reserved. No part of this book may be reproduced or used in any manner without written permission of the copyright owner except for the use of quotations in a book review. For more information, address:

Nathan W. Landrum
Alienjest Press
1900 New Gallatin Rd, Scottsville, KY 42164
or visit the website
www.alienjestpress.com

First paperback edition

Illustrations and Book Design by Bailey Vidler
Illustrations Copyright © 2022 by Bailey Vidler
www.baileyvidler.com

Edited by Susan Chang

ISBN 979-8-9865300-0-0 (paperback)
ISBN 979-8-9865300-1-7 (ebook)
(Alienjest Press)
www.alienjestpress.com

Library of Congress Control Number
2022912088

This book was written because my father took me to every national park in the southwest, and a few others elsewhere, and because my mother encouraged me to read at a young age and to make my own stories as I grew.

It fits in your hands because my first beta reader and backgammon coach, Michelle Mason, encouraged me to keep the wordcount down and story manageable.

It is dedicated to them.

PREFACE

Dry Tortugas was the second to last park where my father worked. He literally wrote the book on it: *Fort Jefferson and The Dry Tortugas* by L. Wayne Landrum. I lived in the old house standing in the parade ground. I've snorkeled barrel wrecks, brick wrecks, and the supposed site of an old pirate ship. I've burned my feet racing across the brick path, and I've climbed Loggerhead Lighthouse losing count of the steps. My favorite ghost stories are actually of the ghost in the rec room. (Sorry Private Winters.) And my favorite view on earth is the sunset behind Loggerhead from atop the westernmost corner of the fort.

This book is my first full length novel. It's the first Junior Rangers Investigative Club Story. My introduction to Justin, Lucy, and Rudy, as it is for some of you. Having a published book has been my dream for a long time. I could not have done it alone. Which is funny because this is a *"self-published"* work. That means very little, and I needed lots of help.

Which is why I have lots of people to thank. My dad, whose job allowed me to spend almost every school holiday in some of the most amazing places on earth. My mom, whose constant support and encouragement made this a possibility and who had to help with the bulkiest edits. My many editors and beta readers, including Pat, Casey, Robyn, Emily, Wes, Harry, Sarah, Monica, Reef, Randi, and Kara, along with the other members of my extended family and friend group who helped along the way. Thanks to the park rangers and other park employees I've known from the Dry Tortugas and to everyone who helped me conquer my indecision through online poles and questions.

Thanks to the professionals who worked with me to make this something more than I could have on my own. Bailey's illustrations really capture the characters, scenes, and actions. Susan's editorial advice took an incomplete manuscript and helped me improve upon it greatly. And thanks to everyone who reads this book and shares it with others. I hope you will look for more, check out the website, or visit the park yourself to trace the steps, safely, of my favorite group of National Park Investigators.

Nathan W. Landrum, Author

Fort
Jefferson
Dry Tortugas National Park

DRAMATIS PERSONAE

JUNIOR RANGERS INVESTIGATIVE CLUB

Justin Case. New co-leader of J.R.I.C. Loves mysteries, also photography and birdwatching. Too trusting. Intimidated by muscles.

Lucia "Lucy" Benitez. New co-lead. Strong of body and heart. Loves to swim. Always ready for adventure.

Rudy Sheer. The second youngest member. Up for any adventure which will make him rich and/or famous.

Miguel Benitez. One of the founding members of J.R.I.C. Would rather be inside studying.

HONORARY MEMBERS

Luke Manning. Liveaboard on the *La'sei Fairy*. Volunteer on Loggerhead.

Nina Manning. Liveaboard on the *La'sei Fairy*. Volunteer on Loggerhead.

Spud Manning. The Manning's Chestnut Labradoodle.

RANGERS

Gabriel Benitez. Lucy and Miguel's father. Dry Tortugas District Ranger.

Wendy Carter. Dry Tortugas Law Enforcement Ranger.

Trevor O'Donnell. Dry Tortugas Maintenance Ranger.

Mr. Ishii. Dry Tortugas Interpretive Ranger.

UNDERWATER RESEARCH SUBMERGED ARCHEOLOGISTS (URSA) AKA DIVE BEARS

Dr. Carmen Benitez. World renowned Archeologist. Lucy and Miguel's mother. Supervisor of U.R.S.A.

Dr. Alexa Kapur. Archeologist of Maritime History.

Dr. Alan Erickson. Professor of Marine Archeology.

Chet Bowman. Doctoral student under Dr. Benitez.

Gwen Duncan. Doctoral Student under Dr. Benitez.

Kit Nixon. Doctoral Student under Dr. Erickson.

Sophia Yang. Masters student under Dr. Erickson.

OTHERS

Captain Levi Straus. Captain of *Neptune's Trident*.

Captain Tobias Whitmer. Captain of *Horned Devil*.

Renee Manning. Liveaboard. Volunteer on Loggerhead. Luke and Nina's mother.

Shawn Manning. Liveaboard. Volunteer on Loggerhead. Luke and Nina's father.

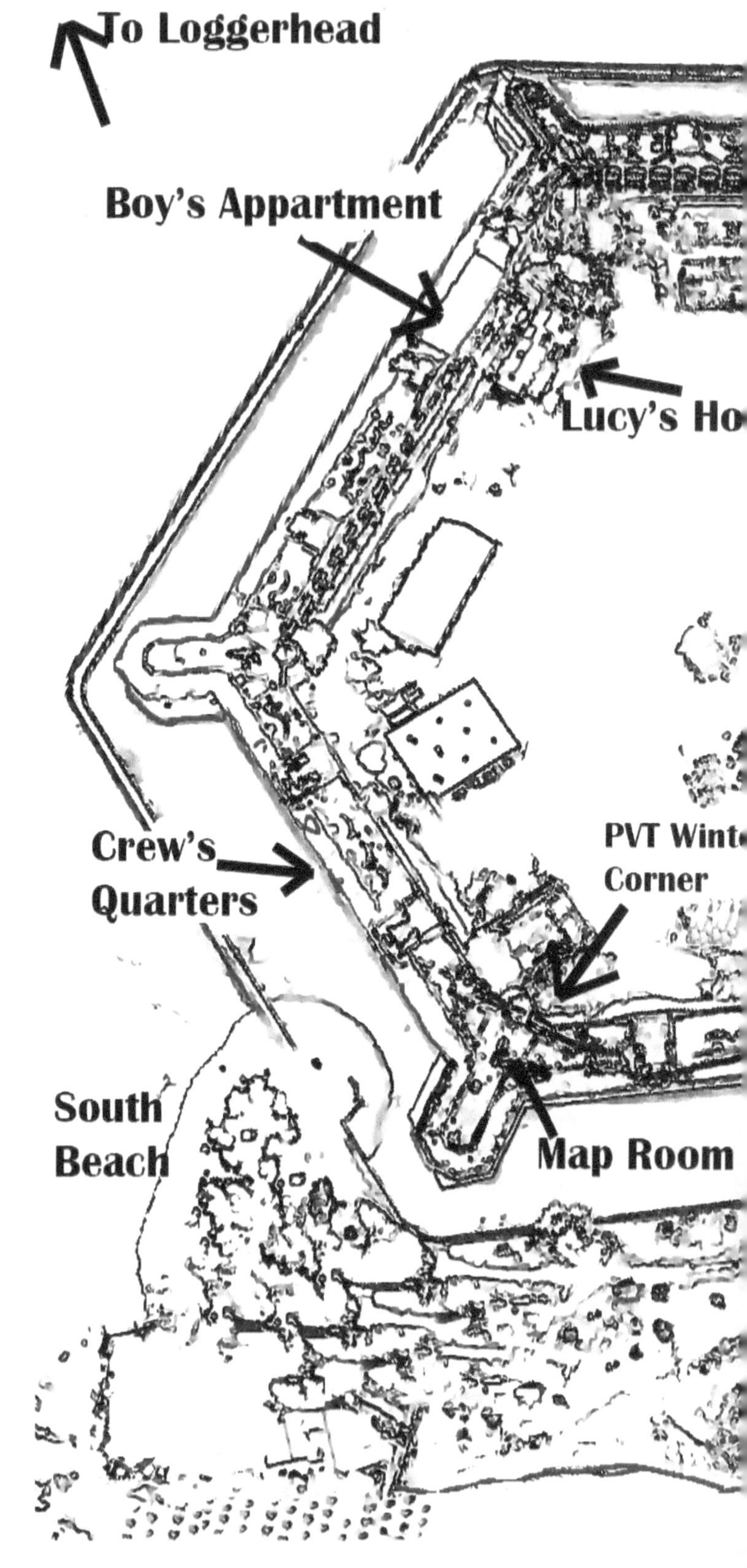

To Loggerhead
Boy's Appartment
Lucy's Ho
Crew's Quarters
PVT Winte Corner
South Beach
Map Room

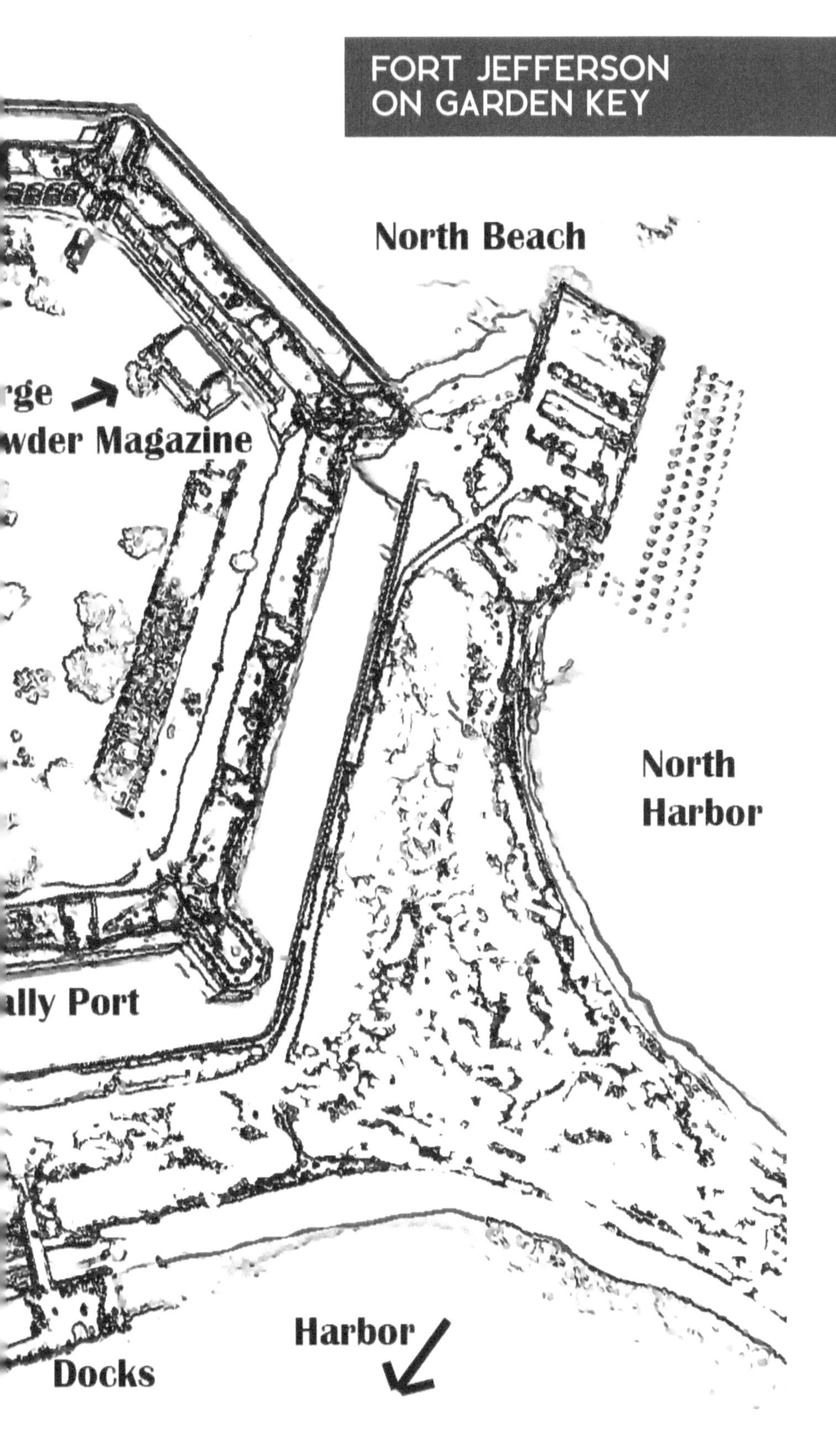

FORT JEFFERSON
ON GARDEN KEY
North Beach
rge
wder Magazine
 lly Port
North
Harbor
Docks
Harbor

TABLE OF CONTENTS

PROLOGUE

DRY TORTUGAS

COOL WATER WELLING UP FROM THE DEEP BLUE caused Lucy to suck in a healthy breath. A swift hiss of air from her tank was followed by gurgling bubbles as she blew out. Kicking forward gently, she watched her breath froth upwards in little spiral air jellyfish. It was strange breathing while surrounded by turquoise water on all sides.

She was thirty feet down. She'd held her breath and dived even deeper before, but it was freeing to be able to stay down here, without any fear of running out of air. There were more frightening concerns in open ocean. Namely, a host of sea life potentially hiding just beyond view, waiting to swoop in and eat her.

Visibility was good today. Hopefully, she would see any incoming sea monsters or sharks long before they got close. She might not be able to beat them back to her family's boat, currently anchored in a large sandy patch nearby. She wouldn't have to race any sharks though, just the other divers.

Her mother's entire team of underwater archeologists was scattered about the sea around her. If Lucy could get past them then any prospective monsters would have tastier targets to gobble. She was confident she could out swim a bunch of her mother's science nerds.

Lucy was a good swimmer, so she was probably safe. Proving her wrong, a dark shadow suddenly blocked out the sun above her casting a sinuous form on sand below. She took in a sudden breath. Her heart rate quickened, and her muscles tensed. As she prepared to sprint off, a dumb smiling face in a round mask entered her field of view, upside down.

Miguel! Cheeks puffed out, he gave her a wave and kicked, his flippers propelling him swiftly towards the surface. Lucy bit down on her regulator fighting an urge to chase and berate him. He was supposed to be dive training too! That could wait. It was time to see what her mother's students were up to.

Swimming with a massive oxygen tank on her back was definitely something to get used to. Lucy had to kick her flippers in little circular movements to avoid running into Chet. Her mom's star student was using his massive arms to help a woman with dark hair, Sophia, lift a rusted metal chain—kicking up clouds of sand. They each wore diving equipment similar to hers but had two tanks strapped to their backs instead of one.

While her mother supervised, they had been documenting and recording every minute detail about the chain and the wooden boxes beneath it. Lucy had been doing lazy loops to get used to the diving equipment, giving Miguel the opening to scare her.

"What do you think we'll find in those boxes?" Miguel had asked Gwen when they were both topside with the university's designated student lookout. "Treasure?"

"Why would there be treasure aboard a Civil War era Union vessel?" The redheaded student, Lucy's favorite from her mom's class, had looked up from her waterproofed tablet. "I'll give you my share if they find something so miraculous. After all, they need a big find to prove to the university that we should stay."

Gwen's frustrated look soured Lucy's mood, reminding her of the late-night conversation she'd overheard between her parents. Her mom's expedition was in trouble. She wanted to help but knew her mother wouldn't allow it. When her friends arrived, they could do something.

Gwen must have noticed her hesitation. "You good, Lucia?"

"I'm fine. The water's deeper than I expected."

"Blame Professor Erickson." Her mom grumbled while checking Lucy's dive equipment. "We were supposed to dive his wreck. It's on a pristine, shallow, sandbar which would have been perfect for an introductory dive."

"Professor Erickson's been awfully protective of his pet project." Gwen yawned.

"He's a perfectionist, and probably afraid to have another professor, and her kids, looking over his shoulders while he works." Her mother had given Lucy's air tank a solid thump, "That's ok. My daughter always jumps into the deep end first. Right, mija?"

The students were working forty feet below. Deep end had never felt so accurate. While they removed a layer of sand, her mother knelt nearby, documenting their excavation with a fancy underwater camera.

Chet and Sophia caused a momentary flurry of activity by removing a rotten—centuries old—slab of wood. Their action caused an explosion of bubbles obscuring Lucy's view and scattering the school of fish which had been curiously circling her mother.

As the water cleared, Sophia set the large wooden slab aside for Kit to test when he returned. Time to see what they had discovered. Holding onto her breath, she floated higher to see two long, encrusted, metal tubes tapered at one end. Each had two round protrusions about halfway along their bodies.

"Huh." Lucy thought, watching Sophia swim excitedly past Chet to probe a cylinder with a gloved finger. Lucy's mom was leaning forward on her knees, emitting a near constant stream of bubbles. She must be excited. Were those, cannon?

CHAPTER 1

BOAT THROUGH CHARTED WATERS

JUSTIN

"*O*FF THE COAST OF THE FLORIDA KEYS, *70 miles west of Key West lies a ...*"

The woman dressed in the white and blue ferry crew shirt was hard to hear. Revving boat engines muffled numerous conversations inside the air-conditioned interior deck. Justin scanned the larger than expected crowd. They were dressed in everything from swimsuits to colorful T-shirts. Many were carrying small day packs or coolers. A lot had heads down on beach towels on tables.

It was too early for announcements. Steaming cups of coffee and the breakfast buffet were far more interesting for all awake passengers except one. A young man with crazy hair was wearing headphones and gripping a metallic briefcase. He looked bored.

Rudy yanked on Justin's sleeve, pointing. A woman in a bright pink tank top and floppy hat loaded her plate with bagels. There weren't many left, and there were thirteen people in front of them. He watched the diminishing bagel pile. "Your dad said we should eat a big breakfast to avoid sea sickness. By the time we get there, we'll be lucky to get half a banana."

"Not everything is about food." Justin replied.

Reaching the buffet, they found only a single raisin bagel remaining. Justin reached out with alacrity and snagged the waiting snack, prepared for Rudy's frustrated sigh. "Justin! I don't want a plain bagel."

"Grab some fruit, Rudy. It'll be good for you."

"All they have left is cantaloupe. I hate cantaloupe." Rudy was very opinionated about food. "I don't want to make my stomach all acidic before we set out on the high seas." An older man behind Rudy chuckled. The younger boy visibly shivered in annoyance.

"Rudy, it's a two-and-a-half-hour ride, not a twelve-week voyage."

"It only takes a couple minutes to get seasick." Rudy filled a plastic tumbler with coffee. Talk about an acidic stomach!

Seating options were limited, so they took the table across from the crazy haired man. They ate their breakfast as the engine hummed and the man's head bobbed slowly to music they could not hear.

A few minutes later, Rudy stood with his tumbler. Justin frowned. "More coffee?"

"Yep!" Rudy stumbled away as the boat lurched with a wave. He returned with a full tumbler and more energy. "Justin, do you think those are the treasure boats?"

"Treasure boats?" Justin asked.

Rudy pointed out to a line of small mangrove islands. "Those are the Marquesas, where one of the biggest sunken treasures ever was discovered. In 1622 this big treasure fleet was sailing from Havana to Spain when a hurricane hit sinking several treasure ships, including the *Atocha*." Rudy shifted to point out two small ships. "They found her somewhere out there and are still digging up the treasure."

Justin shook his head. "How do you know?"

"There's a museum in Key West about it. Dr. Benitez took us when my father and I came to visit." Rudy's grin grew wider. "Maybe we'll find treasure in the Dry Tortugas."

"So, that's why you are excited about snorkeling with Lucy's mom!" Justin realized he was too loud and lowered his voice. "Dr. Benitez won't let us keep any treasure we find."

"Let me dream!" Rudy protested, causing the man with crazy hair to chuckle. At some point during their conversation, he'd straightened up and pulled back his headphones.

"You two must be the visiting brothers Dr. Benitez mentioned." The man loosened his grip on the briefcase. "I'm Kit."

"We're not brothers." Rudy frowned. "Our parents just work in the same park."

"You argue like brothers. Where do they work?" Kit asked.

Rudy sipped his coffee before answering. "Biscayne National Park. Before that, Mesa Verde, and Grand Canyon. And before that—hey!" Justin took Rudy's tumbler to interrupt a long speech.

The man raised an eyebrow. "I'm envious, Biscayne has some fascinating maritime archeology. So why are you guys coming to the Dry Tortugas?"

"To visit Dr. Benitez's daughter, Lucy. You must know her." Justin smiled. "You're obviously one of Dr. Benitez's students."

"How'd you guess?" Kit rubbed his face to muffle a yawn. "The briefcase?"

Justin shook his head. "The way you haven't even looked out the window once, like you've done this trip lots."

"My job sends me back and forth quite a bit." Kit nodded.

"What's in your briefcase?" Rudy asked.

"Thousands of dollars and countless hours of research." Kit smiled back, "Have you ever heard of carbon dating?"

"It tells you how old things are, right?" Justin asked.

Kit pursed his lips, "I'm impressed."

"We have a friend who loves fossils, rocks, and dinosaurs." Rudy explained. "You have money in there?"

"My work doesn't go back that far in time." Kit tapped the briefcase. "No money, just interesting archeology results." He gave them an unreadable look, shaking his head. "But I should probably share them with my mentor first."

"Awe." Rudy frowned.

"Makes sense to me." Justin smiled, noticing Kit yawn again. "Anyway, it was nice to meet you. Rudy, let's go to the top deck, we'll get a better view of your treasure boats."

Kit waved after them appreciatively. "Take it easy."

An hour later, they were crowded on the bow with several tourists. "Do you see it yet?" Rudy asked. All eyes were searching for the first sign of seven islands.

"I see something." The pink shirted woman from breakfast called to a friend. Justin could see a tiny black tower on the horizon, but she was pointing to a sandy key drifting up on the starboard side.

"It's so small and empty." Rudy opined. "Where's the fort?"

Reaching into his pocket, Justin fetched his newest acquisition. The heavy metallic compass had seen better years, but it still pointed north. "We're approaching from the east. Meaning that's probably East Key. We've got a few islands to go."

Confirming his navigational skills, a crewmate spoke from the intercom. "*We will soon pass Hospital Key, the northern-most nesting ground for rare masked boobies. There have even been sightings of their vibrant cousin: the red footed booby.*"

Justin leaned over the rails, exactly like Rudy earlier, trying to glimpse the birds. With funny rounded body, masked boobies looked ridiculous. Hence their name, which was Spanish for clown. He reached into his pocket to grab his bird list, but the boat made a swift turn taking them away from the island.

"*Our most eagle-eyed passengers should be able to see the Loggerhead Lighthouse. Left of that is our destination: Fort Jefferson on Garden Key.*"

Loggerhead lighthouse was the tower Justin had seen earlier! Beside it was a low brown plateau in the middle of a deep blue plain. There seemed to be a small forest and large coastline left of the fort. Even surrounded by masts from sailing vessels and short trees, the fort's long walls and turreted corners were distinct. Above it was a second large black lighthouse. "That must be the harbor light."

The ferry slowly circled Garden Key. Outer walls were a patchwork of differently tinted bricks. Through arched windows Justin could see treetops and smaller brick structures. Where beach stopped, a low brick barrier surrounded the fort blocking incoming waves. "So there really is a moat."

Red and green markers lined the channel, their posts looked weathered by time. There was another beach surrounded by buoys marking a swim area. Up from that was a small spit of land with low lying trees. Within a harbor bay protected by three islands, many vessels sat at anchor pulled away from the fort by retreating tides. A large motor vessel painted park service green maneuvered away from the dock.

In the space it left, Justin caught his first glimpse of Mr. Benitez dressed in his gray and green ranger uniform. The fort entrance and harbor light towered behind him. Standing beside him were their friends Miguel and Lucy. "Well, we're here."

CHAPTER 2

MEETING THE TEAM

LUCY

L
UCY SHIFTED HER WEIGHT TO HER LEFT FOOT, to her right, and
back again, trying to find a comfortable way to stand in her flip-flops. This morning, she had tested her willpower by walking barefoot around the hot brick path circling the fort's interior. When the soles of her feet began to burn, she'd resorted to sprinting from shadow to shadow. Somewhere along the way she had stepped on gravel.

Her brother leaned over to gently elbow her. "Stop fidgeting." Making a point to study her face, "you seem unhappy or in pain."

"If you must know, I bruised my feet." She rolled her eyes.

"Both of them? How'd you manage that?" Miguel didn't sound surprised.

"It doesn't matter." Lucy managed a convincing smile. "I am excited to see Justin and Rudy." She had to raise her voice as engines flared when the green park service boat pulled away so the *Yankee Freedom III* could approach.

Miguel leaned closer to whisper. "You were pretending to firewalk on bricks again, weren't you?"

"Miguel, are you disappointed that Cassidy couldn't come?" Lucy raised her voice so their dad could hear. She was rewarded with a bright red flush across her brother's face. Their dad pretended to ignore them.

The *Yankee Freedom III* crew rushed to secure her so people could disembark. The naturalist's voice echoed from ship's speakers with daily directives, interrupting ever-present squawking of birds around Bush Key. Lucy had grown accustomed to the daily rhythm, but this time two of her best friends were somewhere on board.

Tourists carried sacks of snorkel gear and small day bags. Lucy's dad walked forward to greet and answer questions. "The best part of my day is coming out here to say hello." Because they were picking up friends, he'd left his gigantic coffee thermos at home.

The boat was nearly empty before Justin and Rudy appeared at the gangplank shepherded by ferry's naturalist. She helped them carry a large white cooler. The boys each had large backpacks and smaller cases in their free hands.

"Lucy! Miguel!" Rudy rushed past Justin. "This place is like an island castle!" Miguel reached down to ruffle Rudy's light brown hair. He ducked away. "Don't do that. I'm too old."

"Alright, sorry dude." Miguel apologized, stepping around him to help Justin carry the cooler into the shade of the big sea-grapes between dock ramps.

Lucy reached out to give Rudy a big squeeze. "Good to see you, bud. I hope you're ready for adventure." Rudy fished a park brochure from his pocket. It was heavily altered with pen-drawn lines, circles, and shipwrecks.

"I've made notes about possible buried treasure location." Rudy handed the map to Lucy then turned to stare out towards Bush and Long Key. He pointed to a grove of trees on the far island. "I want to dig over there."

"Those islands are closed for nesting." Lucy stared at more than twenty places circled on his map, several were out in deep ocean. "But we can compare this to U.R.S.A.'s chart."

"Is that noise all from sooty terns?" Justin asked as he and Miguel rejoined them.

"It's been that noisy since February." Seeing her brother and friend side-by-side, Lucy realized how long it had been. Miguel had only been slightly taller than Justin in Arizona. Now he was taller by a couple of inches. Justin was as lean as ever. His skin was tan, and his hair sun-bleached blondish.

Justin pulled out a small notebook. "I'll be one species up on my sister." He noted the date, location, and species of bird.

Miguel stared over his shoulder. "Actually two. There are noddy terns flying over the island as well."

"Are they causing bad fishy smells?" Rudy raised his nose.

Lucy had almost forgotten the stench. "Still better than mangroves. Wind usually blows the smell out to sea. By the way, hello Justin." Sneaking up from behind, she startled him with a hug. "It's been a while."

"It has." Justin nodded. Glancing around, making sure no-one else was looking, he mouthed silently. "We have to talk."

Lucy's dad was finishing with a group of tourists. She nodded, "Later."

"It's nice to see you two." Her father extended his hand to shake theirs. "Lucia and Miguel are thrilled some friends were finally able to visit."

"Hello, Mr. Benitez." Justin stepped forward.

Her dad's eyes were elsewhere. "You're timing is perfect! How many students get to take geography and history from a world-renowned archeologist?"

"Where is Dr. Benitez?" As Justin asked, a rusty yellow cart with a large flatbed swerved around a group of tourists.

The woman behind the wheel was smiling. Her long dark hair was tied back in a ponytail. She was dressed in a long pair of cargo shorts and a T-shirt with a turtle. Lines from her wet swimsuit showed through her 'work clothes.' She took flip-flops off the dash and pulled sunglasses up onto her head. With a mischievous smile, Lucy's mother jumped out of the cart as it came to an emergency brake assisted stop.

"Justin Case. Rudy Sheer. Get ready for a soggy hug." As advertised, her hug left wet impressions on their shirts. "My team just got back. Justin, I'm sorry Cassidy couldn't make it. Has she decided on a major yet? Archeology or Anthropology?"

"Well ..." Justin hesitated to answer the question about his sister. *Neither* Lucy knew.

But her mom had moved on to Rudy. "How is my favorite archeologist-in-training?"

"I'm great Dr. Benitez." Rudy beamed. "My mom says thanks for hosting."

"Any time, besides, we need a lifeline to Key West. Work's so busy, I haven't gone back in weeks! Gabriel, Lucia, and Miguel have marooned themselves out here with me!"

Justin grinned. "Don't worry Dr. Benitez, I packed your ice cream myself."

"Fantastic! Put that and your bags on the cart. I'll drive them home." She turned to the crazy haired young man who'd been hovering nearby throughout their reunion, his hands clasped around his briefcase. "Kit, hop aboard. Professor Erickson has been impatiently awaiting your arrival!"

"What about us?" Lucy asked.

"The *Yankee's* naturalist invited you on her tour. She's letting Lucia lead." Her mom winked as Lucy winced. "You do such a wonderful job." That wasn't true.

"I'll ride back with you. I'm done with this heat." Miguel hopped up beside Kit's briefcase. "I'll take your junk to your guest house."

Lucy's dad watched his wife's cart speed off. "I've got to visit new boats in the harbor." Humming, he headed for a park service speedboat bobbing in the shallows. "See you three this afternoon."

"Anything to escape his stacks of paperwork." Lucy shook her head. They watched her dad walk away, juggling a set of boat keys.

Tourists scattered to explore, take pictures in front of the park sign, or beach prep. The ferry crew began their cleanup routine. The three were soon alone. Immediately Rudy had his cell phone out, pacing. "There's no service."

Lucy shook her head. "Duh, we're seventy miles from the nearest cell phone tower."

"I'm supposed to text my mom." Rudy continued tapping his phone screen. "Wait! Wi-fi! Quick, what's the password?"

Lucy smirked. "Employees have satellite TV and Internet. You can call her tonight."

"I know, but…" Rudy angled his phone so she couldn't see.

Lucy stepped closer to stare at his screen. He wasn't making a call. "Are you trying to play a game?" She crossed her arms. "That will wait. We have just enough time to walk around the moat before the fort tour starts in the sally port."

"What's a Sally port?" That made him look up from his phone.

Lucy pointed to a marble archway crowded with tourists. "The entrance to a fort is called a sally port."

"Wait till our friend Sally hears about this." Rudy's smile grew wide.

Pain in her soles forgotten, Lucy led the two boys to the entrance sign:

Fort Jefferson, Dry Tortugas National Park. White words over signature park service brown. "Alright, we can pose here."

"Perfect." Justin reached for his phone. He took pictures in front of every park sign. Most of their friends were children of park rangers. He had a lot of photos. "It's too bad the rest aren't here."

Lucy tried to get into frame. "It's school season and we're all spread out."

"But you have us." Rudy's phone had returned to his pocket. Instead, he was holding his marked-up brochure. "It pays to be home-schooled."

Justin found a willing older couple. After helping them take their picture, the woman was happy to return the favor. She called out in a bright voice. "Smile!" Lucy forced a grin.

With that over, she led them south, clockwise around the fort's exterior. Picnic tables sat near the entrance, covered in unguarded belongings of tourists. Lucy noted a shorter, fuzzy, gray-haired man dozing on a bench in the shade of the tabletop. "That guy's richer than he looks."

"Really?" Rudy wrinkled his nose.

"See that big yacht in the harbor?" Lucy stared at the sleeping millionaire. "It's his. He's helping fund Mom's research. He's out here to make sure his money's not wasted."

"Does napping help him supervise?" Rudy reached instinctively for his phone.

Lucy grinned, wishing she'd made the joke. "Usually, he follows university boats around, but all the students are preparing for a big meeting."

She continued their tour. "That's the campground." Several tents were set up in an area fringed by beech trees and sea grapes. "We don't get a lot of summer campers. It's too hot. People have to bring everything they need, including food and water."

"What's all of that squiggly stuff in the moat?" Ignoring the campground, Rudy balanced precariously on the last row of bricks, staring into shallow waters. "They're like plants, but round, bristly and *pulsing*?"

"Upside-down jellyfish. They can swim, but they like to hang out on the bottom and catch things swimming above them."

"Do they sting?" Rudy asked.

Lucy smiled wildly. "Don't fall in, and you won't find out."

"*Cassiopea*," Justin moved to stand at Rudy's side. "They release floating stinging cells. It's supposed to be a very mild sting. However, they give some people very itchy rashes."

"We have a Moat Club. It's very exclusive." Lucy stepped behind Rudy, standing so close she could almost touch him. "Anyone who falls into the moat can join."

"Whoa!" Startled, Rudy jumped back from the edge.

Lucy laughed. "I'm not a member, but I'll have to tell you Ranger Kyle's and Miguel's stories." A white sandy beach appeared around the corner dotted by tourists, towels, and umbrellas. "This is the south beach. Some people spend their whole trip swimming here, never going into the fort."

Rudy shook his head. "What a waste."

The moat wall extended into the ocean. There were several swimmers snorkeling alongside it. Justin suddenly pulled out his phone. "Is that a frigate bird?"

Lucy squinted skyward, "The one that looks like a pterodactyl?" It was too high up to make out clearly, but Justin was already writing in his bird book.

As the three walked, Lucy pointed out various fish and coral. Schools of angelfish and mangrove snapper cruised inside and outside the moat wall. A small nurse shark swam underneath a group of snorkelers causing shrill sounds of delight or horror.

They continued over a small wooden bridge spanning an intake which let seawater circulate between moat and ocean. "This is where Miguel joined the moat club. We were racing our bikes. I was totally beating him. Out of nowhere he wizzes by me like he was competing for a professional bike team. He missed his turn and ramped right into the sea. He spent two days washing out gears and oiling his bike."

"Miguel taking exercise seriously?" Justin and Miguel were good friends, despite their age difference. "That's hard to believe."

"He's weird now: trying to get into shape, taking up new hobbies every week, even avoiding computer games." Lucy shook her head sadly. "Island isolation is getting to him"

Rudy was a couple of meters ahead tracing his altered map pretending to identify locations at sea. Justin hung back. "Lucy, we need to talk."

"About what?" She paused.

Justin seemed hesitant, even though they were alone, leaning closer, "My mom and dad were on a group call with your dad and a few other parents."

Lucy crossed her arms. "Your mom is chief ranger. She works closely with Big Cypress, Biscayne, the Everglades, and here."

"The Jackson's were on the call, and they've moved up to D.C. Besides, I heard them mention the *Arizona Incident*." Justin whispered like it was covert information.

Despite herself Lucy raised an eyebrow. "Really? You heard those words?"

Justin shrugged. "Well, no, but they were talking about a desert and a big event."

"Justin, *we* were in Arizona months ago. That was a pretty big event! Several of us almost died. Our parents were probably planning ways to keep us out of trouble." Lucy crossed her arms. "Is that why you sent me that cryptic, '*we need to talk*' text?"

"They weren't talking about us." Justin spoke with more determination. "They were talking about the *Big Mystery.*"

Lucy didn't need this right now. She had her own mystery to share. "Mattie and Cassidy have graduated. The *Big Mystery* is old news. I found something closer to home."

"Not this conspiracy stuff again." Rudy had shuffled over. "I want to show you a likely place for a sunken pirate ship."

"What?" Both Lucy and Justin replied.

"I need to show you now! Before we see your mother's charts. That way you know I came up with this idea on my own." Tension from their argument subsided under the weight of Rudy's enthusiasm.

"Sure, bud." Lucy took a deep breath, "where is it?"

"Lighthouse and trees? That's Loggerhead." Rudy looked to Lucy for confirmation. She nodded. "Just south of that island, there's an area where deep water quickly rises." He pointed to the shallow area on his map. "It's a perfect ship trap. A crew could easily miss these shallow corals." His fingers traced dark spots on the map. "If pirates hit them, they'd scraped across the bottom, then sink somewhere over there."

Rudy's finger followed a line from his map to a spot out across the water. "Look! There's already a boat out there. Is that your mother's team?"

Lucy shook her head. "No, that's a commercial diving vessel. They bring people from Key West or Marathon to dive cool wrecks."

Justin stared out at the boat. "Rudy actually found a wreck?"

Lucy shook her head sympathetically, "You're a little too late, bud. That's the Windjammer, the most famous wreck out here."

"Oh." There was no mistaking Rudy's disappointment.

CHAPTER 3

A TOUR

RUDY

RETURNING TO THE FORT'S FRONT ENTRANCE, Rudy was feeling better. "I discovered a wreck. I just wasn't first." They walked slowly across the bridge over the moat so Lucy could keep up.

She balanced precariously on an elevated board marking a short drop into the moat. "I never use the real bridge, only this rail. Dad and his other rangers tell me not to do it in front of tourists, but I haven't fallen in yet."

"I'm surprised Miguel hasn't pushed you." Justin smiled.

"Sally port." Rudy chuckled. A tunnel-like entrance cut through exterior and interior walls. Lucy's slow pace allowed the two newcomers to take in Fort Jefferson's massive size. She pointed out three slot-angled windows on each side of the entrance.

"Those windows were for riflemen. If invaders tried to cross this bridge, soldiers could shoot out, but it would be hard for enemies to shoot in. Now, those windows look out from the park ranger's office left, and visitor center on the right."

"Have we started the tour? What about other tourists?" Justin's raised an eyebrow.

"Consider this my warmup." Lucy's voice echoed through the cool tunnel breeze. "I'm not you Justin. I don't like big groups."

Crossing through the fort walls was like crossing into another world. Tropical vegetation lined the brick path which circled the entire fort interior. The harbor light to their right towered above everything else. In a sandy patch across from Sally's Port, marched several medium sized, awkward looking, white birds.

"Cattle Egrets—" Lucy explained, following Justin's gaze, "—blown out here during storms. They don't have the brains or energy to fly back. These won't impress your sister, sorry."

"I'm not trying to impress Cassidy. I'm trying to beat her." Justin noted the birds in his book.

Lucy shrugged, "There are supposed to be lots of rare birds out here."

Justin grinned. "I'll find so many, she'll wish she'd never left for college."

"Awe, you miss her already." Lucy teased stopping beneath a warped tree beside a brown park guide sign.

The ferry's naturalist herded tourists out of the visitor center clapping to get everyone's attention. "Today, I'm turning our tour over to a native. Lucy Benitez has lived out here for more than a year. She knows this place as well as anyone." She winked at Lucy, "Why don't you take it away?"

Lucy quivered slightly before speaking, "We are standing in the parade ground. When this was a military fort, more than one hundred years ago, it housed a thousand men, women, prisoners, and children. The last two, of-course, were here against their will."

The crowd laughed politely. Lucy continued. "Anyway, the parade ground is about thirteen-acres. It was once home to several large officers' quarters, powder magazines, military tents, a different lighthouse and even a small farm. The tents were packed up after the war. The animals were moved to a different island. The lighthouse was dismantled. The officers' quarters burned down. There's one house left. I live in half of it." She pointed across the fort.

Lucy stamped on the ground. "Most everything you see is Civil War related, but this island has a longer history. It was an ancient coral reef, which became Garden Key. It has been home to pirates, a base for stranded officers from a British naval vessel, then a fort and jail. In World War Two, it became a fueling station for ships and seaplanes patrolling the Gulf of Mexico for U-Boats. Let's see some cool stuff."

Justin leaned over to whisper. "Lucy has her mom's lecture skills."

"Yeah," Rudy agreed. "But those lame jokes are all her dad."

"Depending how you count, there are four hundred and twenty arches. Each was supposed to get cannon." Lucy stopped atop a rusted metal curve inserted into the gray slate floor. Rudy recognized them from a different civil war fort where his father had worked. "These tracks were used to slide heavy cannon back and forth to aim out of these windows." Pretending to operate a giant cannon, both the ferry and the park service boat were at Lucy's mercy.

"Fully armed and operational, with eight-foot-thick exterior walls and bristling with cannon, Fort Jeff would have intimidated any invading force. These lower windows were designed with iron shutters that closed every time cannon fired, so people couldn't shoot in while soldiers rearmed. But the fort never got all of its cannon, and most which made it out here were harvested for metal after the civil war."

A tourists raised their hands. "Where are those iron shutters?"

Lucy replied. "The fort engineers didn't plan for salt air. Rudy, what did you say about the fort walls?"

He looked up when she called his name. "That they look spotty."

Lucy nodded. "Right. The iron shutters rusted inside the brick walls collapsing huge chunks out of them. The park service hired masons to redo entire exterior sections of the fort. Now, you can spot the old and new brickwork."

Lucy continued, sharing more insights. The two turrets guarding the entrance had cannon specifically designed to shoot troops trying to cross the bridge. Rounded staircases inside each turret contained individual powder magazines. On the second level, she pointed out floor sections missing slate. "You can see fossil coral once mined from the island to build this place."

Rudy missed a lot of her talk because Justin kept tugging on his shirt anytime he got too close to the outer edge of the fort. Did he think Rudy was going to tumble into the moat?

They walked into the Large Powder Magazine, now just a brick shell with a maze of lower walls. They stopped beside a hot shot furnace where cannon balls would be heated before being shot at wooden ships.

Eventually, they wound up back above the sally port on the second floor. "See three slits up here and this groove down here?" Lucy asked.

"The windows above the sally port are unique. Those grooves in ground were dug by prisoners to collect rainwater during storms."

"Why are we looking at these?" One of the tourists asked.

"They are how we know this room was home to Fort Jeff's most famous prisoner: Dr. Samuel Mudd." Lucy explained. "He's the doctor who treated John Wilkes Booth, Abraham Lincoln's assassin. Booth broke his leg while fleeing from Ford's Theatre. Dr. Mudd treated him and was convicted for helping the criminal. He claimed not to know Booth, but there was evidence they had met before."

Rudy raised his hand. "A sign said Dr. Mudd's cell was the other way."

Lucy smirked. "Dr. Mudd kept a journal of his time out here and described looking out through three slit windows and collecting rainwater in the floor. Most historians think this was actually his cell."

"I'll have to investigate that later." Rudy frowned.

Lucy tried to ignore him. "There's a lot more to Dr. Mudd's tale, you can learn from the visitor center's video. This is where our tour ends because it's lunch time."

The naturalist gave her a thumbs up. "Feel free to give my tour any time. Just don't tell my boss, or I'm out of a job."

Justin nodded, impressed. "Honestly, you could be an interpretive ranger."

Lucy shook her head. "Blech. No way."

Justin shrugged, "Then why give the tour?"

"Now you can't bother me with questions, and we can get to the good stuff. It's lunch time. I'm hungry. Let's go meet Mom's team!" Lucy turned back towards the small circular stairwell. Rudy and Justin followed.

Once she was out of earshot Rudy protested, "What does she mean: now we can get to the good stuff? History is the good stuff."

"I know, Rudy. Now, please, stay a little further from the edge."

CHAPTER 4

MEETING THE DIVE BEARS

JUSTIN

SPIRAL STAIRCASES HAD STEPS LARGE ON THE OUTSIDE shrinking inward towards the center. On their way down, a family of three was walking up. Justin had to do a funny dance around two blond twins and their father while everyone tried to find a foothold.

Lucy pulled them inside the visitor center. "We have to say hello to Renee before we go to lunch." They all shivered in cold air-conditioning.

"Lucy." Rudy's voice was full of mock protest. "Why didn't we start here? This air-conditioning is awesome!"

A young blond woman was working in the gift shop. She was about six feet tall, and her face was covered in freckles. She looked, Justin thought, a bit like the twins he'd just seen. When she turned to readjust a couple of books and a stack of waterproof disposable cameras, Lucy stepped forward. "Renee, meet Justin and Rudy."

Renee turned with a smile. "Wonderful to meet you! Luke and Nina will be thrilled to make more friends."

"Weird," Rudy picked up a yellow package from the counter. "Why do you sell film cameras?"

Renee smiled, amused, "They're underwater cameras. Waters around here provide great opportunities to photograph coral reefs, colorful fish, and shipwrecks."

Lucy crossed her arms. "Not everyone has thousands of dollars for a good underwater digital camera."

"Thousands of dollars!" Rudy's eyes bulged.

Lucy nodded. "And Mom's team had to buy two."

"Why two?" Justin asked. Lucy glanced behind him. The old rich historian from the campground was standing next to an exhibit on cannon balls.

Lucy lowered her voice. "We'll talk about that later."

"These are much cheaper." Renee grabbed the yellow package gently from Rudy, who'd forgotten to return it to the sales rack.

Justin shrugged. "Why don't people just get waterproof phone cases?"

Lucy ignored him. "Renee and her family live aboard a sailboat in the harbor. They are volunteering through August and September on Loggerhead. Renee boats over some days."

Renee nodded. "The gift shop is a nice break from heavy-lifting and electrical work. Luke and Nina are hopeless solar power assistants."

Lucy grinned. "The twins are our age. They've lived on a sailboat since they were five."

"It's usually a relaxing life, but last year we were nearly caught in a hurricane." Renee stated calmly. "We decided to take this storm season off. Shawn, my husband, is learning new maintenance skills and Luke and Nina get consistent internet."

Lucy looked pointedly at Rudy. "Imagine that: internet only two months a year."

"Mom would never let me live on a boat." Rudy reached protectively for his phone.

Lucy sighed. "Anyway Renee, when will we see Luke and Nina?"

"You just missed them." Renee frowned. "Their over here for the day. Their father's helping rangers with the solar grid." Justin marveled. Hadn't Lucy seen the twins on the stairs?

"What about Spud?" Lucy asked.

"Spud's guarding our boat." Renee replied. "We'll pick him up before we head back to Loggerhead."

"Spud's their labradoodle." Lucy explained as they left. "He's a big curly ball of caramel colored energy." They circled the brick path clockwise. Justin was already getting used to the place. Having giant brick walls surrounding them made it feel like they were in a medieval castle.

Around the first corner, right of the sally port, the brick path squeezed between stairs and a half-collapsed brick building. Two gumbo limbo towered over them. "What's that ruin?" Rudy asked.

"Another smaller powder magazine." Lucy answered.

"How much gun powder did they need out here?" Justin asked.

"You have no idea." Lucy shrugged past a crooked brown sign. "Anyway, Mom's home base is just up those stairs. But we'll talk about that later. This corner is better at night."

"Why?" Shadows from trees in the corner were refreshing. This seemed like a cozy nesting spot. He scanned branches overhead for interesting birds.

Lucy chuckled. "This is Private Winter's corner. He's one of the fort's ghosts."

"It's haunted!" Rudy nearly dropped his phone. That was probably Lucy's intent. "Let's go, now!"

Moving on, they passed a small *STOP* sign. On an island with no cars? Beneath was another sign: '*Park service personnel only.*' They walked swiftly past. "Walking past Do Not Enter signs is going to give me a severe trespassing complex." Justin remarked.

Lucy shook her head. "You already have one. Remember Arizona?"

Three sections of fort wall were blocked off for employee housing, storage, maintenance facilities, and generators. A well-groomed garden welcomed them into the housing area. It spread from brick path into a casemate. Justin recognized a few growing vegetables.

"That's the Ishii's place. Mr. Ishii is our chief of interpretation. He is technically the park ranger in charge of Mom's expedition, but he's currently at a green training event. His wife is working in Key West's visitor center. They come back next week. Miguel has been watering their garden."

Ripening bananas on the tree centered in the garden made Justin's belly rumble. He was prepared, however, for Lucy to walk them past every house and tell them about every ranger out here. Fortunately, the very next stop was their destination. "This is the…"

"Crews quarters." Rudy interrupted.

Lucy looked perplexed. "How'd you know?"

"There is a big sign which says: *Crews Quarters*." Rudy pointed.

"Oh, yeah." Lucy observed the sign. "Boy, you live somewhere more than a year and you stop noticing things." The crews quarters was built into two casemates, contained by wooden walls. A large group, mostly young adults, milled about outside. They were all wearing T-shirts and shorts, although some had forgone T-shirts in favor of bathing suit tops, and one guy was walking around in only shorts.

"Meet Mom's team, U.R.S.A.: Underwater, Research, Scuba, Archeology. I call them Dive Bears." Lucy pointed to the logo on her shirt. "They're the most recent team of underwater archeologists out here. Using new techniques, digital mapping equipment, and satellite imagery they've even found new wrecks from space."

"Yup! This is the best PhD project!" The speaker was the man who'd forgotten his T-shirt. Maybe he'd been unable to find one able to fit his muscular frame. "You must be Lucy's friends. She's been so excited you're coming. I'm Chet." He reached out engulfing Justin's hand.

Despite Chet's big muscles, Justin's hand remained in one piece. "You guys should meet the crew before lunch." He pulled them into the crews quarters to introduce a battery of names and faces.

Gwen was a tall woman with red hair. Lucy made a beeline for her. Sophia's dark ponytail waved as she glanced up from her laptop for a quick hello. Kit was also there, along with lots of others. Justin logged all their names and something distinct about their features.

There were also two professors. Dr. Alexa was older than Dr. Benitez. She towered above everyone despite her small frame. Professor Erickson was half again older. He stroked his gray goatee when introduced.

Rudy kept snagging bites of food while Chet completed introductions. Before long, they were sitting at one of several picnic tables outside with Professor Erickson, Sophia, and Chet— who'd managed to find a shirt large enough to contain his muscles. Each had a plate filled with chips, dill pickles, and a sandwich worthy of a professional deli.

Lucy's mom was last to arrive. Grabbing a plate, she squeezed in beside her daughter. "Join me in welcoming our two newest volunteers. They may seem young, but they've helped me on a number of previous research assignments." The rowdy college students cheered.

She continued once everyone settled, "Now some announcements. First. Thanks for your hard work. Our first season is nearly over, but we're 90% on target, despite many setbacks. We've discovered several new wrecks, and updated documentation on many more. I want you to know how proud I am of everyone. Here's to the summer crew!"

"Here, here." Chet shouted, leading a round of cheers.

Dr. Benitez smile shifted downward. Her voice grew stern. "I'm not done." Justin knew that tone. It had the same effect on her students as on him. The rowdy group fell silent.

"Not everyone deserves accolades." Dr. Benitez's frown matched her steely gaze. She set her plate aside pressing both hands into the table staring over her assembled crew. "We have a traitor in our midst. I intend to find out who it is."

CHAPTER 5

THE MYSTERY

JUSTIN

"Ahh," Dr. Benitez focused her iron gaze on the woman beside Justin, "Sophia, don't get up, this is serious." The young woman froze in a half squat over her seat. Her gaze shifted to Dr. Alexa. "As I was saying, we have a big problem."

Professor Erickson cleared his throat. "Excuse me, Dr. Benitez, perhaps I should take your daughter and show her friends to their quarters before this *particular* discussion."

Dr. Benitez paused, shrugging. "Fine, Alan."

"Come on, guys." Lucy stood urging her friends to follow, leaving students in suspense while Dr. Benitez towered over them.

Around another corner a brick building enclosed the footpath, forming a narrow hallway between it and fort wall. Lucy pointed at the two-story house. "We live in the bigger half of that house. The rest belongs to Ranger Kyle."

It was made of similar bricks to the fort. It had a small, screened porch, and another patio fenced in and facing fort walls. Half the patio was covered by a vast array of flowering plants. Half was covered in replica artifacts. Both sides were decorated by a variety of hanging holiday lights.

Professor Erickson led them up wooden stairs to the second floor where they were greeted with cool shade and a wooden deck. "These apartments are for volunteers, VIPs and old professors who don't want to live with smelly, noisy, grad students." The professor led them under a series of arches. "The first is mine. This is yours."

The rooms were like the crews quarters but smaller and less crowded, built into only half of two casemates each. "This is our place?" Rudy dropped his backpack in the door running to the back room. There were two bunk beds, the top of both were already made. There was a set of packages on each lower bunk. "Cool! Justin, we have our own apartment!"

"It will be nice to have neighbors. It's been too quiet in these drafty brick walls." Professor Erickson smiled. "I'll leave you here. I've got grants to write." The professor let their wooden door snap shut behind him.

Justin waited until he was gone to ask Rudy. "What's in your package?"

Rudy shook his head frowning suspiciously at the box. "I don't want to know anymore." He pulled out his phone. "Does this place have Wi-Fi?"

Lucy nodded. "It does, bud. I'll help you find the router."

While they were busy, Justin stepped out of the small apartment. Around most of the fort, second-floor casemates had large archways open to air. Here, some exterior walls had remnants of brickwork which would have enclosed the fort in a more serious layer of defense.

Justin leaned against a waist-high brick wall. Directly below, a few people in swimsuits were carrying bags of snorkeling gear around the moat wall. Waves broke against brick with a gentle repetitive crash. He reached into his pocket, feeling the circular metal compass he'd brought to show Lucy.

The apartment door closed. Lucy leaned on the archway beside him. "Rudy's calling his mom. Do you need the password?"

"I'll text Dad tonight. Mom is with Cassidy. If I called them now, they'd think there was an emergency. Why did your mom mention a traitor at lunch?"

Lucy's eyes followed the family around the corner. They had never noticed two people watching them from the second level. She sighed. "I didn't think she'd tell everyone."

Justin straightened up. "Is it the mystery you mentioned?"

"Mama's been acting weird since her students arrived. It's only gotten worse. Today was the first time I've seen her smile in a week." Lucy frowned. "She thinks someone is trying to sabotage U.R.S.A."

Justin nodded, "Why? I can't imagine anyone messing with Dr. Benitez!"

"She won't talk about it with me or Miguel around. I only know anything because I can hear them talk at night." Lucy stamped her foot, wincing in pain. "Sound carries really well upstairs from the living room. They're worried about theft and sabotage."

"Who'd want to sabotage underwater archeologists?"

Lucy threw up her hands in a questioning gesture.

"You know what this means?" Justin understood Lucy's worry. If her research were compromised, Dr. Benitez would have to pack up and head back to the university, leaving the Dry Tortugas behind. Lucy's mom worked around the world. Everyone had been excited when she'd found an excuse to work in the park where her family lived. "We have a mystery. Fortunately, I know a couple of world class investigators."

"Oh no. Don't say it."

"The Junior Rangers Investigative Club!"

"We came up with that name years ago, haven't you thought of anything better yet?" Lucy rolled her eyes, "Never mind. There's no mystery here. Let's just do our schoolwork and go snorkeling."

Justin posed heroically in the archway. "You should know. J.R.I.C. never refuses a case."

CHAPTER 6

THE EXPEDITION'S END

LUCY

Justin and Lucy were equally shocked by the new state of the apartment. Packages had been opened exposing textbooks, workbooks, notebooks, and pencils. Their school supplies had been organized and arranged at the table. Rudy was sitting in front of his laptop which was atop an empty candy wrapper. "It was just our school stuff."

"What are you doing?" Justin picked up a piece of shredded brown paper with his name on it.

"I'm researching Fort Jefferson's history with pirates. I'm thinking the best place to search for buried treasure is Long Key, across the harbor."

"Did you eat my candy bar?" Justin grabbed a second, discarded, wrapper off the floor.

"No, I ate my own." Rudy replied. Then he looked up from his web search guiltily. "What? We had to leave lunch early. I forgot to bring mine with me."

Lucy leaned against the doorway. "Mom took that candy from our hurricane emergency supplies. We'll get you another, Justin. Anyway, tell Rudy what we were talking about outside."

Once they had filled Rudy in, he smiled. "This is another J.R.I.C.

mission, isn't it?"

"It's worse when you abbreviate Justin's dumb name." Before Lucy could roll her eyes, she was interrupted by knocking behind her. She turned, swiftly, to see her brother's face in the window. "Miguel, you startled me!" Opening the door, she punched him in the arm.

"Ow," Miguel rubbed his arm. "I came to see how you two were liking your new place."

"It's a lot better than Yellowstone's cabins." Rudy said without glancing away from the screen. "There's running water and inside toilets."

"Fair enough." Miguel shrugged. "Mom wants to see you all downstairs soon."

Justin rubbed his hands together, "Great, maybe we could ask her about what happened at lunch after we left?"

"Lunch?" Miguel looked questioningly at Justin.

Lucy answered for him. "Dr. Carmen Gonzales Benitez was so angry that her grad students were scared silent!"

Miguel shook his head "I haven't seen her yell at students since the sarcophagus incident." He leaned into Justin, "how did Chet take it?"

"Mom didn't yell." Lucy countered.

Miguel nodded. "If it was that bad, I wouldn't mention it. When Mom's quiet-angry, she hands out punishments like candy."

Lucy turned to Justin and Rudy, "when Chet broke the Sarcophagus, Miguel made one joke and lost computer privileges for a month."

"It was terrible." Miguel nodded. "We're on an island without cell service, grocery stores, arcades, movie theatres, or interesting people."

"Hey!" Lucy frowned.

Miguel shrugged. "Don't make Mom mad. Your tech privileges are on the line."

"There's an ocean and a creepy old fort to explore. I could survive." Rudy replied without looking up from his phone, "Especially if you give me a shovel." Justin eyed the Benitez siblings, shaking his head emphatically. Rudy sighed. "So, that means we do what we always do. Solve a mystery, then get yelled at for helping."

Justin laughed. "It's not always that bad."

Miguel frowned. "It is though."

Miguel and Lucy left the boys to unpack. Lucy found her mother sitting in the living room scrolling through her phone. "Lucia, where are the boys?"

"They'll be down soon." Lucy settled uncomfortably onto the padded couch beside her mother. "Mama, what's going on with U.R.S.A.?"

Her mother looked up briefly. "Nothing you need to concern yourself with, mija." She turned back to her email. Lucy continued to stare until finally her mother sighed. "Fine, it's not like you didn't know already."

"What do you mean?" Lucy could feel her face flush.

"That wasn't you I heard eavesdropping the other night?" Her mom sighed back into their family couch. "It's not just the summer crew going home in a few weeks. It's all of U.R.S.A."

"What?" Lucy straightened. "Why?"

Her mother returned her stare. "How much did you hear?"

Lucy shrugged. "I know U.R.S.A. stuff has gone missing, that you and papa think someone is stealing it, and that the Dive Bears might be involved."

"Well, as I just told my students: these problems caused the university to put an indefinite hold on our funding. Our expedition has only continued this long because of Mr. Howard's support, which will not last forever."

Lucy knew how her mother would respond, but she had to try. "Mama, Miguel and I, Justin and the others: we've solved mysteries before."

Her mother stood and began pacing back and forth in the small room. "I know. You and your other friends have been doing this for a while." She stared daggers at her daughter. "Making your parents worry." Her expression relaxed, "but you've helped with some big incidents. Fine. I'll let you all help, on a provisional basis. Let's wait for the boys, then I'll explain."

Lucy eyed her mother with shock. That had been easier than she expected! Why did that feel disappointing?

CHAPTER 7

FIRST OFFICIAL CASE

JUSTIN

LUCY GREETED THEM in the Benitez's narrow but homey kitchen. Decorative flowerpots filled with a variety of colorful plants lined windowsills. The only appliances on the counter were a blender and a microwave beneath with a fishbowl with two goldfish swimming freely.

Rudy jogged over to the bowl. "Harvey, Evian! Lucy hasn't killed you yet!"

"We think microwave radiation might actually be keeping them alive." Lucy, reaching into her fridge, tossed a candy bar to Justin. She dropped a pinch of food into the goldfish bowl. "There you go little zombie-fish."

While Justin opened his candy bar, Lucy led them past a cluttered room which must be Mr. Benitez's office, and into a living room with enough sofa space for everyone. A red and black Navajo blanket hung on the white wall across from an old Ethiopian crucifix. The only other decoration was a big television. A narrow wooden staircase led to a second floor. Lucy called upstairs. "Mama, the boys are here."

Deliberate footsteps echoed down the narrow stairwell. "Wonderful!" The world-famous Dr. Carmen Benitez stepped into the room with mischievous smile. "Justin, Lucia, and Rudy, tell me: did you notice anything suspicious about my students?"

"What do you mean, Dr. Benitez?"

"Please Justin, call me Carmen. You're not my student, yet." Dr. Benitez settled onto the couch next to her daughter. "I want your opinions as the best detectives on the island. Who looked guilty?"

"Well, we…" Justin started, before looking to Lucy, confused.

"It's ok, Justin. I convinced Mom to let us help her," Lucy interjected. Dr. Benitez nodded, confirming her daughters words. *How had she managed that?* Usually, their parents were trying to stop them from investigating.

"What was the question again?" Justin hesitated, thinking about how to respond.

"How do we find criminals." Lucy repeated, turning to her mother. "We let evidence do the talking and try to avoid personal confrontations." The last time they had come face to face with a criminal, Lucy definitely hadn't '*tried to avoid personal confrontation.*' Best he didn't mention that.

"I use my gut to decide who to trust," Justin shrugged.

"Which is a terrible idea." Lucy shook her head.

"Remember Colorado?" Rudy snuffled. "You said we could trust that river guide?" Justin's face flushed with warmth. "Only, she wasn't a river guide."

Lucy continued through Rudy's giggle fits. "She tried to steer our raft from the front."

"Mrs. Benitez," Rudy cleared his throat, stifling his own laughter, "I've actually done research online about detecting guilt. Some people don't seem surprised by accusations at all, and others act too surprised. I also learned how to read micro-expressions, and weird body language." His smile beamed through their collected surprise before he shrunk back into his chair. "But then again, I don't know your students well enough to watch their body language."

Justin leaned forward. "Doctor, um Carmen, can you describe everything in detail?"

Lucy's mom nodded. "It started two months ago when our students arrived with Professor Erickson. Doctor Alexa and I were here early setting up the map room, dividing student schedules and planning a leave and boat rotation." She shook her head. "On our first day of work, our schedule disappeared from all university computers. We had to spend days rebuilding it from scratch."

"A few days later, we noticed that our expensive 3D-imaging underwater camera was missing. When we began scanning the park's seafloor, one of our GPS units vanished. One missing piece of specialized equipment is a terrible accident. Two is a mystery. Each time something disappears, we have to wait weeks for new equipment to be shipped out." Dr. Benitez shook her head. "Fortunately, Mr. Howard funded those replacements otherwise we'd still be cutting through university red tape."

"It helps to have a rich guy fund U.R.S.A." Lucy turned to her mother, "I wasn't sure he knew about the missing equipment."

"That's why you didn't want to talk about the camera in the visitor center!" Justin had wondered why she'd grown silent when they were talking to Renee.

"Mr. Howard has been very patient, but he's set to go home at the end of the summer. We can't keep relying on him." Dr. Benitez nodded. "Missing equipment and erased records aren't all. To save time we decided to use charts left by the previous archeological team to focus on areas they hadn't completed." Lucy could hear her mother's frustration. "The previous expedition head swore he left paper copies in the map room, but they were gone."

Miguel nodded. "You made me download all of their digitized records."

Dr. Benitez continued, "When we finally got back on schedule, a boat broke down." She shook her head. "Some engine cables had frayed to the point of breaking. Ranger O'Donnell thought it might be incidental wear, but our boats were serviced a week before coming out here."

"Dr. Alexa's scanning teams and Professor Erickson's mapping teams have been fighting over boat time ever since. That's why we've been letting students borrow ours." Justin had seen the Benitez's boat bobbing next to the dock.

Justin sat up. "That's a lot happing very quickly."

Dr. Benitez shrugged. "We have lots of moving parts. Thankfully, there have been no problems with the diving equipment. I'd almost expect more delays."

"Except?" Justin knew there must be more.

"Except, even when we moved the expensive equipment to the bat cave, things continued to go missing." Dr. Benitez frowned. "Each problem has been a too convenient setback."

"Bat Cave?" Rudy asked.

Lucy waved him off mouthing, *"I'll explain later."*

"On top of everything else, commercial dive boats are beginning to show up while our students work on sites which are supposed to be secret. Tourists interrupting our work throws our schedule into even more disarray."

"It sounds like someone is trying to stop your team from getting anything done." Justin scratched his chin.

"Worse, I'm afraid one of my students might be involved." She shook her head.

"Why'd you bring all of this up at lunch?" Lucy asked.

"You met Kit this morning. His carbon-dating samples tell us how old our shipwrecks are. He takes two samples of wood from each shipwreck and tests them in a machine back in Key West. Two samples: One to test, one to hold onto for later verification. Today, we discovered that his most recent spare samples were missing from the map room!" Dr. Benitez gritted her teeth.

"He said they were worth thousands of dollars!" Rudy exclaimed. "He lost all that money?"

"That's not exactly how it works. But Kit's research is based on experimental equipment. Those samples were matching pairs. Without them, his original data is useless. He has to start over and recheck every wreck. Most students are using his data. One missing briefcase and everyone's work is weeks behind." Dr. Benitez threw up her hands in frustration.

"So, Carmen, umm, Doctor Benitez," Justin broke the silence. "What do you want from us?"

Lucy's mom allowed an impish grin to break through her funk. "I want you to help me figure out who is doing this. You'll be more objective. I don't want to discover that my students are involved in this, but I'm starting to suspect everyone."

Justin nodded confidently. "We can help."

Dr. Benitez nodded. "Then consider me your first official client."

Justin felt a bubble of excitement as a smile blossomed across Rudy's face. They'd never had parental approval before! "J.R.I.C. is on the case." So, why had Lucy's frown returned?

CHAPTER 8

A STORY ABOUT SWIMMING

LUCY

"OF COURSE, DON'T SPEND TOO MUCH OF YOUR TIME worrying about my problems. Your schoolwork comes first. Schoolwork, safety, and having fun." Lucy's mom made a gesture encompassing the entire park. "If I feel the mystery is taking up too much of your time, or becoming too dangerous, you will stop."

That was it. They were officially helping her mother. Why was Lucy annoyed? Her mom leaned forward. "So, tell me, where do you begin your investigations?"

Justin swallowed under the intensity of her gaze. "Honestly, it might help if we learn more about U.R.S.A. first."

Lucy crossed her arms. "Yeah, it's not there's anyone here who's more familiar with the park or the Dive Bears." Justin looked confused by her sarcastic tone.

"I'll make sure you *all* get to know U.R.S.A. and what we are up to." Lucy's mom's smile was the same one she gave students when asking them to solve a problem. "Two final things. First, let me know before you do anything even remotely dangerous. Second, don't let Gabriel know about this."

"I was crawling through ruins with Lucy's grandfather when I was half your age, but each of your adventures takes years off Gabe's life." Lucy's mom turned to the boys. "This stays between us."

Almost on cue, the screen door in the office closed with a loud slap of wood on wood. Mr. Benitez walked in. "A welcome party. What are you guys up to?"

"We were making plans for the day Papa." Lucy tried to keep the edge out of her voice, "Um, can you take us out on our boat?"

Mr. Benitez sighed. "I'm only back to pack lunch. Shelly asked me to take the turtle volunteers to Hospital Key to count new nests."

Justin perked up when her father dropped the island's name. No doubt he already knew of the funny looking birds nesting there. "Can we come?"

"Hospital Key is closed for bird nesting." He shrugged sympathetically. "It's an afternoon of sitting in a boat under the hot sun, waiting for turtle volunteers to scout with binoculars." His face brightened.

"I almost forgot." He opened a tall cabinet in his office pulling out two large mesh bags, "I didn't have time to wrap these like Carmen, but I also got you two something. I had to ask your parents for your shoe size, but I think I did a pretty good job with the masks."

Both bags contained snorkeling gear. Rudy's had a red mask, black fins with red strips and red dive boots. Everything in Justin's bag was green. "Lucy helped me pick out the colors." Lucy's father grinned. "You three should grab Miguel, try out the new gear at the beach."

Rudy piped up. "Thank you, Mr. Benitez!"

"Well, actually, we were going to research the Dive Bears. Oof." Lucy elbowed Justin. "I could snorkel," he said rubbing his stomach.

Dr. Carmen Benitez beamed emphatically, "Now is a wonderful time. The tide is going out. The ferry is about to leave. You should have the beach to yourselves."

Lucy turned to Miguel who had padded downstairs at the sound of his name. Obviously, he had heard everything. "You're coming, right?"

Miguel hesitated for a moment catching an intense stare from both parents. "I guess I'll supervise, but I won't snorkel, my mask is still leaking." He added, as though he needed an excuse.

"You keep getting your hair stuck in it." Lucy rose to the bait.

"I'll stay dry on the beach and keep an eye out for giant shark fins." He grinned evilly.

"Not funny."

Justin sighed under his breath. "I guess the mystery can wait."

"What's that?" her father asked, sack lunch in hand.

"We'll talk later, honey." Dr. Benitez winked, ushering him outside.

Lucy waited for the boys to leave so they could pick up their swimsuits. Then she turned to her mother. Her mother stared back. "You have something you want to say?"

Lucy fought an urge to roll her eyes by crossing her arms. "Why did you wait until *Justin* was here to talk about U.R.S.A.'s problems? I could have started helping you weeks ago."

Her mom sighed back into their family couch. "Did I ever tell you about when I learned to dive?"

"No? What does that have—" Lucy stopped as her mother held up a single finger.

Her mom held up her hand, measuring her younger self against Lucy. "I was about your age, maybe a little older. Your grandfather was working with a famous Italian archeologist in Alexandria, Egypt. Local anglers lead them to a site which might have been Cleopatra's lost palace. The Italian dive team worked from a boat anchored a mile from the coast. My father and I took a small skiff out to meet them."

"On our way, I caught sight of a Roman column underwater. It was gray and splotchy with age and covered in sediment and seaweed. I kept my sighting secret." She shrugged. "A few days later, after several diving lessons, I was ready to make my own big discovery. I took my new diving equipment and piloted a skiff out to my find, alone."

"You found Cleopatra's Palace?" Lucy couldn't help her skepticism.

Her mother laughed. "Heavens no! No. It only took a few minutes in the water to realize that what I had found was debris dropped from a modern barge helping to build Alexandria's new port. The date inscribed in marble was a good eighteen centuries after Cleo's reign."

"Mama, what's your point?" Lucy asked.

Her mother, fortunately, laughed her off. "The point mija, is that when I swam back up my skiff was gone."

"What?"

"It had dragged anchor. With its low profile, in choppy waters, I couldn't see it. That was bad enough, but I also couldn't see our ship." Lucy felt a tingle creep up her neck picturing her mother alone at sea.

"With your head out of water one foot you should be able to see just over a mile, but the waves around me were more than a foot and a half high. I couldn't see the ship or coast. I panicked."

Lucy shivered. "What did you do?"

"I picked a direction and started swimming. Eventually, I pulled myself onto one of Alexandria's beaches frightening several families." She shook her head. "If I'd swum in any other direction, I'd still be adrift in the Mediterranean."

"Why are you telling me this?"

"Lucia, the Italian archeologist had a daughter and a son aboard that ship. You remember Francesco and Rebecca?"

"Yeah." They were some of her mother's best friends.

"They had been teaching me to dive. I could have invited them to help me, but I wanted all the glory." Her mother crossed her arms.

"So, you want me to share glory?" Lucy pretended she didn't understand her mother.

Her mom stuck out her tongue, "No. My point is, if I'd had a couple of friends on the skiff, I would never have wound up in such a tight spot alone. I knew you would want to investigate this. I know I can't stop you." She shook her head, "but I hoped you would wait for friends to back you up."

"You really want us to find your 'saboteur?" Lucy used Justin's title with air quotes.

"Yes. My students are wonderful. The other rangers are great. But if they are up to something they will be on guard around me and your father. Besides, you little investigators have a stellar track record."

"We're the Junior Rangers Investigative Club, Ma." Lucy shook her head.

"Whatever. You have my blessing," she fixed Lucy with a strong gaze "for now. If I tell you to stop, you must listen."

"Yes ma'am." Lucy gave her mother a false salute before running upstairs.

CHAPTER 9

WATERS NEAR SHORE

LUCY

"**Y**OU'RE NOT SNORKELING?" Justin asked as they reached the beach. "I don't feel like getting wet." Miguel didn't, exactly, sound annoyed.

"The island seems emptier now." Justin surveyed the south beach. A single tourist, a middle-aged woman, shaded her face with a novel.

"That's how I like it." Lucy grinned as they dropped their gear onto the sand at a distance. "Miguel is the people watcher. I prefer to think of this as my own private kingdom."

"I haven't done much snorkeling." Rudy was trying to squeeze his new dive shoes into flippers.

"You live in Biscayne." Lucy stared at him incredulously. "It's ninety-five percent water."

Justin hopped on one foot, flippers in hand, mask pulled onto his head. "I bet you're out here a lot, Lucy."

"She's basically half fish." Miguel dropped a study guide atop his towel. "Which is why the sharks like her."

Lucy ignored him, hobbling into the surf. There was no way to look graceful on land with flippers. "Follow me and I'll show you all the best places."

She led the boys over seagrass scattering schools of small fish in her wake. She stopped in a sandy spot to balance on tips of her fins. "I'll take you to a few coral heads out by the buoys. Then, we'll swim around the corner and over to the coaling docks."

Justin, snorkel still in his mouth, let out a muffled trumpet, "Ok."

Lucy led them towards a swim marker, then dove. Halfway down she signaled. "*Watch me.*" There was a large brain coral beneath her: a bulbous yellow green thing, surrounded by purple sea fans. A school of angelfish swam around it. Growing out of coral like tacky multihued holiday decorations, was her target—Christmas tree worms.

Reaching out, careful not to touch coral itself, she wiggled her fingers. The creatures retracted, ducking into their homes. Smiling over her snorkel, Lucy dolphin kicked deeper. Near sandy bottom was a small overhang. Inches from the sea floor, a tunnel opened beneath the coral. Large red antennae peeked out of shadows.

Justin followed her dive. She pointed to the lobster. He gave her a thumbs up and swam for the surface. Lucy continued in a straight line to a rusted, blackish-red, trapezoidal object about person size. It was tapered on one side and leaning onto a circular propeller.

Flipping, Lucy gave them a thumbs up, motioning "*follow me.*" The boys followed hugging a concrete wall. A series of metallic pillars came into view. The south beach had been almost empty of fish. Here, schools of gray snapper cruised through the collapsed dock. Yellowtail browsed soft corals. Triggerfish, angelfish, and parrotfish nibbled amidst rubble.

Justin followed Lucy to the bottom, going slightly deeper each time, until catching sight of something in the corner of his eye. A flash of metal and shiny bits reflected light out of the murky, deeper, water. He began to swim towards it when he felt a tug on his flipper.

Lucy stared down at him through mask-bugged eyes. He followed her to the surface. "What's up?" He asked.

"That's the boat channel. Someone might hit you." As though to make her point, a speedboat motored past.

Justin felt his cheeks flush in embarrassment, "Oh."

"Why were you headed out that way?" She sounded scolding.

"I saw something shiny down there." Justin wondered if all of Rudy's treasure talk had gotten to him.

"Probably just a tarpon." Lucy was frowning.

"Are there lots of those out here?" Justin asked.

"I'll show you later. Come on, before the next passing boat turns you into shark bait." Over Lucy's shoulder, a dark cormorant stared down at him from the sign. If not for Justin's tightly strapped face mask, his cheeks would have turned bright red.

Back at the beach, the woman was gone. Miguel was reading his book, making animated marks with his pen. "Was that a plane propeller?" Rudy's nose was dripping with seawater and snot. Justin recalled the trapezoidal object.

"Yep, Mom believes it was an extra engine which fell off a boat back when this place was a seaplane base during World War Two. You missed it Justin, Rudy made a barracuda friend." Lucy teased "It scarred the crap out of him."

"You try swimming into a mouth full of teeth." Rudy glared at Lucy. "Bug eyes." She prodded the red indentations from her mask.

Justin tried to change the topic, "How do you hold your breath for so long?"

"Miguel and I are taking diving lessons. I can hold my breath for almost two minutes."

"Well then, expert, do you have any tips to keep my mask from fogging?" Rudy asked.

"Spit in it," a voice interrupted from shore.

A similar voice, with more energy and a higher tone: "Wash it with toothpaste and seawater."

The speakers were a skinny blond boy, hair cut short and unevenly, and an equally skinny blond girl whose hair fell just beneath her shoulders. They looked incredibly similar: same eyes, same nose, same freckles. Justin had seen these two on the steps inside Fort Jefferson. They looked a lot like their mother, Renee. The boy shook his head. "Don't use toothpaste. Your whole mask will smell like salty mint and burn your eyes."

"That's because you don't rinse it afterwards." The girl sighed.

Lucy rushed out of the water. "Luke, Nina! How'd you know we were out here? Come snorkel with us."

Luke smiled. "Your mom told us where to find you."

"We didn't bring our gear." Nina shrugged. "Besides, Loggerhead has better snorkeling."

Luke stepped forward, "You must be Lucy's friends. She's talked about you a lot."

"And you must be the Loggerhead volunteers. I'm Rudy." He grabbed Nina's hand with the same one he'd used to wipe his nose. She didn't seem to care. Luke, however, refused his offered shake.

"I'm Justin." He was standing in water, so he waved awkwardly.

Miguel stretched theatrically. "I see you've met the liveaboards. Can we go back inside?"

"What's it like living on a sailboat?" Rudy asked.

"We've been to almost every country in the Gulf of Mexico, and to each Bahamian island." Luke beamed. "We fish whenever we want. We see vast open sea by day. And we watch stars every night."

Nina rolled her eyes. "Luke posts about our liveaboard life on social media, so he makes it sound super romantic. It's nice to be on dry land, to meet new people, and to make advanced orders from a grocery store." She beamed, as though that was one of the best things in the world. "Satellite TV and internet are much better than playing 'I spy something blue,' day after day. It's always ocean."

"How long have you been here?" Justin steadied himself in his flippers.

"More than a month." Luke answered. "We're waiting for an expensive part for our motor."

"I thought you lived on a sailboat." Justin crossed his arms.

"We do." Nina's eyes followed Miguel back to the fort. "But a motor is better when you want to go when wind doesn't."

Lucy stepped behind Justin, whispering so only he could hear. "Do you have to interrogate my new friends?"

CHAPTER 10

SUNSET

LUCY

LEAVING THE TWINS AT the DOCK, everyone rinsed their snorkel gear setting it out to dry. Justin went to help Mr. Benitez with dinner, while Miguel, Lucy, and Rudy argued over what to watch. Dr. Benitez won and made them sit through the first in a trilogy of archeology movies. She turned it into a lecture about bad movie archeology.

When the forty-seventh archeology rule was broken, Lucy grabbed Justin's shoulder. "Be back in a while," she announced.

Stepping out of their house, Justin shook his head, "I learned more about what *not to do* as an archeologist than I have ever learned about what *to do*."

"Most importantly: do not fight over remotes in front of my mother." Lucy led Justin upstairs. "Don't let her fool you. She loves those movies. Dad says that if he hadn't found Mama in college, she'd have turned to a life of archeological thievery."

"For some reason, I could picture her in a bright trench coat stealing historical wonders." Justin squinted back towards her house, "Maybe we should consider your mom our primary suspect in the case of the Scuba Saboteur."

"Ha, Ha, Ha, ha, ha, ha. We're not calling it that." Lucy looked out the arches. The sky was turning orange over Loggerhead, and golden light illuminated bricks. "Get your phone, hurry." Justin returned, phone in hand. "Follow me." Lucy led him through a wooden gate to the northwest turret and up to the third level.

"I haven't been this way, yet." Justin began snapping pictures of colored sky. "I didn't want Rudy to follow me."

"His problem with heights, I remember." On top, sand and grass had taken over, causing the fort to look like an island unto itself. Lucy led Justin along a small white path carved by years of tourists. She climbed one of the many large brick bunkers positioned around the third story. "This is my favorite place to watch sunsets." The sun hung left of Loggerhead Lighthouse.

Justin took a few more pictures before moving carefully to sit beside her on the raised sloped surface. "Has anyone ever fallen from up here?"

Lucy apprised his cautious movement. "Tourists have fallen before. Back when it was a prison, several prisoners jumped into the moat trying to escape." She leaned forward, rewarded by Justin's startled gasp. "So far everyone who's fallen into the moat has survived." She gestured behind them. "Just don't fall that way."

As the last rays of sunlight disappeared, Justin stretched out his arm and took a shot with them both. "Why'd you bring me out here?"

"To show this place off." Lucy gestured across open horizon. "These islands are great. Don't tell Rudy, but I could easily imagine pirates tromping around hiding treasures."

Justin nodded. "Do you like living out here? It seems quiet and remote."

"That's why this is my favorite park yet." She pulled up her legs, propping her chin on her knees. "But I do miss our adventures."

"Trust me. We don't have as many adventures without you."

"Which reminds me. You wanted to talk about the Big Mystery. Was there more than just our parent's phone conversation?"

Justin was silent for a second. "I think Cassidy's given up. When she left for college, she told me it was our turn to figure things out."

"She was pretty frustrated after that ghost town." Lucy faced Justin. "Mattie, Cassidy, and Miguel were our age when we founded J.R.I.C. to find out what happened to our parents. Now they're all in, or headed to, college. It doesn't feel like we've gotten any closer to figuring anything out."

Justin scratched his chin. "Does Miguel remember anything from back then, about our parents or the month they were missing in Arizona?"

"Miguel was itty-bitty. He was living with Mama while she finished her PhD. All he remembers is that she was very worried because Dad was gone," Lucy shifted causing loose rocks to slide down the sloped magazine. "But then Dad was just, back."

Justin sighed. "A month lost in the desert, and they won't say anything about it."

"Newspapers, interviews, old records, yet the best we've ever found was that picture of all fifteen together, supposedly taken two weeks before the *Incident.*" Lucy made air quotes around her last word.

"I found something while unpacking in Homestead." Justin pulled a round greenish-gray object from his pocket, handing it over. She could feel it's weight. "An old compass. I mean, really old. But it still works." Opening the latch, Lucy watched the needle spin to point north. "Check the back."

She turned it over, squinting at the three letters etched there. "W. A. R. Creepy."

Justin took it from her, returning it to his pocket. "Remember the other photo taken for the newspaper—the one taken after the rescue?" Lucy nodded. "The helicopter pilot who found them was in that picture. His name was William Rapsilber. William *Alexander* Rapsilber."

"W.A.R., You think this is his compass?"

"Possibly! Rudy and I have tried researching him but haven't found much. Maybe, if we solve her mystery, we can ask your mom about him. Or maybe she'll just tell us everything." Justin chuckled, trying to make the last part seem like a joke. Instead of responding, Lucy watched Loggerhead Light sweep across the inky indigo horizon.

"Ugh." Lucy finally sighed. "We always do this. We get to a park and suddenly we're finding lost bear cubs, hunting down missing persons, or saving impalas from volcanos."

Justin scratched his head. "I'm pretty sure that last one didn't happen."

"My point is, we never get to simply have fun in a park." Lucy let her frustration be heard.

"Mysteries are fun." Justin frowned. "And you talked your mom into asking for our help this time."

"I know." Lucy sighed. "And we need to help her. But tonight, No more mystery talk."

"*Mysteriesssss.*" A whisper carried through night air. "*Secretsssssss.*" Both Lucy and Justin shot up, looking for the hissing.

"Miguel!" Justin pointed down to Lucy's brother standing beside their magazine.

Lucy let out a string of expletives in Spanish then English. "Miguel Alejandro Benitez. Don't startle me!" She flung a loose coral pebble. It hit a row of bricks behind him.

Miguel laughed. "I knew you guys were here. This is Lucy's favorite spot."

Justin scanned the darkened fort roof. "Rudy isn't with you, is he?"

Miguel joined. "You think I'm crazy?"

"We were headed down anyway." Lucy glared.

While walking back to the stairwell, a scream echoed from somewhere in the parade ground. The three rushed to the interior wall. "There," Justin called. In the vicinity of Private Winter's corner were five or six shadows. One of them screamed again.

It was a half scream half laugh. They were far away, but there was enough breeze to carry snippets of conversation. "…not funny…really… thought…" This was followed by a round of laughter.

Miguel sniffed. "It's just some Dive Bears coming back from the beach."

"I thought someone was in trouble." Lucy shook her head, annoyed.

"Who's that?" Justin pointed to a lit window above the crews quarters. A shadow figure stood, watching the students from above.

"That's Ranger O'Donnell's apartment." Miguel replied. The three watched the ranger watch the students. Eventually someone opened the door and the group piled into a darkened room. A few moments later Ranger O'Donnell's light went out.

"Hmm." Justin stared elsewhere into the night. Lucy scanned the parade ground. It was dark, with little illumination from stars and a sliver of the moon. She couldn't see anything.

"What?" Lucy asked.

"Oh no." Miguel chuckled as his footsteps echoed down the stairwell, "Justin's getting the Case mystery vibes. "Next thing you know he'll be interrogating everyone."

Lucy sighed. "Probably, but not tonight."

CHAPTER 11

LATE MORNING PLANS

JUSTIN

J USTIN WOKE EXCITED TO START MYSTERY SOLVING. "Rudy, I'm going to eat all the granola if you don't put your phone down and get up!"

A few moments later, the younger boy stepped out of their bedroom, rubbing his eyes. "I don't even like granola."

"Then why are you up?" Justin asked.

"I finished my daily quests," Rudy shook his phone. "Also, I wanted to make sure you didn't put granola in my bowl." Justin paused mid pour. "Why are you so excited, so early?"

Justin pointed to a clock above the door, "It's almost nine o'clock. I bet Lucy and Miguel have been up for hours."

"Lucy, probably." Rudy yawned. "Miguel, definitely not."

"We have a mystery to solve, a real client, and parental permission. This could be a whole new chapter for J.R.I.C."

"If this is how things are going to be, I don't like it." Rudy grabbed a different cereal. His lack of excitement was frustrating. Justin chewed thoughtfully. Lucy's mom had listed lots of problems. Where to start?

They were finishing breakfast when Lucy barged in. "Wake up sleepy-heads!" Seeing them at the table, she glared. "I thought you would be begging to start this investigation."

"You try getting this one to move any faster." Justin pointed to Rudy.

Rudy's head slumped over until his hair hung just above his milk. "Not you too. Guys! We're in a national park. We don't have to keep business hours."

Lucy nodded. "We don't have to be lazy teenagers like my brother either. Cassidy always made us start early."

"True." Rudy replied unenthusiastically. "But she's not here, and I'm not a teenager."

Lucy growled with annoyance, turning to Justin. "Have you come up with a plan yet?"

Justin's sister would have had several by now. "I don't know."

"Then I guess our timetable is up to me." Lucy sighed theatrically. "Let's go to the docks. If we leave now, we'll beat the ferry. After that, Mom said we can bug her students. She called it interactive studies."

Justin nodded, "Look at you, taking initiative!"

"We need to solve this before the Dive Bears leave." Lucy frowned.

Rudy slumped over his bowl. "Why do you have to be a morning person?"

Justin watched Lucy balance-walk across the moat bridge. "It's pretty crazy that we have to walk all the way around the fort just to get out."

"An old park ranger blew a hole in the other side of Fort Jeff with dynamite, to make a shortcut out to the moat. Masons fixed it when they repaired the iron shutters." Lucy pointed to the lower docks. "We're headed that way."

A large group had gathered on the beach. Justin recognized Dr. Alexa, Professor Erickson, and several students. Standing nearby were park rangers dressed in gray shirts and green shorts. Two university boats bobbed between the crowd. "What's that?" Justin asked

Chet and another student shouldered a large white rubber tube. "A sonar." Lucy explained. "Dr. Alexa's team use it plus a magnetometer to find new targets to dive."

Rudy pointed to a massive drone being loaded onto the boat by a man with dreadlocks. "Wow, they even got special permission for that in a National Park!"

"Yep, Travis does aerial surveys of potential wrecks." Lucy led them onto the dock, lowering her voice. Things looked tense. Students loading both boats were working hard to avoid a simmering argument. Some had stopped to watch Dr. Alexa and Professor Erickson square off.

"I don't care if it's your day to go out. My students' work has already been delayed by 'maintenance issues." Dr. Alexa scowled. "We're on borrowed time."

"Dr. Alexa, your own schedule gives my students *Mary Rose* today. Your students are scheduled on *Vasa*." Even while arguing, Professor Erickson seemed resigned to defeat. "All of your mapping equipment is on *Vasa*."

"Which is why I told them to move it." Dr. Alexa crossed her arms.

Students were juggling loads of computer equipment across the dock. Justin leaned over. "With salt water, aren't they worried about those electronics?"

"It's not like they have a choice." Lucy eyed the arguing professors. "It's probably best we don't get involved." She led them to the larger dock. Along the way she pointed. "That guy with the mustache is Ranger O'Donnell."

"Who's that?" Rudy asked.

Justin explained what they had witnessed last night. Rudy turned to stare down at the boat slips and the gathering. "Do people fight out here often?"

"It's an island. Lots of people, nowhere to go. There's a lot of drama. Especially when you mix in stupid college students and broken-down boats." Lucy made a face. "Now, let's see who's out in the harbor."

Justin counted six sailing vessels in the sheltered bay. A large, very fancy speedboat with two engines and orange trim was tied to a massive white ship. "That's the yacht?"

Rudy whistled, "*Neptune's Trident*! What kind of historian can afford a boat like that? And will he give us a tour?"

"Gwen thinks his money is inherited, and he writes books as a hobby. And no. No one's been aboard his boat yet. He and his captain like their privacy." Lucy pointed out two other motor vessels painted in festive colors. "Those are commercial dive vessels. The left one is the *Sylvan Spryte* and that—" Lucy pointed "—is the *Horned Devil*."

It was a motor vessel with two pontoon hulls, two decks, and an elevated captain's cabin. "That's the one your mom thinks might be involved in sabotage?" Justin asked.

Lucy narrowed her eyes. "I wanted you to see it. Captain Tobias has been out here a lot recently. Sometimes he's not even carrying tourists."

"Suspicious." Justin stored images of the ships in his mind. Down below, Dr. Alexa pulled out on a university boat with four students. "I guess the argument is over." Professor Erickson was speaking to Ranger O'Donnell as the ranger set tools around the remaining university vessel. Other students had vanished back into Fort Jefferson. A lot of drama, indeed.

Justin scratched his chin. Sabotage, thefts: small crimes centered around U.R.S.A. That had to mean something. He ushered his two friends away from prying ears, smiling with excitement. "Okay, look. I was afraid that this investigation was too open ended. It's not. We have a limited list of suspects. There are people on this island, and people on boats."

Rudy leaned against the wall. "Well, that seems obvious."

"But listen. It can't be just anyone. The saboteur has to be out here often, at the right times and with access to U.R.S.A." Justin breathed a sigh of relief. "We're looking at a specific set of suspects: park rangers, anyone on boats which have been out here for a long time, and as your mom suggested: the students themselves."

"So, specifically, everyone?" Rudy laughed.

"It's a small island. We can eliminate suspects as we learn more. All we have to do is focus on police officer's standard: M.M.O."

"Massive Multiplayer online?" Rudy asked.

"Motive, Means, and Opportunity." Lucy corrected.

Justin gestured to the docks and harbor, "Our criminal pool is actually pretty small. We'll solve the Case of the Secret Saboteur in no time."

"We're not calling it that." Lucy interjected. "Let's go tour the map room."

CHAPTER 12

U.R.S.A. HEADQUARTERS

LUCY

LUCY'S DAD SAT IN THE PARK HEADQUARTERS, staring out the window. She waved as they walked by. He waved back. From the gumbo-limbo tree's shadow, she led her friends up the southern turret.

In the enclosed brick hallway on the second floor there was small arched wooden door. A mass of wires and cable spilled through its top running along the ceiling. Lucy stopped outside. "Okay. Be cool," she stared pointedly at Justin. "No interrogations."

Justin smiled widely. "This is exciting!"

"*Another* powder magazine?" Rudy asked. When Lucy looked surprised, he pointed to white paint covering every surface. "Whitewash, I recognize it from Ft. Pulaski, where my dad used to work. Was this fort built for people or gunpowder?"

"Well, there were supposed to be 470 cannons out here. That would require tons of gunpowder." Lucy smiled evilly while both Justin and Rudy jumped at the interruption from the suddenly open door. "I thought I heard voices." Chet stood in the entrance with a large smile, "Welcome to U.R.S.A. headquarters. Come on in." Lucy caught a whiff of spice from the muscle-bound student's deodorant as they wedged by. "What interrogations?" He asked.

Chet followed them into a cramped circular room. Curved cabinets and shelves encircled walls crammed with folders, books, and large electronics. The wall directly across from the entrance was taken over by a massive projection which was currently flashing through pictures, while a three-dimensional ship was being pieced together center screen.

Including Chet, there were four Dive Bears crammed around a small central table. One student was ignoring the projection, instead focused on one of two computers resting against the east wall. "That's Sophia." Lucy started introductions, "You met her yesterday." Sophia glared suspiciously up at them, clicking away from her work.

"That's Gwen." Lucy pointed to her favorite member of U.R.S.A. The tall redheaded woman was working on a laptop balanced precariously in her lap. She was manipulating digital images with a joystick in one hand and keyboard in her other. She nodded but didn't turn from her work. "She takes pictures of wrecks and uses them to build 3D digital models."

"Using U.R.S.A.'s underwater cameras?" Justin asked. Lucy hoped that no one else could hear his eager suspicion.

"I'm turning our most interesting wrecks into virtual reality dives." Gwen ignored Justin's question without looking up. "Soon people will be able to dive the *Avanti* from the comfort of their homes."

Lucy pointed to the final student dozing on a pillow of his own intensely curly hair. "That's Kit. He's usually awake."

Rudy surveyed the room. "Your headquarters is crowded."

Chet chuckled. "The more people the better, it keeps Private Winter's ghost away."

Rudy's eyes went wide. "There's no such thing as ghosts." Professor Erickson's dramatic entrance caused Sophia to straighten up and open a different file on her computer. He stepped over to watch her work, his stern frown softening into a smile, "However, there have been some odd occurrences in this room."

Rudy put his hands on his hips. "What do you mean occurrences?"

"You guys fit all of your equipment in here?" Justin asked, oblivious to ghost talk.

"Nope. There are way too many of us. Usually, we work out of the crews quarters." Chet shook his head. "We got lucky today."

"Lucky!" Professor Erickson scoffed. "We're supposed to be out on that boat."

Justin tapped his chin thoughtfully, "How often do boats break down?"

"What do you mean strange occurrences?" Rudy repeated.

Lucy struggled not to smack her forehead. "*Anyway*, Mom promised the boys a tour."

"Then, let's give you guys the rundown." Chet had to squeeze around sleeping Kit. "If I could direct your attention over here." He pointed to a nautical map hanging near the hall. "This is our master plan."

"What are the different colors of pins?" Rudy asked. The map was so perforated by markers it was a pincushion.

"Well, there are three teams out here each supervised by different professors. Blue belongs to Professor Erickson. Red for Dr. Alexa. Green is Dr. Benitez." Chet pointed to examples of each color. "This helps each group focus." He pointed to a place where all three colors were pinned together. "Sometimes our work overlaps."

"That's barrel wreck eighty-seven." Gwen called out.

Chet nodded. "It's important to Dr. Benitez because it's a newly discovered wreck. Dr. Alexa's interested because it sunk early during Fort Jefferson's construction. Professor Erickson wants to learn more about the tools found aboard which might give significant insight into the life of people aboard."

"What are the black pins?" Rudy asked.

Gwen chuckled from behind her keyboard and joystick.

"Well, we run our boats back and forth scanning every map section. We mark each possible target then go back and dive them. Often, instead of something of epic historic importance, we find dropped anchors, garbage dumped in the park, and things washed in from shipping lanes. We mark trash black, so we don't waste our time with a second trip."

"We found an old refrigerator last dive." Gwen added. Chet pointed to a pin exactly between Loggerhead and Garden Key

"Gray pins are sites we haven't been able to dive and might not be able to, now." Chet frowned. Rudy stared up at the map with determination. Brushing aside some papers next to Kit, he set his own map down beginning to mark it with pinned locations.

Justin seized the quiet moment. "I heard you've had some setbacks."

"Well, yeah!" Chet answered enthusiastically. "What do you expect when you mix scuba diving, boating, and archeology? Problems caused by sea, science, and isolation. We're expected to work with precision and delicacy. Even though we can't talk to each other."

"You don't have those fancy dive masks with speakers?" Rudy asked without looking up from his work.

Chet shook his head. "Not in our budget. We have enough specialized equipment corroding before our eye. When anything breaks down or disappears, we wait weeks for replacements."

"Disappears…oof?" Lucy elbowed Justin before the one-word question left his mouth. "I mean with all of those problems it's amazing you get anything done." He stepped out of elbow range. "You must have found something super valuable."

"Not really." Sophia looked up from her work. "There are more than two-hundred wrecks recorded out here, but most were ships carrying construction material for Fort Jeff. Not much monetary value in piles of sunken bricks and hardened concrete barrels."

"Any pirate treasures?" Rudy asked.

"Well," Chet pointed to two purple pins closer to Loggerhead. "Purple is for previous archeological teams. These two sites were thought to belong to the *Nuestra Señora del Rosario*."

"That's a ship from the *Atocha's* fleet!" Rudy exclaimed.

"I'm impressed you recognize it." Chet nodded. "Don't get too excited. All they found were ballast stones and some old swivel cannon. Ballast stones were used to weigh down ships so they wouldn't float too high in the water and risk tipping over. Cannon are cannon."

"Not everyone agrees that wreckage is from the *Rosario*." Gwen added.

"Couldn't you check the cannon for etching or emblems to learn where they came from?" Rudy asked.

"You know your archeology." Gwen chuckled. "Someone should look into that."

Chet shrugged. "The Dry Tortugas was once a pirate haven, but if they left anything behind, we haven't found it. We probably won't. People have had centuries to scour these waters for valuables."

Lucy expected Rudy to visibly deflate. Instead, he perked up, pointing to a blue pin near two purple pins, but further north of Loggerhead. "What about here: wreck one-fourteen? I have it on my map." He pointed to a mark on his own drawing and the pin on the wall. "I want to search it for treasure."

Professor Erickson chuckled. "Good eye! That's a wreck I'm personally mapping."

"Is it a treasure ship?"

The professor shook his head. "Sorry, no. It's a brick wreck."

"A cool one." Gwen again. "I was on the Professor's preliminary dive there. It's not just bricks, there's a ton of different construction materials in well preserved condition." She turned sheepishly towards Professor Erickson. "That reminds me, I have to get back out there to photograph it. I promised you I'd fully document it, but then our camera went—" Looking at Lucy, she trailed off.

"There are more important wrecks," The professor sighed. "We don't have enough boats or time."

"So, there's nothing out here valuable enough to keep secret?" Justin broke the silence overtaking the room. Even Rudy rolled his eyes. "Just construction materials?"

"Just construction material!" Professor Erickson cleared his throat. "The very first recorded underwater expedition uncovered a two-thou-sand-year-old Roman vessel carrying construction material! It's discover-ers found something more valuable than treasure: information. Care to elaborate, Sophia?"

Sophia again clicked away from something on screen, like a student caught playing videogames in class. She cleared her throat. "Well, umm, so, construction materials tell us about shipping lines, what types of tools the builder used and so much more. Even learning where the materials came from can be important. I bet you've noticed a sudden change in brick color near the top of the fort?"

Her friends shook their heads. Lucy sighed, "I showed them yesterday. Lighter bricks lower down came from a southern brick factory before the civil war. Darker red bricks on top come from a factory in the northeast. Fort Jefferson remained Union. When the war started, they had to find new brick suppliers. That line marks the war's beginning."

Sophia nodded. "Exactly. Bricks on a wreck provide context. They tell us when the ships sank. We can use other items aboard to infer more about what happened during the war. Everything we piece together helps us learn about trade and shipping along the gulf coast. These wrecks are key to understanding maritime society in the mid 1800s."

"If you want to talk real treasure: Kit's innovative design will revolutionize the way we sample and date submerged wooded artefacts." Professor Erickson pointed to the sleeping student. "Gwen's 3-D maps will make our work accessible to everyone. Dr. Alexa's students are, ahem, all producing impressive work." He raised his hands "Sophia here recently discovered a set of medium-range cannon aboard a sunken freighter."

"Wreck one-twenty-two." Chet pointed to a blue pin south of Loggerhead. "We've been trying to figure out if they were supplies for Fort Jeff's armament, or if they belonged to Union artillery regiments quartered here during the war. If the former, then perhaps the Union was more concerned about defending this fort than it seems. If the latter, perhaps they are evidence that the Union was preparing for a southern invasion through Florida. Those cannon are an awesome find!"

Sophia blushed. "Professor E's letting me turn it into a secondary research project."

"That's pretty neat, isn't it?" Lucy elbowed her friend.

"Cannon are cool, I guess." Rudy sounded dejected.

Lucy wished he'd sound a bit more excited. Even her mother thought Sophia's find was remarkable. Before she could say anything, there was a snuffling snore. Sitting up, Kit tiredly scanned the room. "Hey guys." He turned to Chet. "Did I hear you all talking about pirates?"

Lucy nodded. "Rudy wants to know where you Dive Bears are hiding your hordes of pirate treasure."

"Wouldn't you like to know?" Kit rubbed his eyes, then aimed to finger guns at Rudy. "Oh, that reminds me." He turned to Professor Erickson. "I forgot during all our excitement yesterday, I have the carbon-dating results from your wreck." He pulled a document from the folder he'd been drooling on. "They don't make any sense."

"What do you mean?" the professor asked.

"Well, your samples came from your brick wreck, right?" The professor nodded. "So, it should be about a hundred and fifty years old." The professor motioned for Kit to get to the point. "Only, the carbon dates I measured suggest its nearly three times that age."

The professor stared at Kit's paper. "Are you sure that you tested it correctly?"

Kit pointed to a line graph Lucy couldn't read. "Every other sample I ran with it was well within the margin of error." That was a long way of saying: yes, the Professor's sample were older than expected, and yes, the test was correct.

"Four hundred years old!" Rudy must have done math in his head. He began to dance up and down. "Your sample's as old as the Spanish treasure fleets!"

"What?" That pronouncement caused Gwen to look away from her work. "No way." She snuffled with laughter.

Professor Erickson ignored Rudy. "Do you have your other test sheets?"

Kit nodded. "They're back in the crews quarters."

"Well then, let's go get them." The professor made for the door, squeezing around Lucy and her friends. "This is impossible."

Kit followed, voice echoing down the hall. "I'm sorry. You took those samples yourself, and with the spares missing I don't have any way to check my work. I'll go out and take another round tomorrow."

"That can wait because…" Professor Erickson's reasoning was muffled by the closing door. Justin stared. He'd obviously noticed the same thing as Lucy. The samples which had made them so excited, were the samples which had gone missing yesterday!

CHAPTER 13

THE RETURN OF THE TWINS

JUSTIN

LUCY STOPPED THEM BENEATH THE MAP ROOM. She poked Justin's chest, playfully but forcefully. "Can you contain yourself?"

"What?" Justin rubbed the spot.

"You couldn't have been more obvious! Every question you asked was clearly about the possible saboteur."

Rudy nodded in agreement. Justin frowned. "You were only interested in your mythical treasure fleet."

"At least that's archeology!" The younger boy crossed his arms. "Bricks and cannon are cool too."

Justin was still skeptical. "That's not what you said in there."

"Guys!" Lucy whispered, starting to walk. "Sound carries through these halls. Don't say anything you don't want half of Fort Jeff to hear."

Rudy threw up his hands, "You started this conversation."

Lucy paused outside the visitor center door, letting Ferry tourists pass. "Why the smile?"

Justin's grin only widened. "Unless I'm mistaken, our mystery just got more complicated!"

"And—" Rudy added "—it might involve a time traveling pirate ship."

The other two ignored him. The visitor center was crowded with tourists trying to buy souvenirs before they had to get back on the boat. Renee stood behind the counter, while her two blond children helped organize a line.

Seeing Luke and Nina, Lucy waved. "I thought you guys would be here."

Luke leaned forward conspiratorially. "Tell us more about your mystery."

Justin felt his heart skip a beat. "How did you know about that?"

"Wait to talk." Nina leaned in to shush her brother. "Prying ears," She scanned the room full of tourists, all of whom appeared more interested in their own business.

Lucy led them out a side door. Luke started. "Now that we're alone, we heard you guys are like detectives."

"Not like detectives, Luke," Nina corrected. "Lucy says you guys have solved mysteries."

Rudy took the bait. "Yep! We even have a cool nickname." Lucy, standing behind the twins, shook her head pleadingly. "We're the Junior Rangers Investigative Club."

Neither twin laughed. Nina picked up the thread of Luke's question. "So, what are you investigating? And how can we help?"

They seemed sincere, but they, or their parents, may be involved? Justin stood in thought for a moment, rehashing everything Dr. Benitez had told them. Finally, he explained everything quickly, concluding with a request. "Keep your eyes peeled, and if you notice anything weird, especially about U.R.S.A., let us know."

Luke gave Lucy a sympathetic look. "I didn't know your mom was having so much trouble. The university students often work around Loggerhead. We'll watch them."

Nina grinned, "Spud can help sniff out clues for sure!"

"When are we going to meet him?" Rudy asked.

"Tonight." Luke nodded.

"Spud is coming?" Lucy's voice went up about two octaves with excitement.

"Yeah," Nina replied. "He's not allowed in Fort Jefferson when lots of tourists are around, but we'll get him from our boat soon. Speaking of that," Nina tugged on her brother's sleeves. "Mom's probably done with work. We should go."

As the two walked off, Rudy and Lucy both turned to Justin with equally accusatory glares. Rudy spoke first. "Seriously?"

"What have we told you about immediately trusting everyone?" Lucy shook her head.

Justin frowned. "They're your friends. Besides, I'm sure they're not involved."

"Not them, duh. But what about their parents?" Lucy asked.

Justin raised his hands defensively. "Your mom's had problems for months. The Manning's weren't here until a month ago. The timing doesn't make sense."

"Just be careful, Justin. Let the wrong thing slip and this could be Utah all over again." Lucy frowned.

"I'm never going to live that down, am I?" Justin reached into his pocket for his bird book. He was sure he'd seen a white-eyed vireo near the docks. "Well, the party's not for a few hours, I need time to think anyway. I'm going bird watching."

CHAPTER 14

GATHERING

JUSTIN

EVEN THOUGH JUSTIN GOT CAUGHT UP SIGHTING BIRDS, Lucy was last to arrive. Outside the crews quarters, the grad-students prepared for a large gathering. While waiting for her, Justin filled Miguel in on their day's adventures.

Miguel nodded along keeping his voice low, "So we don't have a motive or a method, and our list of suspects includes everyone?"

"Everyone except the liveaboards." Rudy chuckled. "Justin's says they are innocent."

"He did?" Miguel's sarcasm was obvious. "I'll have dad arrest them now!"

"I thought you weren't interested in our investigation?" Justin raised an eyebrow.

"I'm not. But a man can only take so much college prep work."

"What man?" Lucy approached from the parade ground.

"Finally!" Miguel made a sweeping bow. "My sister's graced us with her presence!"

Justin surveyed the budding party. It looked like about twenty Dive Bears, nine rangers plus family, and a few assorted strangers. "Is this everyone?"

"It's a small island." Miguel leaned in, grabbing Justin's shoulder. "These are your suspects. Any of them might be sabotaging U.R.S.A.'s work."

Lucy looked around. "I don't see Professor Erickson, but all other Dive Bears are here." Two sullen students sat beside Dr. Alexa. Chet, Kit, and Sophia wove through the small crowd. Gwen conversed with a ranger Justin hadn't met. Other students dipped in and out, helping in the kitchen.

"Is this all the park rangers?" Justin turned to ask Lucy, but she had wandered off with the twins.

Miguel, still beside him, answered. "Rangers usually stay for a week or two out here before breaking in Key West. Right now, we're short because some rangers are away for training. Dad's backup law enforcement, Ranger Kyle, had to go to boat school after crashing a park boat into rocks on East Key."

Justin made a mental note to check the rangers' schedule. Then he would know who had been out here for most of U.R.S.A.'s problem. There were three other people he did not recognize. "Who are those guys?"

"The crew of the motor vessel *Fort Jefferson*, the park service ship which brings out supplies and rangers." Justin recalled the large green ship on the dock. "The second mate is Lucy's and my dive instructor. You can leave them off your suspect list. They're only here three days a week."

Justin shrugged towards two other college age women sitting with Chet. They were young for rangers but, "I didn't see them at U.R.S.A.'s meeting."

"That's because they aren't Mom's students. They're monitoring sea turtles: counting nests and watching baby turtles hatch." The two young women were laughing at Chet. Miguel ran a hand through his hair. "I'll go see if they might be suspects."

Miguel beelined for the turtle researcher's table. Justin sighed deeply. A moment later, Rudy abandoned him for the twins and their dog. He was left alone.

"Looking for suspicious individuals?" Dr. Benitez had snuck up behind him.

Justin nodded. "What do you know about the historian with Ranger O'Donnell?" He gestured covertly to Mr. Howard. "Why's he funding your expedition?"

"He wants first access to our publications to help write his next book, and his financial assistance has been instrumental *especially with recent issues*. I'm trying to convince him to extend his time with us. But our recent discoveries haven't piqued his interest. He has a rather romantic view of history: all swords and swashbucklers. I think he was hoping for more of that." He sounded like an older Rudy. She frowned. "I'm sure it doesn't help that each new *problem* costs him more money."

"Hmm." Justin nodded. "Do you think he might be the saboteur's target?"

"If so, I don't envy the saboteur. I have a distinct impression that his captain might be more than a humble yacht captain. He's pretty intimidating and protective."

Justin narrowed his eyes, trying to understand. "Bodyguard?"

"Something like that." Dr. Benitez winked. "Speaking of, I don't see Captain Levi. He's a big guy with a bushy beard, always wearing khaki."

"Captain Levi." Justin would try to remember that name. "You don't think they are your bad guys, do you?"

"They have only been helpful." Dr. Benitez tapped her empty glass. "Anyway, we shouldn't talk investigation so publicly. I'll expect a full morning briefing!"

Before leaving, she leaned in conspiratorially. "Just remember to have fun. School starts tomorrow. School, fun, mystery, in that order." Justin had forgotten about the school supplies stacked in his apartment. How did Lucy's mom expect them to solve a mystery while doing homework?

Over the next couple of hours, he managed to talk to every ranger, the park boat operators, and each other guest, memorizing names and getting some idea of why everyone was out here. His stomach began to rumble, and he didn't feel any closer to identifying the best suspect.

Rudy was standing over the table deciding between desserts. "Have all three." Justin joked. Before he could reply, a harsh laugh interrupted the party. People backed away, circling two figures in the dark courtyard. Dr. Alexa stood beside the furthest picnic table her face pinched in anger aimed at Professor Erickson. She glared, spun on her heels, and walked away.

Watching Doctor Alexa leave, Justin turned towards Rudy. "What was that about?"

"Island drama?" Rudy eyed his plate full of desserts. Justin loaded his own plate. Making rounds, he'd forgotten to eat. The turtle volunteers left, so the two boys went to join Sophia, Chet, and Gwen at their table.

"Hey dudes," Gwen's red hair was plastered to her head, where it had dried.

She must have gone diving recently. "What do you think of the park so far?"

Justin sat across from the taller woman. "It's pretty cool. There's a ton to do."

"I wish." Sophia groaned, put her head into her arms and collapsed onto the picnic table. "I'm beginning to understand how these islands could be used as a prison."

Chet smiled. "She's just stir-crazy. She's hasn't been back to the mainland since day one."

"I can't afford Key West." Sophia complained from within her arms.

"At least we have internet." Rudy lifted a cookie. "What did prisoners do for fun?" Sophia's only reply was a weak groan.

"Until she found artillery cannon, Sophia's project was all computer work. Now she has to spend equal time on computers and in the field." Gwen crossed her arms smugly. "Not everyone can handle two jobs at once."

"I love it out here." Chet sounded sincere.

"Of course, you do." Sophia grumbled. "You're Dr. Benitez's golden boy." Words of praise spoken sourly. "You have your pick of assignments, control your schedule, and your research hasn't had any setbacks."

Chet scratched the back of his head. "It's a shame that Kit's samples and that other stuff went missing."

"*Other Stuff.*" Gwen interrupted. "I have twenty wrecks to re-photograph."

Chet continued, "We get to overcome obstacles, and improvise fresh solutions. You and Kit are lucky to dive all of those wrecks again!"

"That's a very easy outlook for *you* to have," Sophia aimed her plastic fork. "I heard Dr. Benitez is considering you for Professor Erickson's skeleton shutdown crew. You'll get to stay out here when we leave. Did you want the island to yourself? Maybe you're the problem."

Chet's eyes went wide, as though he were unprepared for the accusation. Gwen stood, interrupting his reply. "Anyway, let's take this party to the beach." She pointed to a distant table. "Kit, you with us?" He and the other students looked up. The Dive Bears made their exit, collecting food and drink as they left. Gwen winked across the empty table. "Crisis diversion time. See you guys later."

Once they were alone, Rudy cleared his throat. "Well, that was interesting."

"Yeah." Justin stared after the students.

CHAPTER 15
A DIFFERENT PERSPECTIVE

LUCY

LUCY'S FATHER HAD ARRANGED HIS PARTY and invited everyone: Rangers, U.R.S.A., and the few others who called the island home. "We need to develop a sense of community." Something they needed to do about once a week, apparently.

"It's a perfect way for dad to bring people together. Mandatory fun to make everyone get along," was how Miguel explained it.

"Or it's just a party." Lucy had replied.

"This is great!" Justin rubbed his hands together like a cartoon villain. "We can put names to faces and ask everyone tough questions."

"Don't do that." Lucy warned. "You'll make us look suspicious or weird."

"No." Miguel smirked back at his sister. "Justin's right. Let's treat everyone as suspects, maybe rough some of them up a little." His joke had fallen on deaf ears.

Once the party began, Justin split off to interrogate everyone. Rudy immediately rushed to bug everyone about old pirate treasures. Miguel left her to follow two turtle volunteers like a lost puppy. Lucy was alone in the crowd.

She headed over to talk with the park boat's second mate. Her dive instructor smiled. "Next week we're picking up equipment for some nurse shark researchers. While your friends are here, get your parents to take you out into deeper water."

Lucy shivered but nodded politely. Turning away, she was promptly ambushed by Spud, his tongue wagging as he bound up to her. Luke and Nina flanked him. "Spud, be polite." Luke whispered through a smile.

"What's up, Spud?" Lucy scratched the dog's curly fur. He was distracted by a morsel of food dropped from where Chet and Miguel were sitting with the Turtle Volunteers. "I've always wanted a dog, but they're hard to keep in parks."

"They're hard to keep on boats too, but Spud makes a good cabin pup." Nina leaned closer, whispering, "We brought him to sniff out your saboteur." Spud had taken up residence underneath the picnic table, waiting for scraps.

Lucy grinned. "Thanks guys, but what exactly does a saboteur smell like?" They spoke for a while. Eventually Spud wandered off.

The twins followed. "We'll let you know if he finds anything." Nina winked. Spud seemed perfectly willing to sniff everyone, but he didn't seem interested in finding saboteurs.

Miguel eventually gave up on the turtle researchers. Rudy kept circling back to the table full of food. It took Lucy a while to realize that he wasn't interested in treats. He was interrogating every archeologist who approached.

Lucy waited until he was alone to sneak up behind him. "What are you doing?"

Rudy didn't even jump. He was becoming too comfortable with her sneak attacks. "I'm learning about archeology." He paused, finally adding, "to help our investigation?"

"I'm not Justin." Lucy sighed. "If you're more interested in pirate treasure, that's fine. Just don't expect anything to come from it."

"Uh hu." Rudy's eyes were focused on Professor Erickson.

Justin wasn't any better. He was talking to everyone. He was good at that. Yet, all his conversations would somehow lead back to their investigation. So much social skill, all wasted.

Eventually her mother wandered over with a plate of food. They sat together observing everyone else. "Justin is a lot like his sister."

"I'm glad I'm not like Miguel." Lucy replied.

"You two are more similar than either would admit. You are also, each, incredibly unique. Sometimes I wonder about the Case family. I love mysteries too. In archeology answers lead to more questions. That's fun. But, when a Case picks apart a problem, they are always looking for something definitive. Anyways, mija, don't spend too much time on this mystery." Her mom stood. "Have some fun too."

"Mama, did anyone ever tell you that you are a really weird mother?"

"You and your brother both have, this week in fact." She was called over by students.

Over the next hour, the party settled as it grew dark. Suddenly, that tranquility was interrupted. "Excuse Me!" Professor Erickson and Dr. Alexa quickly became the center of everyone's attention. Students scattered to avoid the fight.

Ranger O'Donnell, caught between them, stepped back narrowly avoiding Spud's paw. Professor Erickson tried to speak, "Dr. Kapur, Alexa. Might I suggest we talk about this—" but was interrupted "—at another time."

"No, Professor. I am tired of accusations, complaints, insinuations, and suggestions." Interrupting him mid-sentence, Dr. Alexa marched away, "We are done."

"We both want what is best for our students." Dr. Erickson called after her.

"Then you could both leave." Ranger O'Donnell spoke up. It was hard to tell if anyone else heard him.

Lucy scooted up to Luke and Nina. "What did I miss?"

Luke shook his head. "I didn't hear anything. I was helping Spud show off for the turtle volunteers."

Nina rolled her eyes. "Professor Erickson and Dr. Alexa were arguing over which team would go back to Key West first." Her voice changed to imitate the older professor, "he said: *your students have enough data. Leave the boat to those who need more time out here.*"

"Really?" Lucy was impressed by Nina's professor voice.

"Archeologists. Put two of them together and you get three opinions." Ranger O'Donnell stared down towards Lucy and the liveaboards. "The only thing worse than a gaggle of archeology students is their teachers." Several students standing nearby rolled their eyes. "If you'll excuse me."

He walked away.

"Why was he involved?" Lucy turned to the twins.

"I don't know." Nina shrugged, "But we need to stay longer, to get to the bottom of this."

While she and her brother rushed to beg their parents for more time, Justin waved Lucy over. "Let's follow the Dive Bears to see what they're up to?"

"Sure," Lucy agreed, focused on Ranger O'Donnell as he headed away from the party with Mr. Howard. She had a different target in mind.

CHAPTER 16

THE FIRST STAKEOUT

JUSTIN

"How often do the Dive Bears hang out on the beach?" Justin asked.

"Mom says they work hard all day and need evenings to unwind. If we're going, hurry. I want to follow him." Lucy pointed to Ranger O'Donnell.

"They need to unwind after a party?" Luke asked.

Rudy sighed. "Every time I asked about treasure, I mean research, they changed the subject."

Lucy rolled her eyes. "Maybe they weren't expecting to be accosted at a snack table."

Rudy ignored her, reaching down to scratch Spud's chin. "I guess you're officially on this case too, pup. Let me know if you find any buried treasure." Spud wagged his tail.

"Quiet." Lucy raised her hand as a signal. They were rounding Private Winter's corner. "Listen." A pair of footsteps retreated up the turret staircase: Ranger O'Donnell. Cautiously peeking around the small powder magazine beside Lucy, they watched Mr. Howard head for the fort exit. The two had split up.

"What are we doing?" Justin asked. Lucy shushed him. They waited.

Finally, Lucy sighed. "I thought Ranger O'Donnell might be up to something in U.R.S.A.'s headquarters."

Justin stared at her. "Doesn't he live upstairs?"

Lucy nodded. "That means he has easy access to the map room." A light went on in his apartment over the crews quarters. "I guess he went home."

"He's a suspect?" Rudy asked.

"He was in the middle of the professor's arguments," Lucy explained. "On purpose."

Justin nodded. "We'll keep an eye on him, but he's not doing anything now."

"Um." there was a quiver in Rudy's voice, "We're in ghost corner. Can we leave, please?"

"Ghost corner?" Nina asked.

"I guess it's sufficiently dark." Lucy lowered her voice to a whisper. Rudy whimpered when he'd realized they weren't moving. Justin liked her timing, even if it meant they would lag behind the Dive Bears.

"It was during the last days of the Civil War. Fort Jeff was a prison— mostly for Northern deserters. Guards were on the same side as their prisoners, so sometimes they were more friends than enemies and they would hang out."

"No wi-fi." Justin leaned over to whisper. Rudy pushed him away.

"One dark night, Private Winters was upstairs, in one of the cells." She pointed into the dark second floor arches. "He was playing cards with people he was supposed to guard. He finished his shift as two other soldiers were making their nightly patrol walking this very brick path." She tapped the ground. "Witnesses said he'd been drinking, a lot."

"That was why he thought it would be a clever idea to play a prank. Coming down those stairs," she pointed to the map room stairwell. "He hid in these shadows and drew his knife. When he heard other soldiers coming, he jumped out to scare them."

Justin winced, anticipating what was to come. "What happened?" Nina asked. Spud, hearing her worry, whined.

"Well, back then this electric light wasn't here. Prisoner, Guard? The sober soldiers couldn't tell. All they saw was a dark figure holding a knife attacking from prison stairs. Unfortunately for Private Winters, they were carrying loaded guns."

"They shot him?" Luke asked.

"An instinct, a reflex. Two shots and Private Winters lay dying about where you are standing." Lucy pointed. Rudy skittered off the bricks. "Ever since, there have been stories about a ghost haunting this section of Fort Jeff: odd noises, shadowy figures, papers disrupted in the map room, objects misplaced and strange sounds."

Other than Spud's thumping tail, the night was silent. Rudy's face was frozen in terror. Maybe Lucy had gone too far. It might be hard to convince him to help them surveil students. Fortunately, Nina spoke up. "Maybe that ghost is your saboteur."

"Not unless he knows how to sabotage computers." Lucy smiled.

"Not a ghost then." Justin cleared his throat. "We should catch up to the students."

Rudy recovered once they exited the fort's walls, relieved by either the gentle night breeze, stars, or rocking boats at anchor. "That's the historian's skiff." Lucy pointed to a sleek double-engine cigar boat. "Captain Levi's come to pick up his boss." A big man helped Mr. Howard aboard. His muscles would give Chet a run for his money.

Nina chuckled. "That's a speedboat, not a skiff."

"That's a grizzly, not a boat captain." Luke smiled. They watched the speedboat putter out to the yacht. "How does a historian afford a boat like that?"

"Pirate treasure." Rudy suggested. They moved on towards the beach.

Speakers had been placed on the moat wall. One Dive Bear tended to them while his legs dangled above the waves. Other students clustered around the beach or stood waist-deep in water. A few gathered around a cooler.

"They do this every night?" Justin asked.

"Not every night." Lucy replied, "But most."

Rudy surveyed the beach party. "I don't think we're going to learn anything here."

Nina nodded. "Rudy's right. This is just a bunch of people hanging out. I doubt… hey Spud." Nina interrupted herself reaching for Spud as he dashed for students near the cooler.

"Spud. Be polite." Luke called after the pup.

"Hi guys," Gwen reached up from her beachside seat to pat the dog. "What are you doing out here?"

"They're escorting us to our skiff so we can head back to Loggerhead." Nina lied. "Spud heard the music and got excited."

"Alright little party animal." Gwen gave the dog a more enthusiastic petting. His tail wagged energetically. She looked up, "have you guys seen Chet or Sophia?"

"No," Lucy swallowed, "Why?"

Neither were on the beach. "Ugh!" Gwen sighed. "I dragged everyone here so those two would talk. They've been having a bit of friction lately."

"Why?" Justin crossed his arms.

"Professional disagreements." Gwen tossed up her arms. "Their two mentors have been butting heads, so they have decided it's their job to continue the fight."

"But Chet's my mom's student." Lucy frowned. "And Sophia works with Professor Erickson."

"I thought Dr. Alexa was the grumpy one." Rudy added.

"Hey." Gwen lifted a finger to her lips. "Careful. Her students are already in a bad mood." She paused. Under intense gaze of five pairs of eyes, she continued. "Yeah, Dr. Alexa is grumpy. But it's your mom and professor Erickson who are feuding. You know about our problems?"

Lucy shrugged.

"Dr. Benitez still thinks there's a way to save the expedition. Professor Erickson wants to send everyone back to Key West now."

Lucy's face fell. Justin tried to sound hopeful. "I'm with Dr. Benitez. What about Chet and Sophia?"

"They're siding with their mentors." Gwen sighed. "If you see them, tell them I'm expecting them for a peace-making conference."

Taking that as a dismissal, the twins turned Spud around and they all walked away. "That was quick thinking." Justin complimented Nina.

"I figured you wanted to keep your spying secret." Nina grinned proudly.

"Mom and Dad." Luke pointed to two figures crossing the bridge. "That's our cue."

Nina sighed, grabbing Spud, "It was nice investigating with you guys. Come to Loggerhead soon."

"Still think they could be involved?" Rudy asked.

"They are pretty good liars." Justin, copying Lucy, rolled his eyes.

CHAPTER 17

TWO ENCOUNTERS

LUCY

WHILE THE MANNINGS' BOAT puttered out of the harbor Lucy led them to the dock. Rudy stepped gingerly over a mess of fresh fish guts beneath a carving table. Lucy rushed ahead grabbing some fishy bits. "Eww." Rudy gagged.

She ignored him "Want to see something awesome? Justin, do you have your flashlight?" He began fishing through his many pockets. Lucy shook her head. "That's why I don't carry a lot of junk around with me everywhere."

Justin produced: a Swiss army knife, a small pair of binoculars in a felt case, a box of waterproof matches, a sewing kit, three glowsticks wrapped in aluminum, and, finally, a small light fastened onto a keychain. "You never know when any of this stuff will come in handy."

"How about never?" Lucy wiggled the fish guts.

Justin held up a glowsticks. "We can drop this in the water and see what's down there."

"You're not dumping that plastic in the water." Lucy stared at the packaged glowstick which advertised: *High intensity, 60 minutes.* "Why do you have those?"

"I would have tied it to a string first." Justin held up a small spool of yarn.

"Seriously?" Lucy waited for him to cram everything but the flashlight back into his pockets. "That junk will weigh you down when someone pushes you into the moat."

Justin's smile turned into a look of concern. "Please don't, I don't want to be stung by *Cassiopea*. Also, I have my cell phone."

"I have my phone too." Rudy quickly added.

"You've only been on the island for two days. I'll wait until night three, at least." Lucy grinned. "Promise."

Rudy leaned closer to Justin. "I'm never walking around the moat again."

Lucy held up a yellow tail which had once belonged to a snapper of the same name. Rudy stuck his tongue out in disgust. "Follow me." She them to the dock's edge.

"What are we doing?" Justin asked.

Several awkward birds the height of Rudy's knees hobbled out of the shadows, lifting their beaks expecting a treat. Lucy made a shooing motion "Get, get." The pelicans backed into darkness. She pointed into the water below, "Shine your light down there." Justin stepped to the edge.

Dock lights cast rippling reflections, but the flashlight beam carved into the depths. The eyes of gray snapper cruising patrol stared back. Soft coral and sponges grew on pillars which faded into green. "How deep is it?" Justin asked.

"Twenty or thirty feet. Now watch." Lucy tossed a small piece of fish into the water. It sank slowly. Suddenly, a massive round mouth appeared out of the darkness swallowing the morsel and swimming away in a flash. Several larger silver shapes darted by.

"Woah!" Justin nodded, "So many of them."

"The world's biggest minnow." Lucy watched the silvery torpedo disappear fighting a small flutter in her stomach. "They get to be six or seven feet long out here. Is that what you saw while we were snorkeling?"

Justin stared out towards the coaling dock ruins. "I don't think so. It was closer to the bottom, and not moving. Also, the color was wrong."

"Was it treasure colored?" Rudy asked.

"No, but maybe shark colored." Justin leaned from the pillar, hanging over water.

Lucy leaned back. "A few years ago, over on Loggerhead, a shark grabbed a snorkeler. They had to punch it until it to let go. I worry about that every time I get in the water."

"That's not the only incident." A voice almost startled Justin into losing his grip and tumbling into the water. Lucy reached out catching his shirt and pulling him back. "A fisherman out here once found a human foot in a hammerhead's stomach." A lanky man with a prominent shark tattooed on his arm stepped out of a small room in the wooden dock house. His shark had horns. "What are you three doing out here?"

His scraggly goatee and long sun-bleached blond hair stuck out in every direction. He wore a loose Hawaiian shirt with short sleeves to show off his tattoo. One of his hands was balled into a fist around a small piece of paper. The other held a large plastic bag.

"Same question, what are you doing out here tonight?" Lucy tried to hide her surprise.

"Cleaning fish for dinner," he held up the plastic bag full of fish fillets. "And checking tomorrow's weather report. Although I don't see why I have to explain that to you." His gaze shifted towards a larger and muscular figure walking down the park service boat's gangplank.

Chet waved. The grumpy man "hmphed," turning to glare at the three. He took a deep breath. In an instant, his demeanor changed. He stretched out a strained smile. "Want some to take home to your father?" he held up the bag. "I caught more than I could eat."

"*Then don't catch that many.*" Lucy thought. "No, thanks." He tucked the bag into his pocket. "We were here to see tarpon. Now we'll be leaving." She used the muscular student as an excuse to lead the boys away. "Hi Chet, what are you up to?"

"Not much." Chet scanned the dock. "Is it only Captain Tobias out here?"

"Yeah." Lucy replied. She saw Justin's eyes widen in recognition of the *Horned Devil's* captain's name. "Are you looking for someone?"

Chet glared towards the lonely man. "Not really." He stopped before the bridge. "Well, I'm going to join the beach festivities for a while."

Bidding him goodbye, Lucy stepped down to the water's edge to wash off the fish remains. Justin followed her to provide light. "So that was Captain Tobias? He doesn't seem very friendly."

"He's not. That's why Mom suspects him. I wonder why he's out here right now."

"I thought he took people diving." Rudy asked.

"Do you see any people out here with him? Did you see any lights onboard his boat?" Lucy pointed out to the harbor. The only illuminated vessel was the yacht, it's bearded captain a tall silhouette on deck. "Captain Tobias is a commercial dive captain without any clients."

"That's suspicious," Rudy nodded.

Lucy made her disgust plain. "I bet he's out here spying on the Dive Bears." She stepped onto the balance beam/bridge which would take them back into the fort.

"Why is it a big deal if the public knows and dives on U.R.S.A.'s wrecks? This is a public park." Justin reached out to offer a hand as she swayed on the rail. She pushed it away.

"Yeah, that's my plan." Rudy nodded. "I'm going to find a pirate wreck, dig up some buried treasure, and become famous."

"How do I explain this?" Lucy breathed in deeply, "the Dive Bears wrecks are new, uncharted, and sometimes surprisingly well preserved. They are also vulnerable. Take Sophia's cannon. To document them, she's had the team help dig them up, exposing them for the first time in a century. Now, anyone could damage or move them. But it's harder to steal from a documented wreck. Once she finishes her report, she won't have to worry so much about illegal salvage operations."

Lucy stepped down from her balance beam. "Rudy's not the only one interested in old artifacts. You could make a lot of money illegally selling things from an undiscovered, uncharted, wreck. Mom wants to keep her research quiet until the wrecks are recorded properly."

The three paused silently within the sally port. Finally, Rudy broke the silence. "In other news, what was Chet doing on the park boat?"

"Who knows?" Lucy paused. "Check out the dark side." One side of the fort was pitch black. Overhead, the harbor light shone against a sky painted with a vast array of stars. They were even visible through the second-floor arches. "Isn't it pretty?" She would have liked a moment to appreciate the view but jumped when Rudy sucked in a deep breath.

"Do you see that?" he whispered, pointing.

He didn't have to point. There was only one thing on Fort Jefferson's dark side to which he could be referring. A shadowed figure skulked about the parade ground with a dim light.

"Who is that?" Justin asked in his own whisper.

"I don't know." Lucy answered.

"Private Win—" Rudy swallowed his words.

The figure disappeared in shadows cast by the Large Powder Magazine. The three waited for it to reappear. It didn't. "Come on!" Kicking out of her sandals, Lucy sprinted silently around the brick path.

Her friends' shoes flapped on the bricks behind her. The dim light jostled in the distance disappearing into deeper shadow. Rudy huffed, "Why are we chasing a shadow?"

Lucy shrugged him off and raced around another corner. Slowing to tiptoe into the shadows cast by the fort's walls she tried to control her breathing. Hopefully, she was hidden from anyone in the Large Powder Magazine. She raised a finger to her lips as the boys approached.

"Who are we chasing?" Justin whispered.

"If I knew that, we wouldn't have to chase them." Lucy hissed in hushed reply. "Go around that side. I'll go around this one." She pointed right and left of the powder magazine. "Rudy, stand back and watch. Yell if they try to escape."

Rudy looked to where Lucy was pointing. "What if they aren't in the powder magazine? What if they are a ghost?"

"Ready?" Lucy and Justin skulked around opposite sides of the building. She crept a circular approach to the magazine's entrance. Seeing no one, she stealthily sprinted past, so anyone hiding behind the structure couldn't slip away.

She lowered into a crouch and listened for breathing. Turning the corner, a figure froze against the brick wall. She was equally startled until she realized it was Justin. "No one on my side." He pulled out his flashlight.

They stepped into the Large Powder Magazine. Two sets of scuffling footprints echoed in the large open space. Justin aimed his light around the room, scanning every corner and all six alcoves. "No one." Lucy shook her head. They rushed back to Rudy's lookout position. "Did you see anyone?"

He shook his head. "Maybe they are in the fort?" They checked through the first-floor casemates. Empty. If the shadow had retreated upstairs Rudy would have seen them.

Lucy's brow furrowed. "We're all in agreement we saw someone, right?"

"Yeah." Rudy's voice waivered, "Where did they go?"

CHAPTER 18
MUSINGS ON A GHOST

JUSTIN

"**T**HERE USED TO BE A LIGHTHOUSE inside Fort Jeff. It's keeper and his family had a house in the parade ground. When the fort walls went up, they tore down the original and replaced it with the harbor light." Lucy pointed into the courtyard, "All that remains is the concrete circle of the old foundation over there."

Justin followed her gesture to a lone marker standing in the field. "I see the sign."

"Actually, that is a monument to all the people who died out here during a yellow fever outbreak. A lot of them are buried near that big stone memorial under those trees."

"Gugg." The noise escaped Rudy's lips. "Are you trying to creep me out."

"It wasn't a ghost." Justin crossed his arms.

"Are you sure? We saw someone. Lucy chased them. When we got there, they were gone. The experience gave me nightmares." Despite the high temperature, Rudy shivered over a cup of cocoa.

"Is that why you didn't want to wake up?" Justin asked. He turned to Lucy. "What time where you up?"

"Before sunrise." Lucy yawned.

"She doesn't count." Rudy protested. "She ran towards a ghost. She's obviously insane."

"What ghost?" Miguel walked in rubbing sleep out of his eyes. "The one in the rec room, or Private Winters?"

"Miguel don't mention the rec room ghost. We're meeting Mom there for class." Lucy threw a dirty napkin at her brother. "We don't have time to scare Rudy."

"Who said we had to study today anyway?" Rudy asked with wide eyes.

Lucy sighed. "See?"

Justin had been holding onto a chart he'd made last afternoon, hoping for ghost talk to die down. "Miguel, check this out."

"What is it?" Miguel asked.

"Lucy said that using my gut to choose our suspects is a bad idea. This will help." The chart had taken Justin a while to draw because he wanted straight lines. "There are five columns: Suspects, Motives, Means, Opportunity, and Other. I've made twenty rows for names and left room for more."

"What do we do? Write down the names of everybody out here and then fill in the boxes?" Lucy took the chart to begin sketch pictures over each section.

"You make it sound like a bad idea." Justin cleared his throat. "We name our top suspects, and whenever we learn something important about them, we add it to my chart. The more categories we fill in, the more likely someone is guilty. We can also write down anything which might exclude a suspect." He squinted. "We should use a different color of ink for that."

"You don't want to try a Venn diagram, or a pie chart?" Miguel snarked, grabbing a cup of yogurt and riffing through the cabinets. "Where's you a column for Evidence?"

"Um," Justin felt embarrassment creeping up his cheeks. "There's room. I can add it."

"Justin's onto something." Lucy glared at her brother. "This can help." Handing his chart back, she bumped into his arm spilling some cocoa, "Why's Chet's name first?"

Justin reached down to clean up the mess. "Chet's research hasn't been impacted by any sabotage. Gwen couldn't find him on the beach, and later we saw him on the park boat."

Rudy reached for the chart. "Good. Sophia's on this list." He nodded to himself, then tilted his head. "You included the turtle volunteers?"

"What?" Miguel asked through a spoonful of yogurt.

"Lucy, what are their names?" Justin gently took his chart back from Rudy, shaking off drops of cocoa soaking through the paper.

"Mina and Shelly." Miguel answered too quickly. "It wasn't them." Justin wrote their names on his chart anyway.

"You should write down that Sophia talked a lot about money." Rudy suggested.

"Money makes sense as a motive." Lucy pointed to a different place on the chart. "But I think Ranger O'Donnell outright hates the Dive Bears."

"This is all good." Justin began diligently writing down their suggestions. "Lucy, should I show this to your mother before we start school?"

"Go for it." Miguel didn't sound particularly interested.

"You won't be there." Lucy crossed her arms. "Chet's her best student." That muscle bound guy? "She won't like seeing him on top of your list."

"I'll help you carry stuff to the wreck room. You don't want to be late." Miguel pointed to the clock, ushering them outside.

The wreck room turned out to be the 'rec room.' Meaning: recreation room. It was a short walk across the path from the Benitez's home. Like their apartment upstairs, it was walled into the fort. Unlike their apartment, it took up two whole casemates. There was a laundry room and a small sitting area in the first casemate. The second casemate contained a pool table and a large area with a huge television. Even with lights on, the room seemed dark.

Justin marveled. "This would make a perfect investigation headquarters!" The main sitting area had couches and a large coffee table. A massive corkboard hung behind a deeply pitted dart board. "This could be our mystery board."

"Of course." Miguel laughed, setting Rudy's stuff down on the coffee table. "All we need is colored yarn, more push pins, and construction paper. Then we can start lining up clues."

Lucy shook her head. "Everyone does laundry here. Anyone could see our plans." Emphasizing her point, a dryer buzzed startling them all.

"But we can still put something together now, to present to your mom." Justin hung his chart on the corkboard.

Lucy scribbled one change out, "don't mention our sighting last night."

"Speaking of ghosts." Miguel looked past his sister to focus on Rudy, "Remember, this room is haunted too." His smile growing wide, he slipped outdoors.

"What does he mean?" Rudy sat upright.

"Thanks Miguel!" Lucy shouted after her brother as the door slammed shut.

Justin ignored Rudy's wide-eyed concern. "Let's see what we can add before Lucy's mom comes."

Working on clues, Rudy slowly forgot about ghosts. Once Dr. Benitez appeared, they took a step back so she could observe their hard work. "I wasn't expecting a chart. Maybe a list of clues or a notebook full of observations. Is this how you always work?"

Lucy smirked. "When Cassidy was in charge, we kept notes on construction paper and made papier mâché sculptures of suspects."

"Ha, ha, ha."

Justin shrugged. "This was my idea. When we find clues, I'll also make a clue chart."

"No clues yet?" Dr. Benitez cleared her throat when she saw their disappointed looks. "Anyways, this is not why we are here." She held up her copies of their textbooks. "Your parents would kill me if they discovered that I asked for your help on an investigation. They will absolutely murder me if I neglect your studies."

The next couple hours were a slog through schoolwork. At some point, Miguel came back. Dr. Benitez roped him into helping Rudy with math, while she helped Lucy and Justin with more advanced problems.

That afternoon, Dr. Benitez began making her own notations to Justin's chart. "Paul was in Key West when the GPS disappeared. Barbara was gone half of July. I'll double check with Gabe, but I can help you eliminate half of my students and most rangers. It couldn't be Travis. He can't keep a secret to save his life."

"Mama, leave the investigation to professionals." Lucy said.

"Sorry. You have your methods." She rubbed her hands together. "Well, I think that's enough studying today. I need to check on my less mature students. Get out of here and do something active!" In a flash, she was off to supervise U.R.S.A.

"I don't want to be active." Rudy complained hefting his books.

"How about we go swimming!" Lucy suggested eagerly.

"We did that yesterday." Rudy shook his head. "I'm going upstairs to play games." Opening the rec room door, they were hit by a wall of heat. "Come get me when it's cooler."

Justin turned to Lucy, holding up his chart. "I know what we can do."

"Why don't I think it has anything to do with swimming?"

CHAPTER 19

THE FIRST CLUE

LUCY

JUSTIN DUMPED HIS SCHOOL STUFF with Lucy's in her dad's office. "I want to interview anyone we can find." He had two speeds: trust everyone or be suspicious.

Lucy couldn't fault his enthusiasm. "Fine. Just be polite. Also, I have an idea about how our *ghost* got away." She put air quotes around ghost. "We should check it out."

A few Dive Bears were hanging around the crews quarters. Every question Justin asked them lead back to Chet. Lucy had to change the subject multiple times. They didn't learn anything new.

"It's hard to investigate, when you can't ask direct questions." Justin complained.

They wound east around Fort Jeff. While Justin added a blue bird to his diary, Lucy explained the hill of bricks and brambles. "That pile of rubble is left over after the old Officer's Quarters inside the fort burnt down. This way, there's something I want to show you." She pointed to the Large Powder Magazine through the fort's windows.

Sand clogged the moat making a small hill connecting fort and moat wall. Lucy's dad was always complaining about how hard it was to clear.

There was a small brown sign warning that the area was closed. They were worried someone walking down there, could be hit by a stray fort brick, or falling tourist.

"Our '*ghost*' might have escaped here." Lucy pointed. "Someone could squeeze through a first-floor window and drop down. I've thought about sneaking out this way. You could play fun pranks on people who didn't realize you'd left the fort."

Justin's eyes locked onto deep indentations in the sandbar. "Footprints? You're right! It looks like someone dropped down from up there!"

Lucy squinted. "Yeah. Probably."

"They're too messed up." Justin held out a hand to measure against loose sand. "Those prints could belong to a big burly criminal or someone small like Rudy."

Lucy shook her head. "If those footprints do belong to our *ghost*, it still doesn't prove they're our saboteur. The dark side of Fort Jeff has nothing to do with underwater archeology."

"Hmm." Justin pulled out his phone taking pictures of the prints. "Still, let's call this our first clue." He flashed a satisfied smile. "Now, I want to talk to Mr. Howard."

"Not so easy." Lucy grinned. The historian was on the deck of his yacht next to his bushy bearded captain. "Want to swim out there?"

"You can drive your dad's boat, can't you?" Justin turned to her eagerly.

Lucy frowned. "We've only been investigating three days. Let's wait until at least day four before we start acting crazy."

CHAPTER 20

MORNING SWIM

LUCY

PRE-DAWN SUN STRETCHED PINK FINGERS over Fort Jefferson turning scattered puffy clouds orange. Lucy was out of her house before Miguel could pull himself from the sofa where he'd fallen asleep watching TV. It would be hours before the boys woke up. Perfect.

She hurried past the generators and desalinization plant, thankfully quiet this early. A single student sat outside the crews quarters reading. Her father was the second person she saw, in the park headquarters. He liked to get an early start on paperwork.

Outside sheltering fort walls, the morning became a barrage of bird noise from Bush Key. Ranger O'Donnell was on the docks already at work on a university boat.

The crew of the MV *Fort Jefferson* were preparing for today's departure, the first group of students would be going home. Trying to ignore how much that worried her, Lucy surveyed the water. It was low tide and calm seas.

The water was warm as a bath. Angling close to the wall, no snorkel gear necessary, Lucy opened her eyes to a momentary saltwater sting. She began breathing in a steady rhythm. As long as she kept the moat wall close to grab onto, she didn't have to worry about something appearing out of the open water.

It was a good day. The waves were barely a light chop. Around one last corner and she was headed towards the north beach. Closing in on shore, she turned to swim out to the north coaling dock. There, she stopped. Water beyond that point was darker, deeper, and there were no handholds.

In her third lap, just before the moat opening, she heard voices calling out to her. "Lucy, Lucy, up here." She lifted her head to look into the rounded glasses of one of Dr. Alexa's students. Beside him was Sophia. Lucy could make out a wet impression of her university swimsuit beneath her tank top. The other student had wet hair, but he'd changed into dry clothes.

"Hi Paul, Sophia."

"You do this every day, kid?" Dr. Alexa's student leaned over the edge of the moat wall to talk. Lucy bristled at his use of 'kid.'

Sophia shook her head, "She's out here every morning, sun or rain."

"I just wanted to say goodbye." Paul smiled. "Dr. Alexa is taking red team back to Key West." He yawned stretching out his arms. "Sorry, we spent all last night packing."

"All of Dr. Alexa's students are going home?" Lucy frowned. That was more than she expected!

"Well, since we just discovered that Sophia's—" Paul began before Sophia's grabbed his shoulder anxiously. He fell silent.

"It's not something we're supposed to talk about." Sophia interrupted. "We'll let you get back to your swim." She grabbed Paul's arm, leading him away. That was strange. Lucy swam on, more annoyed than intrigued by their interruption.

Sun crawling into the sky. She climbed out of the water. Relative silence had been replaced by daily park activities. A seaplane sailed overhead to make its first landing. The docks were bustling as the M.V. *Fort Jefferson* was loaded with supplies and passengers, including all of Dr. Alexa's students.

Her dad was filling a park boat with gas before his morning patrol, and her mom waved from an U.R.S.A. boat pulling out to sea. Lucy watched her parent's two boats travel together out of the harbor. What were they up to? "Huh." Then she rolled her neck, enjoying the start to another Dry Tortugas day.

CHAPTER 21

CHANGE IN THE AIR

JUSTIN

J USTIN WOKE TO LOUD REPETITIVE BEEPING. It took a moment to confirm that it wasn't a fire alarm and was, instead, a large forklift. From his top bunk he watched it back down the small brick pathway below his apartment. Sliding out of bed, his feet hit cold brick floor. Out the window, he recognized Ranger O'Donnell and an older maintenance ranger.

Rudy was awake in bed playing something on his phone. Wrapped in his covers, he ignored the noise. According to Justin's phone, it was 9:23 in the morning. His mom had sent several new pictures: his sister's new dorm and a few with his sister standing next to an array of strangers. He wondered which was Cassidy's new roommate. His dad had sent a single message: *hope you're having fun.* That was more than he'd expected.

Rudy stretched. "It sounds like a factory out there. I'm hungry."

Breakfast was scrambled eggs and a rolled tin of biscuits. Rudy had wanted to cook bacon too, but they couldn't find a second skillet. As they finished eating, Lucy barged in. "I hope you weren't planning on asking Dr. Alexa any more questions."

"Why?"

"One of her students told me *all* of red team is leaving." Lucy looked concerned. "Mama's expedition is already falling apart."

Justin frowned. "Did that student tell you why?"

Lucy shook her head. "He seemed sad, and maybe surprised? I think he was going to tell me more, but Sophia interrupted him. Like it was a secret." That was interesting.

"We should go ask him more questions before the boat leaves." Justin grabbed his bird book, frowned, and grabbed a school notebook instead. He didn't want to mess with his birding notes.

"We don't have time." She sighed. "Mom sent me to get you ready for class!"

Justin rubbed his hands together. "That works too. I have lots of questions for her."

Those questions would have to wait. They found Lucy's mom drying off on her front porch, but she was in no mood to talk. "Dr. Benitez, good! I wanted to show you our list of main suspects." Justin's words died in his throat.

Dr. Benitez squeezed more water out of her hair. "Not now. Take your books to the rec room, start with Math. I'll be there in a second."

"Math again!" Rudy complained. When Lucy's mom frowned deeper, he swallowed his complaints.

The next couple hours were weird. Lucy's mom hovered over them unwilling to let Justin distract her with questions about their investigation. Things only got stranger when Lucy's father arrived.

"Hi guys!" Gabriel Benitez's smile looked uncomfortable. "Remember the other day, we talked about going out with the turtle volunteers?"

Justin was the first to nod. He wanted to see the birds on Hospital key.

"Great! Today's your chance. We're headed to East Key. Why don't you come out with us now?" He turned to Lucy's mom. "With your permission of course."

Dr. Benitez practically pushed them out of the rec room. "Fine by me. Applied science is the best science."

"What's going on?" Justin whispered as they awkwardly packed their books.

Pausing at the rec room door, Lucy grabbed his elbow holding up a finger, so they could listen while her dad spoke cryptically to her mom. "You can take your students out now. Do a complete survey." A survey of what? "Wendy will ride out to supervise."

Letting the door shut before they were caught, Lucy explained. "Wendy is another law enforcement ranger. She must have come out on a seaplane."

"Is this about our mystery?" Justin asked, "And if so, why wouldn't your mom tell us?"

CHAPTER 22

TURTLE HUNT

LUCY

THE PARK BOAT HAD TAKEN DR. ALEXA'S STUDENTS HOME, but the rest of the Dive Bears swarmed the docks prepping both university boats. They glanced worriedly at Lucy and her friends, breathing a sigh of relief when they saw that Dr. Benitez wasn't with them. Before Lucy could march up and ask what was going on, her dad arrived with turtle researchers in tow.

There wasn't time for mystery talk as he called Justin and Lucy to help them hand equipment onto the boat. Rudy waited until everything was loaded before joining them onboard.

"Alright, first mate," Lucy's dad turned to her. "Cast lines!"

"Aye, aye, Captain." Lucy called back. Justin distributed life jackets while she untied lines from cleats. Before long, their boat circled Fort Jeff headed east.

Rudy leaned to shout over the wind "These islands feel so small from the ocean."

"The Park is 99% water." Mina, one turtle researcher, replied. She ducked down beneath the wind beside the other researcher. Lucy moved to join them. "Which makes it a wonderful place to find sea turtles."

"So, you guys are out here counting sea turtles?" Rudy asked. Lucy smiled. The more questions the better, her mother had warned them of a turtle quiz when they returned.

Mina replied. "We count nests, identify turtle species, and track as much information as possible about species nesting out here: loggerhead, green, hawksbill, and a rare leatherback."

A few minutes later and Mr. Benitez was pulling back on the throttle. "Almost there." Without a big brick fort, lighthouse, or loads of vegetation, East Key was nothing more than empty sand tufted by sawgrass.

"Where's the dock?" Justin asked.

"There is no dock." Lucy answered. "We're swimming."

"Really?" Rudy glanced skeptically into the ocean. They were about seventy feet away. No one had a swimsuit.

"Hold on." Mr. Benitez interrupted. "I just need to find my way past rocks. We're going to beach her." Her father slowly pushed their boat forward grinding the bow into sand, stopping above waves breaking on the beach. "Welcome to East Key."

Rudy jumped off the bow, his flip-flops splashing in surf. "Where's my big red X?" Lucy followed him, wading into shallow water to help the turtle researchers with their equipment.

"I don't think that pirates made their treasures so easy to find." Justin, at Mr. Benitez's direction, opened a compartment under a bench pulling out a heavy anchor. Aiming for an empty spot he tossed it into dry sand.

Rushing to top the small island, Rudy's feet slid a half step down for every step up in loose sand, "There's got to be something buried somewhere."

"Is he joking, or have videogames fried his brain?" Lucy stepped out of the way as Justin jumped off the boat, scattering sand and salt water.

"Alright guys, gather up here." Mina had a pile of flags scattered at her feet. Crouching next to two shovels Shelly, the other researcher, sat on the beach with her notebook open.

Rudy returned reluctantly. "Anyone marooned out here would starve to death."

Shelly looked up from her notebook. "If you were stranded back here during pirate days, there was a plentiful source of food. You wouldn't even have to leave this island."

"Where?"

"Think about it." Lucy elbowed Rudy. "It's turtle season."

"Oh. Gross."

"Yep." Shelly nodded. "Almost every night, sea turtles crawl onto this island to lay their eggs. You could keep yourself fed like an olden days sailor."

"Ponce De Leon was looking for the fountain of youth when he found these islands full of turtles. So, he named them Las Tortugas. Not to be confused with the island of Tortuga south of here, which was also a famous pirate haven." Lucy's dad grinned at Rudy leaning on his shovel. "At the time, sea turtles were considered great eating. Lots of meat, easy to find and easy to keep—even without a fridge."

"How?" Rudy asked.

"Sailors dragged turtles on deck and flipped them on their backs." Mina made a scooping motion. "They could keep them alive for weeks."

"That's terrible." Rudy shivered.

"Fortunately, we're here to protect sea turtles, not eat them." Mina handed everyone a stack of flags.

Shelly stood, brushing herself off, "You'd die of dehydration long before you'd starve. There was a reason they changed the name to Dry Tortugas."

Mina gave her friend a shoulder squeeze. "Let's get to work. Any questions?"

Rudy raised his hand, "how deep would pirates bury treasure?"

They walked around the small island looking for signs of new turtle crawls. Turtle tracks were hard to recognize, but Shelly pointed out several new trails. Each had two rows of flat impressions left by flippers and a line from a giant body dragged across the beach.

They followed each crawl looking for depressions. Then Lucy, Rudy or Justin would mark boundaries around nests with flags. While they worked Justin kept both turtle researchers busy with questions about their time in the park, not about turtles. Twice, Lucy caught Rudy climbing through sawgrass. He claimed to be looking for nests.

"There won't be any nests that high." Mina explained. "The bank's too steep, and turtles would have a tough time digging in grass."

Rudy grumbled under his breath. "Pirates wouldn't."

Lucy's father helped keep everyone on track, peppering their conversations with questions about turtles. Eventually Rudy became interested in their primary goal. "Different temperatures cause boy or girl turtles?"

"Yep." Mina nodded.

"How?" Rudy squinted confusion.

"It's called temperature dependent sex determination. If the average temperature of an egg is less than 82 degrees, babies will be male. If the temperature is above 87 degrees, babies will be female." Shelly answered.

"What happens in between?"

"Well, then the nest will have a mixture of male and female turtle babies." Mina answered.

"It doesn't work like that for people, does it?" Rudy asked.

"Nope, only for some egg laying reptiles like turtles, crocodiles, and alligators." Mina stood, surveying their work. "How about we get on to our second job?"

Shelly led them back to shovels. Rudy's energy picked up.

Lucy's father shook his head. "Pirates understood that these little sandy islands change with every storm, too much to be a reliable treasure hiding place. East Key was a different shape last year. Two hundred years ago, it was probably a different island entirely."

"Rudy's used to easy loot." Justin pulled Lucy aside. He pointed to the turtle volunteers, "I don't think those two have anything to do with your mom's mystery. They don't have access to the map room. They also take breaks back in Key West for weeks at a time."

"I could have told you that myself." Lucy sighed. "Come on."

"Why do we have to dig up this nest?" Rudy asked Shelly, shovel in hand.

"See that line of seaweed?" Mina pointed to a drying black-brown line, "That's the normal high tide line. However, that line back there," she pointed to another line of seaweed, almost gray from sun, further up the beach. "That's the maximum high tide line. Sometimes, mother turtles lay their nests below it, where the nest might be swamped."

Shelly nodded. "We are going to relocate this nest above that line."

"Why?" Justin asked. "Most parks don't want people interfering with wildlife."

Mina and Shelly shrugged. "Well, turtles are endangered. It's partially our fault. Helping them every now and then probably won't hurt."

"It won't make the babies get lost or forget their mothers?" Rudy asked.

"Nope." Shelly shook her head.

"Now I see why you were so excited to have us along." Lucy's father cracked his knuckles theatrically. Just as he was about to start digging his radio crackled.

"DT07 to DT01, can we talk on channel 09? Over."

"I'd better take this." Lucy's dad handed his shovel to Rudy and stepped away.

The team spent an hour excavating and relocating. Rudy and Justin were both amused by turtle eggs, which were like leathery ping pong balls. Afterwards, Mina showed them how to lightly shift sand back onto eggs. "Like their momma's flippers, gently spread it out so you don't crush them."

Although they were having fun and learning a lot, Lucy's dad seemed rushed. With one final toss of sand, he nodded. "If we're done here, we need to hurry back so I can drop you off."

"Where are you going?" Lucy asked.

"To Loggerhead." He replied cryptically. She turned to Justin. He must have caught it. Something was off.

CHAPTER 23

ADVANCED PLANNING THE CASE WAY

JUSTIN

TIRED FROM WORKING UNDER THE BEATING SUN, everyone slumped into their boat chairs. Justin leaned against the wind to watch Ranger Benitez's face. Lucy's parents were acting weird. Her father hastily dropped them on dock, helped the turtle volunteers remove their equipment and pulled away without so much as a good-bye.

"What are we doing now?" Justin turned to his two friends, only to realize that it was the turtle volunteers standing beside him.

"We have a show to binge while we crunch these numbers. Your friends are over there." Mina pointed to Lucy and Rudy on the beach with Spud.

The labradoodle was running back and forth, tail wagging. Justin ran to join them. "Hello boy," he reached down to scratch Spud. "Where are Luke and Nina?"

"On Loggerhead playing video games with their father." Renee replied. "I'm here picking up groceries the people on the ferry kindly brought out, and to invite all of you over tomorrow. Luke and Nina are excited to give you an island tour."

"Well, we just started our schoolwork." Lucy replied.

"Your mom's the one who suggested it." Renee smiled.

Justin frowned. First the turtle hunt, now a trip to Loggerhead. There was a mystery to solve, and it was only growing more urgent. Why would Dr. Benitez send them away? Renee loaded Spud back into her boat, and the two pushed into the harbor.

"What are we going to do?" Rudy asked, turning to Lucy, "Don't say: walk around the moat. It's too hot."

Justin expected Lucy to suggest another snorkeling session. Instead, she sighed. "Fine, let's go back home and cool down." Rudy stared at her in shock. "What? I get hot too. Besides, my parents are acting weird, and I want to know why."

"Maybe there are clues in the map room," Justin suggested as they passed Private Winter's corner.

Lucy frowned. "Make it quick. Mom will be expecting us."

"Fast," Justin agreed. How fast, he couldn't have suspected. As the three approached, they heard several elevated voices.

"I don't care! I need you to find those photos!" Sophia's angry voice echoed from the locked room.

"Give me time." Gwen sounded calm, despite her friend's anger. "I have a lot of files to search. Breathing down my neck doesn't speed things up."

"Now guys—" Chet opened the door when Lucy knocked. "Oh, hey." He turned into the room shouting. "Keep your voices down!" He turned back to Justin and crew. "Now is not a good time."

"I've got them!" Gwen called excitedly.

"See. I told you." Sophia sounded angrier after getting what she wanted. Justin leaned into the room. Chet's bulk blocked his line of sight.

"Sorry guys, you'll have to come back later. If you see Professor Erickson or Dr. Benitez, though, send them this way." He shut the door before Justin could respond.

"That was weird." Rudy watched the closed door.

"Maybe Mom will have answers." Lucy sighed. "Let's go. We don't want to get caught eavesdropping."

Dr. Benitez was neither at home, nor waiting for them in the rec room. "She must be out with a dive team." Justin scratched the back of his head.

"Yeah, but why? We have afternoon class." Lucy slumped into the larger couch in her living room. "Whatever. I'm fixing lunch. Then I'm going to the rec room to work on our mystery."

Justin stared at the board with his updated chart. It now included evidence. It still didn't seem adequate. "Maybe we should add a list of every problem U.R.S.A.'s had."

"Crimes chart!" Rudy scrawled that title on a blank sheet of paper before Justin or Lucy could think of a better one. "What should I write on this list?"

"Missing equipment, missing research," Justin called out while Rudy wrote, "and commercial boats diving on secret wrecks."

"Kit's missing research samples are their own thing." Lucy added.

"Right." Rudy added the fourth article to his list, then tacked it on the board.

Justin took a step back. "We also need a timeline."

Lucy nodded. "Now, you're sounding like Cassidy."

"It's useful." Justin admitted begrudgingly. "Do we know when these crimes occurred?"

"The underwater camera went missing day one. That was two months ago." Lucy tapped her chin. "The GPS unit went missing soon after that. I remember because dad took Miguel and me to U.R.S.A.'s lab in Key West to look for everything." Lucy pursed her lips, thinking. "After that, Dr. Alexa moved U.R.S.A.'s remaining heavy equipment to the bat cave."

"Dun, dun, dun." Rudy turned to Justin.

"You guys know 'bat cave' is just a name for a fancy storage room, right?" Lucy stared at the list. "A lot of the stuff which has gone missing is large, or so important it's hard to miss."

"What's your point?" Rudy asked.

"The Dive Bears would have noticed anyone else using their equipment or trying to take it back on the park boat."

"We're on an island!" Justin tapped his forehead. "The equipment might still be out here! If we can find it, we may find the guilty party!"

"Unless it was all dumped into the ocean." Justin had seen Miguel approaching, but had remained silent, expecting something like this. He felt good about his decision. Justin had never seen Lucy jump so high out of her seat.

CHAPTER 24

GRINDING GEARS

LUCY

"**M**IGUEL!!" LUCY TURNED TO SHOUT AT HER BROTHER, "Don't!" Justin pretended to ignore them by writing down her brother's suggestion.

Miguel stared up at the board. "You are definitely related to Cassidy. That looks like one of her endeavors. Just not as colorful."

"I only have three colors of pen." Justin complained.

"Fair enough." Miguel slid onto the couch, leaving Rudy between him and Lucy. It was a good idea. She was still angry.

"Where have you been?" Lucy asked sharply. "Where's Mom?"

"Studying in park headquarters. Dad's super comfortable desk is unoccupied. As for mom, I'm not sure. Something weird is happening. She told me to find you guys and promised to be back soon." Her brother checked his watch.

Justin had still been thinking about one of Miguel's suggestions. "Do you really think our bad guy dumped stolen equipment, research, and samples at sea?"

"It depends." Miguel leaned forward. "Think like Cassidy. Brainstorm. Come up with good questions and they will help you solve the mystery."

"What are the right questions?" Justin asked.

Miguel sighed, "Alright, one freebie: 'Why steal all that archeology junk? Think quickly, mom's back in thirty minutes." Spurred on they began brainstorming.

"Maybe they stole expensive equipment to sell it." Rudy pulled out his phone. "I'll see how much that stuff is worth."

"We've been calling our suspect a saboteur. Maybe that's all they are." Justin frowned, "If they just want to hurt your mom's expedition, then they might really have dumped everything at sea."

"There is a third option." Miguel leaned forward eyes flicking to Rudy. "Maybe our saboteur wants to use this equipment to find something."

"Like what?" Justin asked.

"Pirate Treasure." Rudy answered without any hint of irony. Lucy rolled her eyes.

"There you go. You have several different paths to follow. With mom's help." Miguel smiled. "I'll bill you when you catch the guy."

Justin smiled, "We'll have this mystery solved in no time." On cue, the rec room door opened, and Lucy's mother walked in.

Dr. Benitez managed only a half-smile. "Sorry I'm late. Are you ready for your turtle quiz?" Her hands were empty. "I'm kidding. I didn't have time to make one. Why don't we call it early so you can prep your dinner?"

"Actually, Dr. Benitez. We're hoping you'd help us figure out our next step." Justin made a sweeping gesture to their presentation board.

As Lucy's mom surveyed their work, Justin stepped back with a proud smile. Dr. Benitez pursed her lips quickly glancing over the chart. "It looks like you guys put a lot of thought and effort into this. I'm sorry, I shouldn't have wasted your time."

There was an awkward pause before Justin could find courage to ask, "What do you mean?"

"I was a bit too eager for a mystery, so I jumped to conclusions." Lucy's mom shook her head, pointing to papers pinned to the board. "This is all nothing."

Lucy asked. "Mama, what do you mean?"

"The equipment was probably lost on our way out here." Her mom pointed to number two. "The previous archeology team's missing work disappeared long ago." She sighed, "Captain Tobias and the others have been out here for decades. Of course, they know some of our uncharted wrecks."

"What about Kit's samples?" Justin ventured.

"Kit was under pressure to finish those samples quickly. I'm sure Dr. Alexa will find his briefcase in our Key West office." Dr. Benitez shrugged, sympathetically, "I'm sorry guys, but your investigation is over."

CHAPTER 25

THE MYSTERY DEEPENS

LUCY

AFTER THEY WERE DISMISSED FROM SCHOOLWORK, Justin found Lucy sitting on her porch, beneath a cheerful assortment of lights. "What's up with your mom?" He asked sullenly.

Lucy had tried to talk to her mother, but she'd been shut down faster than Chet proposing another polar expedition. "One third of her team left, how could our mystery be over?" She waved at her dad, watching them through the kitchen. "We'll talk later. It's a good thing it's game night."

Lucy took Justin inside, so they could assemble a tray full of snacks for dinner. Her mom was happy to help carry everything over to the rec room. She seemed eager to get them out of her house.

The rec room had undergone a transformation. Miguel had been working on this for a while. There was an entire miniature world built atop the pool table. There were castles, forests, and a box full of miniature monsters ready at a moment's notice. "Are you guys ready to quest?"

Smiling, Lucy's mom dropped off her tray and left.

"It looks good." Lucy felt sorry to disappoint her brother, "But there are more important things happening tonight." Before Miguel could protest, she grabbed Justin's wrist and yanked him out the door.

"What's up?" Justin asked. Lucy raised a finger to her lips and mimed sneaking. They tiptoed slowly and quietly past Ranger Kyle's array of colorful hanging lights and around the house, crouching below overhanging windows.

On the parade ground side, the Benitez's kitchen and living room windows cast squares of light. They stealthily stepped onto the brick patio beside her dad's office. Lucy pulled Justin into a corner. They were hidden so long as her parents didn't step outside. With some concentration, she was able to hear her parents talk.

"… she's just the first to leave." They must be talking about Dr. Alexa. Lucy could hear her mother's frustration. "Even if I could somehow get the university to release our funding—which will be harder than ever now—once Mr. Ishii returns to discover how poorly I've taken care of the parks resources, he will send us all packing." Mr. Ishii was the ranger who had approved her mom's expedition.

"It's not your fault dear." Lucy's father countered.

"U.R.S.A. is my responsibility!" Lucy's mother rarely raised her voice. "How am I going to turn things around?" Footprints echoed off wooden floor. Lucy crouched lower pulling Justin with her.

"Are you positive all the cannon were taken?" Her father's voice was calm, despite his massive revelation.

"*What!*" Lucy mouthed to Justin.

"Gwen and Sophia hadn't photographed wreck one-twenty-two yet. We only have one underwater camera, remember." Her frustrated sigh was loud enough to be heard in the quiet night air, "I trust Sophia's assessment, every gun has been moved."

"I'll have Wendy send her report to the Everglades tomorrow." Mr. Benitez cleared his throat. "And our kids?"

Lucy felt her ears burn. "I shouldn't have gotten them involved. I thought we were dealing with a student acting up, or a bad practical joke. But now…" She stopped mid-sentence. "Don't worry, I've told them to leave it alone."

"You think they'll listen?"

"Ha!" Her mother's bitter laugh sent shivers through Lucy's spine. "They had better." Then her tone changed completely. "I'm sorry, Gabe."

Lucy's father chuckled. "Carmen. They are smart and capable. Now they will be more vigilant."

"We're dealing with antiques smugglers. I want them as far away from this mess as possible."

The silence lingered. Lucy tugged on Justin's shoulder. As quietly as possible, she led their escape. Once they stood in lights outside of the rec room Justin put a hand up blocking Lucy from the door. "Are we going to stop investigating?"

Lucy clenched her teeth, staring hard into Justin's eyes. "Why would we do that?"

"Your mom told us not to. She's worried about us."

"Well, we're definitely not stopping now." Lucy pushed past him grabbing the door handle. She paused, "Mr. Ishii comes back soon. Mom's right, if we don't solve this, he will cancel her research even if the university doesn't. I am not letting anyone ruin her reputation or take her away from me early."

Justin smiled "You don't have to convince me. I'm in. We should tell the others."

Lucy nodded, pushing open the door. "Yep, but I get to tell everyone about the cannon."

CHAPTER 26

J.R.I.C UNDERCOVER

JUSTIN

"**M**IGUEL IS GOING TO BE DISAPPOINTED ABOUT GAME NIGHT." Justin was speaking to himself. The slap of a shutting door was his only reply. He sighed, following Lucy.

Miguel had set up an impressive miniature world. He'd taped up sketches from several of their past adventures. There was sheet of paper pinned over the dart board he could use to draw combat maps.

Rudy sat opposite Miguel rolling and rerolling dice beside a plate of food. He stopped to offer them figures for their characters. "Ready?" Lucy ignored her small rogue. She took down Miguel's adventure drawings, replacing them with Justin's charts. "What are you doing?"

"We've got a mystery to solve." Lucy answered.

Miguel looked around at all his work. "I spent hours prepping for this game."

"Miguel." Lucy crossed her arms and stared at her brother. "Our game will wait."

Miguel stepped back, sighed, and collapsed onto the nearby sofa. Resting one arm over his face, "Alright then, take it away."

Lucy recounted what they'd heard. Rudy did not look surprised, but Miguel sat up, disappointment forgotten. "That, honestly, explains a lot. The Dive Bears have been acting crazy today. Dad ambushed Ranger Wendy the moment she stepped out of a seaplane. And mom's angry." Miguel nodded, "Professor Alexa even looked happy to leave. Glad her students are avoiding the trouble."

"Mom doesn't want her students in trouble either," Lucy countered.

"Which is why we need to figure out who stole the cannon and find them. Fast." Justin interrupted them. "So, um, where do we begin?"

"Who is our cannon thief?" Rudy asked.

Justin cleared his throat, "Mr. Benitez thinks it's Captain Tobias, but it doesn't sound like he has all the evidence. We should add stolen cannon to our list of crimes."

Lucy added it to their *crimes list*. "This crime is on a whole other level."

"Which is why mom told you to stop investigating." Miguel stared at his sister and their list. "Are we sure this recent theft is even related?"

"Either that, or we have two criminals." Justin's smile widened at the tempting thought. He tapped the board. "Cassidy always says we should pay attention to our timelines. What's changed recently?"

"Kit's samples!" Rudy jumped up. "Kit was on our Ferry when we came out. His samples disappeared that same day."

Lucy asked. "What, about Kit's samples, makes them so important?"

Rudy replied eagerly, "he told Professor Erickson that his boat was 400 years old?"

Lucy crossed her arms. "If you're going to make this about pirates again, I swear."

"I'm not." Rudy grumbled, "Even though pirate treasure would explain everything."

"But maybe our saboteur needed some kind of information from Kit's samples. Is that what you meant?" Justin asked. Rudy nodded slowly. It was a clever idea! "I'm impressed! But I can think of something else which happened that day."

"What?" Lucy asked.

"That was when we started our investigation. Just one night later, we were chasing someone through the dark side of the fort."

Miguel slumped back into his resting position on the couch. "If you're saying that your arrival made criminals nervous, I'm going to puke."

Justin wobbled his head. "I mean, we did scare someone sneaking around the fort. But more importantly, Dr. Benitez told her students about the sabotage and the end of their expedition. She let her bad guys know she was onto them.”

Lucy countered, “or maybe the cannon theft was always their big plan? And everything else was leading up to it.”

“Real civil war cannon are super rare.” Rudy held up his phone scanning through an article. “This rusted Union cannon is selling for ten thousand dollars!”

Justin stared at the listing on Rudy’s phone. “The cannon were their plan all along?”

“That’s, literally, exactly what I just said.” Lucy rolled her eyes, “But Sophia only found her cannon weeks ago. Most of U.R.S.A.’s equipment went missing before that.”

“Not Sophia’s cannon necessarily, but something.” Now Justin’s friends were all frowning. “Think about it,” he gestured to Rudy’s crimes list. “First, someone, like Captain Tobias, takes equipment and research to help find valuable artifacts. Then, when Dr. Benitez’s students discover something valuable, they steal it.”

“But how did Captain Tobias know about the cannon?” Rudy asked.

“Sophia told everyone about them.” Lucy exclaimed. “It was a big deal! She was super excited. Professor Erickson let her make it a huge research project.”

“That would actually be a bonus for our criminal.” Miguel nodded. “Even without the cannon, Sophia will still publish a research paper. Then there will be news stories about the theft. A black-market buyer could use all of that to prove the stolen cannon were real.”

“Like the time we found that treasure chest!” Rudy exclaimed.

Justin found himself nodding along, artifact theft was familiar territory. “I think we need to find those cannon.”

Lucy turned to her brother. “Should we sneak onto every boat in the harbor and look for them ourselves?”

Miguel shook his head. “We’re not going to be that dumb.”

Lucy shrugged. “If I was the cannon thief, I’d be in Key West by now.”

“Hmm.” Justin staring at their list of suspects. “Even with Chet’s muscles, stealing heavy cannon is not a one-person job. They’d need someone with a boat, plus someone in U.R.S.A.”

Miguel rolled his eyes. “So instead of one suspect, we’re looking for two?”

“Or more!” Rudy cheerfully added. “And don’t forget, now we will have to do it without getting caught!”

Justin scratched his chin. “You make it sound like we’re delinquents.”

“We are.” Rudy replied. “So, how do we catch a bad guy on a boat?”

“We let Lucy swim after them.” Miguel grinned.

CHAPTER 27

THE NEXT PHASE

RUDY

For the second day in a row, Rudy woke to a blaring forklift alarm. He tried hiding under the covers, to no avail. Justin was making breakfast. Sighing, he dragged himself off the top bunk and into the kitchen.

Out their window, he watched the same two maintenance workers unload heavy awkward looking containers off a large tractor. Rudy rolled his eyes. "If I'd known they were going to work so early, I wouldn't have agreed to stay up and play through Miguel's adventure."

"He took a long time to put that together. Besides, taking breaks gets our brains back on track."

Rudy settled on a cereal with lots of cinnamon. "Well, I would have killed his boss faster."

Justin laughed. "How would you have done that? We were facing the Phoenix King. Phoenixes are, by definition, hard to kill."

"I would have used a spell to send him to another plane of existence."

Justin paused, "That would have worked. Why didn't you say anything?"

"Miguel obviously wanted an epic battle. And that was more fun."

They ate in silence. Justin was probably organizing a list of suspects and plans. Rudy imagined he was always thinking about mystery solving. After a while, Justin stretched. "Ready for a boat ride?"

Rudy furrowed his brow. "It's Friday."

"So?"

"That means it's Saturday, gaming day, in China."

Justin frowned. "You're in a park on the edge of the world, there's a mystery going on right outside, and you want to play video games?"

"It's cooler in here. We've been told not to investigate, and this is the one day this week I can hang out with my friends across the globe." Rudy held his ground.

"At least walk out to the dock with us."

"I can do that." Rudy slid reluctantly from his chair.

Lucy and Miguel were downstairs. Their father gave them a measured smile. "How's it going guys? Coffee, anyone?" Rudy rushed to draw himself a cup. "Ready for your trip to Loggerhead?" Ranger Benitez seemed eager to get them moving. Justin had theorized that the parents had planned this trip to keep them away from the investigation. Jokes on them: they were going to Loggerhead to investigate.

"Actually, I'm staying here." Rudy took a nervous sip of his coffee almost spitting out the hot liquid. He rushed to the fridge in search of milk.

"You're not coming?" Lucy stared at him intensely.

"I'm going to stay here and play videogames." Rudy explained.

"That's fine." Lucy's dad straightened his tie, turning to the others. "As for you two…" Wasn't he worried that Rudy would investigate on his own? Did he think Rudy was too young? "I can't take you. I have other responsibilities." He was staring at Miguel.

Miguel sat up. "Can Wendy take them?"

"No. I'm doing boat checks, she's my back up." Miguel's dad stared at his reluctant son. "So, co-captain?" Rudy wondered if they were searching boats in the harbor for missing cannon.

Miguel sighed, "I knew there was a reason you helped me get the boat card and added me to your insurance."

"Wait, what?" Rudy asked over his coffee. "Miguel has a boat license?"

"And I get to use it to shuttle Justin and Lucy." Miguel stared despondently.

His father didn't budge. "Hey, I didn't say you had to."

"It was implied."

Mr. Benitez stated firmly, "I could imply that any good brother would be happy to drive his sister and friends around. It's a good story. It's definitely cooler than the story about how you lost your boat license."

Miguel sighed. "Fine."

Rudy, watching their back and forth, turned to Lucy. "If Miguel is driving, I'm doubly excited I'm staying here."

Ranger Benitez already had his boat prepped at the dock. It was a decent looking little speedboat with extra bow seating and a snorkeling platform on the stern, not as flashy as the orange and black boat tied up nearby.

"When we moved out here, Dad said he would take us snorkeling and fishing every weekend." Lucy sighed.

"Instead, he just complains about how hard it is to clean and maintain. Meanwhile, mom loans it to her students." Miguel put his hand on Justin's shoulder. "They must like you. This is the first time we've used it in weeks."

Ranger Benitez was doing his final radio, engine, and equipment check. While the four waited on the docks, an U.R.S.A. student approached. Rudy recognized scraggly haired Kit. "Hey guys what are you up to?"

"We're headed to Loggerhead." Lucy replied.

Justin stared. He must have noticed the same thing as Rudy. Kit had a briefcase. "Did you find your missing samples?"

"Uh. No. These are new samples." Kit raised his briefcase. "Professor Erickson found them. They're from his wreck. I'm shuttling back to Key West to figure out what went wrong with my last batch."

Rudy perked. "You have samples of wood from the 1600's?"

"Presumably," Kit's head wobbled. "Which doesn't make any sense." He opened his briefcase, "hopefully with these we can figure out what's really going on." Rudy stared at the two green vials. They had been talking about the samples for so long, but he'd never seen one before. They looked like big wooden splinters in oil.

Kit left them to catch his seaplane as Lucy's father returned. Ranger Benitez tossed Miguel the boat keys. "Stick to the channel until you're away from Fort Jefferson. Radio in before you dock, and again when you come back." He called out to the others. "Life jackets?"

"Life jackets," Miguel nodded. "Got it."

Lucy managed the lines. Justin handed out lifejackets. Miguel worriedly motored into the harbor. He only bumped against two pilings. His dad winced both times. Rudy asked, "Ranger Benitez, where's Professor Erickson?"

Lucy's dad frowned. "Why?"

Rudy didn't have to lie. "I want to ask him about his old wreck."

Ranger Benitez sighed. "Probably in his apartment going over paperwork."

"So, I shouldn't bother him?"

Ranger Benitez smiled. "Professor Erickson is always happy have someone stop by and ask about his work." Rudy would go see him after his games.

CHAPTER 28
LOGGERHEAD

LUCY

"I CAN'T BELIEVE RUDY CHOSE TO STAY." Justin shook his head sadly.

"We'll drag him along next time." Lucy smirked back at their reluctant boat pilot. A clump of hair, still wet from her morning swim, blew into her face. "Since we have a chauffeur now, this won't be our only nautical adventure!"

Miguel ignored them, gunning out of the channel. Motors hummed as Lucy watched Justin think. "Why didn't Kit go back with Dr. Alexa yesterday?"

Lucy shrugged. "Do you think it has something to do with the cannon theft?"

"He didn't look guilty." Justin said thoughtfully.

"What do criminals look like?" Lucy laughed. "Kit looked like a sad puppy."

They closed the gap between the two islands. Miguel slowed their boat. "Alright Lucia, sit up front and look out for coral heads." Lucy shifted forward, keeping watch for purple and black patches in otherwise sandy seas. The ocean lightened as coral gave way to sand. Once they were out of danger, she looked up.

Loggerhead Lighthouse towered above the island. It's top third was painted black while the rest was painted white. Large palm trees were scattered around it, partially shading both houses on the island. Shrubs and sand continued from there in both directions.

Luke and Nina stood on a tall pier. Spud sat between them, his tail thwapping against wood. The dock was taller than their boat. It took Lucy and the others several tries to climb onto solid deck. "This would be easier at high tide," Luke and Nina offered hands to help them up. Miguel waited until the bow was lifted by a wave and leapt onto the dock.

Lucy bent down to bury her face into Spud's soft curls while Justin surveyed the stark island. "What do you guys do out here all day?"

"Before dawn we walk Spud looking for turtle nests, then we watch T.V. until mom or dad ask for help. Then homework, snorkeling, and golf."

"Someone left golf clubs in our closet," Nina explained. "I like hitting balls into the ocean. Later we snorkel out to find them."

We also climb the lighthouse at least once a day because the view is cool." Luke pointed. Lucy stared up to at the lighthouse. There was a small metal walkway outside around the top. If Rudy were here, he would climb it just to give Justin a heart attack.

"Mom's working on the solar grid." Luke pointed at a small shed near the tower.

"Dad's napping. He was up late last night making sure no more boats anchored around the island." Nina tilted her head.

"Boats around the island?" Justin confirmed.

"Yeah, why?" Nina raised an eyebrow. "Does it have something to do with your investigation? Tell us while we show you around."

"I'm staying here to read." Miguel held up one of his study manuals. Lucy had forgotten he was with them.

"Let's go." Low shrubs made an inland hike challenging, so the twins let Spud lead them down the beach. While they walked, Justin explained their dramatic shift from hired investigators to rogue agents.

Loggerhead was the largest island in the park. Its shape changed often but, in general, it stretched northeast to southwest. The twins lead them around the north point where, at the tip, sand reached far out to sea. There were several places where sand rose above the surface making small bars.

"There's a picture of old Loggerhead in our home." Luke confirmed.

"It used to be completely covered in tall trees."

"Australian Pines were an invasive species." Lucy pointed to some rotten buried roots. "They would trap sea turtles and prevent native birds from landing." A small dark bird hopped through low bushes behind the roots, catching Justin's eyes.

"It looks better this way." Nina reached down to give Spud a scratch.

"Rudy's going to be sad he missed this." Justin watched the bird fly off.

"Why?" Luke asked.

"This looks like the perfect place for buried treasure." Justin answered.

"Rudy's convinced he's going to find gold out here," Lucy explained.

"I haven't seen any yet—" Luke nodded thoughtfully "—but there's a surprising amount of ground to cover. I would know. I have to find all of Nina's random golf balls."

Nina chimed in, "Changing the subject. Yesterday, your dad radioed over to ask about the unusual boat we saw."

"Unusual boat?" Justin frowned thoughtfully.

"It was anchored over there." Nina pointed to an open spot of water, between them and Fort Jefferson, near the windjammer wreck.

"That's about where Sophia's cannon wreck is." Lucy confirmed.

Justin leaned forward suddenly interested, "tell us everything! Was it a commercial dive vessel?"

"It was too dark to recognize." Nina shook her head.

"We heard a loud motor running, and then saw a big spotlight come on over the ocean." Luke turned to Lucy, "we told mom and dad and they radioed Lucy's dad. He told them to keep an eye on it."

"Why?" Justin asked.

"Boats aren't supposed to anchor near Loggerhead after dark." Lucy frowned.

"The next day, we took Spud for his usual pre-dawn walk." Nina watched Spud run off to play in the surf. "Right as Luke and I opened our door, an engine started up from that same spot. We heard the boat drive back towards the fort."

Luke suddenly frowned. "We did also see a university boat in the same place after dawn, but we figured your dad knew about that."

"That would have been Mom, or her students, when they learned that the cannon were gone." Lucy explained.

"You guys saw the cannon thief!" Justin turned to the twins. "Are you sure there aren't any details you can tell us about the boat?

Nina held out her arms to indicate size. "It was bigger than a speedboat, smaller than a battleship. We might be life-long sailors, but we can't recognize boats in the dark using engine noise."

"The boat was out from dusk to dawn." Justin tapped his chin, "that's a long time."

Lucy countered. "Maybe the thieves needed lots of time to load the cannon."

Justin smiled at the twins. "Thanks. This will help. Let's continue our tour."

On the island's west side, they stumbled upon the collapsed remains of an old wooden hut abandoned decades before. After passing the lighthouse, Luke and Nina pointed out large rocks, and a stretch of beach. "This is where we usually like to snorkel. There's a big reef out there called Little Africa."

"Why is it called that?" Justin asked.

"We'll show you from the lighthouse." Luke replied.

The south end of the island was anticlimactic. Except when Justin jumped up and rushed into the scrub. "A red-legged thrush!" He exclaimed in excitement the others could not share.

On their return, Lucy pointed to two boats on the horizon, "That's Mom and her team."

"Is that Sophia's wreck?" Justin pulled binoculars from his pockets to watch the boats.

"I think so?" Lucy turned to Justin, with excitement. "That gives me an idea! Seeing the Dive Bears work might help us investigate. I'll ask if we can observe them. We'll say it's part of our history lessons. If we're lucky, maybe we can snorkel Sophia's cannon wreck."

CHAPTER 29

ENCOUNTER IN THE ARCHES

RUDY

RUDY THREW OFF HIS HEADPHONES IN FRUSTRATION. His gaming friends across the globe had retired for the night so he'd swapped over to try and learn anything which might help with Dr. Benitez's mystery. He'd checked prices of various pieces of missing U.R.S.A. equipment. The underwater camera and GPS unit were valuable, but a couple thousand dollars didn't seem worth the risks their saboteur was taking. The stolen cannon were worth far more.

A real sunken treasure would justify all previous thefts. So, Rudy was reading about pirates, treasures, and missing shipwrecks associated with the Dry Tortugas. He'd found a few stories about treasure ships sinking in or being discovered out here, but mostly when he searched: *Dry Tortugas* and *treasure*, he got advertisements about dive trips.

He could find more academic articles in the map room, but he was not going into that haunted place alone. Rudy would never be able to solve mysteries through observation like Justin. He couldn't keep up with Lucy as she single-handedly saved the day. He needed to provide something that the others couldn't. But what?

He tried typing in names of each of their suspects into a web search, looking for clues. He finally found a book about pirates written by a J. Edgar Howard. It was listed as: *out of print*, with a price of $400! "I can't afford that!" He grabbed his phone, resisting the temptation to open one of his games. "If I can't figure out why U.R.S.A. is being sabotaged, maybe I can figure out how they stole cannon."

Cannon like that weighed thousands of pounds, it would take a lot of people, or specific tools to lift them from the sea. Specific tools… an idea began to form in Rudy's mind. This idea was interrupted when a neighboring apartment door slammed. His ears perked up.

Professor Alexa was gone. Their only other neighbor was Professor Erickson. Someone who might know more about valuable wrecks. Rudy hesitated. He felt close to developing an idea which might help their mystery. However, interviewing Professor Erickson would be more fun.

Leaving his research behind, Rudy marched over to knock on the professor's door. There was a moment of silence, followed by rattling dishes. "Oh, hello." Professor Erickson held his door open, looking confused. "Rudy, is it?"

"Hi professor." Rudy stepped through his door before he could react.

The professor looked around, "What brings you over, and where are your friends?"

"They're on Loggerhead." Rudy's eyes drifted around his room over massive stacks of papers, a few esoteric bits of equipment leaning against walls, a pile of junk blocking half the archway into his bedroom. "Anyway, I came over because I have questions."

"Really?" The professor left his door open, returning to his dishes.

Where to begin? Rudy couldn't just ask him if there was something worth stealing. "Well, you see, I've been interested in Spanish treasure fleets for a long time."

"A fascinating topic of interest." Any suspicion or concern on Professor Erickson's face was replaced with that look teachers get when they find an interested pupil. He stopped scrubbing.

"I want to find buried treasure. A pirate treasure would be coolest, but Spanish treasure fleets had boatloads of gold, silver, and other treasures."

Professor Erickson leaned against his sink. "Both the 1715 and 1622 fleets were famous disasters, losing ships carrying millions of dollars' worth of goods destined for the Spanish Crown."

Rudy nodded. "I learned about the *Atocha* from a museum in Key

West. Then, today I was reading that some of those sunken treasure ships had been found near the Dry Tortugas. I want to find one of those."

Professor Erickson chuckled. "Heck, so would I! It would be a stellar academic discovery, and it would make any discoverer rich and famous."

Rudy nodded. "You found that really old wood on your wreck!"

The professor's smile faulted. His voice lowered in pitch. "That was error. Kit must have gotten his samples mixed up." He sounded suspicious. Suspicious of his own student?

Rudy asked. "What if that sample really was from the 1600s and you and Kit found a clue to a new treasure ship?"

The professor began shaking his head before Rudy could finish his question. The shaking slowly turned into a contemplative nod. "Well, the Dry Tortugas were discovered in the 1500s. Ships traveling the Gulf of Mexico considered these islands prime anchorage. Which explains why the U.S. built a fort here centuries later."

Rudy's tummy began to bubble with excitement until Professor Erickson chuckled. "Wreck one-fourteen is a civil war era barge. Old Spanish wrecks do not contain stacks of American-made bricks. I am convinced that Kit's new samples will confirm my shipwreck is from the 1800s."

Rudy recalled meeting the student on the beach that morning. "Why didn't you tell Kit you had extra samples the other day, when he seemed so worried?"

"I wasn't sure I had them." Professor Erickson's voice turned stern. Was he covering for his student? Maybe Kit lost his samples on purpose? To hide that mistake!

Disappointed, Rudy began poking through stacks of equipment stuffed in the archway between the kitchen/living room and bedroom. "Don't touch that, please." The professor snatched a long pole away. It was an odd tool, like a spear gun, a hollow plastic vial with a needle—like a giant syringe—at the end. "It's dangerous."

Rudy swallowed, imagining that long needle poking through his arm! "What is it?"

Professor Erickson moved the vicious weaponlike instrument out of sight and reach. "One of Kit's sampling tools. We use it to take core samples of ancient, submerged, wood without exposing them to outside air."

Rudy nodded. "I see." He didn't. "Why does it matter if old wood is exposed to air?"

"Older samples, without protection, might break down before they reach Key West. Kit's samples can be preserved for months." While Professor Erickson relocated some of his more dangerous looking equipment, Rudy noticed something interesting atop a stack of papers next to his laptop.

It was an old book with a yellowing cover. "Is that Mr. Howard's book?" The title was *The Pirates Caesar*. "I saw it online. It's super expensive!"

"He loaned it too me." As Professor Erickson pulled the book away, two sheets of paper fell out.

Rudy picked the first up to hand back to him. It looked like a photocopy of a really old letter hand-written in beautiful script with large looping D's and large scrawling P's. He couldn't read most of it because it was Spanish, but he recognized one word. "Professor Erickson, does that say: *Pirates*?"

"What?" The professor reached for the paper and glared when Rudy didn't hand it back. "Can you read Spanish?"

"*Un poco*?" Rudy bent over the paper for closer look. "I practice with Lucy and her family." The Benitez's spoke both English and Spanish comfortably. Rudy mostly just listened. Professor Erickson held out his hand expectantly, "I can't read most of this." As he passed the copy away, he noticed a scrawling signature at the bottom of the time-stained letter: *Caesar*. "What is it?"

Professor Erickson stared down at his feet. He seemed uncomfortable talking about it, almost embarrassed. "A foolish dream."

"Really?" Rudy reached for the next paper which was conveniently labeled: Translation. Professor Erickson reached it first, and tucked both papers back into the book, which he set atop his fridge.

He turned frigid eyes on Rudy. The gaze of a professor whose students had stopped listening in class. "That's enough browsing through my documents without permission."

Rudy took a hesitant step backwards. "The letter looked old, where did it come from?"

For a second, Rudy thought Professor Erickson wasn't going to answer. He prepared to be kicked from the room. The professor let out a long-drawn sigh. "I found it hidden among a series of documents in the National Spanish Library. It was in a section related to the Spanish Crown's new world governance, in a stack of documents labeled as having *dubious origins*."

Rudy knew what that meant. "So, it might not be real?"

"It's probably not." Professor Erickson exhaled slowly. "You see, supposedly that letter was from the early 1600s, 1622, in fact."

Rudy could barely control his voice, almost shouting, "is it about the *Atocha?*"

Professor Erickson nodded, "There were twenty-eight treasure ships which left Havana that with the *Nuestra de Atocha*. Boats full of gold, trade items from the new world and Asia, and tons of silver. The 1622 fleet got a late start and was caught up in a hurricane."

Rudy nodded. "I knew most of that."

"Well," Professor Erickson gave a professorial smile, "That letter is from a man claiming to have traveled with the fleet. His letter begs a man named Gaspar De Vargas to help him recover treasure from a ship sunken in *las Tortugas*, um, before it could be stolen by Pirates."

"*Las Tortugas?*" Rudy nearly shouted. His eyes strayed towards the top of the fridge.

"It's probably a scam." The professor chuckled, shifting Rudy's attention. "Spanish treasure fleets carried near unimaginable wealth, so when one was hit by a hurricane it became big, international news. Word didn't travel as fast back then, but big headlines still meant big rumors."

Professor Erickson grinned as Rudy stared agape. "There was no shortage of hucksters, professionals, and yes, pirates hoping to make wealth off plunder from those sunken ships." He pointed to the stack of papers. "Gaspar de Vargas was responsible for the first rescue and recovery operation sent after the 1622 fleet. Many in the Spanish Caribbean would have known him. I suspect that the man who wrote the letter was trying to trick de Vargas."

"Caesar?" Rudy recalled the signature on the letter. "Like in Mr. Howard's book?"

"Well, it's complicated." The Professor seemed startled that Rudy had read the signature. "But no. Anyway, the Caesar in that letter was probably fishing for a reply from de Vargas. He was hoping de Vargas would reveal the location of any treasure ships sunk in *las Tortugas*."

Rudy could feel goosebumps rising on his arms. "So, did treasure ships actually sink out here?" That would be so exciting!

Professor Erickson nodded. "According to historical records, de Vargas lead a salvage operation for the *Nuestra de Rosario* on Loggerhead to recover her treasure and rescue her surviving crew."

"Really?" Why hadn't anyone told Rudy about this? Maybe he should have gone with Justin and Lucy!

"A previous archeology team found several silver pieces and a couple bronze cannon over there." The professor stepped to his open door, peering out through a brick archway. He shrugged. "It's probable that the Caesar who wrote that letter wanted to learn from Gaspar De Vargas if there was any treasure left worth scavenging."

"Is there still treasure out here?"

Professor Erickson's frustrated sigh killed his enthusiasm. "I'd say no. De Vargas burnt the *Rosario* to the waterline to prevent pirates from harvesting it. Anything left would have been picked over a million times before the Dry Tortugas was even established as a National Park."

"Then why did you copy and translate the letter?"

The professor rubbed his hands together and shrugged. "A small interest of mine? A ridiculous dream of a grand new discovery, new publications, and more research for my students. Lucy's mother, ahem, Dr. Benitez believes it's nothing. Dr. Alexa laughed. Honestly, they are probably correct. Not that it matters now. Because of Sophia's cannon, we are being sent home."

Rudy tried to keep his face slack. Professor Erickson covered his mouth. "Oops, I probably shouldn't have mentioned that. Dr. Benitez asked us to keep you three out of our mystery garbage. She explained that you kids have a propensity for investigating trouble."

"We were investigating." Rudy admitted. "But Dr. Benitez told us to stop."

"Quite right!" Professor Erickson nodded. "If you want to talk treasure Rudy, those cannon Sophia discovered were worth a great deal of money. People would do dangerous things to get them. Better to stay away." The professor breathed out heavily. "Sophia is my student, and this could ruin her research. Can you do me a favor?"

Rudy nodded. "I guess."

"If you learn anything about those unscrupulous cannon thieves, will you tell me?"

"I'll try."

"Good." Professor Erickson studied Rudy's face. "I want to catch whoever did this." He turned to his stack of papers. "Also, please don't mention that letter. It's an embarrassing topic. I don't need more ridicule."

"Don't worry Professor." Rudy leaned in with a conspiratorial whisper. "I'm part of the Junior Rangers Investigative Club, we never give up our sources. Just, don't tell Dr. Benitez, please."

"I guess we both have our secrets." The Professor winked. "Yours is safe with me."

CHAPTER 30

SPUD'S CLUE

JUSTIN

AFTER LUNCH, THE TWINS LED JUSTIN AND LUCY TO THE LIGHT-HOUSE. "Better go now, without Rudy." Miguel joked, but he declined to join them. Mr. Manning rested his hand atop Spud's head and also waved them along. "I should save my energy. Renee is expecting help with repairs."

At the bottom of the stairs, Lucy signed their names in a visitor log. On the way up Justin began counting steps. He lost count halfway and gave up. There were several windows along the way to take a breather and look outside.

They had to climb a ladder to get into the room beneath the light. The only windows were small portholes in both doors leading to the outer walkway. Sunlight streamed in from above. There was another ladder, but the hatch leading up to the light was locked. Luke opened a side doors and Nina led them outside.

"I'm incredibly glad Rudy isn't here." Justin could see the Manning's temporary home below, along with whole of Loggerhead. He could also see Fort Jefferson, and the white specks of further keys. There was a lot of boat traffic. "I can see the Ferry."

"Several ships are diving the Windjammer." Lucy pointed to a small cluster of boats surrounding the park's most famous wreck.

Nina stepped closer causing a slight sensation of vertigo to shiver through Justin. He got nervous when he saw other people near edges. Nina pointed west outlining a dark shape under the water, "see, that coral looks like Africa."

The dark mass in light sand had a distinct African continent shape. "You're right."

"It's a great reef to snorkel." Luke added. "Bring your gear next time."

Below, a tiny park service boat circled the reef piloted by a tiny ranger. "From here you can see almost everything going on in the park," Justin noted.

"Yeah, it's pretty cool." Nina smiled.

"Actually, it's pretty hot," Luke countered. They were all sweating in direct sunlight, amplified by black paint. "Let's head down."

Miguel and Spud met them outside. The dog wagged his tail. Justin's friend tapped his foot impatiently. "Hurry! If you don't make it back for afternoon classes, I'm in trouble."

Lucy turned to Justin. "We should stick around, play a few games of golf."

Nina nodded excitedly. "I can show you the best spot to hit balls into water, so they usually land in sand and not sea grass!" Miguel rolled his eyes.

He was saved by the twin's mother Renee. "Are you guys ready? Miguel offered me a ride over to open the gift shop for the after-lunch rush."

"I thought you were working on the solar grid?" Luke asked.

"I'll leave that to your dad." She winked. "Don't tell him, but it's mostly cleanup."

Spud raced ahead of everyone padding up the dock.

Justin turned to Luke. "He's especially playful."

"We usually play after lunch. Baby coconuts are perfectly sized for Spud's mouth, and they float." Luke walked over to a pile of brown and green baseball-sized objects stacked under the island's welcome sign. "Want to see how we play fetch?" As everyone stepped onto the dock, Luke heaved a small coconut into the water.

Spud watched it arch into the ocean, his tail wagging. "Okay, go get it." With Nina's encouragement he leapt eagerly in and began swimming. Grabbing the coconut gently, he turned for shore. He ran from the beach to the dock waiting until he was back to shake vigorously spraying everyone with sea water.

"Good boy!" Nina took the coconut from Spud and handed it to Justin. "Toss it as far as you can." Justin made sure Spud's eyes were on his *ball* and then threw it. Spud's tail thwapped heavily against the dock, but he didn't move.

"Spud is a good boy. He won't go into water without permission." Nina smiled.

"A necessary trait for a sea dog." Renee added.

"Okay, go." Spud had been watching the coconut bob in the waves. With Nina's encouragement, he sprang into action.

"Alright, ready to go?" Miguel was nervously checking his watch.

"Let's wait until Spud's back, so we don't hit any diving doggies." Renee cautioned. Miguel nodded, heading towards their boat. It didn't take long for Spud to reach the coconut, but instead of catching it, he swam past it.

"Where's he going?" Luke asked.

Spud stretched his neck grabbing something else. Turning, he swam for shore again. "I wonder what that could be." Lucy asked. Spud climbed onto the banks.

Nina reached out to catch the object from his mouth. A green plexiglass cylinder with a rubber stopper. Justin and Lucy shared a look. It was one of Kit's sample vials.

"I'll take that," Lucy held out her hand, trying to sound casual. "It's from U.R.S.A. Someone is going to be in trouble for littering."

Renee seemed satisfied with Lucy's explanation. What was a vial like that doing out here? Could it be a clue? They couldn't discuss it with Renee around, so they left the twins with meaningful glances. Spud's tail wagged farewell.

"Lucy, keep lookout again please." Miguel, under his sister's guidance, aimed for the distant channel markers pushing the boat's throttle forward gently picking up speed.

Renee turned to ask Justin. "How long has Miguel been operating boats?"

Justin beamed. "I didn't even know he could drive one until this morning!"

Renee nodded, "Could you hand me a lifejacket too?"

CHAPTER 31

WRECK ROOM TWO

LUCY

RENEE DIDN'T HAVE TO WORRY. Miguel kept the boat running at a safe speed all the way to the harbor. As Lucy worked with the lines, her mother pulled up in an U.R.S.A. boat full of exhausted and worried students.

"Go get Rudy." Lucy's mother locked onto them with a no-nonsense gaze. "It's time for schoolwork."

"Okay." It wasn't time to argue.

When their mom entered the rec room, Miguel split like a prison guard released from duty. Lucy's mom was all business. No one dared mention their investigation until she had assigned homework and left.

It was a couple of hours before their schoolwork was complete. Staring around a now empty room, Justin began pulling out charts hidden in his notebook. "We learned several things today."

"I investigated too." Rudy beamed.

"We should play a game in case anyone walks in." Lucy uncovered the pool table.

"What did you learn?" Justin asked, digging pool balls from their pockets.

Rudy grinned. "For one thing, U.R.S.A.'s disappeared equipment is all expensive. But Professor Erickson told me Sophia's missing cannon are worth a lot more."

"You spoke with Professor Erickson about our mystery?" Justin frowned.

"Relax, we were talking about treasure fleets first." Rudy grinned. "He's the one who brought up the cannon."

"I wonder if he suspects the students too." Justin scanned his chart. "We should see what each Dive Bears was up to the night of the cannon theft."

"Already ahead of you." Rudy grinned. "According to Professor Erickson every student was helping Dr. Alexa and her team pack."

"I'm impressed!" Justin nodded. "Anything else?"

Rudy beamed at his encouragement. "That's it. What did you guys learn?"

"Loggerhead is awesome! You're coming next time." Justin grinned. "Also, the twins saw the cannon thief's boat."

"Then they watched the Dive Bears come to discover that those cannon were stolen." Lucy rolled pool balls down the center of the table. "Wait, how did U.R.S.A. know to check the cannon wreck?"

"That is a good question." Justin began gathering pool ball into the triangle.

"It would have taken more than one person to lift a bunch of sunken cannon out of the ocean." Lucy grabbed a cue stick taking aim at the white ball. "If all of the students were busy, who could have been helping Captain Tobias?"

Rudy frowned. "Are we sure we're looking for a student?"

"Let me think." Justin winced at the crack of Lucy's powerful first shot. He was too distracted to notice it was his turn. Finally, he lifted his head, "Everything happened because of U.R.S.A. So, a Dive Bear has to be involved, but maybe Captain Tobias, or whoever, has another outside accomplice."

Rudy grinned. "This is starting to sound like a conspiracy."

"Unless…" Justin sighed. "We need to make sure that every student was accounted for and figure out which boats out here could have stolen the cannon."

Lucy lined up a third shot. "I can help with the boats. There's a dock log with information on every ship and captain that anchors in the harbor."

"We should also spend more time with the Dive Bears to find our student conspirator," Justin turned to Lucy.

"I'll talk to Mom." Lucy nodded, lining up a third shot. "She loves to let her students show off."

"Good." Justin winced again at another sharp crack as Lucy's shot connected. "There's just one more thing." He pulled Spud's greenish glass vial from his pocket. "We need to figure out if this is one of Kit's lost samples."

CHAPTER 32

UNDERWATER INVESTIGATION

LUCY

NONE OF THE BOYS LOOKED READY for their early morning start. Rudy was yawning relentlessly from late night gaming. Miguel was grumpy about his second day as chauffer. But why were Justin's eyes drooping?

"Every night! You do this every night?" Rudy shouted as they were jostled by the waves.

"What's he doing?" Lucy asked.

"Last night, he was staring out into the dark parade ground." Rudy answered.

"I was watching the Large Powder Magazine, waiting to see if our mysterious creeper would come back." Justin rubbed sleep from his eyes.

"He sets alarms," Rudy added, "Checking three or four times a night."

"Have you seen anything?" Miguel asked from the wheel. "A ghost maybe?"

Justin shook his head. "I've watched a couple of U.R.S.A. students and park rangers out really late but only in residential area. No new shadows."

"Did you guys notice? The *Horned Devil* is gone?" Justin had asked everyone to look out for Captain Tobias's boat. "It's seeming more likely that he had something to do with the cannon disappearance."

"The only boat I recognized was the yacht, wearing a speedboat." Rudy countered.

"What?" Lucy stared at him.

Justin was used to explaining Rudy's random descriptions, "He means that the speedboat has been pulled onto the yacht's back deck. That's probably how the bearded captain works on it."

"That's it!" Rudy grinned. "Mr. Howard's hiding the cannon under his speedboat! We should check."

"You just want a fancy yacht tour." Lucy rolled her eyes. "We're headed out to snorkel two wrecks and interrogate Dive Bears. Let's focus on that instead."

Rudy fidgeted with his life jacket. Lucy had only been able to find one his size. It was bright yellow, and he looked ridiculous. Justin began to lather sunscreen into his arms. He wouldn't have to worry about a sunburn, but he was getting oily, coral safe, liquid everywhere. Lucy leaned over to Rudy. "When dad asks us to solve 'The Case of the Mysterious Handprints,' we have suspect number one."

Miguel steered them towards an U.R.S.A. boat drifting in the waves. Unfortunately, it was not the cannon wreck. That was off limits. Instead, they were snorkeling sites Lucy's mother considered perfectly safe. Hopefully, they could still learn something to help with the mystery.

On the university boat, Chet was checking his dive gear. Another student, Barbara, dangled her flippers in water. Sophia held a foam float with a medium sized red and white dive flag. It was attached to a line to be pulled through water. She looked surprised when they pulled up. Miguel shut the engine off letting their boats drift together. "Hello Miguel and crew. I didn't realize you'd drop by this early."

Miguel perked up when Sophia called them *his crew*. "It's Justin and Rudy's first time snorkeling with U.R.S.A. I thought we should start in shallow water." Lucy rolled her eyes.

"What is this wreck?" It might have been Justin's first sincere, non-mystery question. The surprisingly earnest moment was undercut when he lost balance as both boats collided.

"This isn't really a wreck, per se." Barbara gave them a bug-eyed dive mask grin. Her dive regulator dangled over her shoulder. Despite warm water, she was wearing a sleeved wetsuit.

Sophia clarified. "This is a debris pile. Someone got their ship caught up in the reef and dumped heavy stuff overboard to keep afloat."

"Did that work, or did they sink?" Rudy asked.

"That's what we're trying to find out. We'll lay out a grid and map everything, get the orientation and spread, then see if this detritus relates to any nearby wrecks."

Miguel was already digging through his study aids. "That sounds like a lot of work."

"It's a small site. Which is why it hasn't been touched yet. With any luck we'll be able to finish it before we leave." Chet hefted two dive tanks onto his bare shoulders with ease and sat with a thump, back to water. "We need to get started. Come on Barb." He fell, back first, splashing into the ocean.

Everyone watched both divers rise to the surface and give ok signs before disappearing in a series of bubbles and a flash of fins.

Rudy pulled out his small map, marked with potential treasure locations. "What do you call this site?"

"This is site one-eleven." Sophia said, reaching out of the boat to hand gear to Chet: the dive buoy, U.R.S.A.'s last long-handled underwater camera, and a whole pile of yellow lines and metal stakes.

Rudy stared quizzically down at his map, then up at Sophia. "That's not right."

"What?"

Rudy pointed to his map. "Isn't this where we are?" Miguel leaned over his shoulder to nod. "If I copied your map correctly, this is either one-twenty-nine or one-thirty."

"Oh," Sophia looked surprised again. "You're probably right."

Rudy frowned when she agreed with him. "What's down there?"

"Extra anchors, heavy ballast stones, cannon or cannon balls, anything which wasn't vital to their ship's ability to sail, or to making a profit." Sophia answered.

"So not treasure." Lucy smirked at Rudy.

Justin narrowed his eyes. "Interesting. Are there cannon at this wreck?"

Sophia shrugged. "This is our first time here since Dr. Alexa's initial survey. I'm not sure what we'll find. But Travis flew his drone over this site, and we found lots of symmetry."

"Symmetry?" Rudy cocked his head.

"Nature doesn't often make straight lines, right angles, parallel lines, or repeating patterns. Something too perfectly straight could be evidence that it is manufactured. Why don't you guys see for yourselves?" Sophia suggested. "I'll watch our boats. I'm stuck up here anyway."

"Miguel will keep you company." Rudy was already putting on his snorkel gear. "He has a lot of studying to do. I'll go help look for artifacts."

Miguel helped them into their gear. "If you get into any trouble, wave with one arm, Sophia and I will be out to help in seconds." Justin slid into the water.

Chilled by deeper waters between Loggerhead and Garden Key, Lucy shivered. This spot was cooler than her usual swim. Their boats were floating in a large stretch of sand between rows of rocky coral.

Barbara pushed a camera along, kicking with long slow strokes. Below her, blowing bubbles at regular intervals, Chet placed a grid of stakes into the ground. Unlike land excavations, his equipment was oversized, designed for easy use and to be sturdy underwater.

Despite his enthusiasm for treasure, Rudy kept a respectful distance from the working archeologists. With so many people around, Lucy could almost ignore smaller parts of her brain warning of monsters in the deep.

Once or twice, Rudy tried to dive deeper to inspect the sand within Chet's markers. Probably looking for gold. Each time he dove, he rose to the surface to empty his snorkel.

Justin seemed entranced by undersea environments and archeology. Made sense, he couldn't ask Chet and Barbara tough questions while they were underwater. Sooner than expected, Chet began gathering loose equipment. Barbara swam back towards the boats. Lucy motioned for her friends to follow.

Rudy complained aboard their boat. "No cannon, no treasure, just one rusty anchor."

"Maybe you weren't looking in the right place." Sophia winked.

"Lots of rusty metal and crusty rocks." Rudy complained.

"What did you expect?" Miguel asked. "Everything's been stuck in saltwater for more than a hundred years."

Sophia pulled out a black and white aerial photo of the water around them. "There's a lot of stuff out here." She pointed to several black lines, "I'm hoping some of it will be interesting." Behind her, Chet and Barbara pulled themselves into the boat.

"Speaking of interesting, what could you tell me about this?" Justin pulled Spud's green glass vial from his pocket. Barbara, Chet, and Sophia stopped what they were doing and turned to look at the object.

"Where did you get that?" Chet asked.

CHAPTER 33

AN INTERVIEW AT WRECK 2

RUDY

SINCE RUDY HAD YET TO SEE A GIANT BARRACUDA, tarpon, or shark, he was having fun. The coral heads were beautiful, and he expected to find treasure. Exploring Chet's boundary, he found a massive rusty anchor sitting on sand. A cluster of sponges had made a home on one of its prongs. Two finger-like sea whips were growing near the ring where a chain would have been attached.

A bubble of excitement grew in Rudy's stomach, saltwater tinging each breath. This was a piece of history. People had dumped it overboard to save a sinking ship. It had lain here for more than a century. Maybe they had dropped other, more valuable, things nearby.

However, as the day wore on, it seemed like the anchor might be the only interesting thing out here. Rudy snorkeled over the newly placed grid of yellow marine rope. Every now and then Barbara would stop and place a small flag within this grid. Chet followed her, holding a shiny metallic clipboard and an absurd looking pen, marking each flag on a laminated page.

When Rudy tried diving down to see what they were marking, his snorkel filled with water. He enviously watched Lucy effortlessly dolphin kick around the site. Justin hovered around the edges watching both archeologists work, he was probably just waiting to grill them.

No sooner had Rudy pulled himself from the water than Justin was already showing off the glass vial the others had found on Loggerhead. "What can you tell me about this?" Justin held it out as though presenting a prize.

Rudy surveyed the three students' reactions. Barbara's nostrils flared. Chet glanced side to side at his peers. Sophia tilted her head, looking perplexed. "Where did you get that?"

"We found it on Loggerhead yesterday." Lucy crossed her arms.

"A blue cap." Sophia remarked quietly, to herself.

"Odd." Chet scratched at his chin.

"Well, it's definitely one of Kit's vials, from the Blue Team." Barbara nodded. "But Kit is very particular with his samples especially since..." She stopped.

"How much is it worth?" Rudy recalled their conversation with Kit on the ferry. "Is it enough to save your expedition?"

Barbara laughed. "That vial of wood and oil is practically worthless. It's the carbon dating test which costs money." Rudy slumped in disappointment.

"Barbara, that's enough," Chet crossed his arms. "Dr. Benitez warned us not to share too much with the junior mystery solvers."

Justin shook the vial causing the chunk of wood to float in the oily substance. "We know some of Kit's samples went missing. Is this one of them?"

"It's impossible to tell." Chet crossed his own arms, flexing his chest. "I don't know why one of those would be floating around Loggerhead."

"Mom said Kit had to retake every sample which went missing." Lucy explained. "Maybe he lost one at sea?"

Barbara shook her head. "Since those samples went missing, Kit and I double checked all the new ones, together. They have all been accounted for."

"Could someone else be taking samples?" Justin asked.

"No." Sophia answered. "It's a complex tool and Kit only has two of them. Since one went missing, he hasn't let anyone else touch them."

Justin hesitated. "I wanted to ask. When Dr. Alexa's team went home were you all there to help her pack?"

Chet frowned, clearing his throat. "Alright. I know you guys have another wreck to scout. Why don't you head on over there?"

Once the boat was underway, Justin sulked, "They didn't answer my question. I still wanted to ask them about the stolen cannon and the boat we saw."

"If they are our cannon thieves, would they have answered honestly?" Lucy smirked.

"No, but maybe we could catch Chet being suspicious." Justin frowned.

"Or Sophia." Rudy had to shout over the engine noise, "She didn't know her wreck number. Aren't archaeologists supposed to be careful about that stuff?"

Justin ignored him. "Also, Chet didn't seem surprised by that sample vial."

"What about Barbara?" Miguel asked. "Wasn't she suspicious too?"

"How?" They all turned to look at Miguel.

"You're seeing suspects everywhere. I'm just trying to help."

Lucy rolled her eyes. "Enough. Let's go enjoy wreck eighty-seven. It's one of my favorites: a barrel wreck!"

As Miguel drove, the ocean became a deeper, darker, blue. There were four people standing on deck of the second boat. Miguel breathed a sigh of relief. "Dive flag's down. I don't have to worry about hitting someone."

Dr. Benitez and her three students wore matching sleeveless wet suits. "You guys are incredibly lucky." She shouted, grabbing the railing as both boats bumped together with a bit too much force. "I'm sure Lucy told you, this is her favorite wreck?"

Justin nodded, "she said it's a barrel wreck? What's that?"

"You'll see." She watched them put on their gear. "Stick close together. The water is deep. The sunken stern is around forty feet below. The bow is closer to fifty-five or sixty."

The three beat all Dive Bears into the water. The seafloor was so far below! Rudy was glad he wasn't afraid of heights. The outline of a long rectangular ship deck was stretched across the sea bottom. Loose, rusted, artifacts covered the curved stern. On the triangular bow, anything not covered in rust was instead covered in the small beginnings of coral heads.

The most impressive artifacts spanned the wreck's width and breadth: pillow-shaped, molded, perfectly smooth rocks. They were the remains of rounded cement barrels. Wood had long since rotted away, but cement mixture had solidified to preserve them in straight rows.

The three U.R.S.A. students swimming over the wreck looked tiny. It was cool, and Rudy spent a couple of minutes admiring it, but he wasn't here for construction material. His two friends occupied watching the work, he swam off to see what else was nearby and found: another anchor. This one was much larger and more encrusted with living things. Nearby, a large dark shape hovered beneath an overhang.

It was the size of a small car with a mouth large enough to swallow Rudy whole! It had a huge, rounded, body with large dorsal fins and a giant tail.

Rudy's heart leapt through his throat. Forgetting any possibility of hidden treasure, he turned and kicked for the boats. In an explosion of air and water he fell onto the deck of U.R.S.A.'s boat. Taking a hefty breath, he turned to see if the monster had followed him. The water was clear and empty.

"Probably a Goliath Grouper." Dr. Benitez helped him off of his belly. "They aren't dangerous. When you bother them, they'll usually grunt and run away. They don't eat people on purpose."

On purpose? Rudy pulled off his fins, "I'll stay up here for now. Maybe, I can ask you some archeology questions?"

"Your questions should be better than these reports." Dr. Benitez settled into the captain's chair beneath her boat's sunshade, setting aside a tablet and stack of papers. In the other boat, Miguel was asleep, study book draped over his face.

"Well, first, about this wreck. Why did it sink?" Rudy swallowed, "and did anybody die?"

Dr. Benitez smiled, "You will be happy to know that everyone aboard survived."

"Good." Knowing someone died down there would make it a lot creepier. "How can you be so sure?"

"Given her location, and contents, we're pretty confident we've identified this wreck." Dr. Benitez shifted in her seat, her focus switching back and forth from Rudy to her student's bobbing dive flag. "*Lady Madeline* was a transport bark which usually carried passengers. Her crew mistook Loggerhead Light for Garden Key and dashed her against the rocks. Fortunately, they had time to gather on life rafts and row to shore."

"How can you learn all of this from a wreck?"

"We're archeologists. We draw the best conclusion possible from all evidence we have," Dr. Benitez winked. "Also, we have the captain's log."

"Oh." Rudy watched Justin spiral around the dive flag, probably analyzing archeologist's methods for any sign of treachery. He should start asking Dr. Benitez mystery related questions. Instead, he had another thought. "Where do you find paperwork about old wrecks?" He didn't want to mention Professor Erickson's letter. "Can you use it to find treasure?"

"There's no international shipwreck library, but there are many useful sources of documentation, if you are willing to put time and effort into research." She smiled. "Take the treasure fleet you're interested in. Finding records dating back to four hundred years is surprisingly easy. Captain's commonly kept logs and the Spanish government was incredibly interested in the movement of their treasure ships."

"However," Doctor Benitez continued. "There is also lots of misinformation. Captains in a treasure fleet often underestimated or hid some amount of treasure to avoid taxes to the Spanish crown. The more they could hide, the more they could keep. Sufficive to say, their records weren't always accurate."

Rudy decided to press his luck, "Could there be a secret treasure wreck out here?"

Dr. Benitez frowned in thought. "Well, given the *Nuestra De Rosario* remains found scattered around Loggerhead and that *Atocha* sank in the Marquesas keys, it's possible." She bobbed her head as though bouncing ideas around inside her head. "But that was four centuries ago. Waters out here are very shallow. Islands change. Storms move sand and shipwrecks. Pirates, soldiers, and sailors have combed and scavenged these shallows. I'd highly doubt an undiscovered pirate horde could remain hidden."

Rudy nodded thoughtfully, "What if they hid a treasure underwater on purpose."

"Most sailors back then couldn't swim. They definitely didn't have diving equipment."

"So, probably not." Rudy had let his side quest distract him long enough. "If you're not worried about treasure, why are you worried about commercial dive vessels finding your sites?"

"Given recent events…" Dr. Benitez stopped, frowning. "Never mind. I'm not worried about anyone coming out here to scavenge *treasure*. Most tourists diving wrecks simply want to witness history. I'm an archologist.

I sympathize." She spoke solemnly, "But I worry about relic hunters, or well-intentioned people who don't understand the damage they cause by taking a piece of that history home: a sunken brick, a rusty nail, a rusted cannonball."

"Is that really so bad?" Rudy asked.

"I understand the desire to hold onto pieces of our past. But what value is there in turning a rusty cannon ball into a lawn ornament? When you set a rusty nail from a wreck on your mantle does it maintain any meaning?" Dr. Benitez raised a thoughtful eyebrow. "When people take items from these wrecks, they lose context, and we lose clues about our past. Even trash can be significant."

"Like that debris pile Chet, Barbara, and Sophia are working on!" Rudy thought he understood, "I thought it was just a bunch of garbage dumped off a boat."

"Debris pile?" Dr. Benitez asked. "Sophia's not supposed to be out today. Chet and Barbara are supposed to be photographing Professor Erickson's brick wreck. Where exactly did you see them?" She stood, scanning the ocean, for the other anchored boat. Her search was interrupted by an eruption of bubbles.

"Mama. We're hungry." Lucy reappeared on the side of the other boat. "Let's do Lunch."

CHAPTER 34

INVESTIGATIVE FILING

JUSTIN

MIGUEL AIMED FOR GARDEN KEY. Dr. Benitez had been assembling her dive equipment as they left. "Finally, it's my turn in the water!" Justin watched her hastily shove her remaining paperwork over to a student before eagerly jumping in with a splash.

Lucy spent their return trip trying to convince Miguel to give her a shot at the wheel. Rudy gave Justin an odd thumbs up as they pulled away from U.R.S.A.'s boat. "I learned a few things. I'll tell you about them later."

As they hit the harbor, Rudy pointed for Lucy. "Told you, the boat is so big it has a baby."

The orange speedboat had been lifted from the water with a small crane. It was lashed down so the elusive Captain Levi could work on its engines. "It's too bad you're mom says that there isn't any treasure out here. If I found some, I could buy that yacht." Rudy sounded wistful.

"Of course, you asked their mom about treasure." Justin sighed.

Rudy raised his hands. "I also asked her about the investigation!"

"You asked Mom about our investigations?" Lucy raised an accusatory eyebrow.

Miguel proceeded to dock the boat while Rudy filled them in. "You're not very good at this are you?" Lucy teased as her brother reversed three more times. Miguel winced as the boat scrapped against a piling. "Want me to put out bumpers?"

"No!"

Justin ignored them to quiz Rudy, "Chet and Barbara were supposed to be photographing different wrecks? Sophia wasn't supposed to be out." Hopefully he could write those facts down soon, they seemed important. "Anything else?"

Rudy shook his head. "That's it."

"Focus captain!" Lucy interrupted. She had one line lassoed around a cleat and was trying to pull the boat closer. Miguel put it in reverse. "I don't want to fall." Her feet slid across the deck. Justin rushed over to help.

"I think I'm finished." Miguel shut off the motor.

"What are we going to do now?" Justin asked once the boat was secured.

Rudy sighed. "I'm beat. That was more sun than I've had in three months combined. And more exercise than I've had, well, ever."

Lucy stared at Rudy with open skepticism. "You live in Southern Florida, and I happen to know you ride your bike everywhere."

"That's not exercise. Exercise is out-swimming giant man-eating fish." Rudy followed Lucy onto the narrow edge of the bridge across the moat, took two steps, lost his balance, and stepped onto the main path. "I'm going home to play a game where I can catch and cook the man-eating fish."

Lucy cast a pleading glance at Justin. He yawned. "I'm up for something else. What did you have in mind?"

"Most Dive Bears are out right now." Lucy smiled, "Since Professor Erickson works in his apartment, the map room should be empty. We should explore."

"Ug." Rudy scratched his back. "Now I'm definitely going home."

They had to stop by the rec room first. "I'll get this back to you once we're done." Lucy called in to Gwen before shutting the door. She turned to him and held up a key.

Justin lowered his voice. "When you said break in, I was hoping to see you pick a lock."

"Borrowing Gwen's keys is much easier." Lucy smiled.

"She was fine handing them over?"

"I am the boss's daughter." Lucy crossed her arms.

"What kind of work is Gwen doing anyway?" Justin gave the rec room door a suspicious squint.

"Nope." Lucy scowled.

"Nope what?"

"Gwen's cool." Lucy gave Justin's shoulder a hearty pat. "You can suspect everyone else out here, but not her—" she paused for a second "—or Ranger Wendy, or Ranger Kyle."

"You always warn me about making character judgements."

"That's because you are terrible at judging character. I am not." Lucy spun towards their destination. "Don't worry. I'm sure you're good at other parts of being a detective." She unlocked the map room and reached for a light switch. "Gwen works in the rec room because she doesn't want to be up here alone. Jokes on her, the rec room is the scariest room in Fort Jeff."

Justin had to admit, when it wasn't crowded with students the dim and dusty room was creepy. "I thought you weren't afraid of anything— besides horror movies." They could never watch a scary movie with Lucy around.

"You'd be surprised." Lucy frowned.

Justin watched flickering florescent lights warm up, giving the room a weird ambiance. "Really? What else do you find frightening?"

"The ghosts in the rec room when I'm alone, really sticky candies getting stuck in my teeth," Lucy mimed pulling something from her mouth. "The open ocean."

"You swim every day."

"Miguel makes me watch every horror movie about the ocean: giant sharks, giant squids, poison jellyfish. Any time I'm in deep water I imagine sea monsters just out of sight." Lucy circled the room. Reaching between the computers, she bumped a mouse, waking a monitor and casting the password screen's blue light onto her face. "Weird. Normally students turn these off to prevent the fans from sucking in even more brick dust." She ran her finger over the desktop, leaving a streak of gray powder to make her point.

"They must have been in a hurry to get out and dive." Justin shrugged

"Or Private Winter's ghost turned it on." Rudy would have rewarded that comment with a high-pitched yelp. Justin simply smiled. No fun. The file cabinet keys were hung behind the computers. She tossed them to Justin. "What are you afraid of?"

"Nothing." Justin dismissed her question as he began to sort through files. "Why even print all of these records?"

Stepping away from the computer, Lucy pulled an exceptionally thick sheet of paper out of one file. "These are waterproof diagrams, magnetometer readings, drone and satellite photos of wreck sites, and records of research." She waved files in Justin's face. "All stuff useful to identify and document a wreck."

Justin leaned against the file cabinet. "Wow! You know a lot about this. Are you planning to become an archeologist?"

"Don't even joke!" Lucy rolled her eyes. "I live with this stuff, so I've absorbed a lot." She moved to an older, more dented filing cabinet and opened a drawer, "Anyway, this is where the previous team's papers should have been. See the difference?"

Justin glanced into the empty drawer. "Those missing files seems like a pretty big mystery, where could they have gone?"

Lucy shrugged, "Maybe Private Winters ate them. I don't think Mom cared much until everything else happened. Let's focus on the files we do have."

Justin nodded. "Maybe we can find clues about why Chet, Sophia and Barbara were working the wrong shipwrecks."

Lucy began organizing U.R.S.A.'s files on the tabletop, pushing scraps of paper and a box of pens away. "There are all two hundred and seventy-five shipwreck files. You have a better head for memorizing numbers, where should we start?"

Justin balked. "That's a lot of wrecks."

"Ships have been sailing here for a long time." Lucy spread files out in order.

"Let me think," Justin stared. "Get rid of every wreck that's not near or around Loggerhead. Other's may be important, but we don't have time to search them all."

Checking files against numbered wrecks on the wall, Lucy grabbed files one through one-hundred and put them all away. Justin scooped up everything over one-hundred and sixty explaining, "All of these are gray pins, which means they haven't been dived yet, right?" Lucy nodded. "Still too many."

They were left with about fifty shipwrecks around Loggerhead. "Maybe we can compare them to files on the computer." Lucy theatrically cracked her knuckles in front the login screen, "I'm no good at hacking, but I know all Mom's passwords."

Justin moved the remaining files closer. "We'll do ten at a time."

"That will take forever. Instead, let's just see what files the students have opened recently!" Using her mother's password Lucy searched: recent documents. "Look at this!" she exclaimed, opening a colorful document.

"Davy Jones's Dives." Justin read the title aloud. "It's an advertising pamphlet!"

"Charter your historic dives," Lucy continued reading. "Spend five days at sea in our most historic maritime park. Dive uncharted pirate wrecks from the 16th century to vessels from World War Two." She repeated the last part excitedly. "*Dive uncharted wrecks.*" Skipping to the bottom, "All chartered tours were designed and curated by a professional archeologist!"

"The end isn't very good." Justin scratched his chin.

"It's a draft." Lucy pointed to many blank spaces. "See, you can even tell where pictures will go." She pushed back in her seat. "There is no way Mom would let anybody on her team make something like this!"

"Davey Jones Dives." Justin read it twice, "Have we heard of them before?"

Lucy shook her head. She opened an internet browser. "When I search that name online, I get diving clubs in the Canary Islands, Indonesia, Boca Raton, but nothing in the Florida Keys."

"I doubt Davey Jones's Dives is the real name." Justin pointed at the title. "See how the words look out of place?" He grinned. "Look at the logo, familiar?" The bow of a pontoon boat with horns over the Captain's Cabin.

"Horned Devil Tours." Lucy frowned, "Captain Tobias."

"That's my guess too." Justin tapped the screen. "But why is this here, now? And how'd you find it so easily?"

"This is the only file listed in recent documents. Like it's the only thing anyone has ever worked on using this computer. Which can't be true." Lucy grabbed the mouse. "This computer was on when we came in. Like you said, someone was in a hurry."

She clicked through the search bar. "I saw Amelia do this once." Using their absent friend's trick, she checked the computer's activity history. "This should show us every program the Dive Bears have ever worked on." It was, "Empty, except for today. Someone is erasing all logs of work done on this computer."

"Sabotaging university files?" Justin asked.

Lucy began opening files at random. They all seemed full of documents. "It doesn't look like any work has gone missing. But someone is hiding evidence of which files have been worked on when."

"Our student accomplice?" Justin stared at the computer for a long time. "Maybe they wanted to hide that brochure, since your mom wouldn't let her students work for a dive charter."

"It would have worked, if they'd only closed the document." Lucy pointed to the empty recent files.

Justin hummed. "Can you find any other hidden activity on this computer, bring back any data that was erased, or trace who was making it?"

Lucy rolled her eyes. "I already told you, I'm not a hacker."

"That's too bad." Justin leaned over her chair. "But that brochure is a start. Email it to me."

Lucy nodded. "It's proof that a student is working with Captain Tobias. Are we done here?"

"Which student?" Justin grinned, "We haven't even searched the files yet."

Closing the digital file and her email, Lucy cleared the activity log like their suspected saboteur. She opened the file for another wreck. "Alright, let's start!"

CHAPTER 35

THE HAUNTING

LUCY

JUSTIN WAS LEANING OVER THE TABLE HALF ASLEEP while Lucy absent-mindedly searched computer files. An hour and a half had passed. Suddenly, a box of pens crashed to the floor! The loud clatter was followed by hundreds of plastic pens clicking across wood.

"What the heck!" Justin, eyes wide, stared down at the pens. "Wasn't that box in the center of the table?"

"Even Private Winters' ghost is bored." Lucy slid from her seat crouching to pick up pens and returning them to their box. "Have we found anything yet?"

"We're not going to talk about what just happened?" Justin's lifted his hand to his throat checking his pulse.

Lucy tried to shake out sleepy fuzz. "You probably moved them and forgot. Back to our search, have you noticed any patterns? Because, I haven't."

Justin lifted his sheet of notes. "Well, I've noticed some files are much bigger than others. This is Professor Erickson's wreck." He dropped a folder with a heavy thump onto the table. "He's obviously done a lot of work. Compare that to Sophia's cannon wreck." Justin held up the thin file. "See the difference?"

"All that's in here is a sketch of her cannon wreck showing the location of every cannon, before they were stolen." Lucy lifted a single, laminated, drawing. "Twelve missing cannon. That's fifty to one hundred thousand dollars."

"Wow! That might be enough to pay for the yacht's gas bill. But for a student or commercial dive operator, it's a lot." He stared at Sophia's sketch. "Our thief would have found this helpful! Can your dad dust it for fingerprints?"

"No?" Lucy laughed, turning back to the computer. "Anyway, Sophia has more records on this computer. See, she even has draft of her research paper." She clicked on the file.

Justin scanned the opened document. "There's only a single paragraph."

"She'd only just started her survey. But there's also academic papers about shipwrecks and civil war artillery, spreadsheets of dates and charts of old shipping route. There's a lot of research into civil war cannon here. It must suck to start over from scratch. Hmm."

"What?"

Lucy had opened a small document. "This is an email from one of Dr. Alexa's students, Paul. He's answering a question about wrecks one-twenty-two and one-twenty-nine."

"Rudy said we were snorkeling one-twenty-nine today."

"Yeah." Lucy nodded. "According to this email, Dr. Alexa's survey found several big magnetic objects on the sites. He thinks some of them might be cannon."

"Chet, Barbara, and Sophia are looking for more cannon?" Justin asked. "Suspicious."

"More cannon found means more to sell." Lucy stared at the stacks of files, and the computer clock. "Speaking of those guys, they could come back at any time. Put those away. I'll email all this junk to myself so we can read it later." Justin began stuffing stacks of files back into their drawers.

He was shoving the last files into their drawer when there was a loud scrape against the door. Lucy recognized Sophia's voice. "Mapping one site doesn't even scratch the surface." She quickly clicked away from her email, clearing the activity log like their mysterious suspect. "What if Dr. Benitez finds out?"

The monitor went blank. Lucy began to breathe easier. "This is triage."

Chet replied outside. "We'll find something, I promise."

Justin stealthily slid the last drawer shut and moved to stand beside Lucy. She pulled up a random web browser and typed the name of their friend Bethany's favorite TV show into the search bar. Sophia's voice echoed into the room. "We won't find anything as historically significant as my cannon wreck. Not before it's too late."

"Maybe Mr. Ishii will get stuck at the conference, or his flight will be delayed." Barbara's slender face was frozen in surprise. "Holy cow you guys scared me!"

Chet and Sophia pushed past her. All three had changed into dry shorts and university T-shirts. Chet's arms bulged through his sleeves. "Hi guys. We weren't expecting anyone in here. What's up?"

Lucy swiveled in her chair "We wanted to watch the most recent Coffee Chronicles episode, but Gwen's in the rec room."

"Say no more." Barbara's blond curls bobbed up and down. "Her reality TV tastes are terrible. Speaking of wayward scientists, have you seen Professor Erickson? He's supposed to meet us here."

"He's not at home?" Lucy asked.

"Professor E's apartment is empty. Anyway, archeology is fifty percent excavation and one hundred percent documentation." Chet's shrug showed off his muscles as he eyed Lucy's computer. "I'm gonna need that computer. It's paperwork time!"

Justin's eyes met Lucy's. He smiled. "So, um, were you guys the last ones to use the map room?"

Barbara crossed her arms. "Probably, why?" Sophia and Chet both raised curious brows.

Lucy scanned the room looking for something to distract them. "Nothing big, we just had a Private Winters visit earlier. An entire box of pens was knocked to the floor."

"Creepy!" Sophia took a step back.

"Cool!" Barbara smiled.

"Someone probably just left the box too close to the edge." Chet shrugged. "Now step away please. We need to get work done before your mom comes to interrogate us."

"About what?" Lucy wondered silently. She leapt up motioning for Justin to follow her. Chet quickly took her vacant seat. Barbara moved to take the other computer. Sophia remained in the hallway suspiciously

scanning the room.

Lucy waved, squeezing past her, "See you guys later."

"Definitely." Chet nodded.

In a muffled voice, as they walked down the steps, Justin whispered. "So, it was one of those three who left the computer on and was working on the brochure. Also, what did Chet mean triage?"

CHAPTER 36

INSIDE INFORMANT

LUCY

LUCY PUT HER FINGER TO HER LIPS and led him to the dungeon underneath the map room. A sign hung over the small, dark, interior room warning readers to: *Abandon All Hope, Ye Who Enter.* She nodded. "Okay, I don't think anyone can hear us."

Justin looked at her. "Were you able to send yourself those files?"

Lucy nodded. "Yeah, but I don't know how we're going to interpret them."

Justin tapped his chin, "you said Gwen was cool. Do you think we could ask her to help us look through them?"

Lucy shook her head. "I swear on my life that she's not up to anything shady, but if we ask for her help then she'll tell Mom."

"We keep getting more questions than answers. Why did Sophia say she owes Chet and Barbara? Where is Dr. Erickson? Who made that brochure?" Justin went quiet. "We need to share all of this with Miguel and Rudy."

"While you do that," Lucy straightened up, "I'm going to find Ranger Wendy."

"The new law enforcement ranger?" Justin asked. "You think she'll help us?"

"No." Why did Justin think any adult would help them investigate? "But I have a better idea. Meet you in the rec room."

Lucy went to the visitor center, but instead of finding Ranger Wendy, she bumped into a different, older face. "Hello, Miss Benitez." Mr. Howard stared down at her through curved glasses. "How is your mother holding up under her recent cannon crisis?"

"Fine, I guess. Wait! How did you know about that?" Lucy frowned realizing that she, technically, wasn't supposed to know about it either. Panicking she blurted a different question unthinkingly. "What's wrong with your speedboat?"

"Captain Levi is just making sure it's in tip top shape for our return voyage." Mr. Howard's smile carved big dimples in his cheeks. "Between you and me, he likes to play with the crane. Anyway, I heard that you and your friends were helping your mother's mystery?"

"How did you know about that?" *Too?* It took Lucy a moment to notice the other thing he had said. "You're still leaving?"

"I can't stay out here forever." Mr. Howard's smile vanished in an instant. "Especially not when your mother's students demonstrate so much incompetence." As though the missing cannon were the Dive Bears fault! "As for how I know about you and your friends, I have my sources." Lucy followed his gaze to Ranger O'Donnell who was bent over the parade ground bird bath. "Miss Benitez, I do hope you'll solve this one for us."

"That's our plan." Lucy stated calmly.

"Good. Because I've committed a small fortune only to have your mother's most interesting find snatched away." He was smiling as he stomped away, headed towards the crews quarters. "I'd like her expedition to yield *some* valuable results before I leave."

Lucy tried to think of some response. Instead, she huffed, "I'll see you later." She finally understood her mom's concern. Mr. Howard wasn't just a sleepy old guy.

The maintenance ranger's hair was a mess sticking out from under his NPS ball cap. He didn't stand when Lucy approached. "Mr. O'Donnell, did you tell Mr. Howard about the missing cannon?"

"Say I did." Ranger O'Donnell didn't look up, "so what?"

"If that information goes public, U.R.S.A. could get in trouble."

"Oh no." His nose wrinkled, pulling something slimy and smelling of rotten plants from the fountain. "I need to get back to work. Where are your uh, friends?"

"Napping." She answered unbothered by his gruff voice. But maybe she shouldn't be so direct. "What's up with the bird bath?"

"First, it's a bird bath on an island without water, so it's incredibly popular." He gestured to the trees around them. Many different birds were perched in branches watching and waiting. Too bad Justin wasn't here. "And I'm here pulling sticks, leaves and bird, um, poo out of it. I should be helping Tom with boat repairs."

"Which boat needs repairs?"

He harshly jammed a dirty screwdriver into the drain. "Which boats don't? The whaler is down an engine, the 18-footer isn't draining water, and the Parker's annual maintenance overhaul is two years overdue. On top of that, we're expected to help keep your mother's university boats running." He slung another clump of drowned mushy plant matter onto the ground.

"The university doesn't write my paychecks. If some rowdy students get in trouble over a few lost cannons, my job gets easier. Next time your mom can bring a boat mechanic with her." He tried to force a light and jaunty tone. "While you're at it, ask her to bring professionals not a bunch of hooligans. My wife is six months pregnant. Their noise sent her back to the mainland."

So that's why Mrs. O'Donnell was in Key West! Lucy frowned. "Are they really that bad?"

"Worse than you can imagine." He growled. Pulling out another clump of mush he sighed. "Sorry. Your mom's a nice woman. She does not deserve this."

Lucy sighed, "Then, if you have a problem with the Dive Bears, you should tell her."

"Heh, no way. She intimidates me. Besides, all I have to do is bide my time and that problem will take care of itself." He locked a wrench onto the water spigot and twisted. "See you later, kid."

Lucy was still pondering their conversation on her way to the dock when she bumped into Professor Erickson, "Hi Professor, some students were looking for you in the map room."

"I thought everyone was busy on boats." Professor Erickson paused, "wait, how did you know they were in the map room?"

Lucy smiled awkwardly, "We were reading the charts up there. Rudy is still convinced there's a pirate treasure out here."

"Don't I wish!" Chuckling, the professor focused on Lucy, "Are you sure that's all you're investigating?" She nodded. He sighed, "Well, let me know if Rudy finds his pirate treasure. I'll help him publish. That's my kind of archeology."

"Will do." Lucy never did find Ranger Wendy, just an empty space in the dock where her boat should be parked.

CHAPTER 37

THE USUAL SUSPECTS

JUSTIN

"**R**ANGER O'DONNELL MADE IT CLEAR that he wants U.R.S.A. to leave." Lucy stared at the others. "I also don't like that he's gossiping about missing cannon."

"Then why cross him off the suspect list?" Miguel asked. They were standing in the archway outside the boy's apartment. Rudy was inside snoring, and Gwen was still in the rec room binging her show.

Lucy sighed. "He's way to obvious. Also, he wouldn't make that brochure."

Justin nodded. "I agree with Lucy, we need to start removing suspects, or we'll never solve this. Let's focus on the remaining students."

"We found that brochure today. Dr. Alexa's red team is gone." Lucy affirmed.

"Why is the brochure so important?" Miguel asked.

Lucy turned to her brother. "It proves a student was working with a commercial dive captain, probably Captain Horned Devil Tobias, and sharing U.R.S.A. information."

"Information about *uncharted* shipwrecks." Justin added. "You heard Chet. He promised Sophia that they would 'find something.'"

"You're sure the logo you found was for the *Horned Devil?*" Miguel sighed. "Why would a Dive Bear work with them?"

"Maybe someone, like Chet, thought they were helping Captain Tobias find fun new wrecks and didn't know he was planning steal artifacts." Justin sighed. "We need more evidence than just a brochure and a glass vial. Until we find something definitive, it could still be anyone from Ranger O'Donnell to Mr. Howard."

"Yes!" Miguel rolled his eyes, proving it was a Benitez family gesture. "Let's suspect the guy who's money is carrying Mom's expedition. He's sabotaging that expedition to: *make new dive tours?*"

Justin had picked Mr. Howard because of Lucy's encounter, but hearing Miguel's argument made him scratch his chin. "Maybe he's not just a historian. Maybe he's a smuggler, stealing artifacts from research he funds to sell on the black market."

"A Rudy level theory!" Miguel chuckled. "If you're right, it would be our biggest case ever!"

Justin bristled. "I guess *that* doesn't make much sense, but we still need more evidence."

Lucy cleared her throat, "I've been thinking. Spud's glass vial seems like a dead end, but maybe we can use it to help us find more clues."

"How?" Justin asked.

"We use it to get into the bat cave."

"Can I come?" Rudy opened the door rubbing his eyes. "You guys are way too loud. Every fish in the moat knows about our investigation by now."

"They don't gossip." Miguel sniffed.

"How are we getting into the bat cave?" Justin rolled his eyes.

"Follow me." Lucy motioned to let Rudy know he could come along.

Downstairs, they bumped into Gwen leaving the rec room. She carefully stepped around the group, holding onto her laptop. "What are you guys up to?"

Lucy stepped forward. "Hi Gwen, how's the research going? You, um, weren't in the map room earlier today, were you?"

"Nope, I refuse to be in there alone. Why?" Gwen scanned the group. "This doesn't have anything to do with missing equipment and artifact thefts, does it? I assume you've heard: Sophia's wreck was vandalized?"

"Yeah, we heard." Rudy spoke up.

"The night before Dr. Alexa left with her students." Justin tilted his head, trying to sound natural. "You didn't notice anything weird, or anyone missing, did you?"

"We were helping red team pack. Anyone trying to sneak away faced Dr. Alexa's wrath. This whole thing is a mess." Gwen shifted items in her arms to better aim her raised eyebrows. "Who would steal old cannon? They definitely can't be sold legitimately."

"You mean the black market?" Rudy asked too eagerly.

"Pretty dangerous stuff." Gwen blew a loose strand of hair out of her eyes. "Well, my work's done for the day. I'll leave you guys to your investigation."

"What investigation?" Justin's heart leapt into his throat.

"You guys are cute, but really obvious. I hope you figure this out." Gwen leaned in conspiratorially, "I can work at home, but my friends need more time out here. They definitely shouldn't be accused of crimes they didn't commit. So, I guess I'm saying: good luck." She began to walk away but paused on the brick path, "Also, be careful!"

Lucy smirked as Gwen walked away. "See, Justin. I told you she was cool."

CHAPTER 38

THE BAT CAVE

RUDY

"HOW ARE WE GETTING INTO THE BAT CAVE with a vial of wood?" Rudy had been looking forward to seeing the mysteriously named room.

"I have a plan." Lucy grinned. "We just need to find dad."

"Make sure you don't mention the brochure, cannon, or J.R.I.C." Justin responded.

"Don't worry, dad will help." Lucy sounded confident. It was like Rudy's friends knew the plan without communicating. Except the only person in the office was a young woman in a park service uniform with a gun strapped on her waist.

"Ranger Wendy. Even better." Lucy turned to Justin, "Give me the vial."

"Ok." Justin handed it over.

Ranger Wendy was a shorter woman with dark brown hair. She didn't look much older than Cassidy Case, Justin's sister. "Lucy!" she wildly swiveled her chair to face them. "You must be the friends. What can I do for you?"

"Well, we found this yesterday floating on Loggerhead." Lucy held up the vial.

Ranger Wendy grabbed the vial, bringing it closer to examine the tiny sliver of wood inside. "One of Kit's samples?"

"Really, Spud, found it." Justin added. "It was floating near Loggerhead dock."

"The Manning's dog? Curious." Wendy turned to look at them. "You didn't find any more, did you?"

"Just the one." Lucy answered.

"It's not valuable enough to save their expedition," Rudy sighed.

Ranger Wendy fished through her key chain. "It takes the smallest amount of material for carbon-14 testing. What's challenging is finding an uncontaminated sample. Kit's sample tool carves out a sizable chunk of wood." The small sliver didn't look big. "In his lab he peels away outer layers to get a clean core."

Rudy stared at the young ranger. She smiled, "I saw Kit carrying this big spear gun looking thing around one day and made him explain his process."

"A speargun looking thing?" Rudy thought back to Professor Erickson's room.

"Yeah, I didn't think his sample tool was a weapon, but I had to be sure." Ranger Wendy took them into a small arched doorway right from park headquarters. "Well, valuable or not, I'm sure Kit will be happy one of his samples is back."

Lucy asked, "Do you think this really is one of the missing samples?"

"Maybe. He lost twelve separate samples." She frowned. "If he can't tell which one this is, he might not be able to use it."

"Couldn't he compare it to the rest?" Justin asked. "There were twelve identical samples in Key West."

"He destroys the samples to run his tests." Wendy's frown deepened.

Lucy pointed to the cap. "At least we know it's from the blue team."

"We'll see what Kit has to say." Wendy led them through a narrow hallway. "Welcome to the bat cave." She shoved open a wooden door leading deeper into Fort Jefferson.

"No bats." Lucy replied. "No butler."

Wendy reached into the dark room, "But a room full of toys." Sudden lights illuminated metallic shelves full of equipment designed for rescue, construction, and storm monitoring. Some of items looked new, some looked ancient. There was enough marine gear to outfit everyone on the island for a year long voyage, including a dusty box full of military rations marked: *hurricane supplies.*

Rudy gagged, imagining the taste of old M.R.E.s. Justin pointed to something in the back corner. "Are those night vision goggles?"

"Yep." Ranger Wendy stepped underneath a brick archway next to a large metallic cage. Inside the cage was an array of expensive equipment. A locked box, in a locked room, tucked away in thick brick walls. "They're ancient. I don't think anyone's used them in years."

"Do they still work?" Justin asked as Ranger Wendy swung open the metal door.

"Hand me the vial." Lucy passed it over. Ranger Wendy grabbed a tin box before answering Justin's question, "Lucy helped me test them last month. Why?"

"I've never used real night vision goggles." Justin lied. "How do they work?"

Ranger Wendy set the vial gently in the box. "Well, it's hard to describe without using them. Basically, they amplify low light so you can see in near darkness."

"Can we try them?" Justin asked. Rudy realized he was distracting Ranger Wendy while Lucy tiptoed into the locked container, reaching for the bin with the sample vial.

Ranger Wendy, noticing her shadow, turned. Resting a gentle hand on Lucy's shoulder, she ushered her out of the metal cage. "What are you doing?"

Lucy grinned sheepishly. "I wanted to see if there were any other vials in there."

"There aren't," Wendy put her hands on her hips. "Not that it's any of your business."

Lucy looked abashed. Rudy almost felt sorry for her, and he knew it was an act. Ranger Wendy sighed. "You know what? Take those old night vision goggles. Try them out. Bring them back when you're done. Just leave this investigation to professionals."

Justin nodded eagerly. "Are you sure?"

Lucy smiled. "Thanks!"

Before Wendy could retract her offer back, Rudy grabbed the headset. It was heavier than expected. Beside it was a battery pack. He grabbed that too. Unlike Justin, he didn't have to fake his interest. He'd never used them before, "Are you sure it's ok?"

"My dad used to let me play with outdated park service equipment. It's one reason I'm a ranger now." Ranger Wendy pointed back into the metal cage, "Besides, we have a newer, better, pair. Those are ten years old. Still, don't break them, and don't walk while wearing them."

Lucy laughed. "That was the second time Ranger Kyle fell into the moat."

"I hope I can trust you three to be more responsible." Ranger Wendy eyed Lucy and Justin. "You understand, right? This is a bribe. You have something interesting now, so stay away from our investigation."

"Yes Ma'am." Justin nodded. Lucy bowed her head. Rudy had never seen his friends tell a more blatant lie. They left.

"What was that about?" Rudy held up his prize.

"Well," Lucy explained as they walked away. "There weren't any samples in that box. Wendy's right, if that vial belonged to Kit, then it should have a code written on it."

"I meant these." Rudy held up the night vision goggles.

Justin glanced around to make sure there wasn't anyone listening. "They were just a distraction, but they could be useful for stakeouts."

"Wendy gave us these so we wouldn't investigate." Rudy hugged their new toy to his chest.

"So?" Lucy asked.

"Did anyone else notice that the bat cave had weird dimensions?" Justin asked.

CHAPTER 39

DISCOVERED

JUSTIN

"WHEN I SAID WE NEED TO USE OUR EVIDENCE, I didn't mean trade one piece for something else." Justin held up the night vision goggles.

"Don't pretend you aren't excited." Lucy turned everyone back to her house. "Also, I didn't *trade* our evidence for goggles. Now you know that equipment in the bat cave should be secure, Kit's vials are still missing, and Spud's clue might be one of them."

"If not, someone else is taking samples." Rudy added.

"I don't know why they would. Kit's the only one who knows how to use his special carbon dating machine in Key West." Lucy hummed thoughtfully. "I guess someone could send samples to another lab, but that would cost a lot of money."

"What about the tools themselves?" Justin frowned. "Are they valuable?"

"I don't know. Kit's testing machine is super expensive, but no one is going to steal that monstrosity." Lucy turned to Justin. "Now, let's go home, I'm hungry."

Mr. Benitez loved to cook. "My mother and I used to argue about every little thing, but we'd set it all aside to make dinner."

"Abuela's meals are the best!" Lucy swiped a pepper slice from the chopping block. "It's hard to believe you two didn't always get along."

"I was a hard-headed kid growing up. Always getting into trouble." Mr. Benitez's knife cut into a second pepper. "Like a certain group of young men and women."

"What do you mean?" Lucy asked, playfully grabbing another slice of pepper.

Ranger Benitez raised a single eyebrow. "I know your mother asked for help finding out who is causing U.R.S.A. trouble."

"Well, yes. But then she told us to stop," Lucy stepped into her father's harsh gaze.

"So why are you still bothering her students and pestering my rangers?" Justin felt a lump in his chest when Ranger Benitez's questioning tone shifted.

"Wendy told you about us?" Lucy stopped before grabbing another pepper.

"Ranger Wendy is concerned. As am I. You three might get yourselves into real trouble." Ranger Benitez sighed. "Okay, I'll level with you. We are currently looking for the *Horned Devil*. We believe Captain Tobias was involved in the theft of artifacts and we are investigating how he learned about them."

Lucy father's gaze softened settling onto the boys. "I say *we*, but I mean *my* law enforcement team, the Coast Guard, and relevant authorities. Not you." He set down his knife. "Let me explain how things are going to go."

"Dad." Lucy sighed.

"No talking." He extended one finger. "Listen. You guys are going to drop your investigation and stop hassling your mother's students and my rangers."

Justin looked away. He didn't know what to say. Rudy was nodding in agreement. Lucy's head lowered.

Mr. Benitez continued. "If you do not stop, I will tell your parents, and we will cut this visit short. Do you understand?"

Rudy was first to respond. "Yes, Mr. Benitez."

Justin swallowed the lump in his throat. "Yes, sir."

Lucy bowed her head. "Fine."

So much time passed that Justin began to feel uncomfortable. Suddenly Mr. Benitez reached for a vegetable, smiling widely. "Wonderful! Now who wants to get shrimp from the freezer?"

Dinner did not make Justin forget the tension. Dr. Benitez returned, and absorbing the mood, she said nothing. When the meal was over, Justin pushed away his plate. "I need to email my sister."

"Ooh, if you're sending a message to Cassidy, let me come." Lucy sat up. "I have questions about her new college!" She turned to Rudy. "Are you coming?"

Rudy rubbed the back of his neck. "I'm going upstairs but only to fall asleep. I'm beat."

"You're starting to look like a beet." Lucy flicked his reddening skin. "Are you sure you remembered to use sunscreen today?"

Rudy winced. "I missed a few spots."

Mr. Benitez followed them into the kitchen. He lifted two fingers to his eyes. A gesture without words: "*I'm watching you.*"

CHAPTER 40

PRINTING A TRAP

LUCY

LUCY SLAMMED THE APARTMENT DOOR. "This changes nothing!" She stared at the boys, waiting for a response.

Rudy shrugged. "We've never listened to our parent's before. Why start now?"

Lucy could hear his sarcasm. "You sound like Miguel."

"Maybe Miguel has a point." Rudy stuck his tongue out.

Lucy fought the urge to reach for and pinch it. "I'll ignore that."

"Guys!" Justin interrupted their feud, "we have to assume anyone we talk to will tell your parents. No more questions. We keep these hidden," he grabbed his charts from the table.

"Ranger Wendy told your dad about us, just like that." Rudy frowned.

"She didn't know we were questioning students," Lucy countered. "A Dive Bear must have told him about that. It wasn't Gwen." She protested too quickly.

"When I went to see Professor Erickson, I told him about J.R.I.C." Rudy bashfully raised his hand. "But I only mentioned our investigating because I was trying to reassure him."

"I doubt Professor E takes us seriously." Lucy tried to make Rudy feel better. "It was one of the three students from the map room."

"Sophia, Chet, or that other one, um, Barbara?" Justin asked. "We're close to the truth, so they told your dad to stop us!"

"What do we do now?" Rudy asked.

"We act natural, go about our daily lives, and wait for someone to slip up."

"That will take forever!" Lucy threw up her hands. "We don't have time."

"We should set a trap." Rudy sighed.

"Who are we trapping?" Justin stared at his charts. "We still have a lot of suspects. Chet was eager to get to that computer. To see the brochure?"

"Brochure, brochure, brochure," Rudy's voice was strained, "I haven't even seen it yet."

"Give me your computer." Lucy called up her email.

"Red, blue, and teal, like Captain Tobias's boat." Rudy leaned over his laptop.

"I hadn't noticed the colors," Justin nodded approvingly. "But there's no name on the brochure. The *Horned Devil* isn't even mentioned. The logo is not enough proof." For a while they sat staring at their biggest piece of evidence.

"Not enough." Slowly, a plan bubbled into Lucy's head, "but we can use it. We need Miguel's printer." She rushed downstairs.

"Couldn't this wait until tomorrow?" Despite Miguel's protest he pushed through his cluttered room to grab his small printer, closing his eyes as she printed multiple copies of the document. "The less I'm involved the better."

Lucy rushed back upstairs. "Rudy gave me an idea." She held up copies of the unfinished brochure. "A trap. We'll leave these where the Dive Bears can find them and watch how they react."

"We're setting bait." Justin realized her plan. "How do we make sure our student suspects see them?"

Lucy stared down at their three circled suspects. "Barbara is usually the first student up in the morning. When I go swimming, she sits at a picnic table reading and drinking tea."

Justin picked up a brochure. "So, if you get up a little earlier then you could leave a brochure for her and watch her reaction from the second floor."

Lucy glared, "Are you waking up with me?" Justin shook his head. Of course not. "Fine. I'll set my alarm."

"What about Chet and Sophia?" Rudy asked.

"I did most of the brain work." Lucy sat up stretching. "You guys figure that out. Apparently, I have to go to sleep early."

Lucy fell asleep with ease and woke with plenty of time to leave the brochure, like a secret message, on a picnic table outside the crews quarters. She then crept upstairs to watch the picnic tables.

What she witnessed was anticlimactic. Seeing the brochure, Barbara set down her cup of tea to pick it up. Reading it without any reaction she crumpled it and tossed it, unsuccessfully, towards a nearby trashcan. Shrugging, she turned back to her book.

"I'm so glad I got up thirty minutes early for that." Lucy left to swim. Her return trip was delayed by a crowd of park rangers gathered in the headquarters. Stealthily, she opened the door.

Everyone was gathered around the radio. Her father was in mid-conversation with the Coast Guard. With every word, Lucy grew more excited. Then, as realization dawned, she was hit with a wave of disappointment.

CHAPTER 41

LITTLE AFRICA

JUSTIN

LUCY WAS GONE AND IT WAS LATE. Ranger O'Donnell's window was shut. The crews quarters were dark. It was quiet outside. Justin frowned thoughtfully. "Chet and Sophia hang out with other Dive Bears on the beach. Maybe we can use that?"

"You don't sound very confident." Justin heard the shrug in Rudy's voice as he lazily pulled himself up to brush his teeth.

"I'm not." Justin picked up the night vision goggles to watch the parade ground with a highlighted gaze.

"Do they actually make a difference?" Rudy asked, taking a picture with his phone.

"Yeah." Justin stared through the enhanced lenses, "Everything is super bright, and super green. I see a very empty fort."

"Any ghosts or secret saboteurs?"

"None of those." Justin racked his brain, trying to figure out how get brochures to Sophia and Chet. Lucy's plan was ingenious. He had to match it somehow. He fell asleep still thinking about how.

"Justin, wake up!" For the first time since arriving Rudy's shout, not maintenance workers, woke him. Smells of blueberries and butter tickled his nose. "I made muffins."

"Guys!" Lucy pushed past Justin as he opened the door. "Good, you're up!" She was breathing heavily, like she'd been running. "They found Captain Tobias and the *Horned Devil!*"

"What?" Her announcement roused them both.

"That's not all," Lucy's breathing had calmed. "Dad's shipping us back to Loggerhead!"

"Why?" Rudy asked while snagging a third muffin.

"Since they've caught the bad guy, they're going to do more investigating here. They don't want us in the way. Dad's coming." Lucy pointed to stack of brochures and the night vision goggles. "Hide those."

They had barely finished hiding everything when Lucy's father appeared, smiling. "Hi guys, something came up and Carmen will be busy all day. She asked me to take you over to Loggerhead." Ranger Benitez turned to Rudy, "Grab snorkel gear. I called over. The twins want to show you Little Africa."

They quickly assembled their things under Ranger Benitez's watch. Rudy pulled Justin aside to whisper, "does this mean our investigation is over?"

Ranger Benitez drove them to Loggerhead in complete silence. The twins met them on dock. All five turned to watch Lucy's dad speed South. "It looks like he's headed to the other side of the island." Lucy commented.

"That's where we're headed." Luke smiled.

"Why are you all here?" Nina had two sets of snorkel gear cradled in her arms. "We're excited to show you Little Africa, but shouldn't you be investigating?"

Lucy gave Spud a sympathetic scratch. "They found the cannon thieving boat captain."

"Is that bad?" Nina asked.

"Yes. Now they can simply ask Captain Tobias about his accomplices." Rudy moped. "They don't need us."

"Snorkeling will make you feel better." Luke was trying to sound sympathetic.

"As we walk, you can tell us everything." Nina suggested, leading them across the island.

"That is Little Africa?" Rudy stared out towards dark patches of coral.

Justin had forgotten this was Rudy's first time on Loggerhead. "From the top of the lighthouse, it looks like Africa."

"Why are Lucy's parents around Madagascar?" Rudy pointed to a park service boat and a university vessel floating in the distance.

Luke squinted out over the ocean. "I don't know, but Dad has been watching that spot for the rangers."

Nina nodded. "We've seen lots of U.R.S.A. boats out there recently."

Justin scratched his chin, "There was a park service boat there when we were on the lighthouse other day." Did it have anything to do with the mystery? Not that it mattered with Captain Tobias caught. Clearing his throat, he turned to Lucy. "There was dive gear on our boat when your dad drove us out here, right?"

"So?" Lucy was already in her snorkel gear. "No use worrying now. Let's swim!"

Despite other concerns, the reef was beautiful. The twins led them around massive coral heads, scattering fish and skimming over a menagerie of sea life. Spud sat patiently on the beach until they returned to the shallows, then doggie paddled out to them.

After snorkeling, Justin felt better. He was almost ready to admit that their mission was over, even though they hadn't solved anything. They trudged slowly through the sand to meet Lucy's dad and return to Fort Jefferson.

On Garden Key, they found Miguel in the rec room. "Did you hear?" Rudy ambushed him while playing video games. "Our investigation is over!"

"Not quite," Miguel sighed. "I was listening in on gossip in the headquarters. They didn't find Captain Tobias, only his boat abandoned in Key West. No cannon aboard."

"That's great!" Justin exclaimed happily. "It means we can still solve this mystery!"

"And that Mom's job is still at stake." Lucy's glare tempered his excitement. "Let's get those brochures to Chet and Sophia."

CHAPTER 42
CASTING BAIT

LUCY

"HOW DID THINGS GO WITH SUSPECT NUMBER ONE?" Justin followed Lucy along the brick path. Rudy had refused to join them, retreating to his room for more video games.

Lucy recalled her experience watching Barbara. "Unless she's a really good actor, it's not her."

"So, it's Sophia or Chet." Justin fell silent when Lucy grabbed his wrist. Pulling him with her, they crept quickly into the maze-like small powder magazine. "What are you doing?" he lowered his voice as Lucy put a finger to her lips.

"Sophia's out there." Lucy peaked out of the brick entrance. Sophia approached the corner, eyes focused on her phone. "Now's our chance." Grabbing a brochure from Justin, she crept to the entrance and carefully slid the paper onto the brick path.

Backing up, Lucy bumped into Justin and stifled a squeak. Seconds passed. Out of sight, Sophia gasped. Her footsteps resumed at a hastened pace. Creeping back to the entrance together, they watched Sophia jog past the crews quarters towards the apartments.

"Where is she going?" Justin asked.

"Let's see." As Lucy took her first steps, Chet emerged from the crews quarters to watch Sophia sprint away. She elbowed Justin, "follow my lead." Snagging a second brochure, she thrust it towards the big Dive Bear. "Hi Chet, do you know what this is?"

Chet's normally kind face morphed into a disgruntled frown. He snatched away her brochure. "Where did you find this?"

"Back there," Lucy pointed to Pvt. Winter's corner. "Is it important?"

"No." Chet was not very convincing. He folded the brochure into his pockets. "Thanks. I'll take care of this."

"Fast thinking." Justin whispered as Chet rushed back into the crews quarters.

"We're not finished. Follow me, quickly!" Lucy led him to the archway she'd used earlier to spy on Barbara. "Wait for it." A few moments later, Chet appeared again headed their way. "Hide." Lucy braced herself, concerned that he might climb the stairs. Instead, his footsteps faded. "He's leaving Fort Jeff."

They moved across the hall, from archway to harbor. Chet crossed the bridge pausing to scan the dock before heading towards a boat slip. Several U.R.S.A. students were carrying gear back to shore, but Chet walked past them to approach a ranger, waist deep in water repairing a boat. "That's Ranger O'Donnell." Justin observed as both figures spoke animatedly, "I can't tell if they are angry, or excited."

Conversation complete, Chet returned to the fort reaching the crews quarters in time to collide with Sophia. The two students froze, locked in a staring contest. Lucy wished she had Justin's binoculars. Before anything could happen, Gwen opened the door. Chet's shoulders slumped and Sophia retreated inside.

"Interesting." Justin was scratching his chin again.

"They won't do anything with other Dive Bears around," Lucy shrugged. "But we should be ready for tonight, when they head for the beach."

CHAPTER 43
ARGUMENT IN THE ARCHES

RUDY

RUDY SAT AT THE KITCHEN TABLE ignoring lunch and thinking mystery. He was trying to find something they had missed. "Boring!" Justin's chart was a complicated mess. Rudy was about to give up when he heard knocking. A few seconds later, he heard the professor's door open. "Did you print this?" Sophia voice echoed through the arches.

Professor Erickson replied calmly. "You should come in. We can talk."

A door shut. Their conversation continued. It was muffled, but it sounded like an argument. Rudy inched towards his door and turned down his blinds. Voices settled and a door opened. The professor spoke with a clear harsh tone. "You must get this under control."

"I didn't do anything wrong!" Rudy watched Sophia's ponytail bounce in protest. "Professor, you have to believe me! I can fix this."

"I want to." Professor Erickson's words sounded cold. His sigh echoed. "Fine. I'll leave it alone, for now. Just be careful."

Silence stretched on. Rudy was tempted to lift the blinds. He resisted. Moving to the kitchen window he watched Sophia rush downstairs. Justin and Lucy would want to hear about this. Prepared to follow Sophia, he opened the door, stopping immediately. Professor Erickson was leaning against a picnic table in the archway.

"Hello Rudy, I didn't expect you here now. What have you been up to?" Professor Erickson probably wanted to know what Rudy had heard. "Not taking a nap I hope?"

"No, I was listening to a podcast about pirates and treasure fleets." Rudy mimed headphones, hoping the professor believed him.

Professor Erickson nodded sagely. "We didn't interrupt you, did we?"

Rudy shook his head. "No, was someone else up here?"

"You just missed Sophia. She's been acting odd." He trailed off, changing the subject. "Anyway, how goes your investigation?"

"Pretty good." Rudy beamed. "Find any pirate treasure yet?"

The professor shook his head sadly. "Nothing exciting."

If Rudy followed Sophia now, Professor Erickson would know. Instead, he lingered in the doorway. "I'm just getting some fresh air," he swallowed his explanation.

Professor Erickson raised an eyebrow. "Breaks are an important part of research. They give you time to think." Did he sound, sad?

"Yep." Rudy walked awkwardly over to an arch to stare across the ocean, taking in a few theatric breaths. The air was salty. He shuffled around for a while then returned to his apartment.

Professor Erickson called after him, "I'll see you later then."

"Yep, see you." When Lucy and Justin returned, Rudy made sure to keep his voice low, now that he knew how well sound carried. "Is the professor still out there?"

"Nope." Lucy shook her head. "Why?"

"You wouldn't believe what just happened." Rudy eagerly shared everything he'd heard.

CHAPTER 44

STAKE OUT

JUSTIN

JUSTIN IMPATIENTLY PACED AROUND THE BENITEZ'S KITCHEN. He wanted to begin, but dinner came first. "Dive Bears have to eat too." Lucy reassured him as her family gathered on the porch.

Over dinner, the three investigators stared at each other awkwardly while Lucy's parents chatted about weather and food. Everyone was on edge except Miguel, who happily discussed his day online. "I talked to Cassidy, by the way."

"Really?" Justin sat up when his sister's name was mentioned. "She must be having a fun time." Too much fun to call him.

Miguel nodded, "You need to call her soon, before classes begin." So, it was Justin's responsibility? She hadn't even answered any of his emails!

After dinner Lucy excused herself. "I'm going to hang out with Justin and Rudy." She might as well have said nothing. Her parents waved them off without comment.

"Come on." They hurriedly picked up the goggles, snuck passed Professor Erickson's door, and took second floor hallways to the south wall. They found a position in the south-western turret where they could watch the Dive Bears assemble on the beach.

"Can they see us?" Rudy asked with a slight edge in his voice. Justin wondered if he was worried about being seen, or about a potential Private Winters ghost encounter.

"No. It's too dark." The brick archway was nearly pitch black. They had to walk with arms outstretched to avoid bumping into walls. "Perfect conditions for night vision goggles." Justin watched the evening in highlighted green. "Chet's sitting beside the cooler. Sophia's next to the speakers. Everyone else is swimming."

"Can I try?" Lucy reached for the goggles. After scanning the beach, she handed them to Rudy, who examined the dark fort around them. "Looking for Private Winters?" She teased.

"No," Rudy protested, turning to the beach. "He's not here."

Chet finally made his move: approaching Sophia by the drinks. Before he could say anything, Gwen joined them. Their conversation was short. When it was over, Chet stomped off. "Where is he going?" Rudy asked with a yawn.

"Hopefully somewhere incriminating." Justin stood with Lucy's help. They walked across the turret following the muscular student. The island's harbor side was bright enough that goggles were unnecessary.

The dock house was well lit, but two figures sat in the shadows looking out at the stars. "The turtle volunteers." Justin observed. The two turned as Chet approached. They spoke for a couple minutes. The big student eventually turned away.

Lucy whispered, "Stay back, in the shadows." Chet walked directly beneath them. At one point they were looking down on his head. "He's coming this way! Hide!" They waited out of sight. Chet's footsteps leveled off. Then came knocking.

"That's Ranger O'Donnell's apartment." Lucy whispered. A door opened. Silence. Lucy peeked around the corner, goggles on her head. "Chet is inside."

"We'd nearly cleared Ranger O'Donnell. Now this." Justin hummed. Then he went back to scan the beach again, "Where'd Sophia go?"

CHAPTER 45

HIDDEN ROOM

LUCY

Lucy aimed the goggles. Justin was right! Sophia was gone. "Maybe she followed Chet." They moved inside. The interior path was empty. The crews quarter's windows were dark.

"Is she out by the dock?" Justin asked.

"No." Rudy had taken the goggles. "She's not in the campground either." He gasped.

"What?" Lucy tensed. "Did you find her?"

Rudy's voice waivered, "Is that a rat?"

"Probably," Lucy sighed. "There are wood rats in the campground."

"Gross."

Justin whispered, "Focus. Where is Sophia?"

"Maybe she's walking around the moat." Rudy handed over his goggles.

The moat! Lucy felt her eyes widen. "I know where she might be." Grabbing the goggles, she jogged along the fort's front wall, knowing the others would follow. She ran past the turtle volunteers' apartment and through a small archway into Dr. Mudd's cell above the sally port.

"Where are we going?" Justin asked.

"Remember the footprints we found in the moat?" Lucy asked. "What if Sophia was the one sneaking into and out of the fort?"

"Why?" Rudy asked.

With night vision goggles, Lucy could see everything: green grass, green trees, and green shadows. "She could sneak into the fort, do whatever and then tell her friends she'd been walking around the moat."

"An alibi!" Justin nodded.

Lucy shushed him, pausing her scan to linger on the Large Powder Magazine. Was something moving? In the added light, there was no mistaking the small human form with a bobbing ponytail. "It's her."

"Let me see." Lucy handed Justin the goggles. "That's Sophia alright." He passed them to Rudy.

"Where is she going?" Rudy asked.

Snatching the goggles back, Lucy watched Sophia duck into the first floor. A minute passed. Another minute. "I think she climbed back out of the fort."

The three shifted to the exterior wall and watched Sophia return from the north beach. "Huh." Justin said.

"She was our ghost!" Rudy barely managed to keep his excitement to a whisper.

"What was she doing?" Justin asked. Sophia headed back to meet up with her friends.

"There's nothing over there but ruins." Except for a secret entrance and exit. Lucy thought back to the night they had chased Sophia around the Large Powder Magazine. "I have an idea." She handed Justin the goggles. "It's good we have these. Come on."

"So, Sophia is definitely our bad guy?" Rudy struggled to keep up. "What about Chet and Ranger O'Donnell?"

"I don't know." Lucy ignored the Large Powder Magazine, instead heading for the fort's interior beside the stairwell. "There." She pointed to a hallway leading beneath the turret. "Go past the Area Closed sign and keep walking."

"Where does this go?" Justin donned night vision goggles and followed the hallway.

"You don't know by now?" Rudy asked smugly. "Another powder magazine."

"He's right." Lucy whispered into darkness. "There's a room like the map room, but not refurbished."

"It's very dusty," Justin's footsteps echoed through brick halls. "The floor is broken."

"Be careful. That wood is almost a hundred years old." Lucy turned to Rudy. "I forgot about these closed off powder magazines. They're not really good for anything except gathering dust, spiders, and scorpions."

"Scorpions!" Justin called out. "It's too dark, even with night vision."

"We should have brought a flashlight." Lucy sighed.

A sudden beam of light flashed out of darkness. She'd forgotten about Justin's pockets. "Do you see any treasure?" Rudy called. Lucy resisted an urge to elbow him, hard.

"You need to see for yourself." Justin called. "Come on in."

Justin angled his light towards the floor so she and Rudy could step around broken boards into the dilapidated room. Bricks showed through holes in wooden walls. Dust kicked up by their footsteps hung in the air. Littered across the floor was U.R.S.A.'s missing equipment.

Expensive pieces sat openly on the dirty floor. The large underwater camera rested beside a missing GPS unit which balanced atop shiny dive equipment. Lucy picked up a single walkie-talkie. "She was talking to someone."

"I think I know who." Justin lifted a sheet of paper. It was surprisingly glossy for its place on the dusty floor, glimmering in the light.

Lucy snatched it from him. "It's a finished version of our brochure." She read the title printed in Captain Tobias's colors. "Undiscovered Archeology! Historical dives in the Dry Tortugas brought to you by *Horned Devil Tours*!" Lucy squinted at the color pictures. "Now we know why Sophia needed an underwater camera. She was taking glamor shots of U.R.S.A.'s wrecks."

"Your mom said they didn't have pictures from wreck one-twenty-two." Rudy leaned in to point at a picture of the water bound cannon.

"Obviously, Sophia did." Justin waved the paper. "This proves she was working with Captain Tobias!"

"We're not really surprised, are we?" Rudy asked. "The guilty parties are a guy who looks like a pirate and named his boat the *Horned Devil*, and a mean student."

"She's not mean, just grumpy." Lucy felt a heavy weight sink into the pit of her stomach. "Mom will be incredibly sad that Sophia is the student saboteur. What do we do now?"

CHAPTER 46

LIGHTS IN THE DARKNESS

LUCY

"LET'S BRING MY MOM AND DAD HERE. Show them what we found." Lucy took a careful step. It was hard to tell stone floor from rotten wood. She bumped into the sign blocking the entrance. She reached out to stop Rudy behind her. "Watch your head."

Justin ducked under the sign speaking rapidly. "Nothing back there proves Sophia is our criminal."

"Why do we need evidence proving it was Sophia?" Rudy asked, ducking. "We saw her."

"From halfway across Fort Jeff, in the dark." Justin stood in the hallway. "We didn't see anything in there with Sophia's name on it."

Lucy squinted into the beam of Justin's light, "Right. This will show Mom that someone's messing with U.R.S.A. But she will want hard proof it's Sophia. She'd rather let her expedition fail than accuse the wrong student."

"Meanwhile, we'll get in trouble for continuing to investigate. Ok." Rudy stared at them, "Hear me out. We lure Sophia here. Then we drop something behind her, blocking the door and trapping her."

Lucy smacked her forehead. "This isn't a cartoon."

"I've got a better idea." Justin interrupted loudly. "We need Miguel, and we have to hurry."

Lucy found Miguel in the rec room playing games. He pretended to ignore her. "Come with me, or I'll tell Mom and dad that you've been helping us." He set down his controller. "Grab a flashlight and meet us by the Large Powder Magazine."

Miguel surveyed Sophia's stolen goods. "You didn't find twelve missing cannon, but you found everything else. Impressive." Was that a genuine smile?

"Come on." Lucy led him back outside. Justin was watching the sally port with the goggles. "Sophia hasn't come back yet, has she?"

"No." Justin shook his head.

"Walk me through your plan again." Miguel leaned against the brick wall.

"Rudy's outside waiting for the other Dive Bears." Justin took Miguel's much larger flashlight. "When they come through the sally port, I'll wave this around. Rudy will point it out to Sophia. Hopefully, she comes to investigate."

"You want her to run towards danger?" Miguel frowned.

"We're hoping she'll need to see who has discovered her cache." Lucy countered.

"Where do I come in?" Miguel crossed his arms.

"Tell Mom and dad that you overhead us talking about investigating the Large Powder Magazine. When you see Justin's signal, point out his flashlight and say you think it's us."

"That will definitely bring them here." Miguel turned to look at her. "Then what?"

"I'll be waiting in there." Lucy pointed to the closed room. "If Mom and Dad drag their feet, hopefully I can prevent Sophia from escaping before they arrive."

"It's a bad plan." Miguel scowled. "We've got to come up with something better."

"Rudy's going to come back into the fort any second." Lucy stared at her brother. "Fine, I'll go instead."

"Wait." Miguel sighed, "I'll do it."

"Hurry!"

"You could say thanks!" Miguel trudged across the parade ground.

"Ready?" Justin handed her the night vision goggles. "There's enough light so long as you stay near the back of the room."

"Ok." Lucy left him, creeping into a small dark room. She stood away from the wall, in green near darkness, afraid of scorpions. "I hope I don't have to wait long."

She didn't. A few minutes later she heard the scrape of feet on brick and a hushed whisper. "She's coming." Justin dashed away, sprinting upstairs to hide.

A couple more moments and a dim beam of light pierced the darkness. "Chet?" Came a tremulous whisper. "Professor Erickson? I can explain." A small figure entered, blurred by a bright flashlight beam sweeping across the floor. Its first pass barely missed Lucy, making her heart hammer.

The flashlight beam lifted, and Lucy removed the goggles blinking into bright light. "Um, hi Sophia."

"Oh God!" Sophia's hands leapt to her chest as her flashlight clanked to the floor. It took her a second to recover. "Lucy! What are you doing here?"

Lucy smiled. "Ghost hunting."

"I thought you were a ghost." Sophia burped out a laugh. She reached for her flashlight. "Where are your friends?"

"Justin heard you coming." Lucy didn't want to give her time to think. Sophia's eyes darted around at the equipment. She kept talking. "We decided to play a trick on you. Um, sorry."

"Oh," Sophia hesitated. "Okay?"

More footsteps approached. Sophia stepped back, beginning her retreat. Lucy cleared her throat, "By the way, look what we found. Isn't that U.R.S.A.'s missing camera?"

"What?" Sophia asked. She almost sounded believable.

Lucy pointed. "That's U.R.S.A.'s missing GPS unit and that's some general mapping equipment."

"Oh, really?" Sophia tried to sound disinterested as she backed from the room.

"Sophia." Lucy narrowed her eyes, "Why are you here?"

"I saw a suspicious light." Her guilty face was obvious even in dim light.

"So why didn't you get a ranger?"

Sophia's expression fell. She looked mortified.

"Does it have something to do with this?" Lucy held up the printed advertisement. "Were you working with Captain Tobias to steal artifacts and equipment from U.R.S.A?"

"No!" Sophia snatched the brochure, looking confused. "We weren't supposed to steal anything!"

"I hope not!" Lucy's mother stepped into the dark room. A massive flashlight beam speared Lucy, then scanned across U.R.S.A.'s goods before landing on Sophia.

Sophia's face fell. "Dr. Benitez, it isn't what you think."

"What is it then?" Lucy was glad she wasn't the subject of her mother's harsh tone. "Let's get out of this dark, musty, place before you explain."

"Ok." Sophia hung her head.

"Now!" Lucy winced. Her mother sounded so angry! "Lucia." Lucy felt herself snap to attention. "And the boys." Her two friends stepped bashfully from the shadows.

Lucy's father was standing sternly in his wrinkled Park Service uniform. He'd skipped a button, causing his undershirt to show through. When Sophia stepped out, he pursed his lips. "Hmm."

"Most of our missing equipment is in there." Lucy's mom pointed back to the room. "No artifacts." She turned to Sophia, "I imagine your co-conspirators have taken any stolen antiquities with them." Sophia's head sank even lower.

Lucy's father nodded, "Ranger Wendy is on her way. When she arrives, escort our delinquent investigators home."

Rudy leaned over whispering to Lucy. "It feels like we are in as much trouble as Sophia."

CHAPTER 47

CONSEQUENCES

JUSTIN

"WHAT DID I SAY WOULD HAPPEN if you continued to investigate?" Mr. Benitez stood in the doorway. Despite his question, Justin was happy he'd returned. Miguel had managed to dodge trouble by slinking upstairs, but they had been stuck in awkward silence on the couch under Dr. Benitez's contemplative gaze.

"Do you have to call our parents?" Rudy kicked his feet under his chair. "We helped you catch Sophia."

Ranger Benitez crossed his arms, gaze hardened. "Look, it's really cool that you guys like to solve mysteries." He looked over at his wife, who remained silent. "When those mysteries don't involve dangerous people."

"Sophia is dangerous?" Lucy asked.

"Anyone stealing equipment from their own expedition is behaving irrationally." He settled beside his wife. "Did you ever consider that she had partners? People willing to steal property from federal land might not be as gentle as a delinquent student." He sighed, "We can talk later. I have calls to make." He quickly squeezed his wife's hand, then left.

"Dangerous partners? Captain Tobias?" Lucy asked.

"Is that who you think Sophia was working with?" Dr. Benitez raised a single eyebrow. There was something frightening about her expression.

"We found your stuff. Did we save the expedition?" Rudy asked. "Is Sophia under arrest?"

"I don't know. Now, explain why you were in a closed powder magazine." Dr. Benitez leaned forward expectantly.

Justin spoke first, explaining everything leading them to the hidden room.

"I see." Dr. Benitez frowned. "Why did you suspect Sophia?"

Lucy attempted to describe the clues which had led them to suspect the three students of working with Captain Tobias. "Barbara seemed innocent, but she was with Chet and Sophia. They have both been acting weird. Then we found a strange brochure on a university computer. We used those to test our suspects."

"So, you all printed those brochures? Chet brought one to me this afternoon."

"Chet?" Lucy asked.

Her mom remained silent, so Rudy took over. "They saw Chet show one to Ranger O'Donnell, so those two became our prime suspects. Then I heard Sophia confessing something to Professor Erickson. We also saw this weird ghost the other night, so Lucy knew to watch the Large Powder Magazine. That's when we witnessed Sophia sneaking around the fort and found U.R.S.A.'s equipment." He hesitated. "It's a little weird."

"Only if you explain it like that." Lucy shook her head. "Anyway, Rudy's right. Chet and Ranger O'Donnell are also acting suspicious. They might all be working together."

"This is why you should have left the investigation to us." Dr. Benitez made a weird face somewhere between a smile and a frown. "Chet and Ranger O'Donnell were working with us."

"What?" Justin squeaked.

Rudy crossed his arms, "Then why was Chet helping Sophia find a new wreck?"

"He was helping a friend. Sophia was looking for a new, significant, find. In her own way she was trying to save the expedition. But Chet also knew Sophia spent a lot of time with Captain Tobias. He came to me because that brochure proved she was working with the dive captain."

"As for Ranger O'Donnell, I asked him to keep an eye on the Dive Bears when things first started going missing. His apartment is above the crews quarters. He's more aware of my students comings and goings than anyone. He and Chet have been comparing notes."

"Wait. You all knew Sophia was guilty?" Lucy asked

"Professor Erickson came to me this afternoon." Dr. Benitez frowned. "We were going to confront her tomorrow. There must be some reason she's involved in this."

"Oh." Justin squirmed in his seat.

"There are several factors you didn't consider." Dr. Benitez rubbed her temple. "I don't know what to tell Dr. Erickson. He was hoping to keep this quiet, to make things easier on Sophia." There was a door knock. "Speak of the devil."

The three remained on the couch as Dr. Benitez went to open the door.

"Dr. Benitez." Justin recognized Professor Erickson's voice. "I was hoping we could talk about Sophia."

"Of course." She answered. Justin heard a closing door.

"So, we really didn't help?" Rudy asked once they were alone.

"I don't know." Justin stood, walked in a couple circles then sat back down.

"Did that make you feel better?" Lucy asked. Justin didn't respond. He was trying to hear the muffled conversation outside.

Eventually, Dr. Benitez returned, rubbing the bridge of her nose. "It's been an eventful night. You thought you were helping." '*Thought,*' was a gut punch. "Without your brochure trap, it might have taken weeks to catch Sophia. Go to bed. We'll figure things out in the morning."

"Yes mam." Lucy jumped up giving each boy an insistent look. "I'll see you guys tomorrow."

Professor Erickson's lights led them back to their apartment. Rudy shook his head. "Well, things have gone worse."

"They've also gone much better." Justin replied.

CHAPTER 48

THE DAY AFTER

JUSTIN

T HEY HAD CAUGHT THE BAD GUY AND SOLVED A MYSTERY. Yet, Justin couldn't shake feeling that they were missing something. It felt like guilt. They had ended the prospects of a budding archeologist. On top of that, while Dr. Benitez used a cup to water plants in her kitchen, they were waiting for her to decide their punishment. "Lucy will be down in a sec."

"You're up early!" Ranger Benitez leaned on his countertop, stirring his coffee. "Mystery solving must be invigorating."

Rudy leaned in. "They're being really nice. Our punishment must be terrible."

Ranger Benitez took a long sip of coffee. His welcoming expression melted away. He let them stew nervously. Moments passed. Dr. Benitez's gaze was no more sympathetic.

Unable to wait under their intense stares, and still curious, Justin tried a different tact. "What's happening with Sophia?" Better the Benitez's think about her punishment than theirs.

Dr. Benitez leaned back in her chair. "Sophia admitted to *borrowing* university equipment," She made air quotes. "It was part of some deal between her and Captain Tobias."

Ranger Benitez set down his cup, "Captain Tobias offered her a lot of money to help develop his new business venture. She was planning a sabbatical to work on his ship, giving passengers detailed history of wrecks and guiding special dives in the Dry Tortugas. Honestly, not a bad plan."

"Except, Captain Tobias asked for the locations of some our best, secret, wrecks." Dr. Benitez sighed. "Sophia claims she knew nothing about his plan to steal from them."

"You believe her?" Rudy asked.

"I do." Dr. Benitez leaned forward. "She's been having financial problems but she's not a bad kid. The night of your welcome party, she even attempted to return our equipment."

Justin tried to think about his next question, "If Sophia knew about the missing cannon before anyone else, doesn't that prove she was involved?"

"Captain Tobias's tried to trick her. The two had taken two-way radios to coordinate their plans. When the cannon went missing, Captain Tobias radioed her. He claimed he'd woken up early to dive wreck one-twenty-two and that's when he discovered that the cannon were missing."

Justin tapped his chin. The twins really had witnessed the cannon theft! Ranger Benitez poured a new cup of coffee. "But Captain Tobias didn't tell Sophia everything." He turned to his wife with a mischievous grin. "Mind if I show them?"

Dr. Benitez shook her head. "Go ahead."

"Lucia, get down here!" Once his daughter arrived, Ranger Benitez led them outside. "The night the cannon went missing, the Manning's saw lights over the wreck. Captain Tobias anchored out there overnight to pull up every cannon."

Justin nodded. "Luke and Nina saw his boat and their parents radioed you."

Ranger Benitez smiled "But then Luke and Nina went to sleep. Their parents watched the *Horned Devil* until about three am, when it left wreck one-twenty-two and circled Loggerhead to anchor beyond Little Africa."

"Why?" Rudy looked at Mr. Benitez.

"That's what I wanted to know." Mr. Benitez frowned. "Early the next morning, because of Captain Tobias's radio call, Sophia took a student named Paul to dive wreck one-twenty-two. They discovered that the cannon were missing then rushed back to tell Carmen."

Justin frowned. The twins said the boat had been out at the cannon wreck all night. They saw it at wreck one-twenty-two before they went to sleep, and again when they woke up. If their parents had seen the boat move in the middle of the night, how was that possible? Something about this story did not add up.

Ranger Benitez continued. "Carmen confirmed the missing cannon. But when the Manning's told her about the boat's strange movements, she went to investigate the other side of Loggerhead." He led them to the casemates beneath their apartment, winding through old detritus, dry buoys, rusted out bikes, and old engines.

"Anyway, even though it was dark when the *Horned Devil* stole the cannon, Rene Manning was able to show Carmen where it parked the second time: a sandy patch near Little Africa." Ranger Benitez stopped over a large rubber container. There were several of a matching massive size nearby. They were dark green with rubber sides bulged out. Ranger Benitez put his hands on a lid. The container quivered as though full of jelly. "That's where Carmen found these."

He lifted the top. Sunlight shone in at odd angles through the casemate, so it took a moment for Justin's eyes to adjust. "We're keeping them in water because, well, we haven't decided what to do with them." Inside the container was a brown conglomerated mass of rusted tubular metal. "At least we know they haven't left the park." The missing cannon!

Ranger Benitez tapped the plastic container, sloshing water inside. "Captain Tobias figured the guns would be too conspicuous on his boat, so he hid them behind Loggerhead for later pick up. He wasn't counting on the Mannings or Ranger O'Donnell. Lucy's mom found them, then Chet and a couple of my guys brought them back here for safe keeping."

The forklift! Justin and Rudy had been listening to those rangers unloading the cannon for several days in a row! "You asked the Mannings to watch waters west of Little Africa. You were waiting for someone to come back!"

Ranger Benitez crossed his arms. "We're not entirely incompetent investigators ourselves. While you three were off trying to discover Captain Tobias's accomplice, we were simply waiting for him to return and pick up his dumped goods."

Lucy's crossed arms mirrored Ranger Benitez's earlier skepticism. "Sophia didn't know about this?"

"We showed Sophia the guns this morning. She broke down into tears of joy. Makes me believe she's innocent of the cannon theft." He stared into rust-stained seawater. "Although Carmen raised heavy complaints about losing scientific data, it could have been much worse. Better an irresponsible student than a criminal."

Justin watched the cannon appear to shift in the water. "What's going to happen to her?"

"Carmen and Ranger Wendy are escorting Sophia back to Key West. Dr. Carmen Benitez won't throw the book at her students, but Sophia put her entire expedition at risk. There will be consequences."

"What about Captain Tobias?" Justin asked.

Ranger Benitez shrugged. "No one's seen him since the Coast Guard found his boat in Key West."

Justin frowned. "What about Kit's samples?"

Lucy nodded. "Yeah, other than the one Spud found, we haven't seen the rest."

Ranger Benitez scanned the stakes and lines. "That's still a mystery. Probably dumped out at sea."

"Why would Sophia do that?" Lucy asked. Justin stared at the cannon. Something about the way it looked like it was moving beneath the water bothered him.

Ranger Benitez smiled brightly at his daughter. "Now you all know. We had everything in hand. You simply caused things to progress faster than expected."

"Do you think that this will be enough to save Mom's expedition?" Lucy asked.

"Between finding these cannon and catching our culprit, maybe." Ranger Benitez's smile was only a little less spectacular. "I hope so. Now, there's just one question left. We caught the criminals, so what do we do about the investigators?"

CHAPTER 49

MORE CLUES?

LUCY

"YOU'VE PUT US IN A STRANGE POSITION." Lucy's mom leaned against the stairwell entrance. Miguel had walked halfway downstairs, seen her staring over the others and retreated. "I specifically told you to stop your investigation. You didn't. Gabriel told you to leave it alone. You didn't."

"But my lovely and always correct wife reminded me that you were investigating without all of the details, which caused some of our friction." Lucy's dad glanced at his wife confirming their decision. "We're not going to ground you. We're also not going to reward you."

Lucy's mom nodded "You are going to catch up on schoolwork you've been ignoring. We'll also give you extra chores helping U.R.S.A. Think of it as penance. And, of course, we are going to tell your parents about all of this."

Rudy groaned. "Do we have to go home early?"

"That's up to your parents." Lucy's mom crossed her arms. Rudy shivered. Justin looked relieved. Lucy rolled her eyes. The Case family was used to their adventures. He wouldn't be smiling when he learned about her mom's idea of extra chores. Lucy's mom stared. "What are you waiting for? Get your schoolbooks! We need to walk through your assignments before I leave."

Justin and Rudy hustled back to their apartment. Lucy's father went back to work. That left her sitting with her mother, in silence. Eventually her mother sighed theatrically, examining her nails. Lucy raised an eyebrow. Nothing happened. After a moment she finally spoke. "What do you want from me? Another story?"

She frowned when Lucy shook her head. "I can't think of a fitting one. Usually, when I do something wrong, it doesn't lead to positive results. Don't take that to heart. Look, when the boys get back, I'll give you assignments, but I also want you all to take a break. Go play. Celebrate a job well done. Hang out with Luke and Nina."

"The Twins!" Lucy shot up, "We completely forgot to involve them in our final plans!"

"Thank goodness! Two parents who aren't worried about their children confronting criminals!" Her mom laughed. "You can tell them all about it tomorrow night. Your father is planning another big barbeque to put everyone in better spirits." She sighed. "Everyone likes Sophia. This is going to hit them hard."

"Yeah, sorry about that." Lucy sighed.

"Her choices are not your problem. What should concern *you* is that I will hold this disobedience over your head." Her mom raised her hand. "Next time you try to get out of chores, remember that I have this, up here." She pretended to wave an incriminating document.

Upstairs, Lucy found Miguel sitting on the edge of her bed reading something on his phone. "That was oddly unsatisfying."

Her brother grinned. "I thought for sure mom would tell you that story from Egypt when she crawled into a wind tunnel after her dad told her not to."

"That time she found a whole new passage, some crazy hieroglyphics: and another tour group exploring the well-known ruin? A funny story, but I don't know how it relates." Lucy let her smile die. "Where were you?"

"Hiding," Miguel stated flatly. "I haven't been caught up in this yet."

"Coward."

Miguel shrugged her off. "You guys are really close to being in major trouble. Last night, mom was talking about taking the boys back to Key West with her. The only reason she decided not to is because they don't want you on the same boat with Sophia."

"They sounded fine this morning."

Miguel scoffed. "Yeah, they've had time to cool off, but you're walking a tight rope. They're still debating whether or not to send you to Biscayne next month."

"Oh." Lucy was excited to see the boys out here, but she'd especially been looking forward to staying with the Cases soon. "But Amelia and Bethany will be there too!"

"Then better keep on the down low. This exchange homeschooling program could evaporate at any moment." Miguel gave her a sympathetic head pat. He didn't do that often anymore. This time, she allowed it. "Hey manita, do me a favor?"

She backed up and crossed her arms. "I won't like this, will I?"

Miguel snickered. "Tell Justin this is the first time our parents solved a case before J.R.I.C.!"

"I'm not telling him that." Grabbing her books, Lucy left. Downstairs, her mother gave them their assignments. Then she ushered them away.

Throughout the assignment lecture, Lucy could tell something was up with Justin from his serious demeanor. Away from her mom, he frowned. "Grab your snorkel gear. There is something I need to show you."

"What are we looking for?" Rudy plopped himself on the picnic table to make it clear that he wasn't joining them.

"I'm so dumb." Justin frowned. "I completely forgot about the thing I saw in the water." Lucy squeezed into her flippers and waddled after him down to the tide line.

Justin was so excited that he belly-flopped into the first wave. Ignoring schools of tiny fish darting out of their way, he swam past concrete marking the old dock, turning left. Silt and floating bits pulled out of the channel clouded the water. Lucy had to focus on Justin's flashy black and green fins to follow.

Instead of swimming through ruined pilings, Justin carved a straight path out towards the harbor. Reaching deep water, he took a breath before diving. The seafloor sloped sharply until Lucy couldn't see the bottom. What was he looking for? She lifted her head to check around them. No boats, but they were dangerously close to the last swim area buoy. When Justin surfaced, she touched his shoulder. "We shouldn't be out here without a dive flag."

Justin nodded and spat out his snorkel. "We'll go back soon." Sucking an audible gasp of air, he dove again. Following him, Lucy had to pop her ears twice. It only got murkier. She recalled that hammerhead sharks fed on junk collected in deep, murky, channels.

Fortunately, no lurking hammerheads decided to eat her. Justin stopped, nearly crashing mask-first into sand. He pointed to something half buried there: an open metal briefcase. Scattered around it were shards of glass, sparkling with reflected sunlight.

Justin did not resurface until Lucy gave him a thumbs up, proving she'd seen it. Then he arrowed for the ruined pilings and surfaced beside her. "That is what I thought, right?"

"One of Kit's briefcases. And bits of broken vials." Lucy couldn't believe it. "Should we pick them up?"

"Let's leave it for now." Justin frowned. "I don't think diving for broken glass is very smart. Plus, I'm not sure we want everyone to know about them."

Why not? While removing snorkel gear, Lucy informed Rudy of what they had seen.

"A metal briefcase, and Kit's samples?" Rudy asked. "Were they all there?"

"We didn't count shards of wood." Lucy rolled her eyes.

"They were broken. Could the tide do that?" Justin asked.

Lucy frowned thoughtfully. "Probably not. You remember Spud's vial. They are pretty tough."

"So, Sophia smashed them, then dumped them in the harbor? Why?" Justin had forgotten he was still wearing his mask, which made his thoughtful look ridiculous.

"Did Spud's vial float from here over to Loggerhead?" Rudy asked.

"I don't know?" Justin pushed aside his dangling snorkel. "Why wouldn't Sophia simply hide her samples with the other equipment in the hidden room?"

Rudy stared back to the coaling docks. "We should tell your mom before she leaves."

Lucy shook her head, recalling what Miguel had said. "If Mom learns we're still investigating, she'll drag you back to Key West."

Justin frowned. "We are missing something. I intend to figure out what." Lucy recognized his resolve but was more worried about what her mother would think.

CHAPTER 50

OLD SIGHTING, NEW CLUE

JUSTIN

"LEAVE IT ALONE, JUSTIN. The Dive Bears get to stay, and we're not in trouble. The case is over." Justin watched Lucy cram their snorkel gear into a mesh bag storming off towards Fort Jefferson. He turned to Rudy, who still sat atop a picnic table.

Rudy pushed himself up. "Let me know when there are gold doubloons involved. Until then, I've got an afternoon to play games before we start our parole sentence with U.R.S.A."

Justin was left alone and dissatisfied. He couldn't rest until their mystery was complete. He spent the afternoon wandering. He went to investigate the room where Sophia had kept her stolen belongings, but a sawhorse was set up to block the entrance. He could move it but didn't want to get in more trouble.

Dinner was quiet. Dr. Benitez was gone and everyone else kept to themselves. They split-up. Justin tried to call his sister. She finally texted back saying she'd be around to talk the next day. She didn't ask about his mystery at all. He let Rudy rope him into a couple of hours of games online with Miguel, and Amelia in the Everglades.

Chet pounded on their door early next morning. He rushed them through breakfast so they could help move 'borrowed' equipment back to the map room.

They helped U.R.S.A. students for several hours, but none of the Dive Bears seemed to know what to do with them, and no one wanted to talk about Sophia.

Justin knew Mr. Benitez was hoping his barbeque would cheer everyone up, but something still felt off. When Miguel came to collect them for dinner, Justin waved his friends away. "I'll be there in a while." He had to call his sister.

"Let me get this straight." Cassidy's voice sounded tinny, but he could see her confused and freckled face clearly. "You solved a mystery, just the three of you, and that makes you sad?" She played meticulously with the tail of her long braid as a young woman behind her balanced precariously on her bed while hanging a poster.

Justin sighed, "It doesn't feel like we did anything."

Cassidy pursed her lips, crossed her eyes, and stuck out her tongue teasingly. "Not every mystery ends in a big chase, a wildfire, or by rolling down a massive hill into a lake." Cassidy's roommate turned to stare. Justin waved. She turned away. "It's a good thing too, otherwise J.R.I.C. would have been disbanded by the parents years ago."

"I'm not an adrenaline junky, Cass."

"No, that's Lucy's thing." She stared through her monitor. "So, what's bothering you?"

Justin ran his hands through his hair, "Money troubles or not, Sophia might be banned from archaeology forever. Who would risk that for a couple thousand dollars and a job as a tour guide?"

"Well," his sister cleared her throat. "You know our Case family motto."

Cassidy's roommate gave them a brief confused glance. "Trust your gut," Justin nodded.

"Look, you've solved mysteries, rescued animals and people, and uncovered plots without me before." She was speaking truthfully. "Do you think, maybe, you're being too hard on yourself because this was your first turn as lead investigator?"

Justin lowered his head.

Cassidy held up a blue notebook, similar to his orange one, shaking it. "I got the photos you attached from your birders journal. I'm envious: blue-footed booby, roseate spoonbill, indigo bunting, and purple martin!" She made another face. "Although, you don't have to list every separate brown pelican."

"Even if they are juvenile, and still have their white feathers?"

"My point is that you started off with so many bird sightings," She held up her phone, with a picture of a nearly empty page from his journal. "As this mystery continued, your sighting dropped off. Did the birds disappear?" Cassidy shook her head. "I bet you developed an intense laser investigation focus and forgot about everything else."

"Maybe." Justin pulled his journal from his pocket. "By the way, I'm not the leader."

"Neither was I, but Lucy gets bored if she can't run headfirst into suspects. Rudy would be a great leader if every mystery involved treasures, secret codes, and internet searches." She shrugged, "The rest of J.R.I.C. isn't there. That leaves you."

"What about Miguel?"

"Well, I was talking with Miguel a couple days ago."

"I know." Justin smiled. Was that a hint of crimson on Cassidy's face?

His sister sighed, "We, kind of, agreed to stay out of this one, so you guys could solve it."

"Miguel wasn't just being lazy?" Justin tapped his chin. "You told him to leave us alone?"

Cassidy laughed. "Miguel thought you guys were doing a fine job. You saved an archeological expedition!" She waited for Justin to agree. He didn't. She sighed, "and still?"

"Something's off."

"So, trust your gut." Cassidy's roommate was behind her now, sitting on her bed cross-legged, a bag of chips in her lap, and staring. "What is your biggest outstanding question?"

Justin frowned at his investigation charts. He had circled the question about the twin's story of the cannon thief: *Two Boats?* But that didn't feel like the most important question. "Why would Sophia dump Kit's samples in the harbor?"

"Now you have a thread to work with." Cassidy glanced at something on screen. "Anyway bro, I've got to go. Whether you stop here or uncover some grand conspiracy, I'm just proud our mystery solving continues." Justin felt a tingle of warmth from her endorsement. "I have to say it because Dad and Mom worry praise encourages more reckless behavior." Cassidy winked, "They're right. Bye-now."

Before Cassidy closed her laptop, Justin heard her roommate ask. "Your brother solves mysteries?"

Justin didn't hear Cassidy's response. She was gone, but now he knew where to start. If only he knew how. He sat back, enjoying a rare moment alone in the shared apartment. What next?

CHAPTER 51

THE END?

RUDY

Tonight's party was an odd mixture of celebration and mourning. Chet sat alone staring at a solitary burger. Professor Erickson wore a scowl plastered across his face. The other Dive Bears were either excited their expedition was saved or depressed and angry about Sophia and the damage she had done to their work and reputation.

Park rangers and associates, some of whom must have arrived that day—because Rudy didn't recognize them—had picked up their somber mood. Only the Mannings seemed particularly upbeat. Their parents went to speak with Ranger Benitez. Spud began his rounds looking for hand-outs while Luke and Nina beelined for them.

"I heard you guys solved the mystery." Luke took a bite from a deviled egg.

Nina shook her head. "Too bad we weren't here to see it go down."

She sounded too bubbly to be disappointed. Rudy stared. "How much do you guys know?"

"A little," Luke spaced his answer between bites of egg.

"Who was working with Captain Tobias?" Nina glanced around the smaller crowd. Rudy winced, realizing several Dive Bears could hear her.

The End?

"Sophia Yang." Chet answered glumly. "I still can't believe it." Rudy was expecting anger or resentment. Instead, he stared into his plate sadly, "I should, um, thank you."

"Why?" Rudy asked.

"Well, for recovering that underwater camera. I thought, maybe, I had lost it." Chet pounded his fist on the table, "Why would Sophia steal from U.R.S.A.?"

"Sophia meant to return everything." Rudy recognized Lucy's sympathetic voice. "She was just scared of being caught."

Chet grumbled. "We were trying to help her. When the cannon disappeared, we dropped everything to help her find a second wreck."

Barbara sidled over, resting a comforting arm around Chet's shoulders. "We had no idea she was at fault."

"Sophia didn't know Captain Tobias was going to steal anything." Lucy ventured.

"What's your mom going to do about her?" Chet asked.

Lucy pursed her lips but didn't answer. Dr. Benitez had spent the morning typing a list of a dozen rules Sophia had broken. "Sophia will read these on the boat ride back. I want her to know how much harm she's caused!"

Professor Erickson stood, interrupting Chet's depression. "Attention everyone. Attention." He waited for everyone to take their seats, before clearing his throat. "I wanted to address the elephant, ahem, on the island. One of our own was caught stealing university equipment and conspiring to steal artifacts." He hung his head. "Sophia was my student. I feel personally responsible." A low murmur rumbled through the crowd.

He raised his hand, silencing them. "I know you all want answers." He waited for nods and muttered agreement. "Sophia's actions jeopardized our whole trip, but neither Dr. Benitez nor I believe she acted maliciously. We've decided not to press criminal charges. Instead, she will answer to an academic court of ethics."

There were several groans but also some excited rumbles from the crowd. "All three of her mentors will stand with her and encourage her to make amends. It's possible Sophia will be able to avoid any serious trouble."

"Fat chance." Chet whispered under his breath. "They'll make an example out of her."

Professor Erickson cleared his throat, "now, what happens next?" The Dive Bears sank even lower into their seats. "I've spoken with both Mr. Ishii and Mr. Howard." An older ranger, whom Rudy hadn't seen before, moved to stand beside Professor Erickson. "We've also discussed this with Dr. Benitez and Dr. Kapur. In light of everything, we have decided U.R.S.A.'s work is over. We are going home."

Rudy felt something sink in his stomach as the chatter rose around him. "I thought we'd saved the expedition." There were shocked glances from rangers and other guests.

Professor Erickson held up his hands. "It's a hard, but necessary decision. Intentional or not, Sophia has damaged Park resources. We must repair our relationship with the Park Service, recover what information we have, and revise our plans so nothing like this ever happens again."

"What about the rest of my research?" "This is too soon." Several students raised voices in protest. "I can't leave my project yet!"

Professor Erickson shouted. "Enough! This is decided. The motor vessel *Fort Jefferson* is coming out, off schedule, to help us take everything back to the mainland. Work together. Finish what you can. Preserve your work for future follow up. We leave in three days." He turned away, leaving students to process his announcement.

"What about Dr. Benitez?" Lucy turned to Chet.

"I don't know." Chet shook his head. "This is first I've heard about this." He stood to follow Professor Erickson. Lucy rushed after him.

"It seems we missed more than I thought." Nina turned to Rudy, "what happened?"

Rudy pulled the twins over to a table vacated by distraught students. "I'll give you a quick rundown." He told the twins about everything they had done and learned while the students around them were in chaos.

When Lucy returned, the twins were up to date, and Gwen had managed to corral the Dive Bears into order.

"Will your mother be staying, at least?" Nina asked.

"He wouldn't tell me," Lucy frowned.

Miguel had sat in silence since the announcement. "Duh, mom is going back. It's her expedition. She's ultimately responsible for everything that's happened."

Justin suddenly appeared behind Rudy, "What did I miss?"

CHAPTER 52

THE MYSTERY CONTINUES

LUCY

"**D**O YOU THINK WE CAN MAKE THEM honorary members of J.R.I.C.?" Lucy was trying to distract herself. They were watching the twins play with Spud. "Luke and Nina helped us find clues, and Spud would be a great mascot."

"I guess." Justin had been lost in thought since Rudy had explained Professor Erickson's announcement to him.

"So can they join J.R.I.C.?" Lucy waved her hand in front of his face. "Justin?"

Justin shook his head, "Sure, but let's not get sidetracked. We need to talk somewhere private. Let's go to the small powder magazine."

"Do we have to?" Rudy asked.

Once they were in the dark brick corridor and sounds were muffled, Justin spoke. "There is definitely something else going on and Cassidy agrees." Lucy crossed her arms making a face. "Ok," he admitted. "She didn't exactly agree, but she told me to go with my gut. My gut says our investigation isn't over."

"So?" Lucy tried to suppress her frustration. "Because of us, U.R.S.A. is still going home."

"That's not our fault." Justin protested, "Sophia's the troublemaker, we only caught her."

"I…" Lucy paused. Several footsteps echoed in the small corridor with claws clicking on brick. "Spud!" Forgetting what she was going to say, she leaned down to beckon the labradoodle.

Luke and Nina followed in the dog's wake. "We saw you guys sneak off." Nina explained. "What are you up to?"

Justin nodded. "Our investigation's not over."

"How can we help?" Luke asked eagerly.

His excitement made Lucy smile. "See, they would be a fantastic addition to our club."

Justin grinned. "Maybe. First, are you two sure that you saw a boat on wreck one-twenty-two at night, and again in the morning?"

"Yeah." Luke nodded. "Why?"

Lucy quickly explained about the recovered cannon and her dad's plan to catch Captain Tobias. Nina grinned. "So, we were helping his investigation and yours? Cool!"

"But there's a problem." Justin explained. "If the boat moved the cannon, why was there a boat on wreck one-twenty-two when you woke up?"

"What are you getting at?" Lucy crossed her arms feeling defensive. "You don't think they're lying now, do you?"

Justin shook his head. "No, but what if the boat the twins saw in the morning was a second boat?"

"What would that mean?" Lucy asked.

Justin shrugged. "I don't know yet."

"Well…" Nina hesitated. "Couldn't you just ask Sophia?"

Luke nodded, turning to Lucy, "She's staying with your mom in Key West, right?"

"Good investigators interview their suspects." Nina nodded.

Lucy ruffled Spud's ears, "Our suspects are usually dangerous adults. We try not to interview them. We gather info and then explain everything we know to someone with a badge."

Yet, Lucy could see a list of questions already piling up behind Justin's eyes. Nina beamed. "If you need any more advice, let us know. We're staying the night here in the fort so Mr. O'Donnell can help mom and dad install our new engine tomorrow."

"I can't believe that grumpy ranger is helpful." Rudy gave Spud a couple pets.

"Mr. O'Donnell's cool. He's about to take shore leave to be with his wife, so he's taking an entire day off to help us with engine installation."

"Where is Spud staying?" Lucy asked.

"Spud will stay on our boat, since doggies aren't really supposed to be in the guest apartments." The dog turned when Luke said his name.

"Doggie allergies and such." Nina explained through a yawn, "We'll be staying in an apartment beside yours. It used to be Professor Alexa's before she left. Just don't ask us to do anything tonight. We've been up since five a.m."

"Anyway, enough standing in creepy dark hallways." Luke yawned, "We're going to take our pooch back to the boat and then turn in. If you need any help, let us know."

"Starting tomorrow." Nina patted her hip, and her dog turned to follow. "Come on Spud."

"I liked their idea." As they left, Justin turned to Lucy. "Do you think your mom would let us talk to Sophia?"

CHAPTER 53

A RELUCTANT ACCOMPLICE

LUCY

"KEEP IT BRIEF." Lucy's mom glanced down at her phone. Lucy had taken them to the map room so they could use a university computer, "I'm curious what Sophia will tell you, but I'm also incredibly angry at her."

"Understood, Mama." Lucy felt goosebumps conjured by her mother's voice.

"Alright, here you go."

Sophia took her phone. Lucy was shocked by the young woman's new demeanor. She wasn't grumpy anymore. It looked like she'd been crying. "Yeah?"

"Hi Sophia." Lucy tried to keep her voice friendly. "We have questions."

"Okay." She sounded neither enthusiastic nor resistant.

Lucy looked down at Justin's list. They had decided she would ask questions since she'd known Sophia longest. "Why did you take U.R.S.A.'s stuff?"

Sophia sighed. "Like I told your mother, I wanted a summer job with Captain Tobias. I was taking my own pictures and making maps of every interesting wreck."

"All for a brochure?" Justin interrupted.

"No." She looked down. "I was preparing digital presentations for my tours. They were going to be educational and adventurous. Toby wanted to cater to an affluent market."

"Toby?" Rudy asked, leaning into frame. "Oh, Captain Tobias!"

Lucy pushed him out of her way. "Why did you hide everything in the powder magazine?"

"When Gwen couldn't find her camera, she panicked. So did Chet. We spent days looking for it. I wanted to sneak it back to U.R.S.A., but by then Mr. Howard had bought us another. Later, I realized that I needed to borrow other things." She blushed. "It became really hard to take anything back. I couldn't just drag everything out and say: 'look what I found!'"

"Were you just going to leave it all to rot in that abandoned room?" Lucy's mother interrupted angrily.

Sophia looked apologetic, "Once I was done, I was going to leave a letter telling everyone where to find our equipment." She hesitated. "When Dr. Benitez said that we were leaving because of me I tried to sneak everything back, but someone chased me out of the fort."

"That was us." Rudy waved.

Sophia hung her head "After that, I stopped trying."

Lucy leaned forward. "So, why did you steal Kit's samples?"

Sophia shook her head. "I didn't."

Lucy turned her back on the student. Her friends both seemed as surprised as she was. "Did you dump them in the ocean?"

"Dump them? What are you talking about?" Sophia asked.

"Mama," Lucy called. "We found Kit's briefcase in the harbor. It was surrounded by shattered sample vials."

Her mother pulled her phone back from Sophia. "Is that true?"

Justin scooted next to Lucy, leaning in to be seen. "Yes, Dr. Benitez."

"I didn't have anything to do with that." Sophia protested off screen.

Justin let out an audible, "Hmmm."

"I mean, why would I?" Sophia continued. Tired of aiming her phone at Sophia, Lucy's mother gave it back.

"That's a good question." Justin conceded. "Lucy, ask her the next one."

"Did you know Captain Tobias was going to steal the cannon?"

"Absolutely not." Sophia shook her head. "I believed him when he told me that they were missing. It wasn't until he disappeared that I realized he had stolen them." She breathed deeply. "When Ranger Benitez showed me that the cannon were still in the park, I was so relieved."

"Why would Captain Tobias move or steal the cannon?" Justin asked.

Sophia stared into the camera. "I don't know. You printed my brochure. You know my cannon wreck was going to be a highlight of our dive tours."

"How could we know that?" Justin asked. "Your brochure didn't mention them at all."

"Not the draft, the final copy." Sophia sighed. Lucy felt Justin straighten up beside her. "When Rudy pointed out your flashlights, I was afraid Dr. Benitez had found my hiding place. When I saw it was just you, I tried to act surprised so I could pretend to find everything with you." Her sad smile was surprisingly pitiful. "But when I saw my finished brochure, I realized that you had printed evidence."

Lucy recalled the glossy sheets in the dusty room. "We didn't print those finished brochures."

Justin's nervous fidgeting shook the back of Lucy's seat. Sophia's brow furrowed in confusion. "Well, I didn't. I certainly wouldn't have printed anything with mine or Toby's name." She scoffed. "That final draft was in a hidden file." She turned to Lucy's mother. "Dr. Benitez, I'm sorry. Things just got so confusing when the cannon went missing."

"Maybe Captain Tobias stole and dumped the samples." Justin suggested.

"Why?" Sophia frowned. "Carbon dating wouldn't help our dive tours."

"Hmm." Justin hummed again.

"Sophia, I think we're done." Lucy's mother took her phone back politely, sternly kicking Sophia from the room. Once her student was gone, she glared at them through the screen. "I believe her."

Lucy nodded. "I do too."

Lucy's mother frowned deeply. "Lucy. I know you three. Don't do any more investigating without telling your father. In fact, don't do anything. I will be back in two days. We will figure this out then. Okay?"

Lucy's response was interrupted by a frightened Rudy squeak, and another voice, "What are you kids doing in here?"

"Oh, it's just you." Rudy recovered. Standing in the arched hallway was Professor Erickson. "I thought you were a ghost."

Professor Erickson grimaced, but he mustered a smile. "Just an old professor." Lucy hadn't even heard the door open. Judging by her friends' shock, neither had they. "Is that your mother?"

"Hello Dr. Erickson." Lucy's mother responded through her phone. "We're done anyway. Give me about fifteen minutes. Lucy, Justin, and Rudy, remember what I said. I'll be back in a couple of days."

"Okay Mama." With that, her mother disappeared.

"Wrapping up your investigation?" The professor asked.

"Tying up a few loose ends. Anyway, we'll see you later." Turning to Lucy and Rudy, Justin motioned over his shoulder, "Come on guys."

As they were leaving, Chet entered. Lucy heard Professor Erickson scold him. "What did I tell you about locking these doors? Especially now!"

"Sorry professor." Lucy felt the map room key in her pocket—she'd never returned it to Gwen—and felt a slight tinge of guilt.

CHAPTER 54

DEFINITELY NOT TWO DAYS LATER

JUSTIN

THEY SHOULD WAIT. In two days, Lucy's mother would return, and they could investigate together. Instead, Justin settled onto a picnic table outside their apartment. "We need to review our clues. We've obviously missed something."

Rudy nodded sullenly. "If we don't *actually* solve this, Cassidy, Miguel, and the others will never let us live it down." Wind whistled through brick arches.

"And Mama will leave." Lucy watched large waves crash against the moat wall.

"This is frustrating." Justin leaned into the table. "All our clues fit so well, until they didn't."

"If we could catch Captain Tobias, we could ask him about everything." Lucy sighed.

"Let's ask Miguel to take us out on your dad's boat and round him up." Rudy was trying to lighten their mood. "A J.R.I.C. manhunt at sea!"

Lucy shook her head. "Normally, I would be all over that idea, but we wouldn't know where to find him, and this weather is rough. I hope Spud will be alright alone on the sailboat."

Rudy chuckled glumly. "You're right. We'd get lost searching for a ghost ship."

A frustrated growl rumbled in Lucy's throat. "We started this case to save Mom and the Dive Bears, but they're leaving anyway. And now that she knows someone else is making trouble, she'll never bring students out here again!"

A glum mood settled over the table. "We can figure this out." Justin leapt up startling his friends. "Give me a second." He rushed into their apartment to grab their charts.

"First, we need to cross out everything Sophia admitted to." Justin struck those out. "Now list the things Sophia claimed she didn't do: stealing Kit's samples and printing that final brochure."

"Or stealing the cannon." Lucy sighed, "Could Captain Tobias have done all those things alone?"

Justin shook his head. "He wasn't here to print that final brochure. Who else has access to the map room?"

Lucy shook her head solemnly, "Mom's head will explode, but I think we're looking for another student."

"If these were our only two crimes," Rudy ventured, pointing at: missing samples and mapping equipment. "I would think someone was doing a secret excavation."

"You just want to turn this into pirates." Lucy crossed her arms and rolled her eyes.

Justin cleared his throat interrupting them before an argument blossomed. "What if Rudy's right?"

"Yes!" Rudy leaned in excitedly. "What if someone is looking for pirate treasure?"

Lucy slumped lower in her seat, ignoring him. "If U.R.S.A. students were doing a covert expedition, we're looking for at least two people. Mom doesn't allow students to take university boats out alone."

"Students," Justin considered that word while running faces through his mind. No one at the party tonight seemed particularly guilty, mostly sad or angry, but "What about professors? Professor Erickson's excavating wreck one-fourteen by himself, right?"

"You think Professor Erickson is our criminal?" Lucy asked.

"No. But the two students thing is just a rule, right? Obviously, Sophia broke it to photograph wrecks with a stolen camera. If she and the professor can both work solo, so could someone else." Justin slumped on the table, "But who, and why? Do we have any brochures left?"

Lucy pulled out another copy of their unfinished brochures—one without pictures. Not the one they had found with Sophia's stash of stolen goods. "The final version had photos from the underwater camera, Sophia's name, and *Horned Devil Tours*. None of that stuff was in the files we took from the map room."

Justin nodded, "Why would Sophia print one to hide with the rest of the things she'd stolen? Someone who knew about our investigation wanted us to catch Sophia."

"Everybody knew about our investigation!" Rudy threw up his hands, "They were all spying for your parents!"

Justin waved the brochure, "I only care about the people who knew about these."

"That would be Barbara, Chet, and Sophia," Lucy began to count on her fingers. "And the people they showed it to, like Professor Erickson and Ranger O'Donnell."

"Professor Erickson again." Justin stared into a dark, neighboring apartment. "Rudy, you said he asked you about our investigations."

"Yeah. When I didn't go to Loggerhead." Rudy nodded. "I went to ask the professor about Kit's carbon samples. He showed me a crazy letter from the 1600s, then we talked about J.R.I.C."

"What did the professor say about Kit's samples?" Justin asked.

"What letter?" Lucy asked at the same time.

Their voices merged. Rudy hesitated, unsure who to respond to first. "Well, the professor told me Kit's tests were wrong. Then I saw this cool copy of a destroyed letter written in Spanish. Professor Erickson said it was written by some guy from the 1622 treasure fleet."

"A carbon date from the 1600s and a letter from that same time period. Professor Erickson claimed these weren't related?" Lucy crossed her arms.

"Kit's samples were stolen, and now we know they were destroyed." Justin scratched his chin, "But the Professor gave Kit extras from his wreck somehow."

"Yeah." Rudy nodded. Justin frowned again, trying to think.

"I want to know more about the letter." Lucy stared at him.

"It was just a copy written by a guy named Caesar. The only word I recognized was pirate. Professor Erickson told me the translation mentioned a ship called the *Magdalene* which was part of 1622 fleet and sank in the Dry Tortugas. He thinks she was a secret treasure ship."

"Really?" Lucy crossed her arms skeptically.

Staring at their table full of evidence, suspects, and clues, while listening to his friends Justin's mind began to buzz. "Professor Erickson's team uses blue flags, right?"

"Yeah." Lucy answered.

"That sample vial we found had a blue cap?" Justin nodded, answering his own question. "Rudy, when Sophia and Professor Erickson were talking, did she mention her secret room?"

"I don't know. I didn't hear everything they said."

"Professor Erickson is Sophia's mentor. He knew more about what she was up to than anyone else." Justin narrowed his eyes. "He didn't want anyone to see his wreck, and when his sample dates were *wrong*: Kit's samples disappeared, and he got new ones."

"He told me the new dates would make sense." Rudy nodded.

Justin checked his chart, and the small timeline Lucy had sketched at the bottom. He stared at a cartoon dog. "Spud's clue appeared the same day Professor Erickson gave Kit new samples. Maybe we didn't find one of Kit's samples. What if the professor was taking *new* samples from his wreck and lost one?"

Lucy's brow furrowed. "And that lost vial floated to Loggerhead where Spud found it. But why would the Professor need to take his own samples?"

Justin turned back to Rudy, "I want to see this letter."

CHAPTER 55

A CLANDESTINE OPERATION

LUCY

JUSTIN STOOD FIRST. "Sure," Lucy sighed, "why not break into my mom's colleagues' apartment? I want her to ground me forever."

"Lucy has a point." Rudy gathered their charts, crinkling paper loudly. "I don't want to get in more trouble."

Justin exhaled forcefully, "But it makes sense, right? We've been watching students. Well, professors have the same access. And Professor Erickson has more reason than anyone to dislike Kit's samples since his results were crazy."

"So, Professor Erickson destroyed Kit's samples so people couldn't learn the truth about his wreck?" Rudy's voice rose with excitement.

"Rudy, volume!" Lucy loudly whispered. "Why would the professor hide the age of his wreck?"

"Why ask?" Justin shrugged. "Rudy thinks Professor Erickson's samples came from a secret treasure ship."

"Oh, and if he was always driving the boat by himself, it would have been easy for him to dump Kit's samples in the harbor." Rudy grinned.

"Right." Why hadn't Justin thought about that? "Then his spare samples could have come from anywhere, to get whatever dates he wanted.

But he'd need his own sampling tool."

Rudy nodded. "He had one."

"You're only telling us this now?" Justin hesitated.

"I didn't think it was important. Everyone keeps saying Kit's the only one who can do carbon dating." Rudy shrugged. "But you reminded me, I saw a tool like that in there." He pointed to Professor Erickson's apartment.

"Professor Erickson has been working wreck one-fourteen all by himself." Once Justin had a suspect in his sights, he wouldn't let them go until proven wrong. He was like his sister in that way.

"He has been very secretive about that wreck." Lucy nodded, hesitantly standing. "Are we sure? I'd rather investigate someone else: like another student or even Ranger O'Donnell."

Rudy was already ahead of her, pressed against the door, trying to make out anything in the dark. "Then again, what if he's in there asleep?"

Lucy let out a low grumble "He's in the map room, remember?" Frustrated out of her fear of punishment, she pushed past him to grip the door handle. It turned. "Unlocked. If we're going to do this, let's be quick!"

"Come on, I'll show you the letter." Rudy rushed in, phone light first, aiming it at stacks of papers on the kitchen counter.

Lucy scanned the cluttered apartment, "How long will this take?"

"I don't know." Rudy whispered back beginning to sift through a pile of papers.

Lucy's eyes fell on Professor Erickson's laptop. "I'll check incriminating files."

Justin nodded, moving to a kitchen table piled with books and papers, leaving a small space for dirty breakfast dishes. "There's a chart here. Professor Erickson has marked the *Atocha* wreck and the *Nuestra de Rosario*?"

"Ha!" Rudy paused his search. "Those are both ships from the 1622 fleet."

Justin focused on the map. "He's marked a few others too, including his brick wreck, number one-fourteen, and Sophia's cannon wreck."

"Got them!" Rudy pulled a book off the professor's microwave, and confidently slid two sheets of paper from between its pages, handing them to Justin.

Justin squinted at the papers he'd been handed. "Rudy's right, this letter talks about a treasure and pirates."

Lucy took the Spanish photocopy. It was hard to read. The paper was damaged by age and the handwriting was intense. "They really wrote fancy back then, didn't they?" She concentrated. "Rudy, what did the professor tell you about this letter?"

"He said that some guy named Caesar was trying to trick another guy named Gaspar de Vargas into recovering treasure." Rudy furrowed his brow.

"Well, it is from someone called Caesar." That singular name was the only signature. "But I don't think he was trying to trick de Vargas. It sounds like they were working together."

"Really?" Rudy asked.

"He's asking de Vargas to remain silent about a ship called the *Nuestra Senora Magdalene.*" Justin held up the translation reading it's final sentence. "*If you tell others about her, they will inform agents of the crown and we will both hang.*"

Lucy confirmed the translation, nodding. "Caesar claims to be captain of the *Magdalene.* He even thanks de Vargas for rescue, but then he asks to be counted as crew of the *Rosario* and tells de Vargas not to mention his ship."

"Why?" Rudy asked.

"He wanted to keep the *Magdalene* secret. Caesar tells De Vargas that his ship and her treasure are hidden. He says that they will both be labeled Pirates if the truth comes out." Justin cocked his head. "How do you hide a ship?"

"I don't know." Lucy held up the paper, looking at Rudy. "My mom doesn't know about any of this. She loves crazy theories and would definitely have mentioned it."

Rudy frowned. "Professor Erickson said she knew about the letter."

"Then he lied." Lucy waved the paper.

Justin nodded "True. If your mom was hunting a super cool pirate treasure, she'd tell everyone. Then she'd make us memorize a rulebook explaining why everything belonged in a museum."

Lucy took a deep breath. "I'm trying to process a world in which there might actually be a pirate treasure."

"A world where I am right?" Rudy grinned.

"Did Professor Erickson find the *Magdalene?*" Lucy asked.

Rudy shook his head. "He didn't say. He took those letters away after

I saw them. I should have known he was hiding something."

Justin began combing through stacks of papers eagerly. Lucy cleared her throat. "Stop. Put everything back. We don't want Professor Erickson to know we searched his stuff."

"Here, I know where those letters went." Rudy shoved them back into the book, then set it on the microwave. This caused another stack of papers to fall. "Hey guys, what's this?" He held up a document displaying a word: *TRIDENT*.

"It's a check, made out to Professor Erickson, but it's not from the university." Justin dug through some of the other papers on the ground. "Most of these are marked with Trident. Have we heard of them before?"

"No?" Lucy checked the photo-copied letter in her hands. The word *TRIDENT* had been stamped in small print on the back.

"Are they an evil organization?" Rudy offered.

"Let me see," Lucy pushed him out of her way to riffle through the spilled papers. There was lots of stuff about treasure fleets including more documents in Spanish, French and a language she didn't recognize. "Maybe Trident is the group doing the professor's translations."

"Why would they be paying him?" Justin held up the check. "Suspicious." He set it aside, "but not enough."

"Did you find anything on his computer?" Rudy skittered over, taking Lucy's chair.

"I'm not sure we should mess with the computer." Justin glanced out the window.

"Relax, I'll just do a quick scan for: Evil Plans." Instead, Rudy typed 'Atocha' and then 'Caesar.' He clicked on the first document to appear. It was a historical record. The next was a slide show about Spanish history and treasure fleets.

"Look for documents Professor Erickson has authored." Justin leaned behind his chair tapping it with nervous determination, "Maybe drafts of emails."

"You think he types drafts of emails before sending them?" Lucy turned to her friend.

"I do." Justin replied.

Rudy interrupted their teasing. "I found an academic paper?" He turned back to Lucy for confirmation.

"Yeah. That looks like the university's format." Lucy read the title. "*The*

Discovery of a Conspiracy: A Pirate Inside the Fleet of 1622." She breathed in. "This can't be real."

Rudy began to vibrate in his chair. "I told you! Justin, look at this."

Justin's gaze was focused out the window. Following his stare, Lucy saw Professor Erickson and Chet standing outside the crews quarters. "Rudy, open your email and send everything in that file to me. Fast."

"What's wrong?" Rudy asked.

"Just do it." Justin urged. "Professor Erickson is coming."

"Yipes!" Rudy opened the browser and began clicking through files as fast as he could.

"Close his blinds." Justin whispered, "He'll see light from the monitor." Lucy nodded. A few minutes passed. Justin peeked through closed blinds. "How long are those two going to talk?"

"I don't know." Lucy replied. "As the two most senior archeologists, they probably have a lot of planning to do." A tense minute passed with only clacking keys sounding in the darkness. "I think they're finished."

"So am I." Rudy pushed back in his chair.

"Great. Close everything and clear his internet and activity history." Lucy backed away from the window replacing everything they'd touched. "Let's go." She whispered harshly holding the door as Justin and Rudy crept outside.

Rudy shuddered, "I forgot to put his computer to sleep." Inside the monitor blazed into the darkness.

"Too late." Lucy hissed, "come on." They rushed back to their apartment.

Once safely inside, Lucy jumped to sit atop their table, almost knocking Rudy off balance as he leaned back in his chair. "Well?"

"Yeah." It was Justin's turn to take a deep breath.

"If you guys aren't going to say it, I will. There is a pirate treasure, and Professor Erickson found it." Rudy's celebration was interrupted by Professor Erickson's door slamming shut.

CHAPTER 56

ALL SIGNS POINT TO

RUDY

RUDY RUBBED HIS HANDS TOGETHER, excited to explore everything he'd taken from the professor's computer. "I bet there's a secret treasure map, a letter to an evil organization, and a full statement about his plot."

"Dial it down about a thousand." Lucy pushed his chair back to the floor.

"Hopefully, we find something." Justin sucked in a breath of air. "If not, then it looks like we just broke into an innocent man's apartment."

Rudy began opening tons of new documents, pictures, and pdfs. "Where to start?"

"Try that scientific paper we were reading earlier." Lucy suggested. "It should have an abstract."

"The summary at the beginning?" Rudy enjoyed Lucy's look of surprise. "I know what an abstract is." They leaned into the screen. He began to read the introduction aloud. Suddenly, three knocks slammed against the door. He froze, startled.

Had Professor Erickson discovered their trespass? Rudy turned slowly to see a face pressed comically against the window.

"Miguel!" Lucy marched forward slamming the door. "You scared the crap out of us!"

"Good." Miguel rubbed his forehead. "It's late." He stared at both boys and the laptop between them. "What are you guys looking at?" Rudy moved his computer so Miguel could see. "Huh."

The first paper was a bust. Everything was hypothesis this, theory that. Either Professor Erickson hadn't found anything, or he was keeping his secret out of professional papers. "Maybe it's in one of these other documents."

Lucy growled. "It will take forever to find any important bits."

"So, you snuck into the professor's room, hacked into his computer, stole his files, and found nothing?"

"It wasn't hacking." Rudy argued. "Lucy simply turned his computer on."

"Don't pin this on me. You were the one who stole these." Lucy stared at his screen. "There's got to be something here." Most of the papers had been written by other archeologists. Two were translations of salvage contracts written by the Spanish government. Maybe they were secretly interesting, but Rudy was finding it hard to stay awake. He yawned.

"We're not going to find an answer tonight." Miguel cleared his throat. "Dad just talked to mom. Now he's worried about you. He practically tackled Professor Erickson downstairs before sending me up here to get Lucy."

"Professor Erickson?" Lucy asked. "What did Dad say?"

Miguel frowned. "He didn't mention you guys. But he did warn Professor Erickson that U.R.S.A. might still be in danger."

"So, the professor knows our case isn't closed?" Justin shook the back of Rudy's seat.

"I found something!" Rudy opened a file titled: *FINISHED*. "Will this help?"

"That's Sophia's brochure!" Justin leaned in, "But not what we printed. It's the complete copy, like the one we found in the hidden room with pictures of the cannon wreck."

"Professor Erickson has a final draft of Sophia's brochure?" Lucy leaned closer.

"It's proof! He knew about Sophia. He printed this to frame her." Justin stood excitedly.

Miguel interrupted their excitement, "To play devil's advocate, Sophia could have given him that brochure when she confessed her mistakes to him."

"That's possible." Justin conceded.

"Back to work." Rudy rolled his eyes. Minutes passed. Miguel began impatiently tapping his feet. Lucy slumped into her chair. Justin's constant yawning grew annoying. Rudy cleared his throat. "How about this?" Everyone stirred. "There are two different documents labeled Wreck one-fourteen."

His three friends pressed closer. He opened the first. There was a long wall of text. Rudy's scrolled down until he found an illustration mapped out one a grid. "That's the way Mom taught her student to draw their wrecks." Lucy squinted. "This would have been the first thing Professor Erickson did on his survey."

Rudy pointed to the drawing. "A brick wreck should have stacks of bricks, right?"

"Right." Lucy affirmed. "Those aren't bricks."

"Is it Sophia's cannon wreck?" Justin pointed to two cylindrical objects in the drawing. "Those look like cannon."

"No. There were a lot more than three cannon on Sophia's wreck. You saw the pictures." Lucy shook her head. "Read that caption."

Fig. 1.B Secondary Wreck Found Beneath Brick Wreck 114.

"There's a second wreck!" Rudy exclaimed.

"That's not all." Lucy pointed. "Look at this chart." It was a chart of carbon dates. She read aloud, "_The wood has been dated to the year 1600 plus or minus forty years._ But Kit didn't do these carbon dates." She frowned. "The chart says they came from a lab in New Mexico."

"We've got him!" Rudy exclaimed again. "He has some kind of evil plan to keep a pirate treasure for himself."

"What treasure? I don't see any piles of gold." Miguel shook his head. "Maybe Professor Erickson is saving this second wreck as some sort of surprise."

Rudy did a quick search. "Treasure. Treasure, treasure." He called out the word each time he saw it in the report. "If there's no treasure, he's sure writing about it a lot."

"Okay," Miguel threw up his hands. "You have something, but a couple stolen files won't convince Mom that Professor Erickson is her bad guy.

You need more."

Lucy balled up her fists. "If we show this to Mr. Ishii, we can stop him from canceling U.R.S.A.'s expedition."

"Maybe. Still, here's not a lot we can do tonight, unless you want to sneak back into his apartment, ambush him in his sleep, and force him to confess." Miguel checked the time. "Dad will send out a search party if we aren't home soon."

Rudy nodded. "Justin and I will get up early to read the rest of these. We'll find enough evidence to convince your mom."

Lucy sighed. "Ok."

Miguel led his sister down to their home. Justin turned to Rudy. "Alright. I'll give you five minutes to gloat about pirates, treasure, and shipwrecks. Then I want to sleep."

"I told you so." It was all Rudy really wanted to say.

CHAPTER 57

NEPTUNE'S TRIDENT

LUCY

L UCY WATCHED THE SKY SHIFT INTO A VIBRANT INDIGO DAWN. She wished the boys would come down soon. This was frustrating, they finally had some hope, but now the boys were taking their sweet time. Until last night, she hadn't noticed how suspicious Professor Erickson was being. Now she was angry and couldn't do anything about it.

How could Professor Erickson keep a whole wreck hidden from even her mother?

In low early morning light, Lucy watched Rudy's computer screen through his window. Professor Erickson definitely could have noticed them in his apartment last night—if he'd looked the right way. Two pairs of footsteps hammered downstairs interrupting her reflection. Instead of the boys, she looked up to see the twins.

"Good morning!" Nina beamed.

"Hi." Lucy sat up in her chair. "I forgot you guys were here."

"It was weird waking up to a brick ceiling." Luke stepped up beside his sister. "I forgot we were here too."

They looked wide awake despite the early hour. "Why are you up this early?" Lucy asked.

"Early?" Nina asked confused. "We've got to get Spud. Our poor pup's been out alone all night. Want to come with us?"

Lucy checked the boy's window. "We were supposed to do some early morning mystery solving." She stood, brushing breakfast crumbs from her shorts. "But why not? I don't think they know how to get up before sunrise." She lowered her voice. "Want to know what we learned last night?"

"Sure! Tell us while we walk." Nina skipped down the path. Which is what Lucy did.

"We heard Professor Erickson's door open and close lot last night." Luke walked beside them as Nina balanced on the bridge behind Lucy. The sky was brighter outside Fort Jefferson's brick walls. Clouds on the horizon were turning pink. Winds had died down and waves looked more manageable. "If he is hiding a pirate treasure, how will he get it out of the park?"

"And how will he use it?" Nina lost her balance and stepped down onto the main bridge. "It's an old treasure, with old pirate coins. He can't just take them to a bank. Can he?"

Lucy shook her head. "We don't know what he found. Rudy found the word *treasure* in a document. But we didn't find any description of what it was."

"It would be useful to know exactly what Professor Erickson is hiding." Luke pointed out as they stepped onto the beach.

Lucy nodded. "I'll try to get dad and Chet to dive wreck one-fourteen. Rudy will insist on going with them." He wasn't the only one interested the potential adventure.

"Can we come?" Nina asked. She and Lucy helped push their skiff into the ocean. "We can't dive, but we can snorkel. Then we get to say we helped discover a treasure."

"I don't see why not." The skiff bobbed up and down. Luke hopped aboard taking position beside the engine.

"We'll bring Spud. He could use an archeology credit." Nina called out as she and Lucy splashed ankle deep pushing their boat deeper. Once they had jumped in, Luke aimed for the channel.

The water was still slightly choppy, but the rubber boat absorbed most of it. There was a smattering of boats in the main harbor. Was Captain Tobias Professor Erickson's accomplice too, double dealing with him and Sophia?

Captain Levi was securing things atop the Historian's boat. That's right, they were supposed to leave soon! Their speedboat was nowhere to be seen. Lucy squinted at the yacht's name plastered across its stern in decorative letters: *Neptune's Trident*. "That's weird." She thought aloud.

"Huh?" Nina asked.

"Probably a coincidence, but a lot of papers in Professor Erickson's apartment mentioned a group called Trident." Lucy shrugged. Nina's response was lost in engine roar. They were headed to a small harbor between Garden Key's north beach and Bush Key. Which meant they had to go around Fort Jefferson.

Outside Garden Key's main harbor, waves were much larger. In the rubber dingy, it felt like riding on a bouncy waterbed. Luke let off his throttle. "Huh."

Nina stumbled bracing herself against the boat's rubber sides. Lucy reached out to steady her then turned to see what had captivated them. The sun's first rays had awoken hordes of terns, who flocked above Bush Key squawking. It was a beautiful sight of Fort Jefferson, two keys, and open water. There was only one problem: the Mannings' boat, *La'sei Fairy*, was nowhere to be seen!

It took twice as long to get back around Garden Key and beach their boat. All three kept their eyes peeled as Luke navigated the coastline, looking for any sign that their boat had been blown onto an island. "It must have dragged anchor in last night's storm."

As Luke beached their boat, a loud noise cut through the morning air. It was Mr. Howard's speedboat pulling up to his yacht. Captain Levi rushed across the deck to cast a line to the smaller vessel.

"Poor Spud." Nina's voice waivered pulling Lucy's attention back to the emergency at hand. "How could this happen?"

Luke tried to comfort his sister as they tied the dingy and began to jog towards the fort. "Spud's got food and water, and he's been alone on our boat before."

"What if he gets impatient?" Nina's voice echoed in the sally port.

"He won't leave the *La'sei Fairy* without permission." Luke replied calmly.

Nina, however, wasn't ready to be reassured. "But what if he does? He'll be lost at sea." Nina asked. "Why now? Out boats been anchored our there safely for more than a month."

Why now? Lucy also wondered. *Oh Crap!* "Oh! Sorry." Reaching the end of the tunnel, the three had to skitter around a figure standing outside the park headquarters. *Mr. Howard?* If he was here, then who was on the speedboat? No time to worry about that now.

"We'll find Spud soon." Luke attempted to reassure his sister.

Lucy led the twins across the parade ground as a shortcut. "I'll get my dad. You guys get your parents. Luke's right, your boat must be close." *Unless it was towed out to sea.* Mr. Howard's presence, and the timing of the speedboat, seemed odd.

CHAPTER 58
SEARCH FOR SPUD

JUSTIN

THE DOCK BUZZED WITH EVERYONE involved in Spud's search and rescue mission. Ranger Ishii was relaying with the motor vessel *Fort Jefferson* which had been diverted from her trip to pick up U.R.S.A. and was now driving search patterns around the Marquesas.

Lucy's father, Chet, and Ranger O'Donnell had taken three available speedboats to search nearby waters for boat or debris. The Manning's were organizing a search party of campers and Dive Bears to walk Bush and Long Key. Lucy's dad had given special permission to walk the usually closed islands.

Professor Erickson stood beside an electric cart loaded with U.R.S.A. equipment, watching the chaos. While Justin and Lucy watched him, Gwen stepped up to greet them. "This was our last day to do research. I was supposed to photograph every wreck one last time."

"Are you disappointed?" Lucy asked.

"I was hyped for one more day on our wrecks. Both Chet and Professor Erickson seemed stoked about that idea last night." Gwen shrugged, "But when they learned Spud was missing, they put us all on search and rescue detail."

Justin, failing to sound unsuspicious, scratched his chin. "Were you going to photograph wreck one-fourteen?"

"The professor's wreck? Of course. Anyway, I need to talk to Mr. Ishii." Gwen left them to frown after her. Mr. Ishii sat on a bench with several radios.

Lucy ducked into the small room on the dock to check ships' records. "*Neptune's Trident* is the only boat which has been out here since the beginning. Why didn't we notice that earlier?"

Justin shifted his gaze from Professor Erickson to the yacht. "I checked. No one saw Professor Erickson early this morning. He could have been driving the speedboat."

"Well, it wasn't Mr. Howard or his captain." Lucy counted them off on her fingers.

"I thought we were helping rescue a dog." Rudy crossed his arms. "What am I missing?"

"I hope Spud is ok, and that the Mannings find their sailboat. But think about it: they disappeared just when U.R.S.A. is about to go home." Justin watched Gwen prep her boat. "Professor Erickson wants to keep wreck one-fourteen secret."

"What does that have to do with a speedboat?" Rudy asked.

"The weather was not that bad!" Lucy explained. "Someone purposefully pulled Spud out to sea, and that speedboat arrived back in the harbor just as we rushed to tell everyone."

"Plus, have you noticed his yacht's name?" Justin pointed.

"*Neptune's Trident!*" Rudy uncrossed his arms lowering his voice. "*Trident* like those letters in the professor's apartment?"

Lucy nodded. "Sophia said Captain Tobias was never going to steal any cannon. What if she was right?" Rudy's brow wrinkled in confusion.

Justin cleared his throat. "The twins did see two boats around Loggerhead! The second was Captain Tobias. He told Sophia the truth: he went to dive her wreck and discovered the cannon missing. Then he warned Sophia and ran away. The first boat, the one which took the cannon and dropped them by Little Africa, might have been *Neptune's Trident*."

Rudy glanced out towards the yacht. "I thought we cleared Mr. Howard."

"That was before we learned Sophia's cannon were moved, not stolen." Justin explained. Then he smiled. "It helps answer another question. Remember, we couldn't figure out how someone like Captain Tobias could move the cannon by himself."

"Yeah?" Rudy asked.

"Well." Justin pointed to the giant boat. "Do you notice anything which might help move cannon?"

Rudy frowned. He watched Captain Levi, who was currently scrubbing the deck, unconcerned with the chaos on shore. Then he saw it. The tool that Captain Levi had used to pick up the fancy speedboat: the crane on the yacht's lower deck! "Oh!" What was it Lucy had said earlier? You stop noticing things you pass by every day.

"Exactly." Justin grinned. "Now we know how they lifted those cannon."

Lucy leaned against the dock railing. "If there is treasure, Professor Erickson needs to sneak it out of the Dry Tortugas." She gestured to the dock activity, "Only, right now, while everyone is distracted searching for Spud, Mr. Howard and his captain don't seem to be in any hurry." The old man was sitting under an umbrella watching his captain clean.

"They'll probably wait until dark. Professor Erickson had all night to hide the Mannings' boat. When Spud is found, everyone will be exhausted from the search." Justin pointed to the *Neptune's Trident*. "Even if it's not them, Captain Tobias or whoever could still be waiting beyond the park boundary for Professor Ericksons' radio call."

Lucy shook her head. "If they aren't going to do anything until tonight, I'm going to help search for Spud. After that, I have a plan."

Justin raised his eyebrows at her confident determination. "I hope that your plan isn't too dangerous."

"Mr. Ishii is busy with the search now, but this is our last chance to find Rudy's pirate treasure, or whatever, before he remembers to send the Dive Bears packing. We don't have time." Lucy stared forcefully towards Professor Erickson still watching the search party without getting involved. "But we'll take Miguel with us, to be safe."

CHAPTER 59

A RIDE TOWARDS ANSWERS

LUCY

"No way." Miguel sank deeper into the sofa. "It's too dangerous."

Lucy was frustrated. In here it was dark and cool, but they had been out in burning heat looking for Spud. The twins were, at that moment, walking atop Fort Jefferson with binoculars hoping to see their boat from a higher vantage point. Miguel had been playing games.

"Aw, Miguel, are you worried it might be hard? You've been straining yourself trying to avoid us."

Her brother turned from his laptop. "Avoiding your trouble. I don't have time to be grounded right now. Or worse." He shook his head. "Worse is exactly what will happen when Mom or Dad learn you broke into Professor Erickson's apartment."

"It's not about what we did." Justin cleared his throat. "It's about what we found. You saw it. Professor Erickson is the saboteur."

"No, that was Sophia. She confessed." Miguel shook his head. "Your evidence otherwise is a load of academic espionage."

"Miguel, Sophia's in Key West. How could she make a sailboat disappear?"

"You assume I believe that someone did that on purpose."

Justin tried to reason with him. "We know Sophia borrowed expensive equipment, but she denied sabotaging Kit's samples or helping steal any artifacts."

"Professor Erickson knew everything. Sophia's brochure on his computer proves it." Rudy paused, frowning in self-realization. "He used me to help frame her."

"So, Professor Erickson framed his student and kidnapped a dog. Why?" Miguel sounded incredulous.

"It's called dog napping." Rudy stepped forward.

Lucy interrupted Miguel's laugh. "Miguel, Professor Erickson is up to something. We can prove it. Either we break into his apartment again or…" She waited.

"That's a no." Miguel shook his head.

"Or we take a boat out to inspect wreck one-fourteen." Lucy continued

Miguel's controller bounced with a muffled clatter onto carpeted floor. "It's a bad idea if you are wrong. It's worse if you are right. Because then Professor Erickson has already committed several dangerous crimes to keep it secret."

"Miguel. We need proof." Lucy rolled her eyes. "Dad won't take us. He wouldn't believe us and he's busy with the search."

"So, wait until tomorrow."

Justin shook his head. "If we are right, they will steal the treasure and clean up the evidence before tomorrow."

"Do you know how long it takes to excavate treasure?" Miguel stood. The rec room window was dirty from years without outside cleaning, but it provided a decent view of Loggerhead. Miguel pointed. "No boats."

"They're not dumb enough to do anything during daylight." Lucy sighed.

"If you're right, then why did Captain Tobias disappear?" Miguel countered.

Justin shrugged. "We don't have every answer. And we won't until we see the wreck."

Miguel returned to his seat. He picked up his controller. He set it down. He picked it up. He stared at his friends and glowered at his sister. "Ok. I'll take you. But I'll only do it if we are absolutely certain there are no boats near the wreck. *Horned Devil, Neptune's Trident* or any other."

Justin nodded. "The twins are going back to Loggerhead. I'll ask them to keep lookout."

While Lucy and Rudy gathered snorkel equipment, Justin went to find Luke and Nina. He came back smiling. He bragged about a seeing a rare purple bellied wood piper or something. "It's a good sign."

While Justin got ready, Lucy made her way to the gift shop. Mrs. Ishii had resumed her place behind the counter. "What can I do for you Miss Benitez?"

"Could I have a disposable underwater camera?" Lucy pointed to the stack beside the counter.

"Of course." Mrs. Ishii nodded. Lucy liked her. Unlike her husband, she wasn't trying to ship Lucy's mom away. "Why do you want one of these?"

"Well," Lucy handed over cash borrowed from Miguel's room. "We were going to use U.R.S.A.'s big camera, but I didn't want to lose it, *again*."

"Of course." Mrs. Ishii smiled at the joke. Lucy wondered if the woman realized she had dodged her question. Stepping outside, she noticed that the headquarters was bustling.

Several rangers gathered around a massive long-distance radio. Justin had somehow squeezed next to a chart which had been hastily taped to the wall. "Repeat those coordinates for us." Lucy's father spoke into a radio capable of broadcasting all the way to the Everglades.

The voice repeated the coordinates. "…Northeast of Rebecca Shoal…" Was all Lucy understood. Her father made a singular mark and then circle a large area around it.

"What's going on?" She whispered to a maintenance ranger.

"A seaplane spotted a sailboat adrift while flying back to Key West."

"Alright, we copy." Lucy's father replaced the hand-held mike with a smile. "We have good general coordinates. Things will go faster if we spread out. I'll take Renee and Shawn Manning with me. Ranger O'Donnell, Mr. Ishii take a second boat. I'll ask Professor Erickson if U.R.S.A. can spare their boats for our search party."

Ranger O'Donnell frowned. "How did it get out that far?"

"There will be time for questions later." Lucy's dad clapped heartily. Eyes falling on Lucy, he sighed with relief. "I expected you to ask to come with me."

"Well, um." Lucy didn't know how to respond. They had their own plans.

"Don't. This is an official recovery operation." Her father smiled sympathetically, "it's too dangerous." He had no idea! He pointed to the large radio. "We'll be on channel ten if you need anything."

With surprising speed, the entire headquarters cleared out, leaving Justin and Lucy alone.

Lucy grinned ecstatically, "Thank goodness! I hope Spud's alright!"

"I'm sure he is." Justin spoke reassuringly.

"Ready to go?"

"Almost," Justin pointed to the large radio. "Your dad said I could give Luke and Nina the good news."

"I'll meet you on dock." With three mesh bags slung over her shoulder, Lucy followed a crowd to the dock. Hopefully, Miguel and Rudy were getting their boat ready. Instead, the two were sitting on a picnic table watching a gathering of park rangers and Dive Bears. "What are you doing?"

"If dad sees us stocking our boat, he'll ask unwelcome questions." Miguel explained.

They waited. Justin soon joined them. By the time the last park service boat pulled out, the sun had sunk much lower. Lucy was growing impatient. "Come on guys."

The Dive Bears were still prepping their boat. She walked past them briskly.

Chet stopped them with a big smile. "They found Spud's boat! We're going out with the rescue party."

"Cool." Lucy nodded.

Seeing their snorkel equipment, Chet shifted his weight to study Miguel. "Where are you guys headed?"

"Loggerhead, to keep Luke and Nina company." Her lie came easily. Since her mother vouched for him, Lucy trusted Chet but didn't want him to say anything to Professor Erickson. She handed her snorkel equipment to Justin. "Rudy still hasn't seen Little Africa."

"Professor Erickson isn't going with you?" Justin asked. Gwen helmed the other university boat puttering in the harbor.

"He's coordinating packing." Chet turned his back on them. "Have fun guys."

"See you later." Lucy waved. Too bad she wouldn't be there for Spud's rescue, but they had their own mission.

CHAPTER 60

WRECK 114

RUDY

MIGUEL SWITCHED THROUGH EVERY RADIO CHANNEL before locking it on ten. "Make sure you have everything." He opened a cooler and began counting sodas. "Lucy, help with the lines!" Only after quadruple checking everything, did he start the engine. "Let's go."

"Miguel, are you nervous?" Lucy smirked casually.

"This is a bad idea, Lucia."

"Relax." Justin beamed confidently. "We'll check out wreck one-four-teen, then we'll come straight back."

"Do you have a way to record any evidence you find?" Miguel asked.

Lucy held up a package. "An underwater camera from the gift shop."

"That's a film camera." Miguel's concern was quickly replaced with amusement, "Where are you planning to get that film developed?"

Justin passed out life jackets. "We can worry about that after we see what's out there."

"Mounds and mounds of treasure." It was obvious. Rudy didn't know why he had to keep reminding people. He pulled out his pre-marked park brochure. "Have you noticed how far Professor Erickson's wreck is from the rest? Did he plan it that way?"

Lucy cocked her head. "Maybe. Professor Erickson took over wreck assignments when the initial schedule was deleted."

"Interesting!" Justin hummed.

Rudy had added most of U.R.S.A.'s wrecks to his map, including wreck one-fourteen. They were headed towards a patch of white/green in the middle of deeper blue water.

The sun was sinking lower. Their boat arrowed across the water, bouncing against choppy waves. They quickly arrived in a spot as far north of Loggerhead as east of Fort Jefferson. Miguel stopped their boat. "Let me see that brochure."

Miguel squinted at Rudy's map, looked at Loggerhead, and turned to Garden Key. "The place we're looking for is north of White Shoal and south of Texas Rock. There should be a green marker over there to help us find our way."

"You don't know where we're going?" Rudy watched Justin wave his compass around. "Can't you find it with that?"

Miguel rolled his eyes. "I have a faster method. Without internet, our phone's GPS doesn't work. I'm using triangulation. I find three objects above water and put us in the correct place relative to them." He pointed at Rudy's map. "Loggerhead Light and Garden Key are easy, but I need that green marker to be sure."

"Can't you just look for a shallow sandy area?" Rudy squinted at his brochure. "It looks like a sandy U."

"We could try that sandbar." Lucy leaned over the bow to point. "Or that one." She pointed to another. Rudy frowned. There were lots of similar looking places.

"There's the green marker." Justin waved towards something south and east. "It's hard to see because we're perpendicular to the signs."

"Alright," Miguel sighed. "Let's see if I can line us up."

They spent over an hour motoring over various sandbars and coral heads before settling above what they all believed to be the correct place: a shallow patch of sea grass which dropped off quickly into deeper waters. "I see something down there." Lucy pointed.

Curvy wave shadows rippled on the sea floor. Beneath them, Rudy could see parallel lines of rubble. "Straight lines and symmetry," he grinned. "Sophia taught us to look for both." There were also a few jagged bits, "does that look like part of a ship's hull?"

Miguel looked over the edge, "I'm not seeing anything which screams pirate. Guys, this wreck is shallow and obvious, anything of value would have been scavenged decades ago."

Rudy stared into the water. "This has got to be the right place."

Miguel sighed. "I hope you're right. It's late. I want to be back before dark."

"Anchors away." Justin called, throwing the anchor with a splash into a sandy patch.

Lucy was already in her snorkel gear.

"No way you're going to find a pirate treasure without me." Rudy crammed on his flippers.

Lucy handed Rudy the disposable camera. "Put this around your wrist. Photograph everything." She pulled on her mask, flopped to the edge, and jumped. Surfacing, "I'll secure our anchor. Hurry up!"

Justin followed, fins in hand. Rudy was last. Too excited, he sank below his snorkel's range and had to dump salty water out before inhaling. Lucy spit out her snorkel to shout. "Miguel, what are you doing?"

Miguel was hoisting a small dive flag on a boat hook. "I don't want you guys to get run over while treasure hunting."

"If Professor Erickson sees that, he'll know someone is out here."

"And he won't accidentally run you over." Miguel replied.

"Maybe on purpose." Lucy grumbled as they began to explore.

The shallow end of the wreck was propped up over the sandbar. The symmetrical lines were wooden beams covered in algae and soft corals. Larger pieces of lumber were half-buried in sand. The hull sloped downward at a dramatic angle. In deeper water, the straight lines were replaced by jagged tears.

The ship had broken in half. Rudy wasn't good at diving, so he watched Lucy and Justin dive down to inspect the abrupt break. He could not see any evidence that this was a pirate ship, yet. He snapped a picture anyway.

Justin and Lucy swam upward. Rudy asked, "What did you guys see down there?"

"I think her bow is probably buried in sand up there." Lucy pointed back to jagged lines. "Her stern was ripped off."

Justin nodded. "Its contents spilled out in deeper waters, along with half the boat. Wreckage is scattered all around in coral down there."

"No treasure though, sorry." Lucy shook her head. "Come see." After a deep breath, Rudy followed them. They led him so deep that he had to clear his ears. His lungs were telling him to surface.

A sea fan grew atop what Rudy had assumed was the fossil coral bedrock commonly found in the keys. Swimming closer, he realized it was not anchored to dead coral, but to a stack of bricks, mortared together by sand and time.

Suddenly, the other dark objects around Rudy made sense. Rounded by time and waves, scattered as the ship fell apart and after a century of storms, many buried in sand or beneath coral and algae, were bricks every shade of dark red. There were thousands upon thousands of them.

"Wreck one-fourteen is a brick wreck just like Professor Erickson has been telling everyone." Lucy sounded disappointed.

Rudy asked, "Why has he hidden it from everyone? What about all of those documents on his computer, the dumped samples, Spuds clue?"

"I don't know." Lucy replied. "Maybe we missed something."

"Now you decide to have doubts?" Miguel's shout echoed over water. "Thanks guys!"

"Oh man." Rudy couldn't hide his disappointment. He was hovering over a shipwreck. It should be cool but, "This won't help your mom, I'm sorry Lucy."

Lucy smiled softly. "This has still been quite an adventure."

Rudy was not ready to give up. Diving beneath the waves, he aimed for the deepest place he could see. Holding his breath, he followed a trail of bricks to a broken hull. There were more bricks scattered here. Knowing what to look for, he could see heavily damaged planks of wood, a massive iron chain, and scattered, rusted, bits of iron.

Even the front third of the hull, which looked intact from above, was in tatters. Rudy continued to follow it up into the sandbar, to where a pointy bow must lie beneath sand. No treasure. His breath was getting the better of him, and he kicked upward. Justin was right behind him. "Well, this is a pretty cool wreck."

"It's not a pirate ship." Rudy tried to shake his disappointment away.

"Hey guys." Lucy had been swimming at a different angle and was about ninety feet from the wreck. "Come here." She sounded both excited and confused. "There's a second wreck."

CHAPTER 61
THE TREASURE?

RUDY

Rudy bobbed in waves mask down, following the seafloor to the shallowest water. To the left and much deeper, there were several brain corals clumped together on a small rocky overhang. Beneath it, hidden from every angle except one, was a long, green, encrusted metallic bar. He watched Lucy swim above it before coming to the surface.

"What is that?" He asked.

"What do you think?" Lucy asked.

Getting the hang of diving, Rudy swam down into the shadow of the coral. The metallic tube looked out of place, like someone had dragged it there. It was about the length of his body, heavily encrusted with years of white sea-crud and greened by corrosion. There was another one sitting beside it, deeper in shadow.

He swam back to the surface. "A cannon?"

"Definitely. And not civil war-era." Lucy scowled.

"How do you know?" Rudy watched Justin inspect them.

Lucy replied. "According to Mom and Sophia, iron and steel cannon corrode faster than bronze, and they turn black. Bronze turns green. Bronze cannon are usually older too."

Justin burst out of water. His bug eyes were exaggerated by his snorkel mask. "It's a cannon."

"Yeah. We know." Rudy replied.

"That's not all." Lucy swam down beside the cannon so she could be in Rudy's second picture for scale. Then, she flipped over swimming where the cannon pointed: further from their boat to a new sandbar. A layer of grit dusted everything, camouflaging two more green cylinders. Rudy took another picture. Lucy, still underwater, swam to an area which looked like a road made of stacked rocks. Small blue fish swam through sea plants growing around rubble.

Lucy scattered the fish, returning to the surface. Rudy began peppering her with questions. "That's a ballast pile, right?" A ballast pile was usually made up of stones and scrap metal, it was often the only part of old shipwrecks preserved. "Is this a second wreck? Why are those cannon here?"

After catching her breath Lucy replied. "Another ship definitely sunk here. Some of it is still buried. Let me show you." She dove. Justin was about to follow.

"No, wait." Rudy held out the disposable camera. "If we find a real-life pirate wreck, I want to be in those pictures." The ballast pile looked like an organized path underwater. Lucy checked cracks between rocks then jetted towards where the pile was buried in sand.

She pointed to evidence that someone had been working on site. The sandbar stopped abruptly, sloping at an odd angle. Someone, presumably Professor Erickson, had dug down exposing more wreck. The surrounding sand had collapsed reburying parts of his work, but Lucy pointed to several wooden boards wedged between two rocks.

The boards were rotten and decayed, looking older than any Rudy had seen before. Lucy was pointing to an exceptionally warped and ragged one. Cylindrical holes had been carved into it. "Those came from Kit's sampling device," she swam up to meet them.

"Wow." Rudy's voice was muffled through his snorkel.

The three dove the wreck several more times, surfacing to catch their breath and discuss their find. Finally, Lucy smiled. "I think we've seen everything."

Rudy fidgeted, kicking up small waves. "Where's the treasure? We've only found rocks and corroded cannon."

"It's old." Lucy tried to sound conciliatory. "There's not going to be much treasure left."

"Then why is Professor Erickson messing with your mom?" Rudy asked.

"Let's discuss this on our boat. Miguel looks worried." Justin had a point. Rudy could see Miguel leaning against the railing watching them.

They turned for the boat. Rudy lowered his head, kicking hard to keep up, until he caught sight of something out of place. He swam beside a massive brain coral so tall it nearly broke the surface. It was not coral which had drawn his eye, nor the beautiful school of fish around it, but an object beneath them.

A green plastic container, like those being used to store the recovered cannon, was sitting beneath it. Beside that was a fifth corroded bronze cannon. This one was in better shape. It looked like it had been placed next to the container on purpose. Rudy didn't waste time trying to stop his friends. He dove.

The sandbar home to both wreck one-fourteen and the new wreck had a horseshoe shape. The massive coral head stood in its center. The green plastic container was deeper than he'd ever dived before. He took a massive breath.

Coral looming over him, with slight brush of fear, he checked for man-eating fish. None. Swimming down, he reached for the rubber container's lid. Pulling it open, all air in his lungs burst out in a surprised shriek. He kicked up in explosive excitement half-leaping from the water. "Lucy, Justin, come back! Look what I've found!"

CHAPTER 62

THE TREASURE

LUCY

Lucy watched Rudy swim around the seafloor with amusement. The last couple times they'd been snorkeling, he'd barely spent any time below water. Now, he was dolphin kicking like he'd been born at sea. Seeing them, he kicked up to the surface.

It was only about ten or twelve feet deep. He was beside them in no time. "Do you see that box?" he asked excitedly. Shadows were growing longer as sunset neared, but Lucy could see a greenish-rectangular shape beside another cannon.

Justin lifted his head. "That looks like those rubber containers in the storage area."

"U.R.S.A. sometimes leaves them on site to store equipment when they're going to be out more than one day." Lucy watched excitement grow behind Rudy's mask.

"Well, I guarantee that box does not hold archeology equipment. Come see!" Rudy's excitement was contagious. She felt her own enthusiasm growing as she knelt on sand in front of the box, copying the Dive Bears. Justin followed suit. Rudy hovered with fingers perched on the lid. On their nod, he pulled it open.

"That's impossible!" Lucy thought, a string of bubbles leaving her snorkel.

In shadow and low light, the coins did not exactly shine, but some did gleam. There weren't many. They were crudely minted. Many could barely be described as circular. There were two distinct colors. A few loose gold coins, and many more silver coins. Most of the second were clumped together, blackened by time under sea.

There were a couple of large, encrusted, bars of metal—again silver—and smaller objects so caked with sand and cement that she couldn't recognize them. There were also several ceramic cups and bowls—or at least their shards. The largest item was a giant brass bell. It was corroded like the cannon, but better preserved despite its warped shape. Atop everything sat a once fancy dagger now rusted—handle swollen over tarnished metal

Lucy was sure if they dug through the pile, they would discover more amazing pieces. Justin began taking pictures. She pointed up hoping the boys would follow. "That's impossible." She spat out her snorkel.

Rudy was breathing hard. "A real pirate treasure!" He pursed his lips confused. "Although, why is it in a rubber case?"

"If I had to guess, Professor Erickson found all of that from his secret wreck and is storing it so it's easy to collect." Justin nodded down at the rubber tub. "This is why he's keeping people away."

"Maybe." Lucy wondered what her mother would say when she learned about this. Professor Erickson had broken every rule in every archeology handbook. "Do you have enough pictures?" Justin nodded. "Good. We have evidence. And everyone is getting tired." Rudy was getting better at diving, but she didn't want him to wear himself out. "Let's get back to Fort Jeff so we can show my dad."

They swam back towards the boat. When Lucy turned to check on Rudy, she noticed something flash in his hand—the dagger. She stopped, tugging on Justin's fin.

"What do you have there?" Lucy asked.

"It's the dagger from the chest." Rudy lifted it up to show off.

"Put it back." Lucy crossed her arms, kicking to keep afloat.

"Why? Professor Erickson already moved it." Rudy protested. "And it's cool!"

"Rudy." She refused to explain herself. He should know better.

Justin cleared his throat. "It's archeological evidence and evidence of criminal activity. It should remain where it was found."

Before Rudy could protest, they heard Miguel shout across the water. "Guys!" He was jumping up and down, rocking the boat and pointing. Lucy could hear a low buzz.

"That's an engine! Someone's coming!" She shouted.

Spurred by Miguel's urgency, the three kicked faster. What if it was the professor? Worse, what if it was her father? Lucy let the boys take lead to make sure they both made it.

The boat remained out of sight. Lucy heard its engines shift into lower gear. She watched Miguel move to the other side and saw him put up his hands. He glanced nervously back.

Inspired by her brother's desperation, Lucy surged ahead overtaking Justin. She made sure he could see her, then dove. Flipping to look at him, she put a finger to her lips.

From below, she watched shadows as her brother pulled the two boats together. The second boat had a sleek orange and black hull. Footprints from heavy boots thumped on deck. She heard two voices, one high-pitched: Professor Erickson. The other was a deeper growl.

When Justin reached the step ladder behind their boat, he slid the disposable camera from his wrist. He started to climb and was yanked into the boat. Rudy copied Justin, dropping his dagger. It sank quickly. Lucy swam beneath the two boats trying to stay out of site. She couldn't hold her breath much longer. She hoped she could hold it long enough.

CHAPTER 63

PIRATED

JUSTIN

Approaching the Benitez's boat, Justin could see three figures aboard. Miguel stood near the bow, talking to Professor Erickson. The third figure was Captain of *Neptune's Trident*. A gnarly bearded Captain Levi. Lucy caught Justin's attention underwater. He didn't know her plan. He hoped neither man had seen her.

The bearded man stared directly at him. "Son, it's not safe out here all by yourselves." Captain Levi's voice was gruff. He stepped forward reaching. "Let me help you aboard." His other hand rested on his hip, beside a holstered pistol. Justin shook off the disposable camera, then grabbed the step ladder.

Rudy was hauled up after him without protest. Lucy did not appear. Miguel stared hard at him. Justin didn't know how to explain Lucy's location without giving her away. Had Miguel already told their captors she was out here?

"Why are you here?" The professor asked angrily.

"Why are you?" Justin replied calmly.

"I saw you diving my wreck!" Professor Erickson stamped his foot. "What did you see?"

"Your wreck? What do you think we saw?" Rudy sounded equally defiant.

The bearded man groaned. Pushing Miguel out of the way, he snatched keys from the ignition. Justin turned to the professor. "Who is he, really? This isn't university sanctioned."

Professor Erickson scoffed. "I've made more lucrative arrangements." The bearded man unholstered his gun raising it into the sky and slamming it butt-down atop their marine radio.

"My employer, me, who we are, why we are here," Captain Levi slammed his gun down again and again, until the radio was in pieces, "these aren't questions you want to ask."

Justin winced. Rudy scooted closer to him. Miguel opened his mouth to protest but closed it without uttering a word. The bearded man ripped the radio from its mount and tossed it into the ocean watching its remains sink. Hopefully, Lucy was well hidden.

If Captain Levi and Professor Erickson were using the orange speedboat, then Chet and the others must still be helping with Spud's rescue. It was possible neither Dive Bears nor Rangers were around to notice any signal for help.

The bearded man holstered his gun, ensuring it remained very visible. "Now, tell us what you saw down there."

"You weren't mapping the brick wreck. There's another wreck down there." Justin stated plainly. Both men turned to stare at him.

"Is it the pirate wreck from the letters?" Rudy couldn't help himself.

"Why don't you tell me?" The professor glared. "You stole my notes."

Justin's ears began to burn. Rudy asked his question first. "How did you know?"

The professor's eyes flashed to the younger boy. "Spies should know to turn off a computer." He threw up his hands. "I could have done this legitimately. I was going to be the last archeologist out here. In a couple of months, I could have published my new find and become rich and famous, but you had to take my documents, then come out here to find the wreck."

"Those artifacts belong to the park." Justin replied. "You can't just take them."

Professor Erickson dropped his hands. "With the right connections, there's always a way. Never mind legitimacy, I'll still be rich."

"Enough." The bearded man interrupted. "I do not care. There's a more important question." He leaned forward, putting his hand on his holster. "Where is the girl?"

CHAPTER 64

UNDERCOVER, UNDERWATER

LUCY

Lucy's head slowly broke the surface. Nervous sweat fogged her mask, so she lifted it to see Captain Levi's back towering over the boys. Justin was frowning, and Rudy had his hands raised like it was a stickup. The captain spoke in a gruff voice. "Where is the girl?"

Lucy kicked beneath the boat's outwardly sloping hull to hide in the shadows. "We're the only ones out here." Justin's voice didn't waiver. His lie sounded confident.

"Is that true?" The captain gruffly grunted.

Miguel answered next. A flood of relief passed through Lucy's chest knowing he was ok. "She stayed home. We wanted to leave someone to wait for Dad."

"Good… Good."

"How is that good? In a couple of hours Benitez will return. His daughter will send him this way." She recognized Professor Erickson's nervous voice. His presence confirmed all of their suspicions. "We're not going to shoot them, are we?"

An icy spike shot down Lucy's spine. How could she stop the two men above? She could untie the speedboat and pull it away, separating the two boats. She could sabotage their engines. She could start rocking the boat enough to distract them—giving the boys a chance to… do something. Each plan would endanger them more than help. All she could do was tread water and not get caught, otherwise Justin's lie would be exposed.

"Of course not, you idiot. Gun shots echo. We don't need more attention. Besides, who do you think I am? Who do you think I work for? We are not monsters. We do not shoot kids. As long as they behave." His last statement calmly undercut everything else he'd said. "We're simply making them disappear for a while, like the dog. Now, help me with these lines." Both boats shifted as he jumped across to his fancy vessel.

"I didn't sign up for theft or kidnapping." Professor Erickson's complaints were cut short by sounds of heavy lines being thrown clunking atop her father's boat.

"Relax old man. It will be hours before Benitez gets back with his rescue convoy. By then we'll be finished. You, tie this up!" Captain Levi shouted instructions to the boys. "You, get the anchor!" Lucy heard his heavy footsteps pounding just above her. She pushed herself further under the V hull. At any moment, he could look down and see her. "This will all be over before dawn tomorrow."

She saw the toe of his boot hanging over the rail. "We'll take them up to Twenty-five Thirteen." His voice was coming closer. "After that we will…"

Lucy took a silent breath letting herself sink, afraid that at any moment either Professor Erickson or Captain Levi would see her. Underwater, hollow footprints sounded sinister. Suddenly there was a splash behind her.

Her heart jumped. She let out a loud bubble of breath unable to squelch it. Had the man jumped after her? She frantically turned expecting someone behind her.

A boat cushion bobbed gently in the waves. It must have been knocked overboard. She hadn't been caught yet! Another noise, ropes across fiberglass. Someone was pulling anchor. There was a second smaller splash.

A small object floated next to the cushion—their boat key, tied to a small rubber float. She swam for the key, careful to keep under the bow sprit until she heard a sharp electronic whistle.

"Come on!" Captain Levi's gruff voice rang out. The speedboat's engine started with a metallic cough. Panic seizing Lucy's chest, she pushed off the bow and dove swiftly. Reaching the bottom, she watched the orange boat's propellers spin. It took off. After a few seconds, her father's boat followed, lines between the two drawn taut.

Lucy waited for both boats to leave, then she waited longer. Holding her breath for what seemed hours, she finally had to rush to the surface and gasp for air. Two boats jetted into the setting sun. The empty ocean proved she no longer had to worry about being seen. Her new predicament was much worse. She was floating, alone, in the ocean.

CHAPTER 65
BACK ON THE BOAT

JUSTIN

THE TWO CONSPIRATORS WERE BOTH VISIBLY RELIEVED by Miguel's story that Lucy was back in Fort Jefferson. Rudy leaned close. "I hope you know what you are doing."

Professor Erickson and Captain Levi began arguing about their next move. Justin and Rudy slid closer to Miguel. Justin winced when he heard them discussing shooting. The bearded man laughed the idea off.

They resolved their differences, making plans to take their captives further out to sea. Captain Levi moved to the Benitez's boat's bow, resting a foot on the rail. "You! Get the anchor."

Justin's brain raced as he moved to comply. Professor Erickson began throwing lines across to lash the boats together. This must be how he'd moved the Mannings' sailboat. Justin tried to figure out where they were being taken. Was Twenty-five Thirteen another U.R.S.A. wreck?

Never mind that! Lucy was still in the water, and they were about to leave. Justin waited for Captain Levi to search a compartment below the steering wheel. Professor Erickson was attaching tow lines. In one swift motion Justin pulled on the anchor ropes, 'accidentally' knocking a padded cushion overboard. Miguel had given a thorough safety briefing.

The seat could be used like a life jacket. "Oops!"

Captain Levi stood, holding a heavy-duty handheld radio. He eyed Justin as he pulled the anchor rope dragging both boats forward, until, finally, it came out of the water. Captain Levi smiled. "You three go sit in the stern. Don't fall out, we might not come back for you."

Justin took a seat beside Miguel. "I hope you and Lucy know what you are doing." Miguel sounded worried and angry.

He couldn't answer for Lucy. He hadn't told her, or anyone really, about his backup plan. "Don't make them any angrier." Justin replied. "He has a gun."

"Let's go," Captain Levi turned to the professor. "It will be night soon."

Professor Erickson started the speedboat. Night! How hard would it be to find someone in dark open water? The engines came to life with a high-pitched whistle followed by a low rumble of twin props churning water. Justin's muscles tensed realizing how much danger Lucy was in. He had only seconds. Covertly, he reached into his pockets, digging around until he found what he was looking for. In a gentle, nonchalant motion, he dropped one last object into the water.

The lines between both boats squeaked tight as the speedboat pulled away. Justin turned back to watch the cushion floating on top of the darkening waters. Where was Lucy? Terror gripped his heart as the floating cushion disappeared in the waves.

"I wonder where we're going." Rudy said in a faint voice.

"I hope Lucia is alright." Miguel ignored Rudy's statement.

"Guys, it's okay." Justin tried to sound as confident as he should be.

"How is it okay?" Miguel asked.

Justin couldn't answer without being overheard, so he tried to give Miguel his most confident smile. As their boat was towed out to sea, he turned to watch Loggerhead Lighthouse sink below the horizon. "It will be okay."

CHAPTER 66

FAR FROM SHORE

LUCY

Lucy was not ok. "Always, always, swim with a buddy. Make sure someone knows where you are." Those were her father's rules when she and Miguel began their dive lessons. She had broken them both now. That wasn't her intention. Her swimming partners had been kidnapped. Everyone who knew her whereabouts was being towed out to sea.

A man had once been left out here by his diving boat. It had taken park rangers most of a day to find him. Lucy had pictured him before: alone, exhausted, sunburnt, and drying out in salty ocean water.

A kernel of fear began germinating in her mind. "Don't panic. Don't panic." It was easy to recite those words as she lay on her chest, floating in the cushion straps. It was harder to follow her own advice. "Floating is easy." She had done if for hours while dive training, without a life jacket either! "Someone will find me."

But the sky was swiftly darkening, and her words rang hollow. Maybe she should swim. Except there was that famous poster of a monster rising from the depths to swallow a swimmer, which crawled into Lucy's mind causing shivers. Some sharks were attracted to movement. Maybe it would be safer to float.

But floating, even with the cushion, left her legs dangling in pitch black water and allowed her mind to conjure images of tentacles reaching up to grab her ankle. She felt a chill wash over her as a cold current rose out of the depths. Her breathing hastened. That's it! It was over! Something was going to eat her!

That something bumped against her wrist as she floated over the crest of another wave. She gasped and shook her arm. The thing had hold of her and wouldn't let go. She pulled with all of her might, and something cracked heavily against her snorkel mask.

The underwater camera Justin had dropped! It had drifted close, its rubber wrist strap snagging her arm as she flailed. Reaching for it caused the cushion to slide from her grasp, making her kick frantically to stay afloat. She was able to pull it back, but now she was fighting to keep her breathing stable without sucking in salt water. She was supposed to be better at this! Why else had she been swimming around the fort every day?

She had never been in the sea alone after dark. Anything could swim up and snatch her away. She was a mile or more from any solid ground, and only three percent of the park was above water. She had no idea which way to go. She could easily picture herself swimming further and further out to open ocean. That chilled her causing more goosebumps.

Wait a second! What was that? Off to her right there was a flash of light! It was there for only an instant. Lucy waited. There it was again. She slowed her breathing, having been given a reason to remain calm. There, a third time, right on schedule: the beacon from Loggerhead Lighthouse!

Her panic subsided as that distant light slashed across the sky. With renewed resolve, she reached out to grasp the camera's rubbery chord. As she was wrapping it through the straps of her cushion, she noticed an aluminum package floating nearby. A glowstick from Justin's pocket! The boys knew she was out here. She paddled over to grab it. Now she had a floatation device, a light, a direction, and a mission—more than her mother had in the Mediterranean.

She would be fine! Half believing herself, Lucy kicked towards the beacon. The boys were being taken out into deeper water. She needed to get to Loggerhead, and a working radio, if she wanted to save them. It was further than she had ever swam before, but Justin, Rudy, and Miguel needed her. That was all she needed to know. She began swimming faster.

CHAPTER 67

WRECK 2513

JUSTIN

"WHERE ARE WE GOING?" Justin asked the bearded man. Captain Levi reclined in his chair, feet resting on the wheel. He turned lazily to answer.

"There's an old German submarine in the deep waters west of the fort. It was captured, studied, and then sunk in a protected area to make an artificial reef. Boats can't anchor out there, so there are buoys for ships to tie onto. The region only gets a couple dive boats a year."

"What are you going to do?" Miguel asked.

"Simple. We tie you up. The boat of course. Out there, you're out of our way."

"We only have a little water and not much food. That will be a problem if we're trapped on the ocean for days," Miguel tried to be polite about begging for their lives.

"Relax." Captain Levi settled deeper into his chair. "Once we have what we need, we'll radio in your location and make sure people find you. Unless you'd rather we just set your boat adrift."

"Like the Mannings' sailboat?" Justin scowled. The man raised a smug eyebrow. "Why are you doing this? Has your boss told you yet that the treasure on that wreck isn't even enough to pay for your fancy yacht?"

"My boss?" Captain Levi's smile grew very wide. "You have no clue what you've stumbled into—what Professor Erickson has found. The *Atocha* was one of the biggest treasure finds of all time. We're onto something much bigger."

"How could a huge treasure like that be hidden inside a national park?" Rudy asked. "Everyone keeps telling me: the wreck is too shallow, or most treasure was discovered years ago."

Captain Levi chuckled. "You must not know the history of the Pirates Caesar. My *boss*—" more laughter "—wrote about it. Once your parent's pick you up, you should read it."

When Professor Erickson finally killed the engine, it was dark. Captain Levi maneuvered the wheel and both boats collided under shared momentum. The waves had picked up in deeper water, and everyone swayed with a gentle rocking motion. "Professor, idle over to that marker." The bearded captain aimed his flashlight at a large orange buoy. "It's good these haven't torn their moorings yet."

"What if they had?" The professor's voice was strained. *Worried?*

"No reason to speculate." His light dazed Justin. "Take your bowline and tie it to this marker." Justin had to lay across the bow, stretching to wrap a line through a buoy loop.

"Secure it. We wouldn't want you drifting off." Captain Levi sneered through his beard. "See. I'm not such a bad guy." Professor Erickson scoffed. While his back was turned, the captain drew his pistol. "When you are rescued, you'll be tempted to tell everyone about this experience. You'll want to talk about the wreck and complain about the professor here. That's all fine." He didn't aim his gun, but his threat was obvious. "Do yourselves a favor. Don't mention me or my ship."

Professor Erickson watched them as Captain Levi took the wheel his smile morphing into open laughter as he issued his last warning. "Don't fall out of the boat! And don't try swimming for safety. It's two-hundred feet deep and we're miles from anything. You'll disappear, swept out into deeper waters." They motored away.

"Does he consider that a threat?" Rudy asked.

Miguel chuckled. "I found that plenty intimidating." His nervous laughter cut off as their boat rocked violently. He grabbed Justin's shoulder. His grip was stronger than Justin expected. "Now, tell me why we left my sister behind. How is everything ok?"

CHAPTER 68

ALONE ON THE WATER

LUCY

THE SKY WAS COMPLETELY DARK. One, two, flash! Loggerhead Light was brighter but was it any closer? Lucy was kicking as hard as possible, but was she making any progress against the current? She kept her mask pulled atop her head, so she wasn't tempted to stare into the black abyss. She kept kicking. Maybe, just maybe, she was getting closer to shore.

She didn't have time to relish potential success, because a sharp hum cut through sounds of her splashing. Was someone boating nearby? The waters around Loggerhead were supposed to be closed at night. Were they coming for her? No one knew she was missing.

Except the boys and she had their boat key. A dread more powerful than sea monsters shot through Lucy's veins. The professor was coming back to find her! The engine noise grew closer confirming Lucy's suspicions.

She stopped kicking and slid out of the cushion to secure the camera to its straps. It was their best evidence, but she didn't want them to catch her with it. This way it could float along and be found later. The engine noise died.

Lucy froze. She had not been found yet! Professor Erickson and his cohort might know her general area, but they did not know her exact location. The water was dark, if they didn't see her, they would have to give up eventually. She floated as silently as possible.

What seemed like hours passed while Lucy drifted in quietly lapping waves. At any moment, she expected a spotlight to fall on her and a shout when it did. She was growing impatient. "Come on! Get it over with or let me get back to swimming!" She thought this. She wasn't crazy enough to think it out loud.

"At least I have a wonderful view of the stars." She thought, waiting for discovery. There were even more out here than she saw atop Fort Jefferson. Cassiopeia and the Big Dipper, both meant north was… towards the boat and her eventual capture.

Every second she was being dragged further out to sea. That was terrifying! She shuffled that thought back in her mind. It was time to start moving. Capture would be better than drifting further into darkness.

Suddenly a voice broke through still silence. Not the voice she expected. "Lucyyyy…"

Soft, and more distant than the boat had seemed, "Lucy!!!!" The call repeated. It was a sharp voice which didn't belong to Professor Erickson or Captain Levi. Lucy pushed her head up out of water, looking around. "Lucy!!!" the voice called out seeming even fainter.

"Nina?" Lucy asked, calling back into the night. A flashlight scanned the ocean surface. They hadn't heard her. "Back here!" She screamed. The beam continued flashing aimlessly. It was no use. She was too far away.

Wait! Lucy remembered the aluminum package she'd stuffed into her cushion straps earlier. Holding onto the cushion, she tore into it. Grabbing the plastic tube, she snapped it, breaking an inner seal releasing a dim blue glow.

Shaking it, the blue glow grew brighter. "Over here!" She shouted again, waving the blue light high overhead. A boat engine rumbled to life. The noise grew louder. Were they going to hit her? She prepared to dive, but the engine stopped. The flashlight beam quickly landed on her. Its light was blindingly bright. "Here, here!"

The engine revved and the boat pulled closer—the twins covering distance quickly. They were in a small boat sometimes used to ferry people to Loggerhead. At least it wasn't their tiny rubber skiff.

"Thank God, we found you!" Nina was a small shadow on the bow.

She kept her light directed towards Lucy. "Stop the engine. Don't hit her." Nina set down her flashlight, leaning out to offer Lucy a hand. "Your glowstick was a clever idea."

Swimming the last couple yards, Lucy wondered how Justin had known that it would be useful. "Hi." It was all she could think to say. She swung the camera and seat cushion onto their deck. Then, with Nina's offered hand, she was able to climb aboard.

Luke, from behind the wheel, offered a towel. "Sorry it took so long. We had to climb down from the lighthouse."

"Then we had to find you." Nina helped Lucy stand. "You swam a lot further than we expected." She gave Lucy a quick hug.

"How close was I too Loggerhead?" Lucy stared out at her lighthouse beacon.

"You made it about half-way." Luke replied.

Loggerhead Lighthouse flashed. "Huh. I can't imagine swimming twice that far." Thankfully, she did not have to. Which lead to another question. "What are you guys doing out here?"

CHAPTER 69

COVERT RESCUE

LUCY

"**J**USTIN TOLD US YOU WERE INVESTIGATING THAT WRECK. He asked us to keep our eyes out for trouble." Luke's hand rested on the throttle while they waited for Lucy to decide the next step.

"When we saw that fancy speedboat, we thought about radioing you." Nina breathed heavily, "But we were afraid they might hear our warning."

"Also, we weren't sure they were bad guys, until we saw the gun." Luke shook his head.

"Well, I'm glad you were watching." Lucy stared into the dark water.

"We were on top of the lighthouse anyway." Nina smiled, "Watching for Spud's return."

"Justin didn't mention us?" Luke asked.

"He didn't." Lucy frowned. Justin probably thought he was being overly cautious to ask them for help. "But I'm glad you came to get me."

"Justin also gave us these," Luke hefted the night vision goggles. "You were still hard to see, until we spotted your glow light."

"I'd been calling for a long time." Nina shook her head. "We were about to radio for help, bad guys or no bad guys."

"I'm glad you got me out of the water when you did." The towel's texture felt weird in Lucy's hands. "I'm already half prune."

"Here." Luke held out a bottle, sounding embarrassed. "We grabbed sports drinks on the way. It took us a couple extra minutes."

"Worth it." Lucy snagged the drink. "Okay, I can rehydrate later. Right now, we need to save the boys."

"They were headed west towards open ocean." Nina stared into the pitch-black horizon. "Do you know what's out there?"

Lucy nodded. "They mentioned the number Twenty-five Thirteen. That's not U.R.S.A.'s code. The *U-2513* was a German U-boat, captured in World War Two and purposefully sunk west of here. There are buoys out there where they could maroon the boys."

"I hope that's all they have planned." Nina's voice trembled.

"What do you mean?" Lucy turned to her.

"They were willing to abandon you in the ocean, and they had a gun." Nina stopped before saying any more.

"Oh." Lucy shivered. "Not possible. They didn't know about me. I hid from them. Professor Erickson would never." Would he?

"We were only watching from a distance, but it didn't seem like he was calling the shots." Nina frowned.

Luke gave Lucy a confused look. "Why are they doing this?"

"Professor Erickson's discovered a secret wreck. He was planning on stealing treasure and artifacts from it once U.R.S.A. left." Lucy answered. "We blew his cover. He and his accomplices will make a run for it."

Nina crossed her arms. "Does that mean that they're coming back for their loot?"

Lucy nodded. "Probably."

Luke reached for the ignition, "Then we should leave."

"Wait." Nina stopped her brother from turning the key. "Lucy, we should radio your father."

"I want to, but the professor and his crony might be listening." Lucy shook her head. "We don't even know if the rescue team is back yet."

"Fine. If we can't wait for rangers, I say we get the boys." Nina released the ignition. "We can't leave them out there."

"Are you crazy?" Luke stared at his sister. "That's open water. It's dark. There's an enemy boat. How are we going to find them without being seen?"

"We have our GPS." Nina tapped a device sitting atop a small fish finder. "We plot a curve around their path. We keep our lights off. Once we get close, we have these." She lifted the night vision goggles. "I'll wear them to warn you if I see any other boats."

"Do you know where the submarine wreck is?" Luke asked.

"No. But we can use dad's charts and plug in her coordinates." Nina sighed. "You and Mom need to stop second guessing my plans."

"Guys." Lucy said. "My brother and two friends are waiting in open ocean. Let's go save them so we can return to capture the professor." The twins fell silent. "Where are your charts?"

With Nina's help, they soon had latitude and longitude for Wreck U-2513. Nina punched in those coordinates. Luke started the boat. Underway, he kept the engines at a low hum. Nina and Lucy took turns on the bow watching for errant speedboats.

Lucy had the night vision goggles when she saw a flash. The waves had grown steadily to about two or three feet high. Which was a lot for the small boat. As they crested a particularly large wave, she saw running lights aimed in their general direction. She held up her hand, hoping Luke could see it. Fortunately, they had all grown accustomed to darkness. He shifted the engines to idle. "It's them. They're headed this way," she watched as they crested another wave.

Luke turned the boat sideways to slowly idle south, perpendicular the route they had been taking.

Professor Erickson and his partner weren't hiding. Their running lights were on, and a forward light carved night ahead of them. The boats quickly closed distance. Luke shut the engines down completely. Nina threw her towel over their GPS screen to hide even its dim light. The other boat's heavy drone grew louder.

It sped past, knifing through waves and quickly out of sight. The two aboard never noticed a smaller boat off their port side. Luke waited another minute, then reignited their engine. Nina uncovered their GPS. The three continued on.

They reached the U-boat's location much faster than Lucy expected. In choppy waters, Luke had to be careful, but he was a good captain. The sky and water were black, empty, and eerily reminiscent of Lucy's long swim. "We should be close! Do you see them, Nina?"

It was Nina's turn in the goggles. "Not yet." She continued scanning. Barely two minutes passed before she shouted. "I see them. Over there."

Lucy could not see anything. Luke followed his sister's directions until she called out, "Slow down! Can you see them now?" A dark shape, bobbing up and down, resolved into a ship-shaped shadow with three figures aboard. Two of those raised their arms in jubilation. The remaining figure, definitely Justin, stood on bow confidently riding a gentle swell.

CHAPTER 70

REUNION

LUCY

"CAREFUL NOW." NINA AIMED HER FLASHLIGHT at the other boat, while Lucy threw lines to her brother. Luke threw out bumpers, and when both boats collided it was more of a bounce than a jostle.

"Lucia Garcia Benitez!" Miguel shouted when she jumped onto his boat. "Don't ever do something stupid like that again."

"Like what?" Lucy asked. "Hiding from a man with a gun, or going for a swim?"

"You know what I mean." There was both relief and resignation in Miguel's voice as he turned back to their lines. Once they were secured, he looked to Luke and then Nina. "I'm glad you were able to find her." Then he turned to Lucy. "Did you know about them when you decided to hide?"

"I had no idea." Lucy winced as a searing beam of light hit her eyes. Nina was spotlighting them with her flashlight.

"Then what was your plan?" Miguel asked, looming over her. "To swim to Fort Jeff?"

"I hid from the bad guys so I could swim for help. Do you have to be so critical?" Lucy's question was muffled in her brother's shoulders as he enveloped her in an awkward hug.

Justin could swear he heard both twins mutter 'awe.'

"Shouldn't we hurry?" Rudy asked. "Towing us back will take forever."

"Who said anything about towing you?" Lucy lifted something under her brother's arm. It was their boat key! "I grabbed this after you left." She turned to Justin. "By the way, thanks for the cushion and dive light."

"No, um, problem." Justin had dumped lots of things into the ocean hoping something would help. Wait! "Did you get anything else?"

"You mean," Lucy sighed, holding up the camera. "This?"

Justin breathed a deep sigh of relief. "Even if Professor Erickson escapes, we have records of everything they take."

"Yay!" It was too dark to see, but Justin could easily imagine Miguel rolling his eyes. "We'll just boat back to Key West, find a place that still develops film, take those photos to the Coast Guard, and ask them to help us hunt down a pirate archeologist."

"That's our back-up plan. We still have time to stop Professor Erickson tonight." Justin crossed his arms. "With your dad's help. Can we radio him now?" Justin asked. Miguel had already confirmed that the twins had a working marine radio.

Lucy shook her head. "If Professor Erickson hears us. He and his friend will run."

"If they run, they run." Miguel hmphed, "but if they get desperate..."

"Desperate people do stupid things." Justin nodded. "I don't think the professor wanted to hurt us, but I'm not sure the other guy cared."

"So, what are we going to do?" Rudy asked.

Justin turning to Nina and Luke. "Do you guys have Wi-Fi on Loggerhead?"

"Yep."

He looked towards Lucy. "Which Dive Bears would be up and checking their messages?"

"If they are back yet, both Chet and Gwen always have their phones with them, and they are usually up late."

"Oh, sure, but when I carry my phone with me you complain!" Rudy interrupted.

Justin rolled his eyes. "I bet you have it with you right now."

"Of course," Rudy recovered the bag of dry clothes he'd stashed in a front compartment, digging through it to pull out his phone.

"I'm not complaining now. We can use it." Justin nodded. "I bet Chet could take the professor in a fight. Right?"

"Right?" Lucy sounded less than sure. "What, exactly, do you have planned?"

CHAPTER 71
HOW TO CATCH A CRIMINAL

LUCY

"T HAT'S YOUR PLAN?" Lucy crossed her arms. They were following the twins back to Loggerhead. She had traded place with Rudy. Miguel was adamant about keeping her close. Rudy was excited to help Nina navigate using the night vision goggles anyway. "It's almost too simple."

"What were you expecting?" Justin sounded genuinely hurt. "Should we set up a trap? Trick Professor Erickson into chasing us around the fort, trip him into the moat, and time it so he lands on top of his accomplices?"

"That would make for a better episode, if we were cartoons." Miguel called forward.

"Are we sure Professor Erickson will go back to Fort Jeff?" Lucy asked.

"The professor wants his secret wreck to make him rich and famous." Justin emphasized *famous.* "Despite everything, he still thinks he can publish. So, he'll want his research."

"What if Captain Levi is with him?" Lucy crossed her arms. "Or Mr. Howard? Chet might have muscles, but muscles don't beat gun."

Justin shook his head. "If they have any brains, those two will hop on the *Neptune's Trident* and leave ASAP."

"At least, that's what we're hoping." Miguel sounded skeptical. "I don't like rooting for smarter bad guys."

"Trust me." Justin sighed, "We email Chet and he'll detain the professor." Lucy nodded. That was step one. "Then you radio your dad from Loggerhead. Don't mention us. Just say something about our boat. Captain Levi and Mr. Howard will hear. If they race to Garden Key to pick up Professor Erickson, your dad can catch them. *When* they flee instead, your dad can call the Coast Guard."

"I have reservations." Lucy crossed her arms. "When do I get to punch Professor Erickson in his face?"

"You lost that chance when Captain Levi picked up a gun." Miguel cleared his throat. It was late as they motored past the dimly lit park boundary markers. Lucy had passed the time watching the Loggerhead Lighthouse. Its constant flashing beacon conjured a warm and fuzzy feeling in the pit of her stomach.

They slowed, pulling up beside the twins. "There's a ship at wreck one-fourteen right now!" Shouting from the other boat, Rudy pulled up the night vision goggles.

Miguel called. "Head south behind Loggerhead! We'll keep the island between us and potential bad guys."

"Rudy, send your message to Chet the second you get signal." Justin shouted across the space between their boats.

"Roger." Luke revved his engines.

Both boats pulled up to the dock. Lucy and Nina cast their lines in sync to secure them. Rudy leapt up first and collapsed to the ground. He was laughing. "Dry land! I thought I'd never see you again."

"Very theatrical Rudy, bravo." Lucy helped Justin out of their boat.

Justin turned to Nina and Luke. "Take us to your house. Let's send this email and catch our criminals."

"I hope Chet and the other Dive Bears are back."

Rudy nodded. "We were listening to the radio. Everyone is."

It was good to know. Justin nodded. "Did you hear anything else?"

"No." Rudy stopped on the walkway. "Look." He displayed the message Justin had typed. It had been sent. Chet would get it and, hopefully, confront the professor. Rudy balled his free hand into a fist, "I wish I were there! I also want to punch Professor Erickson in his throat."

Lucy nodded. "Right?"

"Yep. We're definitely leaving this one to the adults." Miguel brushed passed them.

After so much time in the dark, the warm light emanating from the Manning's home was welcoming. "Let's check on Operation Spud Rescue." Luke raced for their large marine radio.

"Mom and dad are with him. He's fine." Nina watched her brother with amusement. "Would any of you like something to eat or drink? I know it's hot, but we have hot tea and cookies." She surveyed everyone's eager nods then crammed six mugs into one microwave.

Meanwhile Luke fiddled with the radio trying to find anything besides a static hum. Justin watched Rudy like a hawk, while he continuously checked his phone for updates from Chet. Suddenly, voices broke through static.

Lucy recognized her father's voice. "Zero seven, this is zero one. I've pulled *La'sei Fairy* into harbor. We'll dock her for the night and move her tomorrow before the ferry arrives."

"Copy. Renee and Shawn are eager to get back to Loggerhead. There are two kids looking forward to a reunion with their pup."

"Spud!" Nina had been carefully unloading steaming mugs. Her loud shout startled Lucy. Fortunately, none of the hot liquid spilled.

"Chet just replied to our message." Rudy held up his phone. "Professor Erickson is alone in his apartment. He says he doesn't understand everything, but he promises to keep the professor in Fort Jeff."

"Perfect." Justin helped Nina pass out tea. "Lucy, it's your turn."

Lucy took the handheld radio from Luke. "Dad. It's Lucy. Do you copy?"

His reply came with an immediate radio squeal. "Lucia, good. Where are you?"

"I'm on Loggerhead with Luke and Nina, um, over."

"Are the boys with you?" There was a pause, "Why is my boat missing?"

"Dad, I'll explain in person." Lucy looked around the room. "I'll meet you on Garden Key."

"Right, I'll expect you soon." Did he sound angry? Confused? Lucy couldn't tell over the radio. Soon he would be both—plus surprised.

Miguel grabbed a handful of cookies and started for the door. "What?" he asked, noticing Lucy watching him. "Luke's driving, right? Otherwise, we lose our surprise element." He grabbed a second handful. Lucy had to open the door to let him out.

CHAPTER 72

CASSIOPEA

JUSTIN

THEIR RETURN RIDE WAS SILENT once Rudy stopped complaining. "I can't believe we have to get back in a boat." Justin kept a wary eye on the water, and the mystery wreck. The batteries in their night vision goggles were depleted, so they couldn't see if Mr. Howard and his captain were still out there pulling up artifacts with *Neptune's Trident's* big crane.

As they pulled into the harbor, Justin noted that the park boat was docked and dark. A familiar sailboat was tied to the spot usually reserved for the ferry. Lucy's father stood on the lower dock beside the twin's parents. Spud sat beside them wagging his tail.

The three adults helped secure the skiff while Spud energetically leapt aboard. Turning the wheel over to Miguel, Luke and Nina engulfed their furry friend. Mr. Benitez helped Justin out but blocked his two children on the dock. With arms crossed, he asked, "where is my boat?"

"Loggerhead." Miguel answered.

"And you didn't bring it back? I've told you never to take my boat out after dark. I've also told you to never take it without permission. If you were trying not to break any rules, you've failed expertly."

"Dad," Lucy stamped her foot causing a hollow wooden sound on the dock. "We don't have time. Chet has Professor Erickson cornered in his apartment. We have to catch him before he escapes."

"What?" Ranger Benitez stepped back, confused.

Justin cleared his throat. "Professor Erickson is the real bad guy, not Sophia. He's working with Mr. Howard. We don't have time for detail. The short story: there's a secret cache of artifacts on wreck one-fourteen. Professor Erickson and his associates cut the Manning's boat free to distract everyone so they could steal them. We went out to gather evidence, and they pirated your boat."

"It's true, they threw your keys overboard and dragged us out to sea." Rudy spoke up. Justin watched Lucy's eyes go wide. They weren't planning on scaring him, yet.

"What!" Lucy had never before seen the mixture of expressions currently crossing her father's face.

Justin tried to redirect their conversation. "Right now, Professor Erickson is busy collecting paperwork. We have to stop him before he can escape to the *Neptune's Trident*."

Lucy continued. "Chet can't stall him forever."

"Alright, but I'll need a better explanation later." Ranger Benitez reached to his belt where his gun, radio and flashlight hung. He grabbed his radio. "Zero four this is zero one, are you up and about?"

"Wendy's back?" Lucy asked.

"She arrived by seaplane late this afternoon." He held the radio, waiting for an answer. "Your mom sent her. She suspected you all were up to something."

"Zero four here. What's up boss?" His radio crackled.

"Be ready to go with everything, outside the crews quarters. Fast." Her father spoke cryptically.

"I'll be there in five." Ranger Wendy replied.

Ranger Benitez nodded. "We've got five minutes. Tell me everything I need to know."

Justin and Lucy took turns explaining basic details from their investigation after Sophia. They described evidence found on Professor Erickson's computer and their plan to check his wreck, "We were going to ask you to take us. Then the Manning's boat went missing." They described what they had found on wreck one-fourteen. Then they hesitantly described what had happened once the professor had shown up.

Ranger Benitez patiently accepted their version of events until: "What do you mean he has a gun?" Several birds sleeping around the water fountain were startled into taking flight.

Justin tried to make his comment sound reasonable. "If it helps, Professor Erickson didn't look thrilled about the gun."

"Why would that help?" Lucy's father growled as they walked around the small powder magazine. The Mannings had remained on the dock promising to radio in at any sign of *Neptune's Trident.*

Ranger Wendy waited by the crews quarters. In addition to the normal equipment on her belt, she also had a set of handcuffs. Her determined look sagged into confusion when she saw the entourage. "What's up boss?"

"Professor Erickson has a lot to answer for." Justin had never heard Ranger Benitez sound so angry.

In no time, they were below the wooden stairs looking up into the lights from Professor Erickson's apartment. Justin imagined an impatient professor sitting with Chet as the two discussed inane planning. The professor would be growing more anxious with each passing moment.

"You four go inside." Lucy's father put force behind his words. "You've gotten into enough trouble already." He nodded for Ranger Wendy to follow him.

"Not fair." Lucy complained once they were gone.

"We aren't going inside, are we?" Miguel asked.

"We'll wait here, in case Professor Erickson tries to run." Justin was confident he could justify that decision.

Someone upstairs knocked on the professor's door. A conversation began, and quickly escalated. There was a shout, from Chet, followed by something heavy shifting weight and then Wendy calling out, "Professor, wait!"

This was followed by a splash, then silence. A moment later Chet, Wendy and Ranger Benitez rushed downstairs. Both rangers ignored them, jogging across the parade ground towards the sally port.

Chet slowed, seeing them. "That was crazy!" He turned to Lucy. "When your dad came, Professor Erickson ran outside sprinting right into the moat." He began to jog after the two rangers. "Professor Erickson was carrying a box full of papers and a laptop when he jumped. What's going on?"

Justin and his friends fell in beside him. "We'll tell you later."

Exiting Fort Jefferson, the five watched the law enforcement rangers split up, turning left and right. Lucy sprinted after her father. Justin followed. Rudy and Miguel followed him. Eight more footprints joined pursuit as Luke and Nina rushed to chase Spud, who was chasing them.

"What's going on?" Luke, caught up as Justin slowed down.

"Professor Erickson jumped into the moat! He's trying to escape!" Justin answered.

"Was that smart?" Nina asked.

"Probably not." Justin answered as Spud quickly overtook them. The large group rounded another corner, trailing Lucy, and her father.

The dog parked himself beside Lucy and Ranger Benitez both stopped on the moat wall. He began barking at a bedraggled shape shoulder deep in water. Professor Erickson was standing in the moat only a few arches away from where he had jumped. Grimacing up into the beam of Ranger Benitez's flashlight, he'd stopped trying to swim.

Loose sheets of paper and pieces of a cardboard box were strewn around him. Justin saw a paperback book atop a laptop sunk next to his feet. Professor Erickson's feet were burrowed into the muddy moat bottom. His voice waivered. "I'm stuck."

"The moat is super gross, Professor. It used to be the fort's sewer. Prisoners who tried escaping like you got trapped in muck." Lucy called out to him. "Also, there are *Cassiopea* in there." She turned to her friends. "His skin will itch for weeks."

"Lucy I…" Professor Erickson hesitated, seeing the others approach. "What are you doing here!" His voice rang out in shocked anger. "I mean, it's good to see that you are well."

"Sure." Justin replied.

"I feel better now." Lucy stepped back smiling. "Professor, you look like a drowned rat."

Ranger Wendy jogged up from the other direction. Professor Erickson stopped thrashing and stared up into beams from multiple flashlights. "Could you all, um, help me?" Any hint of fight or flight in Professor Erickson's voice was replaced by defeat.

It took three belts chained together, but they were able to fish the professor out. By that point, his clothes were torn, and half of his ruined research papers were plastered across his face and neck. When Chet dragged him onto the moat wall, Professor Erickson looked utterly soggy and broken.

"You've got a lot of explaining to do." Ranger Benitez glared sternly.

"But first," Justin added. "Tell us when your partners are expecting you, and how you plan to get all of those artifacts out of the park."

Professor Erickson looked at him uncomprehendingly.

Rudy thrust himself in front of Justin triumphantly. "We found your box full of treasure."

Justin pulled him back. "Was the *Neptune's Trident* supposed to pick you up, or were you going to steal a speedboat to meet them on wreck one-fourteen?" Professor Erickson didn't answer. Justin smirked. "It doesn't matter. I'm sure Mr. Benitez is putting together a plan to catch him and his boat."

The professor glared back "You haven't figured it out yet? I didn't hire those men. They were my employers. They won't wait for me. You won't find them or Caesar's treasure."

"Caesar's treasure?" Rudy asked.

At that moment, a distant boat engine rumbled to life. Across black water a solitary light flashed north of Loggerhead. The rumble grew louder. Professor Erickson glared at Chet. "I'd be on that boat, if someone hadn't stopped me."

Chet narrowed his eyes. "Well, I'm happy to help."

Lucy turned to her father. "Dad, are you going after them?"

Wendy answered. "Sorry kiddo. We aren't equipped to confront armed and dangerous suspects on their own vessel. We'll radio the Coast Guard from headquarters." She turned to Professor Erickson. "You jumped into the moat like you had a plan. Where were you going?"

Professor Erickson glared after the retreating lights, "I was going to take *Vasa*. We were supposed to meet at dawn, near the Marquesas."

"You were going to steal a university boat! On top of everything else?" Chet crossed his arms. "Did you even stop to consider your students? You stole cannon, ruined Sophia's dig site, and framed her for your crimes. How much damage are you trying to do?"

"I'm sorry, I truly am," The professor sounded angry, not apologetic. "But I didn't make Sophia do anything. She had her own plans and made her own choices."

"You just used her for your own ends. Destroying two wrecks in the process." Chet frowned.

"I dumped the cannon in an obvious location so they would be found.

Sophia had pictures to help her replace them." The professor moped. "Moving them was a minor disturbance for the greater good. The wreck beneath one-fourteen is much more valuable than rusty civil war memorabilia."

Chet stepped forward with clenched fists. Professor Erickson put up his cuffed hands. "I'm sorry about Sophia, really, but I was on the verge of a discovery which could change history and make everyone rich." He glared at Justin, Lucy, Miguel, Rudy, and the twins. "That's over now, because of you." Spud's tail thwapped on concrete.

"Let's go." Ranger Benitez hefted the professor by his elbows.

Before the sally port, he passed the professor to Wendy. "Take him to headquarters. Contact Everglades. Warn the Coast Guard about *Neptune's Trident* and arrange transport for our professor." His gaze lingered on his two children and their friends. "Make sure he's in police custody before my wife returns."

Ranger Wendy and Chet dragged Professor Erickson across the bridge.

Ranger Benitez turned to them, "say your goodbyes then go to sleep. I'll have more questions tomorrow." His voice was cold. Justin felt something in his chest sink. It didn't sound like there was going to be a reward for solving this mystery.

Justin rested a hand on Spud's head, eying the twins. "Thanks! Without you two, we would still be tied to a buoy in the middle of nowhere."

"I would probably still be swimming." Lucy shivered. "That current was rough."

"No problem." Luke grinned. "We should go though."

"We left our parents on the dock." Nina grabbed Spud's collar. "Plus, this has been a traumatic experience for Spud. He needs rest and treats." Their dog's tail wagged as the twins lead him away.

Once they were gone, Justin smiled confidently. "We caught a real bad guy!"

Miguel groaned. "I wouldn't get too excited, until we discover our punishment."

"Knowing how many rules we broke—" Rudy sighed, "—it won't be pretty."

"Maybe not. But we stopped two secret plots, saved an expedition, and discovered a treasure." Lucy gently elbowed Rudy. "Whatever happens, it was worth it."

"We'll see." Justin replied. "We'll see."

TWO WEEKS LATER

LUCY

"**S**TOP THE BOAT, MAMA." Lucy called from the bow. "We dropped anchor somewhere around here." She leaned over, before turning to Justin, "Right?"

"It's a hard to tell. Last time we were alone out here." Justin pointed to the university boat anchored across the small sandy patch.

"Yeah, Professor Erickson and his goon didn't show up until we were in the water." Rudy sat on the aft deck wearing an eager grin, his snorkel mask, and one flipper.

"Chet and Gwen wanted an early start." Dr. Benitez cut ignition. "The university's extension is provisional. Mr. Ishii is watching us like a hawk, looking for any reason to send us packing."

"It's a good thing you have someone on the inside." Lucy dropped anchor, letting the chain sink into the sand below.

"I'm not so sure we do." Her mother glared. "Your father believes I encouraged your shenanigans."

"He should expect them by now." Astonishingly, Miguel was decked in snorkel gear for the first time since Sophia had discovered the cannon wreck. "Especially from Lucia."

"You boys were the ones pirated, had a gun pulled on you, and were left out at sea." Lucy felt her cheeks warm under her mother's gaze.

Her mother growled. "When I see Professor Erickson, I'll tear him limb from limb."

Miguel ignored his mother to counter his sister. "And you were abandoned at sea."

Lucy fought back a shudder by grinning at Justin. "Thanks again for the cushion." She let her smile become a grimace. "It would have been nice to know you had Luke and Nina on standby."

Justin rubbed the back of his head. "It was a last-minute idea. They were a backup measure."

"Wait." Lucy's eyes narrowed. Justin had taken the bait. "Are *you* telling me that you wanted to hold them in reserve if something happened?"

"Yes?" Justin's hesitated sensing her trap. It was too late.

"So, you asked them for help, Just in case?" Lucy beamed through her delivery of those three words.

Justin winced. "Very funny." Lucy heard a snicker beside the boat. She peeked down to see Rudy hovering at the surface.

"That was very funny, but is someone going to help me?" Rudy smiled.

"I'm coming." Miguel groaned. Lucy had to help. Her brother's long hair was stuck inside his mask.

While Rudy and Miguel expanded their search pattern around the boat, a line of bubbles arrowed their way from the anchored U.R.S.A. vessel. Chet popped to the surface. "Dr. Benitez, we've got most of wreck one-fourteen B mapped. The Professor's rubber chest and the cannon near it are gone. But, thanks to the kid's pictures, we found several other cannon buried nearby. Gwen's photographing everything. We'll find more clues Professor Erickson missed."

"Keep working." Dr. Benitez watched Chet sink back into the water.

"It's too bad Mr. Howard and his thug captain got away." Justin shook his head. The Coast Guard hadn't yet found *Neptune's Trident*.

"Thanks to your pictures, and the files you *liberated* from Professor Erickson's computer, we should be able to put together a decent idea of what they were looking for. You did well." Lucy's mom's gaze narrowed. "Except for risking your lives."

"Only barely," Rudy thrust himself on deck, striding forward with one hand behind his back to keep something hidden from Lucy's mom.

"We found it." Miguel pulled himself out in one rapid motion.

Rudy grimaced. "Here it is," he held up the object he'd been trying to hide. Out of water, it didn't look very impressive. The dagger Rudy had taken from Professor Erickson's rubber treasure chest. Its handle, which had probably been three separate pieces including guards, was warped and rusted together.

"Let me see that." Lucy's mom held out her hand.

Rudy reluctantly handed it over, waiting for Dr. Benitez's conclusion. "Well, it's in impressively good condition. It must have been buried until recently." Lucy was surprised to hear that that much rust and decay could be considered good condition. "I can't say for certain, but it could have come from the 16th or 17th century."

She flipped the dagger to examine a few fingers of gold folded over and pressed into a thin corroded cylinder mounted on its bottom handle. "Someone melted a decorative coin into its handle. Cleaning this up may answer a lot of questions. I'll get it to the Key West lab."

"Can't I keep it?" Rudy asked sullenly. "You said that once an object was taken from its location it lost a lot of its archeological significance."

"It might have been robbed of provenance," Lucy's mom ruffled Rudy's wet hair. "It still belongs with the wreck." She held the dagger up in consideration, "tell you what? I'll include all of you as coauthors in any research U.R.S.A. publishes. How does that sound?"

"Better than nothing." Rudy looked so dejected that Lucy had to swallow a sympathetic laugh. With one last wistful glance at his dagger, he flopped awkwardly to the side of the boat. "I'm going back to watch them map my wreck."

"I'll follow." Miguel jumped in after him.

Justin watched them. "Do you think the treasure in that green chest was everything Professor Erickson found?"

Dr. Benitez scowled. "Once Professor Erickson was turned over to police custody, he called a lawyer and stopped talking." But Lucy's mom smiled, "These waters hold lots of secrets. Why don't you two go check?"

Justin reached for his snorkel gear. "What about you Lucy?"

Lucy thought about her last time out on these waters. "I'm good up here." She smiled nervously ignoring a weird look from her mother.

"By the way, Justin." Her mom's request pulled attention from his gear. "We never spoke about what you wanted as a reward for helping to solve this mystery. Miguel gets a new computer. Rudy will get credit for working this wreck. Lucy will *only* be grounded for a couple."

"Mama!" Lucy turned away from the water.

"But seriously, you all helped save my expedition twice, and you might even have helped one grad student recover from her poor choices before it was too late."

"Sophia gets to stay in school?" Lucy asked.

"We're talking about it." She leaned forward, "So, what do you want Justin?"

Justin's face was serious, despite his goggled eyes. "I want to know what happened in Arizona. Lucy's dad, my mom and dad, Rudy's father, the others who disappeared." His shrug encompassed the many J.R.I.C. members unable to make it to Fort Jefferson, "None of us know why and no one will tell us anything."

"I see." Lucy's mom leaned back into her chair. "That is not my story to tell. I'm not sure it's a story you all are ready to hear." She paused, allowing minutes to pass. "Well, when is anyone, truly, ready for anything?"

Justin reached for his shorts in a dry storage compartment. "I found this when we moved to Florida." He pulled out the old compass he'd shown Lucy on top of the fort, "I thought it might have belonged to William Rapsilber."

"The helicopter pilot? I doubt it." Lucy's mom took the compass, her fingers lightly brushing the etched letters. Lucy was unprepared for any actual answers to J.R.I.C.'s founding mystery. "But I may know who this really belonged to."

Lucy watched Justin watch the compass. Her mother sighed. "Stay out of trouble the rest of your time out here, and I will tell you W.A.R.'s real name." Justin looked disappointed. Yet, Dr. Benitez looked more serious than usual. "It's not much, but you are proven investigators. It will lead you to answers."

For so long, they'd been working to try and learn anything about the Big Mystery. Cassidy and the others had found clues but no real direction. Her mother held out her hand, "Deal?"

"Deal!" With an excited grin, Justin returned the compass. Replacing his snorkel gear, he leapt off the boat with an energetic splash, leaving Lucy alone with her mother.

"You're really going help us with that mystery?" Lucy stared skeptically.

Epilogue

"I'm not a huge fan of secrets." Her mother could only keep a serious look for so long before laughing. "But even I don't know everything. Your father asked for this one secret. I love and trust him, so I agreed. I recognize that compass. However, you'll still have a mystery to solve after learning about it."

"Really?"

Lucy's mother simply nodded. They watched her friends snorkel circles around the site. "You'll have to get back into the water sometime, mija." Her mom pulled herself out of the chair.

"I just—didn't bring my snorkel gear." Lucy's lie sounded hollow in her ears.

Her mother embraced her in a tight hug. "If you want to keep me company, perhaps you can tell me about the adventures you had while I was gone. Your father only gave me basic details. I want to know it all."

"It's my turn to tell you a story?"

"Yep."

"Where do I begin?" Lucy grinned. "Well, after speaking with you and Sophia, we knew there was more to our mystery. Justin was trying piece things together. I knew where they were going to lead. I simply had to let him figure it out for himself…

END

The Junior Rangers Investigative Club mysteries continue in Mammoth Cave National Park in...

Visit www.alienjestpress.com
to follow the adventure.

AFTERWORD AND CLARIFICATION

If you want to learn more about any real historical figures, or about the science or history of the Dry Tortugas, your best source would be people in—and with interest in—the park. Talk to the rangers, historians, researchers, scientists, guides, and hobbyists who take time and effort to learn about these places and share their knowledge. Go online. Each national park has its own website with good up-to-date information. For Dry Tortugas, that is **www.nps.gov/drto**.

I want you, dear reader, to come away from this book with interesting facts, fun questions, and hopefully a deeper understanding of Dry Tortugas. But there are undoubtably things I got wrong, things we just don't have answers to, and things I made up for the plot. So, lets clear up some of the fiction.

Beware spoilers on the next page!

THE PEOPLE

As stated at the front of the book: all characters are fictitious or portrayed fictitiously. I want characters who feel real, and I want to represent the history of these parks and some the significant figures in that history, but all the actions and words of characters in *Treasure off the Coast* are a product of my imagination.

THE SCIENCE

There is ongoing research into the turtles, nurse sharks, birds, marine ecology and more out at the Dry Tortugas. I've tried to represent these as accurately as possible in this story, but there is a lot more to learn if you are interested.

LIFE AT THE PARK

Rarely, the Dry Tortugas is one of the parks I've actually lived in. So hopefully this book gives you a feel for what that is like. However, life changes, policies change, and parks change. Don't use this book as a guide on park life, policies, or practices.

THE ARCHAEOLOGY

There are more than 250 documented shipwrecks in Dry Tortugas's waters. Teams of real underwater archeologist have studied many of them. However, neither U.R.S.A. nor any of their wrecks in this book are real. Sophia's cannon wreck, wreck one-fourteen, and all other wrecks on Rudy's map are made up. You need special permission to use drones in a national park, and Kit's sample tool is something I made up for the story too.

NAVIGATION

Don't use Rudy's maps or my descriptions to navigate the park. I drew the map and chose random locations which worked for the story.

THE CAESAR LETTER AND
THE 1622 SPANISH TREASURE FLEET

The shipwreck of multiple Spanish vessels carrying treasure off the coast of Florida in 1622 is well documented. Wrecks like the *Atocha* and several of her sister ships have their own fascinating real stories. Gaspar de Vargas is a historical person associated with recovery efforts of that fleet. However, there is no wreck similar to wreck 114b or her treasure inside the park. The letter Professor Erickson possessed, and its author, Caesar, are made up for the story.

There's a more complete and up-to-date clarification page on my website **www.alienjestpress.com**, with fun facts and more resources related to each national park. You will also find other information there about the members of J.R.I.C. and word about future releases. Check it out!

And finally, I am a new author and this is my first book. So, if you enjoyed Treasure off the Coast and have a moment to leave a review wherever you found it, I would greatly appreciate it!

Nathan W. Landrum

ABOUT THE AUTHOR

Nathan W. Landrum would rather write a thousand words about a boy drinking coffee with aliens than a single page about himself. This is not to say he hasn't done interesting things. From biking across the U.S.A, to teaching Biology and Chemistry in Lesotho and China: he's bumbled through his share of adventures. (Usually with or in the footsteps of smarter, braver, people.) Perhaps he may share more about some of these antics online. But that doesn't explain these books.

Nathan grew up spending school holidays in various National Parks where his family lived and worked. He would hike desert trails, snorkel coral reefs, explore brick forts, and watch the local wildlife. He couldn't spend all of his time outdoors, so he always kept books on hand.

He began crafting his own stories at a young age. (These usually involved dinosaurs.) He'd journey these parks with friends, real and imagined, and entangle himself in various escapades. While Nathan has never solved a mystery of his own, he knows that each National Park is full of enough natural and historical intrigue to fuel a thousand stories. (He plans to stick to one or two per park.) The Junior Rangers Investigative Club novels are a way to share his experiences in and appreciation for National Parks with others.

Expect to find Nathan cave crawling, river rafting, or bear watching (from a safe distance) in a park near you, researching for the next adventure of Justin, Lucy, and friends. Or check out the website **www.alienjestpress.com** to learn more about what he is up to now, or where J.R.I.C. will be heading next!

www.ingramcontent.com/pod-product-compliance
Lightning Source LLC
Chambersburg PA
CBHW032019310726
48972CB00002B/472